The Lemon Juice Summer

by

Mary Lesser

Mary Lesser lives between the moors in Cornwall
with her husband and their tortoiseshell cat.

Part One - The Photograph

Su Charlesworth has hit a brick wall with the three B's; bereavement, breakdown and burnout and comes home to her late grandfather's cottage near Jamaica Inn to heal herself. She meets Rob the love of her past and future life and learns how to accept the support of friends as she begins to unravel a mystery in her family history.

Part Two - The Date Stone

Daniel Pencraddoc is a successful IT wizard who leaves London to return to life on Bodmin Moor where he meets the fey red lady, an artist called Fiona Rose Frazer. Their relationship becomes serious as Fiona helps him to see what is important in life.

Part Three - Facing Time

Dr Joshua Milton flies back to England for his sister's funeral and takes a holiday cottage for a month on Bodmin Moor to see if he can resolve the unexplained loss of his first love. Events surrounding Daniel and Fiona's baby act as the catalyst for meeting Su Charlesworth, the daughter he never knew he had.

For my mother

born Barbara Charlesworth
adopted Betty Milton
died Barbara Betty Hopkinson

1926 - 1989

The Photograph

Part One of
The Lemon Juice Summer

ONE

Turn left at Jamaica Inn. Not the Satnav speaking but the memory of a voice in my head, my grandfather's voice to be precise. Worryingly narrow in places it was a road I knew quite well, sinking down through an ancient landscape and joined by a rushing winding stream with road signs cautioning otters crossing. After living in suburbia where street signs usually prohibited something, this was a different world. Again I heard his voice, snorting derisively, "Bodmin Moor? When I was a boy we always knew he as Fowey Moor!" The Cornish use of gender to refer to something significant, never the passionless pronoun of 'it'.

I was shattered. It had been a pig of a journey. After stopping for fuel and visiting a supermarket to buy essentials I'd got into the wrong lane, not paying attention and been forced to navigate my way though traffic queues and a one way system before I got back on track. Fog and gloomy skies and miles of roadworks had contributed to the misery. A few more miles and there, almost fronting the lane but sideways on stood Orchard Cottage. Once two cottages, it had grown a little with a sloping single storey back extension which anchored it snugly to the ground. I knew it well, the wide front porch only ever used for the postal delivery, one wall slate hung against the prevailing wet westerly weather. Comfortably modernised, content in its surroundings, it was vernacular architecture at its most honest and unexpectedly my home.

Turning into the farm lane and again into the gravelled parking space, I was relieved to see a light on at the back although it was not quite dark. I reversed, parked and switched everything off, my hands stiff from gripping the wheel. I hadn't been back since grandfather's funeral a few months earlier. Grabbing my bag and fumbling for door keys I hurried through the gate and up to the back porch, desperately in need of the loo. A neighbour from the farm had put the heating on, arranged some flowers in a vase on the kitchen table and left me a plate of egg and cress sandwiches wrapped in clingfilm. There was a biscuit tin with a homemade fruit cake and a note propped against the tin.

You need to order oil. Will call by tomorrow, got parents evening tonight. Jay xx.

I went upstairs, switching lights on and opening doors. Everything was tidy but smelled a little musty. My bed had been made up and there was a hot water bottle under the duvet obviously placed there several hours earlier. It wasn't one I recognised, having a pink fluffy cover with a blue velvet rabbit on it. Back downstairs I switched the kettle on to make tea and ate a sandwich, the bread soft brown and nutty, a hint of mayonnaise binding the eggs, cress with that clean green freshness. I found I had tears in my eyes. Jay had been so kind.

Kindness to oneself and from other people was a topic the counsellor had dwelt on as she'd tried to find a way to help me deal with my pent up frustration and anger.

Kindness is not something to expect from your bosses these days I had raged. I had shouted.

'They expect you to meet impossible deadlines, to drive from one side of the country to the other. They don't care about traffic jams or weather conditions they just want the reports in on time for the sake of their bonuses and you have to make that happen even if it takes all bloody day. You log on and check your emails when you're supposed to be on holiday. You log on at weekends when you're supposed to be having a social life. It's not balanced any more. It's death by bloody email. And HR couldn't give a shit. When I first started they were all helpful smiles and holiday entitlement. Now you're just a number, you're time managed, interviewed if you take a day off sick, performance managed like a sodding battery hen. I hate it. I bloody hate it.'

I'd stopped, my throat tight and my breathing difficult. I remember seeing the look in the counsellor's eye, she'd seen it and heard it all before. Not that she wasn't professionally sympathetic of course, but she couldn't feel what I was feeling.

The job had been relentless. I'd taken the job because I had convinced myself that it was time to move out of my comfortable rut and get out there into the commercial world. The huge increase in salary had been the other factor. What an optimistic fool I'd been to take on something so challenging. I wasn't cut out for the corporate life however swanky the hotel chain which employed me. I'd been so naive, soon realising that this was a bad move. Being on the road left me feeling isolated and lonely. Travelling with its occasional stopovers was a miserable existence. I had thought I would be seeing different parts of the country, visiting pretty towns, but the job left me no time. All I did was stare at the backs of the vehicles in front of me and worry if I would get to an audit on time. As a friend who travelled abroad for work on a regular basis commiserated, all you see are the airports, and they become deadly. I wasted time highlighting natural breaks such as Easter, Bank Holidays and Christmas as something desirable to aim for, thinking that if I could just get through that month and then those weeks, I could have a rest and some decent sleep. I'd started doing admin at weekends and I'd got into the obsessive habit of checking my personal management charts, trying to slice work into bite sized chunks. But it never worked out because revisits and actions on complaints always messed up my system. Then I'd lie awake at night, afraid to sleep in case I didn't hear the alarm. Colour, rhythm and sense of taste had drained from my life without a note of farewell. I was dried out, exhausted and off my food. And I was worried all the time.

After months of increasing difficulty I'd finished an audit somewhere in Kent and driven home in rain via the M25 and M1 in a thirty-five mile an hour traffic jam conscious of the windscreen wipers beating in time with my headache. All I could see was the unlovely face of my latest line manager who had taken me to task and informed me that I should be harder on people, make them sweat a bit.

'You get better performance from worried people Su, don't be their friend, keep them nervous, they stay on their toes that way.' What a power hungry bitch. I shuddered as I recalled her bossy manner, her bulgy eyes shining with zeal and pleasure. What sort of life was it to be afraid of your colleagues. And it was absolutely at odds with the way I had been brought up, which was to be helpful and to consider other peoples' needs. I had been taught that what you put into the universe was what you got back. No wonder I was conflicted, I was torn apart.

I've no idea how I got home in one piece that night.

I recalled sitting on the side of my bed in the almost unfurnished flat, just the light from the hall to one side illuminating my hands. Unable to summon the energy to do anything, run a bath, get something to eat. Sleep when it came was brief, anxious and restless. I finally hit the brick wall unable to breathe and everything stopped. I banged on my neighbour's door and spent a night in hospital and a friend from my previous job in the hospital lab took me home the next day in her lunch hour. The only contribution my employer made was to arrange and pay for counselling, together with a vague threat that my future contribution to the company would be considered fully in due course and to both our advantages.

Then grandfather had died, an unexpected and untimely death. My only relief was that he died outside raking leaves on a sunny November day, in the garden with his boots on. I was his sole heir and the last of our family. In those dark exhausted months I was aware of functioning from a distance. There'd been a small life insurance payout, severance pay from my employer 'generous in the circumstances and with your bonus taken into account' but 'guilt money more like' from a sympathetic co-worker (now not even referred to as colleagues or workmates I'd noticed). Weasel words my grandfather would have called them. And finally the rapid sale of my flat.

It was my breakdown, my burnout, my bereavement. With the Three B's I was a top scoring head case and it was all mine. Not massive and not even spectacular, but frighteningly real to me.

Slowly I ate another sandwich. It was so blissfully quiet here I was aware of my tinnitus. I don't think a vehicle had gone past. I looked around the kitchen, well-used, plain and functional and built by grandfather using his joinery skills. It seemed odd to be owning something like this after my unorthodox upbringing. Even the flat had only been mine thanks to an eye-watering mortgage although rising property prices had provided me with a healthy sum once the sale had been completed. Had I done the right thing, selling up? It all seemed so final but you know that feeling you get when a relationship ends, that loss of trust and satisfaction, that cold sense of finality. I'd felt that when my job sent me pear-shaped. I knew it all had to stop because I just didn't fit there. What I didn't know was where I belonged. I realised I still had my jacket on and a car to empty before bed.

Sleep that night was like being hit with a cosh. Instant, empty silence. I was still in my dressing gown and on my third mug of tea at the kitchen table when a tap at the window roused me. A smiling face with very blue eyes under a dripping umbrella was looking in at me.
'Can I come in?' Jay called, more of a statement of intent than a polite enquiry.

There was a quick flurry of activity, unlocking the door, hesitancy about wet shoes and so on. I asked her to come straight in, I wasn't worried about the floor. She gave a quick glance around with a rapid assessment of my condition all in a flicker of an eye. This wan't a nosey woman, this was an efficient woman accustomed to operating on many levels at once. I'd seen her with a baby under one arm, telephone receiver jammed between shoulder and ear, writing with her spare hand whilst silencing her husband, children and dog with a single look. She sat down opposite me looking pretty in a pink jumper and blue and pink scarf and accepted, interpreting my wordless gestures, a mug of tea.

A sigh, and 'Good to sit for a bit. It is 11 o'clock after all.' She was looking at the clock over my shoulder and making a gentle point about my state of undress.

I liked Jay. She'd been around when I'd returned to the cottage to live with my grandfather as a teenager after mum had died. We'd first met at the stables when I was learning to ride. Blue eyes and straight dark hair betrayed her Celtic ancestry. She was compact, quick, spontaneous and blessed with a generous nature. A happy marriage to a prosperous local farmer had kept the smile on her face. We were as different as chalk from cheese. I felt distinctly chalky.

Jay put her mug down. 'Are you still poorly?'
I thought for a moment. 'I'm not taking any tablets or medicine, and the cuckoo is back in the clock if that's what you're getting at.' I got an old fashioned look in return but there was no hostility between us.

'Did you sleep okay?'

'Well the fluffy hot water bottle was a godsend.' I managed a smile.

'That's Matilda's, she came and helped me get things ready for you.' Matilda was Jay's eldest daughter. 'I'm sorry Mr Charlesworth died, he was a lovely man.' Jay paused thoughtfully. 'And it's a shame about your job and about Andrew walking out on you like that. You've had more than your share of rotten luck this past year Su.'

God. I hadn't thought about Andrew for months. Somewhere in this awful year my boyfriend had decided he wasn't good enough for me, that I deserved better and that he needed to be somewhere else with someone else who had a lot more time for him. Not that he didn't love me I had to understand, but that things had changed and that we had to move on. I'd given him top marks for the run of cliches. After a week of tears, some recriminations and a lot of red wine I'd been at work when he'd moved his things out and left. I'd got home to find his key on the mat in an envelope together with a note, just one word, *Sorry*. I remembered thinking that he could have at least vacuumed after he'd moved his bits of furniture out. He'd been happy to live off me, in my flat, bought with my salary, run with my wages. To be fair he had shopped and cooked and he could use a paintbrush to good effect. But Andrew had been a perennial student, a fair haired charmer and the life and soul of the party. I'd coasted along on his confidence and enjoyed his popularity, his skill as a musician, his effortless ability to get by. Something will turn up, he always used to say, refusing to take any work unless it was to do with music in case his hands got damaged. Grandfather hadn't warmed to him though. "Too quick to please, sails a bit close to the wind that one Su. Time will tell". Time told indeed.

I realised Jay's blue eyes were still on me. 'What are you going to do then love, what's the plan?'

'I plan to live here.' My response startled me. I hadn't really thought it through at all. I'd had a vague idea of doing some travelling but honestly I was just too tired to plan anything. A warm bed and some peace and quiet were all I really wanted.

Jay was talking, sitting back in her chair, smiling. 'Well I'm glad. I'd hate to see the place sold off as a holiday cottage to some rich bastards with lifestyle aspirations. And you belong here really, your family were local even though you weren't born here. It's a sort of homecoming, we should celebrate that.'

Before I could think of anything to say she dashed off into the rain to take a cake out of the Aga or nurse a lamb or something equally worthwhile, while I sat there in my dressing gown desperately in need of a shower. I noticed I was feeling cold. The heating had gone off. I fancied another mug of tea but first I had to order some heating oil.

The next few days found me sorting things out. I'd lived here on and off as a small child, sharing my mother's room which became my room when I returned to live here after her death.

Grandfather's room was at the side nearest the lane, mine at the end overlooking the garden, with a rather nice bathroom and the box room in between. There was a large landing with a skylight, and where the two cottage staircases had once been side by side against the centre party wall there was now a generous oak staircase leading up from the hall. Downstairs the heart of the home, the kitchen, was large enough for a small table, a dresser and under stair storage for the boring stuff. There was a small pantry and off the back porch a boot room to one side and a useful scullery housing the downstairs loo and washing machine to the other. The porch opened onto a large flagstone paved sitting area and a mainly south facing back garden. An estate agent's wet dream Andrew had called it. The sitting room housed the wood stove. Grandfather had built low book shelves against the internal wall in the sitting room. Windows let light flood in when it wasn't raining. The decor was soft creams, blues and greens and very easy on the eye. It was welcoming. I could see Andrew's point.

Grandfather had been a good gardener as well as a decent joiner, sailor and adequate plain cook. After a few years away in the navy as a young man, he'd returned to Cornwall and got a job with a farmers' supplies company where he eventually rose to head of sales. One day he'd met the new girl at the office and it had been a love match. I knew that my grandmother had miscarried a couple of times before my mother was born, a very much wanted baby and for many years their only child. Then a complicated late pregnancy had left him unexpectedly a widower and a single parent, increasingly frustrated by his bright, pretty teenage daughter who ran wild and away for a year and a day or maybe longer, and then came home alone with me. She named me Susannah after my great-great-grandmother.

The garden held two apple trees, one for mum and one for me, the apples of his eyes grandfather used to say. There were also a couple of plum trees, a crabapple and an old cantankerous pear which rarely produced anything. I noticed that the veg patch, neatly fenced against rabbits, had gone to weed but the fruit bushes all looked healthy. Lavender, which had been trimmed and clipped by someone, edged the little fence. *Good for the bees, who will dance on the fruit bushes and then go into the greenhouse to sing to the tomato men;* games and stories I used to enjoy with mum and grandfather, not realising that I was being taught age old gardeners' lore.

Beyond the lawn and a shrubbery the garden sloped down and increasingly wild via a winding stony path to a large long pond, kept fresh by a spring. In summer I knew the path to be a secret way to the pond, disguised by lace cap hydrangeas and hardy red flowered fuschia. It was all bare and twiggy at the moment and in need of attention. I wandered down to a bench at the bottom of the path and overlooking the pond. As a child I'd often sat there with grandfather, being gently taught about dragonflies, damsels and darters, slapping "they blasted clegflies" which gave a nasty bite and watching newts and diving beetle larvae, weirdly pale and usually gruesomely devouring tadpoles. With the arrival of summer we had watched the house martins, swallows and swifts flying and dipping over the pond surface, squealing with joy. Grandfather had profound respect for living things, deplored nature's casual brutality, and questioned why a loving god could let one animal predate another. He was a kind man. He loved his food especially when home grown, a glass of cider, a good joke, a song. I missed him.

I didn't feel like changing much inside the cottage and after some spring cleaning I arranged my own books, CDs and some colourful rugs, my few personal things. With the musty smell gone it had become welcoming and familiar. When Andrew had moved out and taken his stuff I'd realised what little I actually owned, but then a nomadic upbringing had shown me the uselessness of clutter and the attraction of travelling light. The new owners of my flat had been happy to lighten my load a little further.

Of my late unknown grandmother and short-lived mother several photographs survived. Along with his other skills grandfather had been a keen and patient amateur photographer. The box room held a bookcase with albums all neatly catalogued and in date order. There were some framed photographs of us on the pretty little oak bureau in the sitting room, well composed shots of our faces not always looking into camera. A photograph of my grandmother still sat by the side of the bed in his room, a moody dreamy black and white portrait of a lovely girl with her hair up. In my bedroom my mother laughed out at me, wearing a floaty sprigged dress and holding a large brimmed straw hat, turning to camera, surprised, caught in a moment of joy.

It was a travesty that someone so vital could have died so stupidly. We were living at a commune in a valley in Wales when she got a nasty scratch whilst out foraging for mushrooms or nuts and berries to supplement the endless rice and lentils. No one noticed the angry red streak snaking up her arm and when it became a problem they thought that compresses and herbal teas were the answer. By the time someone had the wit to put her in the old van and take her to the inadequate cottage hospital it was too late. A pointless death caused by blood poisoning.

I think that might have prompted my interest in microbiology. After a couple of years at a normal school I left Cornwall for a job in a hospital in the Midlands and via endlessly repetitive tasks involving smelly Petri dishes, evening classes and day release courses, I got to a point where I could build a career in hygiene management. Serious, level-headed, methodical and nothing like my free-spirited vital mum.

Being back at the cottage, the only place I'd ever really known as a home was making me remember things I'd not thought about for years. How kind grandfather had been when he'd taken me in, understanding loss so well and suffering it once again. He'd advised me that the only way he knew how to cope was to somehow turn suffering into wisdom, to meet "they blasted celestial banana skins He throws down" and to learn from them. He'd supported me in every way he could and been pleased by my rapid academic progress and sober, steady behaviour.

I sat alone in the cottage for hours one rainy afternoon, just remembering, and cried and snivelled in a sickeningly self-pitying way. It left me with a faint headache, feeling cross and faintly disgusted with myself. I knew I was going to have to pull myself together and get on with life. The only trouble was that I wasn't sure, now, what my life was supposed to be. I'd been able to define myself by my work and the company I kept but that was all in the past now. I still felt extraordinarily vulnerable.

I found that small routines helped balance things, although I was still tired after the emotional excesses of recent months and didn't want company. As the days lengthened minute by minute the weather showed occasional signs of improvement and I took my tea outside for an hour, pulling up a few weeds and doing a little tidying but sometimes just standing and looking. The pond became a favourite place again. I had already noticed frogspawn in February, indecently early I thought at the time. I even found spawn in a large puddle on the moor one day and fretted about its future as I walked home in a chilly wind.

There were mild sunny days and cold sleety days when hailstones fell in fast furious showers before the sun burst through a gap in the clouds and revealed the garden hung with sparkling decorations. Pale primroses so fragile looking, bloomed robustly in the banks despite the weather. Snowdrops laced the hedge sides and small daffodils poked their heads out of secret safe places. Birds began to sing again, catkins trembled in the hazel and life shouted out. I felt able to breathe again.

Amidst all this burgeoning bucolic splendour the chimney breast developed a small but troubling damp patch. Jay had been calling in quite regularly for a cup of tea and to chat, but I knew she was keeping an eye on me. I showed it to her one day.

'All this bloody wet weather we've been having.' She said. 'The animals hate it and I hate it. Anyway, I'll get Rob to take a look. He knows buildings and if he can't sort it he'll no doubt know some bloke who can'.

Right, so I now had some unknown person called Rob the Builder calling round, which unexpectedly made me giggle. That afternoon I drove to the farm shop in the village and bought useful provisions; biscuits, tea, milk. Builder food. And some vanilla fudge for me.

On the way back the village church faced me square on with a silent reprimand. I pulled over and stopped, mirror, signal, manoeuvre on an empty street. I'm not religious and don't even have a hippy new age pic n' mix religious hangover, but in that churchyard lay my ancestors and two of them were personal and up-close family members. Tending graves wasn't an occupation I'd seen myself doing and I felt a bit out of place walking up to the plot where a new headstone stood out conspicuously. George Charlesworth. His wife Christina Charlesworth. Daughter Tessa Charlesworth. Together United Forever.

For several moments I was breathless, uncomfortable, uncomforted. I had no flowers, no words and no sense of what was right or appropriate for me to do. They were all untimely deaths and I had some unresolved sorrow about that. Nothing there reflected the warmth and vitality of the people I'd known and I felt quite unhappy about the thought of them laying there for an eternity. What on earth was the point, I asked myself irritably. I mumbled an apology and walked back to my car, suddenly aware of a headache, a dull leaden pain in my brow. As I stepped down out of the churchyard into the road a van took rapid avoiding action without stopping. I gazed after it as an arm waved through the window. What that meant I wasn't sure but I suspected it wasn't complimentary.

TWO

A few days later the sun was out and so was I, contentedly hanging out washing, the radio on in the kitchen and a breeze blowing through the open door moving the radon gas out. I'd found an old leaflet from the local Council advising of the dangers of radon in granite houses. My grandfather had been dismissive, doors and windows stood open except in the most inclement weather and anyway, something had to take you if it wasn't cigarettes or too much fat, sugar and booze. Everything in moderation had been the motto of his generation, a little bit of what you fancy does you good. I found myself muttering these proverbs as I pegged things out; waste not want not, a stitch in time saves nine, mumbling away to myself and wondering if it was because I had no-one to talk to for long stretches, when a van pulled into the parking space next to my car. A muffled thump of music was audible before the engine was switched off.

Vaguely irritated I watched as a fit looking brown haired man got out. He saw me looking, lifted an arm in acknowledgement and walked jauntily into the garden, smiling broadly.

'Hello I'm Rob, but you know that.'

For a brief mad second I got the impression he was going to kiss me on the cheek.

'Do I?' I sounded a touch haughty.

'Yes of course you do. We met years ago. I'm Jay's little brother.'

He looked slightly taken aback at my blank stare, then wary.

I remained silent, staring up at him like an idiot. That distinctive arm wave, the van. He took a step closer.

'Isn't this a good time?' He was looking down at me enquiringly. He had dark blue eyes.

'What?' was all I could manage. I realised I'd got goosebumps up my arms.

He regarded me for a long moment. 'Look, Jay said I wasn't to prat about. You've not been well, had some knocks. I can come another day to look at your damp patch, er, damp er chimney, if you like.' He grinned at me and his smile was warm and lively, as though sharing a private joke.

'Oh sorry, you're Rob the builder.' The penny had finally dropped. I was staring at him like a rabbit in the path of the combine harvester.

'Well I can do other things as well, but,' he paused and shrugged 'today yes, I'm the builder.'

'No, yes, please, oh I'm sorry'. I was in babble mode now. 'I don't remember ...' *ever meeting you and how could I forget you.* I don't think I babbled that last bit aloud.

'I don't remember.' I said again, like a village halfwit. And as we stood there looking at each other, I had an odd feeling, like a memory trying to surface. And if I'd been a cat I would have been rubbing myself against his legs by now. As it was I was still gazing at him with slack jawed vacancy.

By now Rob had taken refuge in a change of body language. He slipped into polite meeting a new client behaviour and taking a step or two back he clasped his hands behind his back and looked up at the cottage.

'It's a very pretty place,' he commented, 'there's room for a garden room extension on this side, west facing so it would be lovely in the evening. I can just see it with long windows and a decent slate roof.'

Then his eyes swivelled to some place left of my head and widened slightly. He was looking at my underwear, dancing in the breeze. Oh great. I managed a small stiff smile and invited him in to view the chimney. No way were the words 'damp patch' or 'breast' going to pass my lips.

Rob didn't stay long and left promising to call back and fix the problem when there was an improvement in the weather and when he had the time. I understood that to be typically Cornish, the work would be done but the actual year was not specified. I consoled myself with the thought that it obviously wasn't serious.

Jay called in after the school run with Matilda in the back seat intent on some plinky noisy hand held game.

'I saw Rob down at the farm shop and he said you just needed a bit of pointing scraping out and replacing. He's got some water repellant additive thingy to put in the mortar, works wonders with these old granite buildings. It's such a bugger it's porous and holds water like a sponge. People think it doesn't. All this damned rain these days.' She paused and regarded me closely. 'You ok?'

I nodded. 'He said I'd met him before but I don't remember ever meeting him until today, this morning.' I winced at the memory of my dazed and inarticulate reaction. 'He must have thought he was dealing with an idiot.'

'Yes, he said you seemed a touch confused,' Jay laughed, 'you did meet him once, it was at my 21st, when Phil and I decided we were getting engaged, Rob was down from Uni and you were 18 and about to go off to start training somewhere up England'.

'What, that skinny bearded bloke who tried to snog me on the terrace at your parent's place after saying Uni was all about free love?'

'That was his chat up line?' she was amused. 'Oh I'll enjoy reminding him about that.'

'What on earth did he study if he's a builder?'

'Oh he's not really a builder. He's a blacksmith, an artistic blacksmith, not a farrier shoeing horses. He read geology at Uni, but the commercial world or teaching wasn't for him so he got onto a blacksmithing course someplace. He understands materials and he's good with his hands. It runs in our family, there was a blacksmith somewhere way back. And he can draw and design things, make stuff people like. He's starting to make a good living I think. The London weekenders are placing orders for gates and benches and garden sculptures, and he exhibits small stuff at the craft centre in Devon. He's got a good website which helps.'

I took all this in, lost in thought as I watched her vivacious face.

'What happened?'

Jay looked at me. 'After the attempted kiss? Your grandad took you home.'

'No, I meant what happened to us, it's been 12 years.'

'And I've had three children and got a bit fatter, but you, Su, you're still the same slightly scared girl, you have a lost, funny look in your eyes like a pet that's had a beating. But that's all over now, trust me things will get better, much better.'

And looking at her smiling blue eyes I thought I could believe her. At which point came a wail from the car, 'Mum, I need a wee!'

Country life is not all about baking cakes and bee keeping. It smells, it's noisy and it's dirty. Manure and mud are everywhere, tractors clatter about moving bales, hauling wood and cutting hedges. There are sheep and lambs and cows endlessly bleating and mooing, cockerels crowing at 4 a.m. and the dawn chorus at ear splitting decibel levels until after 6 a.m. Sometimes there are guns going off at night when the local lads are out lamping and shooting rabbits and foxes. Then there's the sheer hard work; wood to chop for the woodstove, ground to be dug for seeds, weeding to do. Slugs and snails, flea beetles and sawflies attack things in the vegetable garden. Rabbits, moles and badgers dig holes and damage lawns. Something gnaws the bark off fruit trees. Grey squirrels, deer and rabbits all get the blame for that. The countryside fights back all the time, inconsiderate and careless, and in a climate as wet and mild as it is in Cornwall everything grows, fast, all at once and almost all the time. Working in it is relentless and hard but for me it was all healing and I worked, planting peas, beans and potatoes, remembering the satisfaction of growing and eating fresh food in the commune.

There were nights when no streetlights showed me the starry skies of my childhood. Days when I stepped outside and new flowers in painterly profusion clamoured for my attention. Fledglings appeared in the garden and at the bird feeder with that slightly daft look young birds have, and new lambs with crazy legs chased each other in the fields and on the moors.

My grandfather had always said that the trick was to work with nature. There was no point in imposing suburban thinking onto the countryside. I began to read about companion planting, understanding that some plants have to be sacrificial to allow others to survive. As I worked I found the old mantra echoing through my head, *one to rot, one to grow, one for the slug and one for the crow*. And using slug pellets was both pointless and cruel. For a start they potentially poison animals further up the food chain, because the snail ingests the poison, the hedgehog or thrush eats the snail, so it's goodbye hog and thrush. I tried beer traps and found them quite effective but there was nothing better than collecting slimy slugs in the evening, after a rain shower. My method was to pick them up using a pair of old tongs and drop them into a pail of water containing a few squirts of washing up liquid and then to pour the lot down the drain. I hoped the septic tank could cope. I couldn't bring myself to kill the snails so I lobbed them over the lane into a verdant patch of grass where nettles and willow herb grew. The thrush living there was appreciative.

I noticed I was sleeping well, eating more and discovering that food tasted good again. The Cornish moorland air smelled sweet and I'd stopped wearing my watch. I had also noticed how friendly people were. In the shop I was always wished good morning or good afternoon, followed by a gentle enquiry as to the state of my health. Standing in a small queue one day I realised that almost everyone got that treatment, but sometimes there would be a kind comment about my grandfather or the fact that I was staying on. Bringing life back to the village as one lady put it.

I went back to the churchyard, this time prepared with flowers and was approached by the vicar with a warm smile and a slightly grubby handshake.

'Sorry about the hands I was just pulling a few weeds up. Hello Su, I'm Vic Ludlow. Victor the vicar. Known as Vicar Vic here.'

'Yes I remember, you were so kind at my grandfather's funeral.' I actually only had a vague recollection of that day, what I did remember was Jay's husband Phil holding my arm and firmly propping me up.

'I knew your grandfather, he took part in village activities. A well liked man I think and a very good Scrabble player.'

I was invited to come to church, join the flower arranging team or help with the little library group, all working for the community and as a good way of meeting people.

'Not many your age Su, but even older people were young once and not all are out of touch and gaga. Come along and help out, you may be surprised and it will get you out.'

I had to remember, this was the country and other people knew your business. I thanked him and said that I would think about it. The deity in my upbringing wasn't one which dwelt in a building.

Jay phoned and invited me to join them all for dinner at the farmhouse that evening. 'Nothing posh, don't dress up, it's just me and Phil and Rob and the mother-in-law and we're all like starving dogs so we eat at 6pm sharp.'

'What's she like?' I asked. I vaguely remembered her from my childhood rounding up their cattle, small black or cinnamon coloured Dexter cows with tiny calves, using a knobbly stick and a very big voice. A slim indomitable figure in a long dirty coat and a yellow woolly hat.

'Martha, oh she's good. Eats like a horse, loves a joke, she's unshockable. I love her to bits and we all eat together a couple of times a week. Matilda adores her. She was great friends with your grandad I do know that, but there was nothing in it.' She was keen to reassure me.

I'm not sure I would have felt that there was anything wrong in grandfather having a love life if he'd chosen to do so.

I made an effort and dressed in clean black jeans (dogs means jeans) with a pretty turquoise top and an opal pendant. It was old and set in a gold filigree, my mother had worn it once or twice, but she gave it to me when I was 15 saying that it suited my unusual eyes and strawberry blonde hair. Her mother had left it to her was all that she could remember. I was pulling on a pair of black ankle boots when there was a knock at the open back door and a shout of 'Anybody home - ahoy the house!' I jumped and my heart started knocking around my ribcage.

Rob was standing there. 'It's okay it's only me. Jay said you were coming up. All right if I leave my van there and we can walk up the track.'

He was wearing a shirt which matched his eyes, clean dark jeans and a v-necked grey pullover with a hole in it. He looked me up and down. 'You look nice, but you'll need a jumper for later, it's colder in the house than it is outside.' Feeling his eyes on me I shivered.

'I'm wearing a thermal under my top.' I picked up my waterproof jacket and a bottle of wine I'd put on the table.

'Merlot. Nice one.' Rob commented. He took a quilted jacket from his van and we set off up the lane to the farm. As we walked I asked him a bit about the blacksmithing. He was easy to talk to, matching his pace to mine, pointing out a muddy bit as we walked.

'I'm getting some commissions which are paying quite well,' he advised me. 'The only downside is driving to bloody London or the home counties with a van load of jangling metal. It's like driving a washing machine with a bag of spanners going round in it.' But he was generally pleased with it all.

He made me smile. Rob was definitely one of life's oxygenators. Matilda had stayed up to say hello before going off to bed, giggling and cuddling a floppy pink rabbit. It was quite clear that she adored her uncle Rob. I remembered to thank her for the use of her hot water bottle on my first night in the cottage. Phil commented that I was looking so much better. Martha looked surprisingly good in a rather county-set get up, with a high Princess Di frilly collar and pearls in her ears. She took my hand and kissed me warmly on one cheek. 'None of that artificial two cheek stuff,' She admired my necklace. 'I've seen that somewhere before, or something very like it.'

Dinner was tasty and substantial with an oven baked pesto and parmesan crusted pollock, Cornish caught of course, and home grown vegetables. A superb apple pie with vanilla ice cream followed.

'From our own orchards,' Phil said, 'eaters, cookers, and what mum and Jay don't cook or freeze I gather up and get them all juiced and pasteurised. Keeps a good year in the garage. I think that in the old days the farm used to pay some of the hands in cider at harvest. The farm next along the valley still has its original cider press.'

Rob made us laugh with some tales from the building trade, describing a couple in their holiday cottage who'd had problems with the underfloor heating thermostat. 'Hopping from foot to foot they were, like hens on a hot brick.'

'I'm envious,' Phil said when he'd stopped laughing. 'It's underfloor cooling we've got here in the farmhouse.'

Jay, looking quite lovely, was looking from me to Rob and back again. To take the attention away I asked her 'Is your name really Jay?' With her love of wearing soft pinks, blues and greens she certainly resembled the plumage.

'No.' She looked at Phil, who smiled back at her. He knew the story. 'It's Jacintha. Bestowed on me by a hormone flushed gas-and-air addled new mother, who had been reading a historical bodice ripper before going into labour and I got lumbered with the heroine's name. It's awful. Phil nearly fainted at the altar when he heard my real name read out.'

Martha looked over the table. 'Do you know why you are called Susannah?'

'Mum said she was meditating before I was born and that the name just came into her head. She didn't know that she was having a girl, but she said she heard a voice saying something like "I'm Susannah, I want to come home".'

Phil snorted, 'Sounds like wacky baccy to me, but with your mum the way she was I'm surprised you're not called Sunbeam or Moonbeam.'

Jay frowned at him.

'I had friends called Stormy and Rock,' I responded, unperturbed. 'They seemed quite normal names to me. Stormy's name described the weather the night she was born and Rock, well he would be called Craig in the Celtic language.'

The evening wasn't a long one. Farmers and farmers' wives get up early. Goodnights were said, backs patted, hands shaken, there were brief kisses. Phil handed me a bottle of his pasteurised apple juice to take home. Rob had a powerful torch ready for the walk back. I stifled a chortle, dying to say the old line "was that a torch in your pocket or were you just glad to see me." But I refrained. He's nice, I thought, but I know nothing about his private life and I am not going to flirt with him. He didn't say much as we walked and he seemed to have something on his mind. At the cottage he saw me to the back door and stood quietly for a moment while I found my keys in my bag. By now it was quite chilly and the sky was heavy with stars.

'Are you free tomorrow?' he asked. He'd angled the torch away to the ground and I couldn't see his face.

'What?' Oh no I was doing it again, going into slack jawed yokel mode.

'I can do your chimney tomorrow if you like, we've had no rain for a few days, ideal for it.'

'Yes that would be lovely' I sounded gushy. 'I mean yes, ideal.'

'OK. About two-ish, got a few things to do and then I'll be over. See you. Night then.' And with that he was off.

THREE

The next morning I tidied up, feeling pleased to be expecting company. There were sufficient provisions of tea, beer, biscuits, crisps, bread, cheese and olives. I didn't know what I was expecting but I was restless and a tiny bit excited. I'd cleaned up an old patio table and bench and with an extra couple of garden chairs and cushions arranged outside it looked welcoming. I picked a few flowers for an old glass jug I'd found and put it on the table, then I stood back and surveyed the scene. It did look pretty and the back garden was looking cared for. Those glossy magazines did have something after all.

Just before two I heard a call and went outside. Two men were standing just inside the back gate. They were very well groomed, both with neat short beards, one with a nice denim jacket and fawn chinos, the other in jeans with a chunky apple green sweater thrown round his shoulders over a pink checked shirt. For a moment I thought they were selling religion.

'Hello Su, we'd heard you'd come down to stay, so sorry about everything but haven't you got the place looking lovely, George would be so proud.' I swear they were both speaking at once, together in perfect harmony. George was my grandfather.

'Oh thank you, did you know him?' Who the hell were these people?

'Oh yes, we used to come over and play draughts and scrabble with him, swap fruit and veg, and bring him these.' One of the beards was handing me a box of eggs.

'Oh, thank you, what do I owe you, I'm sorry, I don't recall your names?'

'I'm Graham.' The denim jacket introduced himself.

'And I'm Oliver.' The apple green jumper was speaking, wearing a rather nice gold earring.

'We live at The Manor House in the village. We were at the funeral, but so was the whole village and half of Cornwall. Such a sad day. But here you are now and looking so much better.'

I remembered my manners, and my Cornish hospitality. 'Won't you stay for a drink and tell me about the times you spent with George, my grandfather.' I gestured towards the table and the jug of flowers.

Graham's eyes lit up. 'So pretty, so inviting in the sunshine and you suit it perfectly. Love to stay and have a chat, anything I can do to help? Sorry we dropped in unannounced but let's have this as well.' And from somewhere he produced a package. 'Home made Dundee cake, been in the tin a day or two so it's come again and is just ready for sharing.'

He talked very fast and I wasn't altogether sure what he was talking about but he bustled into the kitchen, obviously knowing where some things were kept, noticing a few small changes I'd made, keeping up a light friendly chat and making me feel at ease in their company.

Graham, I learned was a keen gardener who liked making home made organic hedgerow wines, (*Oliver quietly commented that they would knock out a few brain cells*). He also loved cooking.

Oliver, the more observant and less ebullient man, described himself as a struggling artist and a casual dowser. I hadn't spent time in a commune without knowing what dowsing was and confessed I'd seen it done and tried it myself. We agreed that there was something to it. Something to be respected. Oliver suggested that I should join him up at The Hurlers one day as there was a strong ley line in that area.

'The St Michael line you mean, but I'm not really into dowsing,' I explained. 'That was my mother and her life. I live a different life.'

I asked him what he painted. 'Oh, abstract landscape mostly. I see colours from beneath the earth when I dowse, it's quite weird but I do get inspiration. You must come over and visit the studio. Don't worry, I won't force you to buy anything, it mostly goes up to our friend's gallery in Cheltenham, does quite well especially in race weeks.'

'That's because the buyers are all pissed.' Graham said.

There was the sound of a vehicle pulling in round the cottage and a van appeared.

'Oh, another visitor is it?' Graham asked, craning his neck to see round Oliver. Rob appeared. 'Oh it's Rob, he's nice, now then, might we be disturbing anything here?' His lively black eyes were on my face.

A bit embarrassed I got up quickly and banged my knee on the side of Oliver's chair. I stood there with my eyes watering as Rob strolled over to us, his hair a bit tousled, dressed in torn dirty jeans, blue t-shirt and a different v-necked jumper this time with holes and burn marks. The contrast with the well groomed boys as I was now thinking of them, couldn't have been greater.

'I think I'm going to faint.' Graham spoke into his tea cup, his black eyes snapping with amusement.

There were pleasantries and smiles. Teasing about Graham and Oliver bringing their spotless car up the rutted track, jokes about muddiness and paintwork, boyish banter. The sun was shining, with sunlight dappling the garden and everyone dressed to play a part. I felt as though I was Alice falling through the rabbit hole, was this really me, entertaining in my garden, after the crappy year I'd had. By now my eyes had stopped watering and I took a reality check, they were all getting along perfectly fine without my intervention. Rob declined the cake, tea, beer and anything else he was offered by Graham while I stood, silent and speechless. He squinted down at me. 'While you're so happily occupied I'll get the ladder and go up for a look.' .

I managed to nod.

'Scream if you fall off and we'll come and save you. But I'll get there first I promise you my love.' Graham said.

Oliver rolled his eyes heavenwards and Rob walked away laughing. I sat down and Graham patted my hand.

'Don't worry dear, I didn't mean it. He butters his bread on a different side and I reckon you could get lucky there if you want to.'

They stayed a little while longer and then at a decent interval made their excuses and left, but not before making me promise to call in at their place. I was brushing crumbs off plates onto the grass when Rob reappeared.

'They're good blokes and Graham is a killer pub skittles player, well respected at the pub he is.'

I absorbed this information without responding. He looked at me patiently for a moment.

'I'm just going to mix a bucket of jallop and sort out that bit of pointing, it's all scraped and ready. Then maybe a cuppa and some of that cake if that's ok with you.'

I managed to nod again and I was ready with his order and a tongue in my head when he reappeared. Again he made some easy small talk and appreciated the cake, not mine I assured him, owning up to the real maker. I did not ask him if he knew what the phrase *it's come again* meant.

He made a lot of noise reloading his van while I stood at the gate watching him. He stopped, patting his pockets for his phone and obviously ready to go. I felt myself droop a little.

'You look a bit tired,' he said. 'Been a bit of a busy social whirl for you, this couple of days.'

'Yes,' I agreed with him, nodding my head like one of those toy dogs you see in the back of a car. 'I suppose it has, but it's good to meet people, especially ones who bring fruit cake as good as that, or fix chimneys'. I added.

He turned round to go and then turned quickly back. 'By the way I'm going up to Devon tomorrow, got a delivery for the craft shop, want to come with me, it's nice over Dartmoor at this time of year, not too busy, tourists I mean.' He spoke quickly.

My droop was banished, I felt a great lift of my spirits and I smiled up at him.

'I'd love to'. My sincerity could not have been clearer.

He looked a bit surprised, then smiled. 'I'll be here at eight sharp then'.

I went indoors and jumped up and down on and off the bottom step of the stairs. I hadn't done that since I was a little girl.

A few days later I saw Jay in the farm shop and we talked a bit about the craft shop.

'You got along with Rob alright then?' she asked.

'I was impressed.' I said neatly side-stepping her meaning. 'I hadn't really appreciated what amazing things people can make. There's glass, ceramics, jewellery, clothes, bags, belts. The standards are really high and things are really lovely quality. And Rob's work is so fine, it's delicate with all those twists and turns and even rams heads.' I was enthusiastic about his candlesticks, fire sets and even coat hooks made with lovely curves.

'I've never been there.' I thought she looked a bit tired. 'Farmers' wives don't get time off.'

'We could go together one day, take the two little ones with us, there's a cafe with an outside space. I could mind them while you walk round on your own for a bit.'

Her face lit up, 'Really?'

'Yes.' I was pleased with myself for having the idea. 'You've been lovely to me Jay while I get back on my feet, let me give something back.'

'Deal.' Jay was pleased.

I told her that I hadn't seen Rob since the trip. It had been a lovely day with a leisurely lunch at a moorland pub where we'd talked about a wide range of subjects. I couldn't gauge his interest though, he didn't flirt at all, didn't ask personal questions, didn't bump into me on the pretext of looking at the same thing. I was intrigued.

'So has Rob got, er I mean, is he involved, in a relationship with someone?' I blurted. Oh that was really uncool and obvious.

Jay paused, thought for a moment. 'I don't think so, not lately anyway.'

I felt uncomfortable. 'God, I sound like a kid.'

Jay smiled at me. 'Gotta begin somewhere I s'pose.'

'Thought maybe he didn't go for redheads.' I tried to make it sound like a joke.

'You're more tawny than red,' she said appraisingly. 'He liked you when you were 18 and I'd say he still likes you, but he's said nothing. Not that my brother usually discusses his love life with me, it's only recently that he's learned to talk properly in whole sentences and not just grunt.'

I drove home feeling much more optimistic about life these days but I urged myself to stay cool and calm. Thinking about the craft shop it occurred to me that I needed to occupy myself better, not just gardening and walking and looking after the cottage. I needed a creative outlet. Painting, I wondered, not really me. Drawing, hmm, another no. Pottery and ceramics weren't my thing and I couldn't see myself sewing or knitting either.

I thought back to my days as a kid in the commune where people tried their hands at things like weaving, wood whittling and rug making. I'd been shown how to do all sorts of things but that was what other people did, not me. I was interested in how things worked, but not necessarily in making them. I made a pot of green tea and sliced some fresh lemon to have with it and went outside. The flowers were really lovely, wild red Campion and white Oxeye daises were jostling in a sunny border and there were early Siberian Irises just breaking bud with a wonderful deep blue showing at their tips. And the light was swooningly beautiful. If only I could paint ... and then it hit me. Photography, grandfather talked about it often enough, surely I must have taken something in.

I finished my tea and went upstairs to the box room. It was dusty and the air was stale, I hadn't paid this room much attention at all. I opened a window, noticing a dead butterfly and several dead woodlice. The blue and white cotton curtains were a bit faded and needed a wash and quite frankly it needed a good clear out. The bookcase was hardly accessible with old photography magazines and catalogues piled up. There were several boxes the contents of which were a mystery, some a bit too heavy for me to move easily. I opened an oddly shaped cupboard built in above the staircase seeing old clothes, old bedlinen and I sneezed. This was going to be a bigger job than I had realised and there was no sign of a camera.

I was back downstairs searching for bin liners and cleaning items when I heard a 'Coo-eee' outside. Martha was sniffing a pale rose growing against the back wall of the cottage. I'd already noticed that it had a good scent. She looked at me, her eyes twinkling.

'You've got a cobweb on your head. Been rooting about have you?'

I told her about the as yet un-tackled box room.

'All houses have their clutter corners and secrets, be grateful you haven't got the crap we've accumulated in the attics at the farm. I'm sure there'll be no skeletons though, George was a tidy man.'

I recalled something Jay had said. 'Do you miss him Martha?' I asked.

'Yes I do, it was nice having someone of my era around, he was a good thinker, you could have a conversation. And if the vicar wasn't free I made up a scrabble foursome when Graham and Oliver came round. But if you're asking was I in love with him, no I wasn't, but I was very fond of him.'

Blimey, she was direct.

'George knew my late husband. We had things in common. He'd talk to me about your grandmother, your mum and of course about you. His ladies, he used to call you. He'd been blessed with his ladies but he was sad that he'd lost Christina and Tessa. He once said that the Charlesworth women seemed to have bad luck. But now I sound ridiculous so let's change the subject.'

I stood, rooted to the spot, seeing his perspective on life for the first time.

Martha had paused, considering what she was going to say next. 'I've got a spare kitten needing a home. She's a very pretty tortie and used to humans. *Please* say yes. She'll be company and if you want to go away I can pop in and see to her amongst my other daily chores.'

I considered the idea for a moment. 'I've never had a pet Martha, but I like cats and I guess this is a cat-friendly garden, and the lane isn't too busy. She'd better stay away from the bird-feeders though.' I indicated the seed and peanut containers in a nearby crab apple. Grandfather had always fed the birds there, understanding their need for shelter when feeding, vulnerable to the ever hunting sparrowhawk.

Martha left, promising to return that evening with the kitten. 'I shall bring you some cat litter and a couple of food packets, then we'll see if you bond okay.'

I went back inside, musing over her odd statement earlier. I hadn't thought about the Charlesworth women as being unlucky. With my background and training I understood that sometimes the human body just couldn't cope. Was there anyone else in the family that grandfather was thinking of, I wondered. Standing at the door to the box room I wondered for the first time in my life, who they were, where they came from and what made me. Were there any photographs of them in this room? Only one way to find out, and I started wielding the hoover, tackling the dusty old magazines and unhooking the curtains.

FOUR

Martha's muddy landrover appeared just as I was getting a simple meal together, my favourite crusty bread ploughman's meal with homemade apple and onion chutney. I liked black pepper on my tomato, a good cheddar with a spring onion, an apple sliced into quarters and a few fat green olives. It looked inviting on grandfather's old white china plates with the dark blue rim. My appetite had improved immensely since I'd moved back home to Cornwall. Martha knocked on the back door and came in with a carrier bag in one hand and a small wicker pet carrier in the other. I heard a protesting mew.

'Oh that looks good.' Martha's eyes lit up.

'There's plenty spare if you'd like to join me,' I offered, gesturing to the huge loaf of fragrant bread. 'The farm shop doesn't do small.'

She accepted with obvious pleasure. Making sure the back door was closed she indicated the basket.

'I think you should do the honours Su, she needs to see you first and start making connections immediately. She hasn't got a name yet.'

I crouched down and undid the two straps. A small, indignant tortoiseshell and white face peered up at me, her green eyes beautifully outlined in black, her markings strongly coloured in ginger and black and with a black tip to her tail. Another mew and what sounded like a huff. Then a delicate yawn, showing that her markings pigmented the inside of her mouth, pink and black. She got out of the basket and without hesitation started exploring, straight under a chair and off round the edges of the kitchen.

'Where should I put her litter tray?' Martha asked.

'Not here in the kitchen, I should think the futility room would be the best place don't you.' I replied, watching the kitten's progress. 'She's a pretty thing.'

Martha giggled. 'Futility it is, the room where a woman's work is never done.'

We spent a companionable hour together eating and watching the kitten, after placing her water bowl and food dishes in a safe place in a corner of the kitchen.

'They're clean creatures, they don't like to defecate where they eat.'

Martha advised me about keeping her in for a couple of weeks, placing the contents of her litter tray around the garden so that when she did go out there'd be a chance she would smell her own boundaries and not get lost. She also recommended the vet she used for the kitten's inoculations, spaying and a reliable flea and worm treatment.

'Her mother has been flea treated so the kitten should be ok, but you can't be too careful. They pick up all sorts of things. And there are too many unwanted cats so don't be sentimental about letting her have kittens of her own, it's just not necessary. I've got almost all the farm cats done now, and her mother is going in shortly.'

The kitten reappeared and approached my hand to sniff it, a soft paw batting my fingers. I put a dab of butter on one finger and she licked it, her tongue rough and warm.

'She'll be your friend for life if you treat her like that,' Martha said approvingly. 'A well fed cat is a happy cat and good hunter.'

After Martha had gone I considered returning to the box room tasks but decided against it. Instead I fetched a pile of old albums, poured myself a glass of wine, and offered the kitten half a pouch of some fishy preparation. She crouched down and concentrated hard on eating. I loved the way she was so in the moment. I noticed she was purring whilst eating. Martha had also provided some cat crunchies. Clever girl, what a clever girl, who's a clever girl then, I started crooning to her. The kitten finished eating, glanced at me, and then wobbled determinedly in the direction of the sitting room, her little belly looking full and round. She sat down and washed, glanced at me again and seemed to be making her mind up about something. I sat down on the squashy little two seater sofa, glass of wine to one side, albums on a small table in front of me. The kitten surveyed the scene, yawned so hard that her eyes almost disappeared and hauled herself up beside me. Finding all to her satisfaction she curled up, gave a deep sigh and went to sleep wedged between me and a cushion. I felt a great smile curling up from deep within me. I needed to find her a name.

Turning to the albums I started with what looked like the oldest one, it had woven dark linen covered boards with crimped leather corners and thick brown pages. The photographs were quite small, four to a page and someone had written comments or captions below each one, in an elegant script and using white ink. People I didn't know and could hardly make out. Boats, a few shots taken on Dartmoor, a woman holding onto a cloche hat with her skirt blowing to one side as she stood before the piled ancient stones of a tor, another showing a village event and people smiling. There was one of a traction engine clearly from the same event.

I turned pages and sipped my wine, aware of the kitten against my side. I examined her more closely. She had white paws and pink toes, a fat white tummy and a dark pink nose which was also outlined in black. I thought about all the cats she was descended from, nature simply intent on reproduction. The cottage was quiet around me, darkness falling. There was a sense of anticipation in the room, as though someone was there with me. All these people having fun inside the album, where was I when they were alive and where are they now that I'm alive?

I got up and switched the lamps on, closed the curtains, poured another glass of wine and opened another album. The room was quiet and cosy. There was a baby, the caption read *Robert William Charlesworth born 10 October 1901 at his Christening.* This album must be older than the one I'd just looked at. I looked closely at the photo, sepia tinged but with what must be some careful hand touching, a delicate little blush of colour on the cheek and lips of a plump baby dressed nicely in what was clearly a christening robe and lying on an embroidered blanket. The picture looked as though it had been taken by a professional, perhaps indoors. Was this baby my great-grandfather I wondered. I had never heard the name before today. I tried to recall what grandfather had said about his own father and had a vague memory of him talking about a hard working kind man. I had no idea what he'd done for a living.

I continued turning pages but they were empty. Then a folded program fell out, hand printed I guessed, advertising that a musical evening would be held at the village hall, with dancing and refreshments, admission One Penny. The event date was Valentine's Day, 1901. There were ribbons and hearts drawn around the top of the bill and the initials, in faint pencil, SP and RW. I wondered who they were, obviously nothing to do with the picture of the baby since their initials didn't match up with the surname Charlesworth.

I finished my wine, suddenly aware that raindrops were hitting the windows. Leaving the kitten sleeping soundly downstairs I decided to run a bath before bedtime and busied myself upstairs. Clean, warm and smelling of my favourite body lotion I walked into my bedroom and switched the bedside lamp on. The kitten opened one eye and stretched out a dainty paw in welcome. She was curled up in the middle of the duvet.

A few days later and I'd made some progress in the box room removing dust, washing the curtains and windows, and sorting out the contents of the cupboard. I had spent some time going through the linens and some old clothes which had belonged to my mother and deciding what I wanted to keep. Pillowslips that were too narrow for modern pillows, some musty blankets, redundant since the invention of the duvet and some horrible flowered sheets and orange fabric table settings, all went on the going-out pile. But I did like two beautifully embroidered heavy cotton squares I'd found. About a metre square they were plain cream with flowers in the corners, bluebells, campion, daisies. Red, white and blue, I thought, very patriotic. I wasn't sure what I would use them for but they were lovely. There was also a paper bag which contained a very large lace square carefully folded in old tissue paper. I'd opened it up and let the lace slip through my fingers, it was very fine and silky in a faded colour like weak tea and with daisies worked into the pattern. It was quite beautiful.

Meanwhile I got the kitten booked into the vets and went to a large supermarket to stock up on goodies for both of us. On the way back I paid another visit to the churchyard. It contained names such as Penrose, Harvey, Williams, Jones, and Griffiths. I sat down on an old bench placed near a wall, my eye roving over a compost bin holding the remains of flowers and grass cuttings. Someone had left a rake and a garden fork there and beyond them I noticed lichen covered slate headstones ranged against the wall. I got up and walked over, they were hard to read but some had traces of beautiful carving, then I spotted *...worth*. I pulled up some grass and rubbed the slate to reveal the name *Joseph Charlesworth died 12 December, the Year of Our Lord 1912. God grant him the Love he deserves.*

Who was this and how did he fit into the family tree, an older brother to Robert William, or an uncle maybe. I became aware of someone calling hello and turned to see the vicar limping over the grass. The man that people affectionately referred to as Vicar Vic.

'Hello again, how are you getting on?' He was looking past me at the gravestone. 'Ah, a relative of yours I suspect. You've got sharp eyes.' He grimaced.

I greeted him. 'What have you done to your leg?'

'Ankle. Rabbit hole on the moor up at Minions, walking the dogs two days ago. My wife was with me thankfully, otherwise I might still be up there.'

I asked him why the gravestones were leaning against the wall.

'Problems with health and safety mostly, not placed upright enough, wobbling about like old teeth. Sometimes the ground subsides a bit over the years which doesn't help, and neither do the rabbits which get in here as well. They'd try the patience of a saint.' He smiled, shifting his weight uncomfortably to his better foot. 'The plus side of course is that the old burial site is easier to mow and maintain. And of course all the graves were identified and recorded before the stones were moved.'

I told him about the early christening photograph of Robert William Charlesworth and how it had stirred an interest in my family origins.

'Popular subject these days,' he acknowledged. 'And it answers a lot of questions for people, it provides a sense of identity or belonging.' He looked at me shrewdly. 'Is that what you are searching for Su?'

I was surprised by the question and it must have shown. 'I hadn't really thought of it like that.'

'We're fortunate here that we still have some parish records, the history group has been researching and digitally documenting the BMD's, grave records and so on. I can put you in touch with someone locally if you like.'

'What do you mean by BMD's?'

'Births, Marriages, Deaths. My stock in trade really, the Victorians did us a huge favour in standardising records and making registrations a legal requirement. Hence the appointment of a Registrar. Prior to 1837 it was the parish duty to keep records, so they were sometimes very good if the person doing the job was diligent, abysmal otherwise. And they were written according to local knowledge, often assuming information, mis-spelling names according to dialect, lots of inaccuracies and so on. Fascinating to look at though.'

I was intrigued. 'So it's possible that someone could help me to put Robert William and Joseph into context then?'

'Oh absolutely. Some of it you can do yourself if you have a computer and join a family research organisation. In your case you'd start with your grandfather, George Charlesworth. You need to find his marriage certificate, that will help you to identify your grandmother's family, then his birth certificate, to identify his parents and so on back as far the records available will permit.

You'd need to get death certificates as well, it begins to get expensive ....'

My mind was leaping ahead, I was already seeing a pattern in the investigative process, my mind accustomed to auditing, carrying out tests, processes. I was thrilled.

'Thank you so much, I'm, well, I'm quite excited by this.' I realised he was still talking.

'And the Welsh names in the churchyard belong to miners who came from Wales during the glory days of the tin and copper mining, they brought incredible skills, knowledge and fortitude. But it was a tough time, villages like Minions and Caradon Town were virtually frontier towns, shantytowns, lawless and dangerous. Thousands of men came to work in the mines.' He waved his arm indicating a direction. 'At St Cleer over there the police station was built with a cell in which to lock up some of the miscreants.'

He talked a little longer and I nodded occasionally, my mind elsewhere. Eventually he looked at his watch.

'I must get on but I'll tell our Mrs Bradley you are interested in finding out about your family. She's in the library volunteers group and does a lot of work on the old records in her spare time. One family she found seems to be able to trace its history back to Tudor times and has a Spanish ancestor. Amazing stuff.'

At home I started with a blank sheet of paper and wrote out the names, birth and death dates that I knew about. It didn't look like much of a start but I added *marriage date?* to my grandfather's name and then realised that I needed to carry out a thorough search of the drawers and cupboards in all the rooms to find his personal papers. That proved to be a longer task than I had anticipated.

I borrowed Martha's cat basket to take the kitten to her veterinary appointment where I was asked for her name. I'd already given it some thought and decided to name her after one of my favourite flowers. Daisy. Her green eyes had already started watching me, tracking me when I walked across a room. She had a sense of humour and would hide at a corner or behind a door, then she'd jump out at me, pretend to be scared and tumble over herself as she turned and ran, looking to see if I was chasing her. She liked to play with a long piece of string to which I'd tied a feather. She mewed, chirruped and burbled in a companionable way and I did my best to make her feel at home. I wasn't sure how she'd feel about me after her operation though, and I felt as though I'd done something awful as I drove away, leaving her with the veterinary nurse.

To take my mind off Daisy I called in at the village library, only open for a few hours in the morning and explained to a rather fat man that I was looking for Mrs Bradley. An attractive woman in tight white jeans with blue varnished fingernails and long platinum blonde hair turned from some books she was placing and answered my enquiry. 'That's me. You're Su aren't you, I'm Liz.' She had a nice voice and a lively enquiring expression. I'd been expecting an elderly, matronly person and she was quite the opposite, probably the life and soul of the party given the opportunity. But she was as smart as a whip and already way ahead of me.

'It's a great opportunity to help you look into your background, because they are village people. So many have moved away to jobs outside the county or even the country, and of course others were lost in the wars. We might find something new or interesting about village life. Have you found anything in your grandfather's papers?' The vicar had, it seemed, already filled her in about my background.

'I'm still going through things, very slowly I'm afraid.' I explained.

'Of course,' she nodded. 'And you'll want to do it respectfully, it's an odd thing going through someone's private papers and things. I know, I've done it and you can find you learn too much about them.'

We exchanged phone numbers and I promised to call her once I had found anything.

'And while you're sorting things out I shall take a look at the parish records and some old parish magazines and photographs, you never know who or what can turn up when it's time for them to be found.' She said.

Mulling over her interesting turn of phrase I walked back down the lane towards my car. It was a lovely day and got even nicer when I heard a voice call my name. Rob was sitting on a low wall, his long legs stretched out in scruffy jeans. There were tools in a canvas bag on the ground.

'What do you think of this then?' He indicated a newly fitted garden gate.

I studied the design, wavy flowing lines, irregular heights. 'Er, I'm getting grass, or is it reeds. I like it, I like it a lot.'

He was looking at the gate, not at me. 'Pondside Cottage this place is. The village farrier used to operate near here, take water from the pond. It's a holiday cottage now, couple who bought it said they wanted to honour its past. I had the hell of a problem talking them out of some vile concoction they wanted made with old horseshoes, it was a nightmare. I sketched this and thankfully they went for it because it was unique.'

'I hope you're charging them a unique price then.'

He glanced at me. 'Feeling a bit cheeky today are you.' His eyes went over me quickly and I felt slightly shy. 'You look well Su, not peaky like you were when you first got here.'

I changed the subject and told him about the kitten Martha had brought me. He seemed interested, smiling at me as I described her cute ways. With his eyes on me I suddenly felt a bit hot.

'Call in the next time you're going up to the farm, if you can,' I blurted, 'come and meet my Daisy.'

His eyebrows rose as I blushed, and then we both started laughing.

'I shall do that. I shall most certainly do that.'

FIVE

I collected Daisy the following morning and was strongly advised to keep her indoors for a week. 'Poor little pet' I crooned to her, 'who'll be the most bonkers then, me or you?' Her enforced containment was already proving a little frustrating for both of us. At home I defrosted a few cooked prawns in hot water and cut them up into small pieces as a treat for her and to assuage my guilt over her operation. I hand fed her and she rumbled her pleasure as she delicately ate them, and licked my fingers. No offence there then, I thought, as she washed herself and examined the little shaved area on her side, where a couple of stitches were visible. I showed her a little padded small pet bed I'd bought from the local farmers' supplies shop. She accepted this with good grace and fell asleep. I breathed a huge sigh of relief.

By late afternoon I was upstairs sorting things out in the box room again when I became aware of tapping on the back door. I poked my head out of the window and looked down onto Rob's head. I called out, 'Ahoy, intruder alert!'

He stepped back and looked up, indicating a carrier bag in one hand. 'Permission to come aboard?'

'Hang on, don't let the kitten out.' I hurried downstairs and let him in, absurdly pleased to see him. 'I have to operate a system of airlocks at the moment so that she can't get out. I think she knows where she is, judging by the amount of time she spends on the windowsills studying the garden, but she's recuperating from her operation and must stay in.'

Rob surveyed the back door. 'Okay I've got the message but does she have a key yet?'

'What do you mean?' At least I'd progressed beyond saying 'what' at last.

'How will she get in and out, or do you intend to run about after her day and night?'

I considered his question. 'Hmm, you mean a cat thing, a cat flap.' I stumbled over my words.

'We are talking cat-thing-flap if your beauty sleep isn't to be disturbed. You can have it in this door and keep the other door to the kitchen shut so she can't bring her finds in any further.'

'You are an expert on cats?'

'Lifelong. My dad is dotty about cats. Some men drink, gamble, womanise, his secret vice is cats. He'll stop in the street to talk to a strange cat. Funny thing is they talk back to him. I spent my formative years in a state of severe, and I mean severe, embarrassment. I'm still having therapy actually.'

He followed me into the kitchen waving the carrier bag. 'Where shall I put this?'

'What is it?' Wow, another coherent sentence beginning with what.

Rob had brought a packet of cat treats for Daisy, a bottle of red wine, because, he explained, he'd never given me a New Home present, and a large bar of caramel chocolate, because he liked it.

'And I shall fight you and cry if you pinch my chocolate.'

This guy was so easy to get along with. I found myself saying that I was hungry enough to eat all the chocolate and that I hadn't eaten since breakfast. 'I can put a snack together if you want to stay and have a glass of that wine.'

Rob accepted without hesitation and once again I found myself assembling a ploughman's plate, but this time avocado and humous with a few cherry tomatoes made it a little upmarket. Rob warmed the wine in a bowl of hot water before he opened it.

'Seeing a wineglass already on the draining board I deduce you do indeed drink, although I'm not sure whether I should be concerned that you obviously drink alone madam.'

Mmm, the wine was rough and red, the sort that spanks you round the kitchen and demands food to complement its flavour. We clinked glasses.

'Welcome home.' Rob smiled. 'I'm glad you're back.'

I liked the sound of that. He was funny, cheerful and once again made me laugh with his stories. I was reminded of Andrew, he'd always been happy go lucky and able to make everyone laugh. Rob noticed my sudden pause in the proceedings.

'You were absent for a moment Su, d'you mind me asking?'

So I told him all about my long term ex-boyfriend, a great relationship at first but a perennial student who never seemed to want to grow up and take responsibility for anything. How he dumped his guilt on me when he met someone else, you know how it goes.

'Sounds like Peter Pan. Did he hurt you a lot?'

'He should have, but, you know, he didn't. I suppose my upbringing made me aware that people move in and out of relationships and there used to be a lot of discussion about how unhealthy and possessive long term relationships were. I used to listen when I was supposed to be asleep.' I added as he raised his eyebrows. 'That doesn't make me special, or saintly or unfeeling, I actually think the relationship had peaked but I hadn't really noticed, which is awful and which is partly why he ended the relationship. And I was so exhausted from work that by the time we split up I was too zonked out, too tired to be bothered, so it was just another sad thing in a bad time, which got a lot worse when grandfather died.'

'Why do you call him that?' Rob questioned, changing the subject. 'And not Pops, or gramps or grandpa. It sounds like Heidi in that growing up in Switzerland book.'

'You've read the Heidi books?' I was incredulous.

He glared at me. 'I deny it. I have a sister not a quarter of a mile away and she lived that life, hid bread rolls in the wardrobe, watched it on Sunday afternoon TV, and was generally a pain.'

Like I said, this guy was marvellously easy to get along with. Suddenly he stretched and I found myself admiring his strong arms, his well shaped hands, noticing a small burn on the inside of his forearm. I had an overwhelming desire to kiss it better. I'd spent the evening talking, looking at his face, watching his mannerisms, liking what I saw. He looked at his watch and sat up straight.

'It's getting late, I'll get off and like the ignorant pig that I am I shall leave you to do the washing up.'

I smiled. 'No problem, I always smash plates after guests.'

His laughter was infectious.

As he stood up Daisy wandered into the kitchen, considered him for a second and walked up to him. Without pausing she folded herself round his legs, flirting her tail, glancing up at him sideways. I watched her, enviously.

'Ah, I have clearly inherited my dad's way with cats.' Rob was smug as he rubbed her head and beneath her chin.

'Nope. She's a tart like most cats.' I responded.

Rob thanked me for an unexpectedly pleasant visit. His words sounded formal and made me stand back a little. I thanked him for calling round and suddenly we were a little awkward, the easy friendship of the evening had slipped away. But he said he would have a think about the cat-thing-flap and that it would be no problem for him to fit it. Then he told Daisy that he was very pleased to have made her acquaintance and left.

I poured myself another glass of red wine. I was sorry to see him go, but the large bar of uneaten chocolate meant he would be back.

The next few days saw me occupied with domestic concerns, I was still getting used to the idea that the cottage was mine and the list of things to do now that summer was almost here seemed endless. I decided I wanted to repaint the hallway in a lighter colour and I had thrown out some ugly old light-shades, preferring some etched glass globes I'd found in a shop in Lostwithiel.

The garden always needed attention and I read more of my grandfather's books on gardening, especially pruning. Everything, it seemed, had a specific time. He had written carefully pencilled notes in some margins, wisteria for example, needed a trim after flowering and again a few months later to reduce whippy growth before winter. Against aquilegia and

Welsh poppy he had noted *let them set seed* and *rabbits don't eat these*.

One day I found that the gooseberry bushes had been almost stripped of their leaves overnight and spent ages picking off plump little caterpillars, drowning them in a bowl of water and washing up liquid in the same way that I dealt with slugs. Again I found a pencilled note with instructions on how to make up a simple garlic spray *against sawflies and others*, and it seemed to have an effect although I wondered if I'd ever get the smell of garlic out of my blender. Wild garlic grew amongst the English bluebells by the hazel bushes, I had recognised the white flowers and the unmistakable scent. But then I thought, do I really want to go to all this trouble for gooseberries when I prefer blueberries? And I was off again, researching whether pests affected blueberries and could I grow them instead. It turned out that in my acidic moorland soil I could.

It was hard to stay indoors as the days lengthened and became warmer, and I formed a habit of taking my mid morning drink down to the pond side. Across the pond and almost opposite the old bench were some huge granite rocks, typical of the Bodmin landscape, smooth and weathered and two in particular I mentally named the cow and calf. The pond path lead around the back of them and past an old stone stile in the Cornish hedge where a footpath went up to Moorstones Farm where Jay lived. Someone, many years ago, had banged posts into the ground and wound barbed wire around them, making the stile unusable. The footpath was only visible because the sheep used it. You could sit comfortably on one and lean against the other, your back against sun-warmed granite. It was a secret place with large ferns providing screening and shelter. Sitting there I felt very small, my perspective altered by scale, green-gold sunlight filtering through soft new birch and hazel leaves. From there I watched unnoticed as a cock pheasant strutted his colours to his somewhat indifferent hen and a stoat busily scouted for evidence of rabbits. A lizard joined me on one occasion and a nuthatch explored the hazel patch, moving up and down the bark with ease. A tiny wren with a big voice often complained about my presence.

With some careful pruning I reopened the narrow path which lead around the pond, removing ankle or eye height obstructions. Working slowly had enabled me to enjoy the spot created by both nature and human hand. My mother I remembered, had felt that the pond was a dark place and didn't go down there much. She said something sad had happened there in the past, but I couldn't recall what as I carried or wheeled clippings up to the bonfire corner, with a feeling of something like contentment.

Finding that midges and clegflies seemed to be most active at around 4pm, I would retreat back to the cottage, to the sunny paved terrace, at home to anyone who called. One afternoon Graham appeared, dressed like a catalogue advertisement with his calf-high brown boots matching the soft leather trim detail on his gilet, a square red scarf knotted gypsy fashion at his neck. It suited his colouring but was practical. Locals out walking wore boots to protect against ticks, and scarves helped to stop the midges from biting soft exposed skin.

'Hello love,' he kissed me on the cheek. 'I've been bothering Martha and raiding her freezer, I wanted some fruit for a pie and I know she has blackcurrants all ready for use. I just can't be bothered with all that poxy fiddly topping and tailing because there'd be my blood in the blackcurrants. I traded her some of my elderflower cordial and I put a bottle in the car for you, here.' A green bottle was produced. Again he busied himself competently in my kitchen, commenting favourably on the few changes I'd made, admiring a pretty blue and yellow jug I'd found in a cupboard and put on display and then he was distracted by the appearance of Daisy.

'Oh who's a pretty girl, oh what a lovely girl, who's a brave little poppet having an operation then.' He'd noticed the shaved patch. Daisy was enchanted by the attention and the tickles and threw herself onto her back, waving all four paws in the air, her fat white tummy gleaming.

'Love to have animals about.' He was chatting, filling up spaces in the atmosphere. 'They give the place movement. Oliver and I have got the hens, two dogs, two cats and I love them all. They put the heart into a home.'

We went back outside, Daisy protesting at being left inside, and I told him all about her, about the gardening, and about meeting Vicar Vic and Liz Bradley. Graham was an attentive and interested listener, and a mine of information about pets, gardening and cooking. He said he wasn't a churchgoer and preferred magazines and newspapers to books, but he was quite interested in family history. His own people had been small farmers locally, working for generations for the nearby big estate before the war killed off the heirs and the National Trust took over the property.

I fetched the old folded programme advertising the Valentine's Day dance in 1901 and he mused over it, holding it carefully.

'Quite an event locally I suppose. Innovative I think because wasn't Valentine's Day a bit of a Victorian invention?' I said.

'Well they really popularised it with the invention of cards,' he acknowledged. 'But I think it goes back a long time, depending on what sort of legend-crap floats your boat. I think even Chaucer gives it a mention. Have you shown it to Liz Bradley yet?'

I answered that I hadn't. 'I still need to find the sort of personal papers she's talking about.'

Graham didn't stay long but before he left he made me promise to join them at The Manor House for lunch on Saturday.

'Lunch is so much more decadent than dinner I always think.' His black eyes were glittering wickedly. 'You can end up between the sheets, have a doze afterwards, and still have plenty of time for fun and games in the evening.'

I spent my evening tackling the contents of the small oak bureau in the sitting room. I'd always loved its warm golden colour and the little bit of carving on the lid, some leaves and what I'd always thought looked a bit like an art nouveau sunflower. On closer inspection it now looked more like a daisy.

I wondered if that had worked on me subconsciously when I'd named the kitten, daisies had always been my favourite flower.

It was cool enough to light the woodstove and that alone was novel enough to give me pleasure as I slowly and methodically sorted through the paperwork, checking through old bills, articles torn from newspapers, some old parish magazines with the name of a local chimneysweep highlighted and various receipts. After a few hours I opened the woodstove and put most of what I'd sorted through onto the fire where it blazed for a few minutes. Daisy sat and blinked into the flames. There were no family papers there. I yawned as the last of the fire died down.

'Time for a bath and bed Daisy.'

She stretched and padded off to her litter tray, glancing at me as she walked by, raising her tail in a friendly way. Her grasp of this new life impressed me, she had her favourite places to sit, liked to invite me to play, enjoyed her food and seemed happy to accommodate what she clearly understood as my rituals, so long as her food bowl was replenished. She was curled up on the duvet by the time I was ready for bed.

SIX

On Saturday I dressed with more care than usual. I'd taken a day out and gone down to Truro, coming home with a few nice things to wear. I'd also managed to get a decent haircut. Selecting some flowers from the garden I made up a rather pretty bunch together with a few rose buds. Remembering that Graham liked to make his own wines, I'd chosen a small selection box of truffles as an after lunch gift. Thus equipped I drove off to The Manor House.

The gates were open and I drove over crunchy gravel to the side of a small circular lawn at the front of the house. The house was basically Georgian in its symmetry, with small paned sash windows under granite lintels and a lovely wide porch with a yellow rose climbing up one side. There were boots and a dogs water bowl inside the porch. Two Lutyens benches enhanced the symmetry at the front of the house. With lavender under the windows and two fat labradors barking themselves stupid behind a gated area to one side it looked like the perfect home. The west side was slate hung against the relentless winter rain in what I knew to be Delabole slate, grey with flecks of gold giving it a soft look.

Oliver came out to meet me wearing rose pink, paint splattered overalls. 'Su you look lovely, in contrast to me! I'd completely forgotten the time and have to change, Graham is pretending to be furious with me. He loves a drama. Come on in. He's creating something marvellous in the kitchen.'

'Wow.' I commented. Indoors the ground floor was a dream with waxed flagstone floors leading along a wide passageway to an attractive red and cream kitchen. There were old latched doors and I caught a glimpse of a panelled study with dark green walls and a leather club chair, a sitting room with a piano, squashy cream sofas and a luxurious oriental rug in front of the fireplace. I could hear Graham shouting something rude at the dogs. He bustled into the kitchen, a striped apron over his clothes. There was a lovely smell emanating from the range.

'Su my dear, you found us.' Graham kissed my cheek, admiring the cottage garden flowers, and thanking me for the truffles. 'Oh, you've got me sussed alright.'

In his usual deft way he had the flowers in an elegant fluted vase and a glass of something from a jug offered before I'd drawn breath. He was like a magician.

'We're eating in the conservatory so come on through, by the way that's non-alcoholic since you are driving, although there is wine as well. Love your dress, that sweetheart neckline suits you, it's very pretty with that opal necklace.' He placed the flowers on a side table in the conservatory.

I was speechless for a few moments. A wide oak and glass room framed an intimate walled garden with a slate paved terrace. There were large pots of flowers arranged in groups, a modern circular slate water feature with water dribbling down its sides, granite cobble edged paths leading invitingly to a door in a wall and to an archway cut into a hedge. It was a modern design but in sympathy with the house.

'It's so beautiful.'

'It's fairly low maintenance and easy to remove the dog shit since there's no grass in this bit, if that's what you mean.' Graham said, but I could see he was pleased with my reaction.

I looked around. From the large and vibrant abstract paintings on the back wall to the comfortable dark red sofas facing each other across a low table at one side and the square chunky table with four chairs on the other, the room was cosy and relaxing. I admired some very large glass bowl candle holders.

'They are cat and dog safe.' Graham advised. 'Too big for waggy tails to knock over and too high for inquisitive cats. We use this room a lot, double glazing and underfloor heating so the cats and dogs love it, an insulated solid roof, it's often warmer in here than in the house.' Graham rearranged a flower stem and straightened a magazine. 'Now make yourself comfortable, step outside if you like but don't go too far, I've just got a few last minute things to attend to for lunch and Oliver might eventually join us if he can get himself cleaned up.'

I went outside and stood on the terrace, holding my drink and feeling as though I'd just walked into a homes and gardens magazine. I'd been brought up amongst people who cared very little for possessions, but the arrangement of this house and garden had been put together with such good taste and love that it created not just an embracing and welcoming atmosphere but made me feel that this was a special moment. I tried to explain this to Oliver when he joined me.

'We worked hard all our lives Su, pleasing other people. Graham was in the NHS and I prostituted my talents in commercial art. We used to talk about what we'd like to create if we ever had the chance, and the time. When Graham found he'd been gifted an inheritance from an uncle down here and property prices went bonkers in London, I sold my flat for a shockingly good price and we bought this and retired early. Twelve years on we're just about where we want to be. And of course it's a homecoming for him, being a Cornishman.'

We responded to a call of 'On the table!' Lunch started with fresh figs cut open and lightly grilled with a little melted blue cheese, served with grilled sweet cherry tomatoes with a touch of basil oil and a few rocket leaves. It was delicate and delicious. Then came fragrant basmati rice perfumed with star anise to accompany Thai green fish curry. I paused while the flavours sang on my tongue.

'Is it ok for you?' Graham's eyebrows were raised.

'It's stunning.' I said. 'So much flavour.'

'The prawns must be cold water prawns, not tiger prawns. And I like to put my own ingredients together but lime juice is essential and lots of coriander and some lemongrass of course. I can give you the recipe if you like.'

I put my fork down and lifted my glass to him. 'And deprive me of the opportunity of coming here to enjoy it? No thank you.'

They were lovely company. I asked them how they'd met.

'I found Oliver lying in a ditch one night.' There was laughter.

'I'd gone off the road near Orpington and this knight in NHS armour was just off duty and tended to my bruises. When you meet a nurse who wants to look after you and who can cook you don't let him go. That was twenty-five years ago.'

There was no pudding but we had coffee and a couple of truffles each, chatting about working life, living in the country and what we missed about cities.

'Certainly not the noise.' Oliver was emphatic. 'But I enjoyed the theatre and I do miss good bookshops.'

'What about you Graham?' I asked him. 'What do you miss?'

'Parties. And being able to buy exotic ingredients on any street corner. I have to travel miles down here to find decent spices. It's a nightmare.'

They invited me to take a walk around the garden. The walled garden lead to a small well fenced orchard with half a dozen hens patrolling. They rushed towards us to see if we had any treats for them.

'Not just now girls. Oh I hate to disappoint them.' Graham was looking at them fondly.

'What breed are they?' I was admiring the iridescence on their dark plumage.

'Barnvelders. Nice layers. I don't know a damn thing about breeds, I just liked their looks.'

A gate let us into a vegetable patch, then round to the back of the double garage where the dogs had the run of a large area. I was immediately goosed by Eric, the large golden labrador while Sally, his black female companion sniffed at my fingers and licked them, her tail wagging.

'They are failed guide dogs, both of them. Completely clueless and brainless but so loving.' Graham was accepting a soggy well chewed old plimsoll.

Above the garage was Oliver's studio, the North end all glass, a couple of skylights adding to the light. Work in progress was on a table in the centre of the room.

'I like to work flat before I move to an easel. I start with the ground and then move to the light.'

His work was bold with orange, red and turquoise on one canvas; green, orange and blue on another. He liked to apply fast drying acrylics using a roller as well as a brush. I studied them for a while. Graham had gone back to the kitchen to find a few scraps for his chickens. Oliver didn't speak. Finally I trusted my feeling.

'It's like looking at music, like feeling music when you hear it played.'

'I always play music when I paint. Sometimes just the titles can get me started. And sometimes I hear sounds when I dowse.'

I was still looking at the work. 'As a commercial artist did you do a lot of work using fonts, lettering?'

'Quite a bit. Why?'

'Oh I just want to write the word *passion* on this yellow one maybe vertically down the right side, in a really nice script.' I caught him looking at me. 'Oh I'm sorry, that's probably crass of me. It's a naff idea.'

Oliver was polite. 'Actually I think you've got something there. It is a passionate piece.'

'And far more exciting than simply having those awful wooden words around the house saying things like bath, love and home.' I said.

We were laughing in agreement. 'As though you were so witless you'd forgotten the use of the rooms.' Oliver relied. 'Though it could be useful for those of us with short term memory loss!'

They sent me off with a bottle of something homemade and a box of eggs. I drove home in a very happy state of mind noticing the abundance of wildflowers on the banks and thought briefly of my once busy life, my tiring, exhausting life, and knew what I preferred. I was feeling so relaxed, so accepted. Inspired by Oliver I decided to get my new camera out and start making a record of this lovely place.

And it really was time to let the cat out. At home I changed into jeans and an old polo shirt. Daisy had raced upstairs ahead of me, keen to play and to supervise whatever I was doing, making her friendly chirruping noise. Normally I would have given her a couple of the crunchy biscuit treats Rob had introduced her too, but I decided it was best to keep her a little hungry until her evening meal. Picking up my new camera, all charged and ready to use I went back downstairs, Daisy in close attendance. I'd already learned to be very careful on the stairs as she liked to hop quickly down a few ahead of me and then pause to see either what lay in front or whether I was following. I opened the back door, fixing it on the latch, and stepped outside. Daisy stood hesitantly in the doorway, all eyes and twitching ears so I crouched down and photographed the moment of her first day outside. She looked at me, looked over my shoulder at something moving which I couldn't see, and then craned her neck to see to her left and to her right. One paw outside, then two, then all four and just as I was about to give her a word of encouragement she seemed to contract into a ball and then explode in all directions.

'Daisy no!' I shouted as she raced off across the small lawn, her tail held in a funny little loop. She stopped, turned, did a little sideways-on dance with her tail crooked and raced back but ran past me and off round the cottage. I followed as fast as possible, but she was darting about, up onto an upturned bucket where she batted a passing fly, off and down under a fern and off again, right round the cottage and ignoring the open door.

I was beginning to think this wasn't a good idea after all when there was a 'Coo-eee' from the gate.

'Oh Martha, thank god, I've just let Daisy out for the first time ...' I was panting.

'And you're having a parental panic I can see.'

Martha was calm, quickly establishing that I hadn't fed her yet, that she had clear access to the cottage and that I'd been putting the contents of her litter tray around the garden.

'That's ok then. Let's sit down here in the sun, if you chase her you'll stress her. Let her find her own comfortable distance on the first day, she can hear and smell us, especially you, even if we can't see her.'

'Thank you Martha, I'm sorry to seem stupid, but I've never owned a cat, though I'm not sure she has any concept of ownership. We seem to be on an equal footing most of the time.'

'Oh don't worry. I've been around animals all my life and they can teach us a thing or two. After all this time she knows an awful lot about you and where she lives. And she's knows when she's well off and comfortable. She'll be back. Be patient and I'll make us a cup of tea shall I?'

I nodded, the earlier contentment of the day quite gone.

Martha returned with everything on a tray and asked me what I'd been up to so I told her about lunch at The Manor House and said how beautiful their house was and then, thinking about pretty things, I went and found the embroidered cotton squares I'd discovered in the box room cupboard. Hand washed and carefully pressed they'd come up really well. Martha held them and put her glasses on to look more closely at the embroidery.

'It's very fine work, the colours have lasted well and the flowers are quite easy to identify. I think this is trousseau work, a girl making things for her bottom drawer.'

I was none the wiser and it showed in my face.

'These are the sort of things a girl would make in anticipation of her marriage, girls were encouraged to have a good stock of things ready for the new home. Social status meant different things might be important. Making something like tray cloths and table linens would mean an expectation of acting as hostess for one's guests, rather than hemming sheets and making shirt collars and dishcloths.' She was musing aloud. 'These are too large for trays and too small for the dining table, although they'd be lovely these days in a small conservatory. Maybe they were for her dressing table. But they are lovely, a real find.'

Then I showed her the ivory lace. I hadn't washed it, being worried I might damage it. Again Martha was fascinated. 'It feels like silk by the way it's catching against my fingertips.'

I sipped my tea. 'How old do you think they are?' I asked her.

'Pre-war, definitely. In fact I think they could be earlier, probably before the first war, turn of the last century even.'

'Wow.'

'The embroideries might have been made by one of your ancestors. George wouldn't have kept them unless he got them from his family, or from your grandmother's family. There you have it, your first heirloom.'

I think I'd already suspected it but nevertheless it was an interesting feeling sitting holding something that someone with my blood in their veins had also touched or better still, made. A connection with this area that I'd not been aware of before stirred within me.

'Apart from mum and grandfather, I know nothing about my family.' I mused. 'Liz Bradley at the library seemed to think I had generations here, but I've never thought about until now. I've just lived where my mum, or my job, has taken me. I've never felt that I had roots, probably because I didn't have a conventional family life. I've no idea who my father was, for example.'

'George wondered when you would start asking.' Her response startled me.

'What?' I was fully focussed on her. 'What, d'you know something Martha?'

She poured more tea, stirring her teaspoon around, deep in thought.

'There was gossip in the village at the time.' She paused. 'You don't have your mother's colouring, although you do have your grandfather's unusual opal coloured eyes.'

'What are you getting at?' I was tense.

'After your grandma Christina died I used to see a lot of your mum, Tessa. She was just a girl then. Lovely, bright, witty, pretty, and very much her own person. She wanted to get away and see other places, and when she was a teenager she had a job at the pub on Friday nights and weekends. She was saving, but to do what or go where, I've no idea.'

'So what happened?' I just wanted facts.

'You have to understand that I can't be sure Su.' Martha was looking closely at me. 'That summer there was a young man staying in the village. He was a working as a temporary doctor in some way and he was with us for a couple of months. He played cricket for the village team that summer and went to the pub and, I suppose, met your mum and one thing led to another as they say.'

'What did he look like?' I asked. 'Did you know him?'

'At the time we all thought he looked a lot like Robert Redford, you know, the actor?'

I was blank. TV and cinema had not figured in my early years.

'A very good looking man, with tawny gold colouring. Your colouring Su.'

I was speechless.

'Su, don't be angry or hurt by this.' Martha reached over and put her hand over mine.

'I'm not.' I said at once. 'I've no reason to be. Mum never talked about my father and I never asked her. We were pretty good together, she loved me and protected me, I never came to any harm, and, and now I think about it I don't remember her ever really being in a relationship. She was either extremely discreet or I was too stupid to notice. Everyone was family. Mum looked after all us kids while other people used their skills and talents to provide.' I tailed off, remembering. Remembering her singing and telling stories, playing games and teaching us about the natural world, her loving kind and generous nature. I realised Martha was watching me, anxiously.

'It's ok, I'm ok Martha. I'm interested though. I'd be interested to see a picture of this actor.' On impulse I went inside and found my phone, typed his name and looked at a handsome face, scrolling through looking at images of a young and then a handsomely ageing man I thought wow, he really is attractive. I found myself smiling as I went back outside.

'No wonder she fell for him if he looked anything like Mr Redford.'

Martha sat back, 'Life's a funny old business isn't it.'

'What drew you and Phil's dad together?' I hoped to take her attention off me.

She smiled happily. 'My family go back a long way here and I grew up just over there, higher up the valley.' She indicated a direction. 'And one day when I was out on my pony I looked down and saw this beautiful spread of colour, all pink and white and kind of foaming. It was the cider apple trees in flower. It was the loveliest thing I had ever seen and I told my mother that I was going to marry the man who owned the orchard. That was Phil's dad. We had many happy years and three lovely boys. Phil looks a lot like my late husband Mark.'

And then, a rustle in the flower bed and a little inquisitive face looked out at us. A small tortoiseshell body made an appearance and Daisy trotted across the grass, tail held high with a little curl at the tip. I learned forward and held out my hand, which she head butted, purring, clearly delighted with herself. And then she trotted off into the house.

'Dinner time for Daisy, and time I was off too.' Martha stood up. 'Su, I can't add anything to what you've just learned, and there's no proof of course. He was gone, I think before your mum even realised she was pregnant.'

And I'm here, and this is now, and I'm in my life.

Martha left and I went indoors, closing up behind me, making the house safe for my adventurous little companion, who was intent on making me understand that she was hungry, very hungry.

I was making a very light snack when I heard scratching. Daisy was using her litter tray. 'Madam,' I told her, 'with you going outside and behaving all grown up now, this nasty stinky business is going to have to become a thing of the past.'

The following morning I managed to flag Jay down on one of her many trips up and down the lane, ferrying children about and dealing with farm and family business.

'What about our idea of a trip to the gallery with the children?' I asked her.

'It will have to wait until after Matilda's birthday party, it's all I can think about at the moment, it's next weekend. My mind is like a goldfish at the moment.'

'Like a goldfish?' I questioned.

'It always goes round the bowl.' Jay replied.

'Can I help with the party?' I asked her. 'I can make balloon animals you know.'

Jay burst out laughing. 'I was going to ask you anyway, but with a gift like that I shall put you down on the entertainments list.'

I agreed to be up at the farm early enough to be useful. Meanwhile there were more boxes to sort through and since it seemed like a lovely day I advised Daisy that the door would be open and that I would be outside as well. This seemed to be a mutually satisfactory arrangement. I carried a few boxes downstairs and outside and made myself comfortable at the little table, while Daisy capered about madly before disappearing into the bushes.

Again I found myself looking through old receipts, letters about business long since finished and forgotten, some gardening catalogues, old enough to be quaint with their garish annuals. A picture began to emerge of how my grandfather kept himself occupied after my grandmother, Christina, had died and how he had gone about making arrangements to involve his young daughter in riding lessons, swimming club activities and school trips.

I was lost in thought and several times I found myself brushing a tear away, so I didn't hear a vehicle pulling in or see Rob until he was standing over me, his shadow startling me. Like his sister he was very quick to make an assessment of the situation and to my surprise he bent over, kissed me lightly on the cheek and stated that tea was clearly required.

He disappeared into the house while I sat there with one hand on my cheek, touched by the spontaneity of the kiss and slightly irritated by just how many people seemed to be able to use my kitchen. He reappeared with my tray carrying two mugs and the bar of salted caramel chocolate, so he'd searched through my cupboards as well.

'This', he said, sitting down and breaking off a couple of squares and handing them to me, 'is a life saver.'

He put a square into his mouth and sat back with a look of bliss on his face.

'Mmmm, let it melt a bit. Then have a sip of hot tea. It's just gorgeous.'

I did as he suggested, salt and sweet on my tongue, then warm and gooey. It was good.

'It's calorie free after twelve noon you know.' He handed me another piece.

I found myself smiling at him. 'I don't know, you come here, make free use of my kitchen, raid my cupboards and boss me about.'

'And cheer you up a bit you mean. It's all a bit weird I guess, going through stuff all on your own.'

I hadn't thought of it like that, all on my own.

'That makes me sound a bit pathetic doesn't it?' I sounded a bit guarded.

'Nope. It's a fact. There's nobody to help you or to share the burden, or task, or whatever you want to call it. But there's nothing wrong with reacting to sorrow or the emotions memories can throw up.'

I was surprised by his sympathy. I hadn't appreciated these finer points, I had thought I was just viewing this as a job to be done, looking for relevant family papers and understanding that there would be things to clear out. But I hadn't expected to find myself reacting to, what was it exactly, partly a sense of loss, partly a feeling that I was intruding on someone's private life.

'Oh I see!' I exclaimed, 'Liz Bradley said something about how you can learn too much about another person's life. And you're right, it's a weird feeling.'

I liked the way Rob didn't fill in the spaces or ask any questions. He sat quietly drinking his tea, his gaze contemplating the garden, apparently deep in thought. I felt as though he was allowing me to sort myself out, not intruding at all but I realised that he was fully aware of my mood. This is a kind man, I could sense my grandfather's approval. After a while I found my shoulders relaxing, he was right, there had been some tension.

'You know,' I said, 'that tea and chocolate combination is a winner. I do feel better.'

A buzzard soaring overhead made its plaintive whistling call. There was a rustle and a squeak and Daisy emerged, greeting us with the peculiar little chirping sound she made. Once again Rob was the object of her interest and attention.

'I've brought her a present, something she might find quite useful.' He was rubbing her ears and chin. He's graceful, I thought, as I watched him leaning forward. And he's not doing any of this for effect or to impress anyone, he's just being himself.

'Well she's a lucky girl, but I hope it's not something to make her fat, like chocolate mice.'

His canvas tool bag was at his feet, I hadn't noticed because it was obscured by the table and my boxes. He rummaged and lifted out a small box.

'A cat-thing-flap, as promised. Shall we go and measure up and see where it should go?'

I wasn't sure whether he was talking to me or to my cat but we both obediently followed him over to the back door, Daisy flirting madly when he knelt down to look at the door, the level of the low granite step, and the world according to Daisy at approximately 20 cm high.

'She'll obviously grow a bit more but I think this should do it, and the door doesn't face west so she won't get a face full of rain on a winter's day. Shall I go ahead then?'

This was clearly directed at me since all there was to be seen of Daisy was her bottom, her front end busily investigating the contents of his tool bag.

'Please, yes, it's very kind of you Rob.' I sat and watched him at work, measuring, drawing a line, drilling small holes, fitting a slim saw blade, cutting out the square and fitting the cat-flap either side of the square. His movements were precise, he placed his things neatly on an old square of towel as he used them, almost surgically precise.

'Can't stand mess when I work, and I don't want to lose anything. Meanwhile you can be my glamorous helper and hold this side straight while I put the screws in.'

I was happy to oblige. He finished the job with a neat bead of brown mastic to keep the weather out. He'd even chosen a brown cat-flap to match the door.

'All we have to do now is let it dry off, and teach Miss Furry Pants how to use it. There's a switch on the side here by the way, you can set it to let her out and keep intruders from getting in or lock it completely. Handy if you want to take her to the vet and stop her doing a runner the minute she sees the basket.'

I thanked him again, it seems he'd thought of everything. Daisy had investigated everything by now and was squatting by his feet, gazing intently at his shoelaces.

'I should take a photograph,' I said. 'Another episode in the life of Daisy cat.'

I retrieved my camera from the hall table, crouched down and got a few quick shots of Rob's boots, the cat-flap and Daisy's head.

'Nice camera angle.' Rob was interested. 'Most people would have tried it from standing and ended up with nothing worth looking at.'

'I'm going to start recording the garden in its weather moods. It's changing so quickly from day to day, I can hardly remember what was growing and where.'

Rob asked to look at the camera, looking through it as though framing shots and expertly flicking through its options, zoom and so on.

'I've never owned a camera before, I wasn't sure what to buy, so I went middle of the range.' I felt a bit embarrassed. 'I'm still learning what it can do, an awful lot judging by the instruction book.'

'Yeah they're clever things these days.' He was studying some setting on a button on the top of the camera. 'Anyway it's what goes on in the mind and hands of the person using it that gets results.' He was holding the camera at an odd angle, just looking at it, or so I thought. 'Your grandad took some nice photographs, I remember seeing them at an exhibition in the village hall some years back.'

'Really?' I didn't know that. 'I wonder if they are up in the box room somewhere.'

'Be worth a look. There were a couple of you that I recall. I'd like to see them again.'

I didn't know that either. I sat quietly, examining the unexpected feeling of pleasure that Rob's presence and interest evoked. I told him I hadn't found a camera in the cottage.

'Maybe he lent it to someone or chucked it out when everything went digital. Although that age group never chucked anything away, in case there was another war.'

I shuddered, aware of how sudden changes could make life so uncertain. He put the camera down on the garden table.

'Come on then cat, let's post you through the flap a few times and see if you get the hang of it.' Rob stood up.

I followed his instructions, and with the door closed, me inside and him outside, we made a game of pushing Daisy through, rewarding her with a little cat treat biscuit and lots of strokes. Eventually she began to learn that it wasn't a trap and didn't hurt.

We left her indoors with the door shut and went back to the garden table. I eyed the boxes and wondered aloud what else they contained. 'Really I'm searching for the birth and marriage certificates.' I explained. 'I want to start learning about my family.'

'Thinking of families Su, are you going to be at Matilda's eighth next Saturday?'

'Yes, I saw Jay this morning. I gather it's a serious event.'

'Oh thank god. I won't be on my own with hoards of screaming girls then. And that's just the grown ups.'

We were smiling at each other, he really did lift my mood. There was a sudden click and Daisy appeared on the garden side of the cat-flap.

'She's done it! We should celebrate!' We were in complete agreement. I agreed to meet him down at The Wheal village pub that evening and waved him off, smiling broadly. I hadn't even asked him what I owed him for the things he'd done for me.

I spent sometime deciding what to wear and eventually opted for cream jeans, a teal silky top with three quarter sleeves and a floppy collar, and my opal necklace. A touch of mascara was all I applied, I've never liked the feel of make up but I did varnish my nails in soft pink. I've always been quite proud of my hands. I felt twitchy and a bit excited. Was this a date I wondered. I tried to remember what the rules were for dating. I was honest enough with myself to accept that I would, in fact, quite like to go on a date with this man. I really liked his company and there was no doubt about it, he was attractive. If drinks at the pub went well, what would happen next, a trip to the cinema perhaps. I imagined us holding hands in the darkness and having our first kiss. I'd listened to my colleagues in the lab talking like this years ago. I thought back to Andrew. Mutual friends had introduced us at a party then we'd got quite drunk and he'd ended up at my place and somehow never left. It was not, in fact, very romantic. And I was beginning to realise that I had mistaken my enjoyment of his wit and friendliness and musical skills for love.

I drove the short distance to the village and turned the car around, parking so that I was pointing in the right direction for home. I had decided I was not going to make the mistake of compromising myself on the first evening. But what on earth are you thinking you idiot, apart from a brotherly peck on the cheek he's not made any advances. I had the awful feeling he was just being kind, seeing me as a lonely woman recovering from a breakdown and a bereavement, settling down with a cat for company. I had a mental picture of Jay telling him to leave me alone, that I'd had a rotten time and was vulnerable, off limits perhaps. I realised I'd told him about my past life, about Andrew, and yet I knew nothing about him. I didn't even know where he lived. I sat in the car and fretted, beginning to think that this was a really bad idea when there was a tap on the window.

'Are you joining me Su?' Rob opened the car door.

'Oh, err, yes, of course I am, I was just thinking.'

'I could see that. I've just walked right down the street in front of you stark naked and you never even saw me.'

I felt like a fool and made some excuse about having been miles away. Then I asked him if he'd had far to walk. God, I thought, I was sounding like a polite bore.

'I live within a safe crawling distance of this establishment, which is quite handy some nights.' He was perfectly relaxed as he stood back to let me out of the car. I got out grabbing my bag and jacket, feeling terribly nervous. He seemed taller, he'd showered and changed, clean grey jeans and a blue and white striped rugby shirt suited his lean form and his colouring. He smelled faintly of soap and I detected a subtle slightly leathery smelling aftershave. My spirits rose, he'd made an effort. My insides felt squiggly.

'Come on then.' He walked towards the door. 'My dad always said that the only place a man walked into before a woman was a pub, to check that the clientele was suitable for her, so after me please.' He was his usual good natured self.

I followed him in, hesitating at the lights, the unmistakeable odour of village pub, the slightly bitter sweet smell of old woodsmoke and beer. There seemed to be a bit of a crackle in the atmosphere, eyes turning to look at us. A solitary rather tired looking young man was standing at the bar looking at a menu. There were a few greetings which Rob casually acknowledged as he steered me to a quiet corner table. I opted for a mixture of tonic water and orange juice, a long drink, non alcoholic, no ice. I'd spent too long in the lab to want to put ice in my drinks. He returned from the bar, holding two glasses and two packets of plain salted crisps.

'The first course, I'm starving, not had a bite since god knows when.' He was chatting companionably, making me feel at ease. 'Don't you like ice? I had the devil of a job stopping Tim from loading up your glass. Or have you got sensitive teeth?' He started on the crisps.

'There was a national food sampling programme years ago. They got samples analysed from all over the country of bar ice and peanuts from the free dishes some pubs offered and found traces of urine and faecal bugs in both. People often don't wash their hands after they've been to the loo.'

He stopped eating, his eyes wide with amazement. 'You don't say.'

'I do say, but your crisps are fine, straight from the bag.' I thought I sounded like an uptight killjoy so I reached for the other bag and opened it, enjoying the salt and the crunch.

'Does it put you off eating out?' He questioned.

'Not a bit. Although I can't remember when I last ate out.' Oh no, I really was sounding like a sad case.

'Well this place does good food and I need to eat. I'll get a menu.'

I felt so gauche. I didn't feel as though I could swallow anything. He returned holding two menus.

'There's the specials board if you want to take a look.' He was indicating the wall to the side of the bar. I stood up and went to look, soup, locally caught fish, beef and ale pie, moussaka. Lasagne was the vegetarian option. I realised I was hungry. Lighten up I told myself, enjoy yourself for once.

'You're right, there's a good smell coming from the kitchen.' I smiled as I sat down. 'I think I'll have the moussaka, it's something I haven't made for ages.' He chose, rather predictably I thought, the beef and ale pie.

We sat and made light talk about food, cooking and personal preferences. As usual he had a funny take on things, remembering the ketchup years, hating anything white on the plate, finally deciding he liked cheese. I made him laugh with tales of weeks living on lentils and vegetables, not knowing what ice cream was like. We relaxed into the easy, companionable state I'd experienced with him in the pub on Dartmoor, but this time I realised that he was very gently asking questions that informed him about me. I responded in a similar vein, and he quite happily answered my questions, telling me that he'd opted for geology at university but that the course and the job prospects didn't really suit him although he'd persevered and got his degree.

'It kept my parents happy, but I've never used it.'

The food when it came really was good. He finished with a large helping of sticky toffee pudding and sat back, one hand over his stomach. 'Ah, that was proper man food, a proper job.'

I was gazing at his lean stomach, there was no sign of a paunch. I glanced at him, thinking about the question I'd asked Jay, was he involved with anyone. She'd thought not. How on earth did you do this. Perhaps there should be a questionnaire filled out before a date, like with a dating agency. I began to see the ridiculous side of the situation.

Rob was watching me. 'Your eyes are dancing, are you up to mischief?' There was a look of delight on his face that caught me by surprise.

I looked right at him, here goes I thought, and opened my mouth to ask him what his intentions were, what his situation was, and whether he would like to fill out a questionnaire. A giggle escaped but before I could speak a man appeared at the side of the table and clapped his hand onto Rob's shoulder.

'Rob you bloody letch, introduce us to your lovely if not stunning companion.' He was lithe and very strong looking with a shaved head and neat level features. His eyes were like headlights, sweeping over me and over Rob, his tanned face twitching with humour.

'Steve, mate, you are a complete and utter pest. Su, I am very sorry to have to introduce you to Steve Bradley, ace carpenter, village incomer and bloody nuisance.'

They were both grinning and clearly liked each other. Steve shook my hand awkwardly over the table.

'Su hello, you've met my wife Liz I think.' His accent was Northern. 'Nice to meet you, but no offence, I can tell I'm not wanted. I'm playing a skittles game in the back bar anyway, I was just curious to know what this dark horse was up to.' He slapped Rob on the back, winked and walked away.

'Sorry about that, he's a good mate actually. We've known each other a couple of years via jobs and just decided to collaborate on a set of gates. He's going to make a rather fancy frame for a client and I'm going to do the even fancier metal insert, all very arty of course. It might be the start of a new venture for us both.'

I told him about how inspired I'd felt after the visit to the gallery in Devon and said that his work sounded more and more interesting.

'I love it, I guess smithing is in my blood. My family used to own the village forge, I gather my dad's side came from Wales originally, attracted to work available at the mines. Mines always need a blacksmith.'

'Where do you work now?' At last I could ask him a direct question.

'I have a unit in some farm buildings the other side of Caradon. He's a distant cousin on mum's side of the family. The Cornish side. Doesn't mind if I rummage about a bit in the outbuildings and recycle the odd bit of metal lying around. I fix a few things for him and it's off the beaten track so I can make plenty of noise. I'll show you one day.'

I loved the way that made me feel included in his plans.

Rob asked me if I wanted another drink, but I really didn't. I'd had a cup of peppermint tea while he ate his pudding. It felt a bit odd drinking tea in a pub.

'Time for the bar bill then.'

'Please let me pay.' I got my purse out.

'Not this time, since it's such a long time that you ate out.'

'But I owe you for the cat-flap and the chimney.'

He pretended to be offended. 'That is a personal matter between myself and Daisy Fur Pants and I already had the stuff for the chimney from another job.'

While he was paying I went to the ladies. What now, I asked myself. What next? I looked at myself in the mirror as I washed my hands, eyes bright and sparkling looked back at me and I looked quite calm and unruffled. But I felt as though I'd like to be ruffled, considerably ruffled.

He was standing by the bar waiting for me and once again I was struck by his grace, there was nothing awkward about this man, he was completely at home and at ease in his environment. I was aware of a few eyes looking our way but he seemed not to notice, ushering me out of the pub without touching me, out into the fresh night air.

'That was very nice Rob.' I stood next to him looking up at some stars, easy to see because of the few street lights. I was hugely physically conscious of him.

'Good, I'm glad you enjoyed it.' As I was looking up, I could feel him looking down at me and I got that tingly feeling in my tummy. And this is not food poisoning I thought, stifling another giggle.

He casually lifted my jacket, which I had over my arm, and placed it around my shoulders. It was such a sweet gesture that it took my breath away. His hands were holding the tops of my shoulders and I thought I felt him tremble. Actually, it was me doing the trembling. I wanted to fall forward into his arms and I closed my eyes for a moment, my heart thudding in my ears as I raised my face for the expected kiss. As I did so the lights of a car shone fully at me and I winced. I heard the mechanical whine of a car window and a voice I'd not heard for a year.

'Su, Su is that you.' Andrew was getting out of the car.

EIGHT

Rob let go of me abruptly and stepped back. I felt a deep sense of shock. Andrew was right there, his curly fair hair shining in the light from the pub windows, his boyish good looks just as I remembered. He was taller than Rob but somehow had a lot less presence.

'You look great Su, it's so good to see you.' He took my hand.

'Andrew. What a surprise. Oh, this is my, my friend Rob. Rob this is Andrew, I may have mentioned him in passing.' The two men glanced at each other. Almost immediately Rob spoke.

'I was just walking Su to her car. Well, I'll be off then. Seems like you two have some unfinished business to see to. Bye.'

And he walked off down the road and into the night.

I was furiously, coldly angry. 'What on earth are you doing here, at this time of night.' I hissed.

Andrew had the grace to look anxious. 'I'm sorry Su, I've got a gig on at Truro, at some place called The Hall for Cornwall. I'm working properly now and we're doing the Marriage of Figaro, they've got a light opera week, starting tomorrow. The orchestra is in digs someplace down there but I'm so bloody late and I'm exhausted, I just couldn't go another 50 miles. Be an angel and put me up for the night would you. Please.'

'Oh for god's sake.'

'I'm sorry,' he said. 'I did try your mobile but there was no answer. I don't know the cottage landline but I drove there and there was no-one in. I was just going to try and get a room at the pub when you walked out.' He paused. 'Oh god, I've just fucked something up haven't I.'

'Yes, no, oh I don't know.' I was pacing up and down, short angry steps. 'OK, since you're here, you may as well follow me back, though I'm not sure how comfortable I can make you.'

I got into my car, swearing under my breath. Of all the bloody nerve, he was always so skint and tight I didn't believe for one moment that he'd have been looking for a room at the pub. And, I thought angrily, he couldn't have reached my mobile because it wasn't the same number I'd had a year ago and I hadn't kept in touch.

He followed me back to the cottage and parked up next to me.

Once inside he looked around while I searched out some fresh bedding for grandfather's room. Fortunately the room was well aired and clean.

'It's all looking very pretty, you've made some nice changes I can see.' He didn't offer to help as I made up the bed. Well he wasn't going to get much more in the way of help from me.

'There's bread and cheese in the kitchen, tea and coffee in the cupboard above the kettle.' I told him. 'Help yourself.' I threw him a towel. 'Now if you don't mind I'm tired and I'm going to bed.'

'Okay.' He was perfectly happy now that his basic needs were seen to.

Sleep didn't come that night. I was angry, upset and so damn frustrated with events in all senses of the word. I thought about Andrew, he'd been good in bed I remembered. He used to say that all the violin and piano practice had given him good fingering skills.

I couldn't help comparing Rob to Andrew. How considerate Rob was, how mature, how kind, how different. I thumped my pillow. Daisy was not impressed.

I was up early and making breakfast when Andrew appeared, looking fresh and pleased with himself. He happily accepted toast, grilled tomatoes and fried eggs and ate heartily.

'I'm not going to hang around and spoil your day, rehearsals start soonish and it should only take me about an hour to get there I think.'

'A little bit more than an hour.' I responded.

He was looking at me. 'You look amazing Su, better than I've ever seen you, sun-kissed and I like your hair like that.'

I tried, with good grace, to be pleasant. 'Thank you. How are things with you and what's her name, the girl you left me for?' It sounded more bitter than I felt.

He winced slightly. 'Lisa. We're getting married. Her folks have bought us a little house as a present. He's a rather well known conductor. She's pregnant.'

'Wow.' It was all I could say. Typical of the Andrew I had come to know, attaching himself to someone with means.

True to his word he didn't hang about and after collecting his things together I walked with him to his car. He slung everything into the back, turned to me and suddenly grasped both my hands.

'I'm sorry about everything Su, and I really do wish you all the luck you deserve and all good things. We had a great few years, there are no regrets.' He was pleased with his speech.

I was wondering what to say other than thanks, when to my surprise he pulled me into his arms and hugged me. At that point a vehicle turned into the farm track and drove past. Squinting through one eye, squashed as I was against Andrew's shoulder, I saw that it was Rob's van. Oh shit, I thought, could things get any worse.

With Andrew gone, for good I hoped, I moped around the cottage. He had left a wet towel on the bedroom floor, a dirty mug in the bathroom and hadn't cleaned the basin after he'd shaved. Angrily I stripped the bed and washed up the breakfast things, realising I was doing my best to eradicate every trace of him. As I banged about with the vacuum cleaner upstairs I kept looking out of the windows in case if I could see, or hear Rob's van. What was I going to do, rush out and throw myself into the lane, under his wheels? He didn't appear. I couldn't concentrate on anything and I was very tired. Eventually I fell asleep on the sofa in the sitting room and when I woke up I had a stiff neck and felt lousy. The day didn't get any better and heavy rain set in. It suited my mood perfectly. I went to bed early.

The next day was brighter. I shopped for provisions, driving slowly through the village and wondering where Rob lived. I had no idea. I paused on the road for a few moments looking in the direction he had walked that night. There were some nice little detached cottages set off the road plus a terrace of four. What did an artistic blacksmith live in I wondered. There was no sign of him. My spirits fell again.

Back home I walked about, restless and irritable. Finally I picked up the camera and went around the garden and down to the pond, accompanied by Daisy, taking a few photographs, hearing Rob's voice in my head talking about the mind and hands of the person framing the shots. I'd really love to know what's in his mind right now, I thought. The pond was looking good, there were some water lilies coming out and the light was nice. I tried several angles, walking round the path, looking, assessing, being patient. I wasn't sure what I was looking for, tried crouching, but no, it didn't feel like an interesting view. I got to the cow and calf rocks and climbed up. That was it, the height was perfect for a shot down into the water, the view of the lily pads and the reflection of the sky was lovely. I took quite a lot of photographs, pleased with myself. Climbing down I slipped and slid and fell forward, landing awkwardly at the edge of the stones. One leg was in mud up to the knee and I had scraped the side of my hand on the granite. I pulled myself out onto the path and examined the damage. My foot was wet, my jeans soaked and my hand stung a bit, but I was intact and the camera was safe. Swearing under my breath and limping a bit I went back up to the cottage, panting slightly from the shock and feeling sorry for myself. I stripped off in the utility room and shoved everything into the washing machine, then went upstairs and got in the shower.

Later, over tea and a salmon and cucumber sandwich, I told Daisy all about it as she ate a tiny bit of my cold salmon. She purred and rubbed her head against my fingers. I felt lonely but she was so cute that I felt a sudden burst of affection for her.

'This is only cupboard love isn't it you pretty little girl, you'd love anyone who gave you nice things to eat.' Daisy didn't seem to have an opinion.

Finally I decided to upload the photographs onto the computer and sat for a while, making up a folder, going slowly through the procedure, unfamiliar with the process and having to resort to the help button a few times. Eventually it all worked and I smiled, there was Daisy, goodness how she'd grown and changed in a few weeks. I clicked from contacts onto full screen view and started slowly going through them from the beginning. Daisy here, Daisy there, Rob's boots and the cat-flap with Daisy's little face in one corner, a rather cute composition I thought.

I was tormented by the image of Rob's face laughing about the cat-thing-flap and helping to post Daisy through it. How many times had he called by and I hadn't even got his phone number. Then I fretted because he hadn't offered me his number and I decided that must be because I was simply a friend of his sister and he was politely doing her a favour and me a job. But he'd asked me out twice I thought, the day over Dartmoor and again the other night. And he hadn't let me pay for my dinner in the pub. I was confused, I really was out of touch with the dating game.

I clicked again and my face appeared, full screen, soft focus, the zoom lens used to good effect. And again, and again, the sun caught in my hair, my face framed by the sky and clouds. He'd also used different special effects and there were a couple of shots using selective colour which had enhanced my hair at the same time as making my face sepia tinged. They were extraordinary and reminded me of some of the old photographs up in the box room because they made me look as though I was from the past. I wasn't looking into the viewfinder, I was pensive, then smiling, utterly unaware that I was being photographed. Full face, three quarter face, all different angles. Of course, I sat back, the penny dropping. Rob had been holding the camera as we were talking, and he had been photographing me as we discussed techniques. As a masterclass, it was amazing. It wasn't even a week ago yet my world seemed to have changed in an instant. I looked again. He was more artist than I realised. I moaned softly, a primeval inner keening. I finally acknowledged that it was more than simple lust I was feeling. I wasn't sure what it was, but it was new, and boy it hurt.

The next day was Saturday, everything was fresh after the rain and the sun was shining. I got up early, hung the washing out and tidied the cottage, making sure Daisy had everything she needed, a plan half formed in the back of my mind. I dressed in blue jeans and a rose pink t-shirt, grabbed my things and Matilda's present and set off for the farm. Martha and Jay were already in full party preparation mode, and while Phil supplied us with coffee and biscuits I was given the task of inflating balloons with a contraption which made the job fast and easy. There were lots of pink balloons, bunting and streamers, and when Rob arrived he and Phil worked together putting the decorations up, with constant advice from Jay until it was suggested that she should go and see to dressing a very excited Matilda.

Rob said a brief hello to me and I smiled my nicest smile, but he wasn't forthcoming. We were then full on into food preparation and table laying, Martha and I making up little bags of party favours. I'd never seen anything like it in my life and Martha was clearly resigned and wishing that things were more like her day, as she put it.

'We were grateful for jelly and ice-cream and a bit of plain iced spongecake with the family. Nothing like this.'

Matilda ran about, looking very pretty and Phil gloomily predicted vomiting by bedtime. I'd given her the present I'd bought and she had it over her arm, a pink handbag with a little compact mirror and a matching comb. Jay's parents arrived, gave Matilda her present, congratulated us all on our hard work and left pretty quickly, taking the younger two away with them for the night. I'd found myself staring at them, thinking that these were Rob's parents too, seeing a likeness in his father's face. Then the parents started arriving with cute little girls in tow. Matilda stood at the top of the steps to the front porch and graciously accepted presents as she greeted her guests. She was glowing from head to foot in pink spangles, her dark hair in bunches with pink ribbons. Martha commented drily that she looked like Scarlet O'Hara on the day of the ball. Most of the mothers headed for the kitchen and the wine after quickly assessing the standards of the party arrangements. One mother appeared bearing an armful of small gauze wings.

'We're all to wear these.' She trilled, clipping a set onto the back of my t-shirt. I was then crowned with a pink tinsel circle.

'Whoa, not me.' Rob backed off holding his hands up. 'I might be wearing a pink shirt but I'm the help, not a bloody fairy.' Martha and I and several mummies dissolved into giggles as he, Phil and a couple of other dads took themselves off into the recesses of the house.

The woman who had produced the wings seemed convinced that one of the children was mine and quizzed me for several minutes about breast feeding and all sorts of motherly stuff, being particularly focussed on how to 'reduce the celluloid on your thighs after all that baby fat'. I realised that she was already quite squiffy. Fortunately motherhood had been a big thing at the commune so I was fairly able to hold my corner before she wobbled off in search of something she referred to as 'her piggy.' I wasn't sure if she meant her child or her husband.

I helped supervise some games and played waitress, quite adequately, when the little darlings sat down to eat. Then a hired magician turned up and gave us all a much needed break, at which point Jay took me to one side.

'What on earth has happened between you and Rob?' she demanded. 'He turned up here early the other morning like a bear with a sore head and stayed for hours, driving me nuts. He said that your ex fella had come back. What's going on?'

I tried to give her a brief explanation.

'Haven't the time Su.' her eyes were all over the children, assessing how everything was going. 'Just tell me, is Andrew back?'

'No. Absolutely definitely no.'

'Then do me a favour will you and tell Rob that. He's bloody miserable.'

I made an excuse and headed for the bathroom where I locked myself in and sat on the side of the bath. He was upset. I kept repeating it to myself, rocking forwards and backwards. He was just upset. There's hope. There's still hope if I can talk to him.

Back outside I mingled into the party. Rob was sitting with Matilda leaning against his knee. She was talking to him about the magician.

'It's hard to know what's real Uncle Rob.'

'Yes, life is like that sometimes sweetie.' He was looking at me.

'Things aren't always what they appear to be.' I responded.

And then it was all over. Happy little girls were leaving, clutching their party bags, mothers were congratulating Jay and saying well done, only three more to do this month, and rolling their eyes. Phil was muttering that no-one was congratulating him, but then he only put his hand into his pocket and paid for it all. Martha and I began to fill bin liners with party rubbish and then Phil came in with a huge pot of tea and we all collapsed. I gratefully accepted a piece of birthday cake from Matilda. It was very nice. I noticed she was wearing pale pink nail varnish. I saw Jay speaking briefly to Rob but his face remained set and wooden. We finished clearing up and then I realised he wasn't around. Jay walked with me to the porch and down the steps, where she carefully unpinned my crumpled gauze wings.

'I asked him to drop you off at the cottage, but I'm so sorry Su, he's gone. The stupid man.'

'Oh don't worry Jay.' I deliberately misinterpreted her. 'The walk will clear my head of little girls squealing.'

It was a fine dry sunny evening and I walked slowly back along the lane, not sure how I was going to sort this out. I'd meant to ask Jay for Rob's address and telephone number, but in all the fuss and excitement of the party I'd forgotten that had been my plan. Well I'd just damn well drive to the village and spot his van or knock on doors. I rounded the corner to my cottage, and there he was, leaning against the side of the van, watching Daisy swatting flies in the garden. I walked up to him, my heart knocking around my ribcage and my mouth dry.

'Sorry Su, I'm a prat. I should have at least dropped you back here.'

He looked tired, there were marks under his eyes. I wanted to touch his face.

'I saw he stayed the night.' He sounded bleak.

'One night. Yes. On his own in grandfather's room. He's a mean tightfisted skinflint and he's getting married soon. He wanted a bed for the night because he's playing at Truro for the week and was too late to get to the digs and simply wanted a bed and breakfast for nothing. As usual all he considered were his own needs. He's not my boyfriend, it all ended a year ago and there's nothing, absolutely nothing between us.' It all came out in a breathless rush.

Rob was watching my face, hearing what I was saying but still looking like a drowning man. Slowly he caught up and took a deep breath. 'He's not?'

'He's not my boyfriend.' I said again, softly. And I reached up and touched his face as his arms went round me.

Much later I said, 'We can't keep this a secret you know. Your van will have been spotted at my parking space. Fingers will be wagging and the village bongo drums will be banging fit to burst. My reputation will be ruined.' I kissed his neck and nestled up against his fine, firm, smooth skin, stroking his chest and arms and down along his thighs.

He turned and threw a leg over me, putting one hand to the side of my head as he kissed me. 'Frankly my dear I don't give a diddly damn.'

NINE

Sunday was one of those rare, golden days that you know you will remember all your life. Nothing existed except the light in his eyes, the touch of his hands and lips, the weight of his body and the encircling comfort of his arms. He dashed home to get a change of clothes and his razor while I showered and refreshed myself. Everything seemed to be moving slowly, everything I saw seemed to glow. I walked about drying my hair, dressing, thinking soppy things like Rob lay here, he used this towel, his head made this indentation in the pillow, he slept here. I was grinning and feeling simply marvellous.

When he returned we made a late lunch together in the kitchen, not having had any breakfast, agreeing about the things we liked, tasting things off each others fingers, discovering the taste of wine on each other's lips. He made me laugh, saying what a caveman he was, only needing a flame to cook things and a knife to cut things with. He confessed he didn't own a microwave oven or a fancy coffee maker. Neither did I, since I didn't really like coffee and the only kitchen gadget I'd brought with me was an old blender, because I could use that to make smoothies and soup. Grandfather just had the old dual fuel hob and oven.

Rob told me how glad he'd been when he'd learned I had returned to the village, how Jay had advised him to be patient and give me time to recover, how fragile I'd seemed, and how distant. He said he'd made himself hold back and stay away when all he wanted to do was come and see me. We talked and talked, my feet between his as we sat opposite each other at the table, later sharing the small sofa with me sitting with my legs across his, a warm hand on my ankles and thighs. I asked him about his previous girlfriends, there was one at University he told me, and one from school who still lived in the village.

'You've already met her.'

'What?' I was surprised. 'Who?' Was all I could manage.

'Liz Griffiths, now Liz Bradley.'

Oh, I felt a bit odd. I had a sudden flash of her pretty face, her long silvery blonde hair. Rob was watching me, not missing a flicker of expression on my face.

'It was ages ago Su. We went out for quite a while when I came back from Uni, but it was never going anywhere. And then Steve came down here, they met, and the rest is history. They are crazy about each other.'

'Oh.' I took a sip of wine and relaxed. We talked a bit more about life and love, the sort of conversation you can only have at the start of a relationship.

'I feel as though I've been waiting for this to happen all my life.' He said, suddenly serious. 'Not just being with someone, but being with you.' He was stroking my hair. 'I remember trying to kiss you at Jay's 21st, I needed a drink to get my courage up, and I bungled it. You took off like a startled hare, but at least you didn't clout me.'

'I didn't like your beard.' I laughed

'Have you found the photographs of you your grandad took?'

'Not yet, but I saw the photographs you took when I downloaded some I'd taken the other day. Do you want to have a look?'

The computer was set up in a corner of the kitchen near the back window. I switched it on and retrieved the file as he pulled up a kitchen chair and sat as close to me as possible. He put his hand over mine on the mouse.

'This could cause operator error.'

I turned to kiss him. We kissed for quite a while, gentle, soft, loving kisses. He rubbed his nose against mine and we collapsed into giggles. Together we opened the file and clicked over the photographs. Rob studied the ones he'd taken of me, liking them.

'Weaving the sunlight into your hair.' He said, kissing me again.

I wriggled away, smiling and pretending to be gasping for air. 'Let me see these others I've taken, I've not looked at them yet.'

We clicked our way through the photographs I'd taken in the garden, some close ups of flowers, an old mossy terracotta pot holding hostas with their leaves throwing shadows, a butterfly a little bit blurred, more photographs showing my progress down to the pond. They weren't particularly special but he didn't seem to mind, occasionally making a comment and leaning over to kiss my shoulder, one hand lightly touching my back and my neck. I remembered I'd slipped and fallen, telling him about it as he held the hand I'd scraped and examining it carefully for damage, thoroughly kissing the side with his lovely soft lips.

'But seriously Su, you could have hurt yourself. Wet granite is lethal, and who would know to look down there if you'd disappeared?' His eyes darkened and it was as if a jolt had gone through him.

'Yes, I'm sorry.' I didn't know what else to say. The bleakness of my mood that day seemed a lifetime away.

Rob turned me towards him and took my face in both of his hands. 'Life can change in an instant. I don't want to lose you before I've got to know you. Jesus, I don't want to lose you.' His face was sombre.

We sat for a few moments, looking into each other's eyes. I felt as though I needed to remember something, to reassure him that everything was okay now, but the moment passed and we turned back to the computer screen. The shots of the pond and the water lilies were quite good and I flicked through them when he put his hand back over mine and stopped me.

'Go back a couple.' He instructed.

I did as he asked when he said, 'Stop. What's that?'

I leaned closer to the screen and squinted a bit. 'What?'

He moved my hand and zoomed into the photo, obviously well practised with the technology. Then he clicked backwards a few shots, forwards a few shots and returned to the original photograph. I'd taken it just before I'd slipped.

'What is it?' I asked him.

'It looks like the shadow, no, the reflection of someone in the water. Was there anyone else there with you?'

I looked more closely. I could see what he meant, in a patch of sunlit water between water lilies there seemed to be the shape of a man, the upper torso was just visible and he was wearing a hat, a sort of bowler hat. I sat back and stared at the screen.

'I have no idea what that is.' I said.

Perplexed I switched the computer off, feeling a bit unsettled. In silent agreement we moved back into the sitting room, back to our wine and the comfort of a sofa on which to cuddle. Daisy wandered in, giving her little chirrup as a greeting, bumping her head against Rob's leg.

'Does Phil employ men on the farm?' I asked.

'Not really.' Rob kissed the top of my head as I snuggled against him. 'These days it's mostly contractors for silage making, hedge cutting and so on. And they have mostly lost the use of their legs because they almost never climb out of their cabs. And if they wear a hat it's usually a baseball cap worn backwards to show that they are twenty-first century burger eating macho men.'

We didn't pursue the subject. His kisses grew warmer and more urgent, and I succumbed to a sense of utter bliss as I discovered more about this loving, passionate man.

From that point on it seemed that summer was at its loveliest. Cornwall can be very beautiful and the quality of light and warmth around the cottage was wonderful. All my old cares, sorrows and fears were just the result of events in the past. They seemed remote, dealt with and consigned to a part of the many experiences that had formed me and shaped my life. I was just incandescent with pure simple happiness at being with Rob. He felt so right. He made me laugh, a lot. I liked the way he looked, the way he did things. He was generous and considerate, a giver rather than a taker, as I'd already realised when comparing him to Andrew. He was genuinely interested in the things I'd done or views I held and I reciprocated, being fascinated by his own knowledge and experiences. We didn't always agree but that was when we would tease each other, until he gathered me up in his arms and kissed me until nothing mattered. When he wasn't working he spent a lot of time at my cottage, but he didn't leave his soiled clothes for me to wash and when I said I didn't mind hanging out a few of his things he raised his eyebrows in mock horror.

'I use you and abuse you enough already, I am not turning you into a washerwoman and spoiling your looks and anyway, what will the neighbours think if they see my smalls dangling about on your line?'

'But everyone must already know that you are in my clutches.' I laughed at him. 'Your van is always there outside, it's like a huge calling card outside the gate, saying keep away, shenanigans in progress.'

Rob laughed at my use of words, it was something else we shared.

One afternoon I was on my own shelling peas at the garden table, when I heard the gate click and Matilda appeared. As usual she was dressed in shades of pink and wearing pink spotty wellingtons. Her t-shirt had the words 'farmers girl' embroidered across the front in navy blue. I didn't make a fuss about her being on her own. As a child I'd had the privilege of being able to roam for miles in the Welsh countryside.

'Hello Matilda, this is nice, are you exploring?' I asked her as I carried on with my task.

She watched me carefully for a few moments, assessing what my reactions were likely to be.

'Not really. I've been here before when I was little.' She perched on the edge of the bench and asked nicely if she could eat a pea. 'Granny Martha does a lot of this.' She indicated my homely task with an elegant wave of one hand. 'Do ladies always have to do these things when they get old?'

'Only if they want a good dinner.' I replied, smiling a bit, already anticipating Rob's enthusiasm about my cooking. 'So what's brought you all the way down here from the farm?' I asked.

'Granny Martha said you had got the kitten I liked. I had asked if I could have it but mum said we'd already got Tramp and Paws, as well as living in a zoo. I think she meant no.' She added thoughtfully.

'I've called her Daisy, she's out and about on her own right now, a bit like you.' I'd finished shelling the peas. 'Shall we put these inside and get a drink while we wait for her to turn up?'

Matilda politely agreed and followed me indoors. Since Rob had been spending so much time with me the pantry and refrigerator were better stocked. Matilda chose a healthy concoction of red berries that Rob had returned with from a recent trip to see a customer. He was endearingly good at spotting a food shopping opportunity on his travels. We selected a piece each of oat and date slice I'd made and went back outside. I did not ask her about school, or friends, or the summer holidays, but waited for her to make the conversation. For a while she was perfectly happy to sit quietly and eat and drink, which she did with sober good manners.

'That was nice and sticky.' She was appreciative. 'It's really nice here. When I grow up I'd like to live in my own house. Our house gets a bit noisy when the dogs bark and Luke starts crying.' Luke was her baby brother. 'He smells a bit funny sometimes and Mabel doesn't make a lot of sense yet, but she's more fun now that she's walking.'

I looked at her, impressed by her sense, a different little girl to the party girl I'd seen only a couple of weeks ago.

'Do you spend time with Granny Martha?' I questioned her. 'Her side of the house must be quieter I expect.'

'Oh yes.' Matilda was nodding, her feet curled up beside her on the bench. 'Granny Martha enjoys my company so I go round as often as I can. We make decisions about things and I help her make pies and jam and soup, sometimes.' She paused, considering something. 'Daddy was talking to Granny Martha yesterday, he said that Uncle Rob was round here,' again one of her elegant hand gestures indicating the cottage, 'like a dog at a gatepost.'

I snorted into my healthy berry drink. Then I realised that this interested and thoughtful child was waiting for an answer.

'Yes, Uncle Rob comes here to see me,' I said levelly, 'and sometimes stays for tea or dinner. That's why I was shelling peas.'

Again she was nodding. 'I thought so. But if he comes to eat his dinner with you now, should I call you Aunty Su?'

I hadn't seen that one coming.

I was saved from further explanation by the appearance of Daisy, carrying something in her mouth. She trotted up to us and put the something down on the terrace. It didn't move.

'Tramp and Paws do this.' Matilda observed, getting off the bench and going over to have a look, not in the least distressed. She crouched down and stroked Daisy, who was arching her back and flicking her tail and looking very pleased with herself. 'You have to say thank you.' Matilda advised me, as she patted Daisy's back quite firmly. 'She thinks she's brought you some dinner.' I could see Granny Martha's influence in her attitude and instructions.

I walked over and thanked Daisy, as instructed. She'd started bringing little presents home a few days ago and I'd already been grateful that Rob had suggested keeping her activities contained to the back porch scullery area. I'd disposed of a few dead field mice and rescued a live slow worm from beneath the washing machine. This latest offering was a pygmy shrew. I flipped its tiny body onto a piece of slate and carried it over to the compost bin at the side of the veg patch, quietly sorry that its short summer life had ended. Matilda was still making much of Daisy, who was basking in the adulation. Their admiration seemed quite mutual.

'Shall I walk back home with you Matilda?' I thought Jay might be getting a bit worried. 'I'd like to say hello to your mum.'

We put Daisy indoors with a few cat crunchies and strolled up the lane together, Matilda advising me of a patch of ground where violets grew and where to see the best primroses in the spring. She also confided that she was trying to convince her dad that she should be allowed to have a pony.

'Mum takes me for lessons but she's fairly busy so it might be better for her if I had a pony here, then she wouldn't have to drive.' Her logic was impeccable.

As we approached the farm house I could see Jay, unloading the boot of her car. She turned and greeted us, her eyes going over her daughter, Matilda looking back at her, a mini-me of her mother. 'I wondered where you'd got to poppet.' Jay spoke calmly and caressed the top of her daughter's head, her eyes turning to me, carefully neutral.

'Matilda has just paid me and Daisy a visit.' I said. 'She wanted to see that Daisy had settled in and we had a drink together and some date slice and she explained a few things, for which I am grateful.'

Matilda smiled shyly and slipped away as Jay exhaled slowly.

'She's growing up so fast. I had no idea she wasn't here.' I could see the worry in her face.

'Maybe she just needs to be reminded of her boundaries.' I suggested. 'My cottage and no further.' Jay was nodding. 'And thinking of my cottage,' I continued, 'Matilda seems to have gained some knowledge that Uncle Rob and I have an arrangement regarding his meal times.' I paused as Jay's eyes lit up and a huge smile broke over her face.

'Only his meals?' she teased me.

'Well, we have each other's welfare very much at heart right now.' I was laughing.

Jay flung her arms round me. 'Oh I'm so glad, I mean, we knew, obviously with his van there that something was going on.' She paused. 'I think he's had feelings for you for a very long time you know.'

Life just seemed to be getting better and better.

TEN

I hadn't stayed long at the farm, being keen to get back home. I was busy making dinner when I heard Rob's voice and felt a glad moment of indescribable pleasure at his call of 'I'm home'. I was across the kitchen and into his arms before he'd got his boots off.

'Oh wow,' he was smiling happily at me, 'have you missed me today? Oh I can tell you have, that's nice.' He was teasing and laughing, not expecting any sort of an answer, which was a good job because I was curling round him as fast as bean tendrils up a garden cane. 'That means kisses then since she's clearly lost the power of speech.' I was perfectly happy about that as I melted against him.

Back in the kitchen I opened the oven door and put the pie I'd been making in to cook. Later we sat chatting opposite each other as we liked to be, pulling at little bits of toasted cheese adhering to the side of the pie dish. I'd made a white fish pie with onion and leek infused into a herby sauce, jazzed up with a few prawns and a cheesy mash on top, served with peas, braised celery and broccoli cooked together with a little butter and a touch of celery salt.

'That was lovely Su. I'm sorry there are no leftovers to help cope with night starvation.'

Night starvation was a phrase he used after a night of passion, when he'd occasionally fetched us a plate in the small hours with a few grapes, a stick of cheddar and a few oat biscuits to keep our strength up, as he put it. I sat quietly, marvelling how a relationship could develop with such intensity from a casual friendship into an intimate, colourful private world. Did other people experience this, I wondered. I told him about Matilda's visit and Daisy's latest catch. Daisy flicked her tail at the sound of her name, she was lying flat on her back on the mat, her tummy full of cooked prawns, her paws limp.

'And yes, they know all about us up at the big house.' I said, indicating the direction of the farm.

'That means they've put their heads together and made some wicked assumptions.' Rob was miming stirring a witches cauldron. 'So we don't have to break the news to them then?'

'What news?' I was deliberately obtuse.

He took both my hands in his. 'The news that I am clearly having my cake and eating it and enjoying it very, very much. And thinking of cake, are we having anything else after that gustatory excellence?'

'We are not.' I got up to clear the dishes. 'I was too busy walking Matilda home to make anything else and anyway, all this unaccustomed eating will make us fat.' I did not mention her query regarding calling me Aunty Su.

'What do you mean?' Rob was amused. 'I've always eaten well, the pub has provided quite marvellously. And if it's exercise you need I'm sure I can think of something.'

We took our wine into the sitting room. The day had cooled unexpectedly and, typical of Bodmin Moor in the summer time, rain was threatening.

'I was talking to Steve at the workshop today.' I already knew that they were collaborating on some work for a customer. 'He's a good bloke and he was a bit apologetic about disturbing us in the pub that night. Anyway, we thought it might be nice for the four of us to meet up there one night, have something to eat together. I can't have you slaving over the stove every night after all.'

'Yes, why not.' I was happy about that. 'It would give me some incentive to go through some more of grandfather's stuff to see if I can find what Liz might be interested in.'

There was a distant roll of thunder and Daisy, who had followed us into the sitting room and flopped onto a chair sat up, looking about, a little bit alarmed.

'It's okay little girl.' I got up and stroked her head.

Rob went outside to check that he'd closed his van windows properly. He came in just as a gust of rain threw itself at the cottage windows. I inhaled deeply.

'I love those smells.' I told him. 'Rain on dry ground, newly washed and sun dried clothes, the smell of the workshop on you when you've been metalworking.'

'You're all whiskers on kittens and warm woollen mittens as the song goes. And there I was thinking that you were some bluestocking intellectual when we first met.' His eyes darkened. 'Blue stockings, now there's a thought.'

I clouted him with an old photographic supplies magazine. 'Digest your dinner my boy, and while that's happening you could be a gentleman and lug another box of stuff down here for me to go through.'

While he obliged I made a pot of tea and switched the lamps on, loving the cosy glow and the feeling of intimacy the cottage provided. The rain was coming down in sheets, clattering against the windows. We sat together, this box was smaller than the others and contained some folders.

'Bingo'. I had my mother's and my own birth certificate. Mine was small and square and it simply stated my name, sex, date of birth and place of birth. 'Goodness, I was born in Hereford, I didn't know that.'

Rob looked at me, 'How did you get a passport or a driving licence?' he asked.

'I don't have a passport, I've never travelled outside the British Isles. And grandfather dealt with my driving licence application.'

I looked at my mother's birth certificate, Tessa Charlesworth, parents' names George Charlesworth and Christina Harvey, and mum was born here, right here in Orchard Cottage.

'Goodness', I said again, 'I didn't know that either.'

My grandfather's occupation described him as a farm supplies sales manager. I remembered that there had been some Harvey's in the churchyard.

Rob was still leafing through the folder. 'This is a bit sad.'

He was holding two death certificates, one for my grandmother Christina, who died following complications in childbirth. The other for their dead son, Frederick, who had died the day before her, just one day old. I felt deeply sorry, my mood slipping down into quiet contemplation of what my grandfather must have gone through. And there was my own mother's death certificate. Septicaemia. Blood poisoning. I took a long shuddering breath and put everything on the little coffee table.

Rob poured tea and sat down, an arm around me. I could hear the rain beating down outside. 'Are you ok?' he asked.

'Yes, it's all just so odd, people who lived and mattered, people who are responsible for me being here yet I never knew them, people I've lost who I should have known.' I felt a tiny pang of envy that little Matilda knew three of her grandparents and had live siblings and cousins and an uncle, who was sitting next to me, his hand warm on my shoulder.

'Maybe we should do this another time Su. It's getting late and I'm a bit tired to tell the truth.'

For a moment I thought he was withdrawing from me and I felt a moment of anxiety but when I turned to look at him he was watching me, patient, calm and kind.

'It's ok, I'm right here and I'm going nowhere, unless you want to throw me out into this horrible weather. Now drink your tea and snuggle up for a cuddle before bed time.'

With his arm around me and my head against his shoulder I found myself almost purring like Daisy.

A few days later and it was Friday. We were to meet up with Steve and Liz in the pub that evening. Rob had spent the day at his own house as there was grass to cut and a client was calling in to see him. Now that I knew where he lived I was to drive down later and meet him there. His place was at the end of the terrace of four cottages I'd seen when I first wondered where he lived. It was the one furthest away from the road and he had the largest garden which provided him with neatly fenced parking for his van and my car. There was a small granite outbuilding at the side of the garden which used to be a pigsty but which he had restored and rebuilt, turning it into a useful storeroom and wood store. He described it as his man-cave. The garden was simple, he'd levelled and grassed over old vegetable beds and the lawn was separated from a large paved terraced area by a flower bed with a couple of red and purple hardy fuschia and some white hebe forming a low hedge. The terrace held a small red table and chairs which were Jay's choice, I was told, and they completed the picture nicely.

Indoors everything was minimal, surprisingly modern and tasteful, with beech worktops in the small kitchen, grey cupboard doors and cream walls. The sitting room had a few framed posters and a black framed enlarged photograph of how the cottages used to look a century ago, which he'd obtained via the local newspaper archives when they were running a local history story. It was fascinating to see the changes time had dealt. There were a few people standing outside the cottages staring toward the photographer. The women in long skirts, their hair drawn back and pinned up off their faces, the men in working clothes and waistcoats, shirt sleeves rolled up. Some definition had been lost with the enlargement but the result was still pleasing. The cream and grey theme went throughout the cottage, it was masculine and restful, the only colour being a few plain primary colour sofa cushions and a matching rug downstairs and striped bedlinen and towels upstairs.

'Ready made department store sad single man choice.' Rob advised when he'd first shown me round.

I was pleased to see well stocked bookshelves, which he told me he had made from fruitwood. The edges were a bit wavy and pleasant to touch.

'I'd been clearing up an old fallen cherry tree in the garden for the woodstove when it occurred to me that I could put some of it to more permanent use. It turned out rather better than I had expected,' he had explained. 'I like things simple and uncluttered, it's easier to look after that way.'

I changed into the usual pub gear of jeans and a top, this time cream coloured jeans with a silky green top and my mother's old opal pendant. When I got to his place he was coming downstairs dressed and with wet hair, and made appreciative noises as he looked at me.

'I like that necklace, it suits your other worldly look Su.'

'Well I'll take that as a compliment but I don't quite understand what you mean.'

He didn't explain and I forgot the comment as we strolled along the quiet lane in the early evening light to the pub, hand in hand. I swear the curtains were twitching as we walked but I didn't care. I was going out properly, for the first time, with this gorgeous clever man and it felt terrific. We'd just got our drinks from Tim the barman and were debating whether to stay inside or sit out in the tiny garden when Steve and Liz arrived. There was the ritual of hellos and how are you, odd from a couple of blokes who saw quite a lot of each other and I thought I detected a little awkwardness but Liz and I looked at each other and smiled.

'I don't know about them,' I said, 'but we've already met and exchanged phone numbers.'

There was laughter and an immediate release of any tension. Liz was lovely, there were no other words to describe her. Dressed in powder blue jeans and a paler top, with silver jewellery and sandals, her silvery hair glittering, she was a scene stealer. This time her nails were painted dark green, she had a great look and Steve was obviously mad about her, getting her drink, his hand gently on her back as he ushered her to a chair. We had decided to stay indoors because Steve said he objected to drinking and eating with flies and wasps getting between his teeth.

'I'm not a barbecue fan,' he commented, 'all that underdone food and warm floppy salad and swatting bugs off your burger isn't my idea of fun.'

'He has very low horizons.' Liz teased him.

There was some small talk as Liz established how Rob and I had met and how far the relationship had evolved between us. She did this with great tact and didn't mention that anything had taken place between her and Rob in the past. I was quietly amused, remembering the conversations at the commune regarding the terrors and errors of possessive relationships. I glanced at Rob's profile with something like pride, quietly pleased that he'd said nothing tacky like coming round to fix my damp patches. He immediately turned to me and put a hand on my thigh, passed me a menu and smiled into my eyes. My heart and stomach collided and for a second I heard and saw nothing other than the great golden firework explosion in my head.

Decisions were made about food and orders placed. I could have ordered cotton wool and cardboard for all I knew. Steve sat back and regarded us.

'I'm none the wiser, so how long have you two been an item then?' He picked up his beer and solemnly looked at Liz. 'There you see, I didn't ask them how long they'd been shagging after all.'

There were shouts of laughter and Liz put a hand over her eyes, shaking her head.

'This is just his first pint, shall I take him straight home now before any more damage is done?' She apologised.

'Might I ask the same about you two?' I asked, 'But less crudely perhaps.'

Liz was happy to explain that Steve had come along to help a friend with a job in the village and that they'd met and fallen madly in love, stating he fell first of course and that they'd been married for two years now.

'She bewitched and seduced me.' Steve spoke. 'I've still got a bank account and clothes and a string of broken hearted women left behind. There are still people up there expecting me to finish jobs.' He joked, but he reached out and touched Liz affectionately. 'This is a marvellous woman, I've never met anyone like her.'

The evening was friendly, relaxed and funny and once again the food was good. Eventually I told Liz I'd found some certificates but that there were still a couple of folders and some photographs to look through. I also told her about the 1901 programme with the pencilled initials with hearts and ribbons, and the names on the gravestones.

'I haven't made sense of it. The initials don't seem to make sense to me.' I told her.

Liz was intrigued, especially with the dates.

'I have already done a quick trawl through some stuff we have, but I've also been working backwards from the most recent things like 1980s parish magazines and church fetes, that sort of thing. I think it's always best to start with who you know, see if you can find them, and trace things back, fill in the picture a bit.' She said.

Steve, listening to this exchange, asked 'Well what was your great granny's maiden name? She won't have been a Charlesworth so what does the P stand for, assuming the S is Susannah like you?'

I was stunned. 'Of course, I hadn't thought, with me not knowing who my father was I've grown up as a Charlesworth, so I suppose I must have been looking for that name.'

Liz was thoughtful. 'Penrose is a local Cornish name. So is Penive which I've seen in a magazine article but I can't remember what it was about. I'm sure it will come to me.' She was tapping her fingers against the table.

'Yes, I saw Penrose in the churchyard but it didn't ring any bells, no pun intended.' I glanced at Steve who was groaning. 'And Harvey, I've only just found out that my grandmother, George's wife, was Christina Harvey.'

'Blimey,' Rob said. 'You're related to half the village already. And probably to me!'

Steve started laughing. 'Both of you, take your shoes off now, and see how many toes you've got!'

The evening ended with me inviting Liz to call round to the cottage as soon as she was free. Rob and I walked back to his place, his arm firmly round my shoulders, walking slowly in step. He made sure I walked by the verge to protect me from oncoming carts as he put it.

'Proper dangerous they fast carts be.' He parodied the Cornish accent.

'They're well matched and great fun, I've enjoyed myself tonight.' I told him. 'In fact I've been having a fantastic couple of weeks, thanks to you.'

He squeezed my shoulder. 'The feeling is mutual I'd say.'

We stopped in the road and stared at each other in the dim summer night. I couldn't make out his expression, but I could sense his feelings and thought he was going to say something but he just leaned forwards and kissed me on the forehead.

'You deserve nice times and there should be treats.' He kissed the top of my head. 'So I think we should go to the seaside tomorrow.'

ELEVEN

A couple of days later I went out with Jay. We'd abandoned the idea of going up to Devon and instead took the children to Siblyback Lake, just a few miles away. With a pushchair each and Matilda skipping about we fed the ducks and walked and then sat in the sun enjoying soft drinks and ice cream.

'This is blissful. I could do this at home but I feel I always have to be doing something there.' Jay sat back with her eyes closed.

'As a busy mum you've become a human doing and not a human being.' I told her.

Jay sat up and looked at me. 'That's exactly it, I'm a doing not a being. It would be funny if it wasn't so true.'

We sat in silence. Luke was fast asleep and Matilda was playing with Mabel.

'She's a lovely girl, with an old head on her shoulders.' I indicated Matilda. 'Will you be getting her a p-o-n-y do you think?'

'She needs more lessons, and to grow a bit and get stronger, but if she's as keen in 6 months or so then I think we shall. Martha has said she'll help, because I sure as hell haven't got the time, will or inclination to muck out.'

'You're tired,' I agreed, 'but that's natural with this full on motherhood thing. Have you had any blood tests to check that your iron levels and B12 levels are all ok? I mean, the girls who were mothers used to talk about things like that back in the days when I worked in the lab.' I was treading carefully but I needn't have worried.

'I think my GP would do that if I asked,' Jay responded lazily. 'But an unbroken night's sleep is what I really need.'

'Well ask the grandparents for some help then, and get an MoT from the doctor as well. The family won't be able to cope if you aren't functioning properly Jay. Be kind to yourself.'

I had an idea, and added, 'Matilda and I seem to get on quite well, she could come and make decisions with me at the cottage, the sort of things she does with Martha maybe.'

Jay sat quietly, considering what I'd said. 'What she'd like best is for you to take her out shopping I think. I'd give you the money. And mum and dad are happy to take Matilda and Mabel for a night, and Martha would have Luke. She loves little boys, all her children were boys. I might ask them to do that and give me a night off. Phil and I could do whatever it is people do when they have a life.'

I told her about going to the pub and just having a meal and a chat with friends, and I mentioned meeting Steve and Liz.

'Rob told me he and Liz had been an item for a while.'

Jay looked at me. 'Yes they were, but it seems like ages ago now. How did you feel about it?'

'Probably no worse than Rob felt when Andrew turned up that night, in fact a lot less worse because she's happily married to Steve and anyway I'd already met her at the library. What's past is past and actually I like her. I like them both although Steve is a bit of a handful.'

'Rob rates him, he's a good carpenter and they bounce ideas off each other apparently.'

Again there was some lazy silence between us in the sunshine. Jay, like her brother, was easy to be with.

'I'm thinking,' she murmured, stretching lazily. 'Remembering Rob when he and Liz stopped seeing each other, they sort of ran out of enthusiasm, he wasn't cut up at all and it seems they've stayed friends. Whereas that night Andrew turned up, Rob was beside himself. When he came to see me the next day he was in a right old state.'

'I went through something rather similar.' I told her. 'Yet we've only known each other for a short time.'

'Phil and I were friends right through school, but it wasn't until agricultural college that we got together. I saw him looking at a girl and I thought my world was going to collapse. I knew he was special and I decided then and there to make a play for him and gave it everything I'd got.'

'It obviously worked.'

'Yes. But he told me afterwards that he'd only looked at the girl to try to make me jealous or at least notice him. Apparently he'd fancied me for ages.' She laughed. 'I wonder how it will be for my kids when they grow up.'

I changed the subject and told her how nice Rob had made his cottage.

'Did he tell you it's been in our family home for a while?' She asked me, getting a wet wipe out to clean something off Mabel's face as she toddled round us, Matilda following her, caring for her little sister.

'No I didn't know that.' I was surprised.

'We never lived there but our dad did briefly, with his parents. I believe our great grandparents lived there originally. Anyway it came down to Rob and me jointly, so he bought me out since I was already married to Phil by then and we have the farm. He's done a thorough job doing it up, it was a bit of a wreck and very dated.' She paused. 'He wants to build an extension on the side next, there's space and the place could do with an extra room.'

'Rob said something about your family having owned the village forge.'

'Yes, we were Williams the Forge, from Wales originally. It was where the farm shop is now. It became a little garage which grandad ran. But he realised our dad wasn't interested so when grandad retired he sold up. Rob has always been a bit sorry that he didn't get the old garage cum forge premises as well.'

I felt a shock go through me and sat up.

'What is it, what's wrong?' Jay's first instinct was to look at the children.

'Nothing. Well, it's something I've found in the cottage, several weeks ago now,' I told her, stumbling a bit over my words, 'advertising a Valentine's Dance at the village hall in 1901, it has the initials SP and RW on it, entwined in ribbons and hearts.

After talking to Liz and Steve I think that SP might be an ancestor of mine but until this minute I hadn't a clue about who the RW was. The W might stand for Williams. Is Robert a family name?'

Jay's eyes were wide. 'Yes it is. Luke's second name is Robert, and Rob is named after our father and grandfather although they were known as Bob and Bert which sounds horribly like a comedy duo. But there's also an uncle or a cousin Richard somewhere in the past.'

'Is there any way we can find out about him?' I asked her, and mentioned that Liz Bradley was looking into some village historical records.

'I could ask my folks but they're travelling around Scottish Islands at the moment. Dad might know some more about the family background,' Jay mused, 'and with kids of my own I ought to find out about our family story.'

After a relaxing few hours we packed up and got the children into the car. The girls were tired but Luke was just waking up.

'He's a night towel.' Matilda informed me solemnly as she strapped herself in.

Jay dropped me off at the cottage where I made a fuss of Daisy. Rob wasn't coming round because he was up country on one of his trips so I made a quick snack and then sat down with more of grandfather's folders and papers. This time I didn't feel sad at the passing of their lives, there seemed to be a pattern emerging, a thread which connected us all through time and I was beginning to feel as though I had a part to play. I looked again at the professional photograph of the baby in christening robes. Then I heard the landline ring and went into the kitchen to answer. It was Liz.

'Su how are you?' she asked. 'I've found something that might be of interest, are you free tomorrow afternoon? It's my day off.' I had learned that Liz worked four days a week as a beautician in Launceston.

We agreed that 2pm was a good time and I went back to the sitting room, glancing round, checking that things were tidy enough for a visitor. There was a text on my mobile from Rob saying, *"traffic is a mare, missing u rotten, cu 2moro nite"*. I was pleased to get his text but I loathed text speak and responded with *"take care up amongst those english, I miss you more, till tea time then, love Su xx"*. And then I deleted the word, love, before sending it. We had not used that word, yet.

I carried on looking through the folders and soon found my grandfather's birth certificate. George William Charlesworth born 15th March 1936, his father was Robert William Charlesworth, occupation Dairyman, and his mother was Helen Upton. He was born at No 1 Orchard Cottages. That must be right here then, I thought. I'd known that this cottage was originally two cottages but I hadn't known they went that far back in my family. So both my mum and grandfather had been born here, and Robert William must have worked at Moorstones Farm where Jay now lived. I had goosebumps on my arms. I went into the kitchen and made a mug of tea. Then I went and got a biscuit. This family hunting was tiring work.

There was an ornate little certificate showing that my grandfather had been christened in the village church. I hadn't seen one of those before. And then I found myself holding the birth certificate for Robert William Charlesworth, born 10th October 1901, the son of Susannah Charlesworth nee Penrose and Joseph Charlesworth. The initials SP, for Susannah Penrose. But if it was her initials pencilled on the dance programme, who was RW and why wasn't it Joseph? I sat pondering this for a while, I felt as though I was on the edge of something important but something vital was missing. I looked again at the when and where born column and couldn't believe my eyes. The Manor House.

That was my eureka moment. I needed to find their marriage certificate, if they'd had a baby in October 1901 they must surely have been married before Valentine's Day 1901, which would exclude them from this forensic fantasy I was entertaining. I went back to the folder, tipping the remaining contents out in my excitement. Daisy came over and sniffed at what I was doing, flicking her tail at the slightly musty smell. An old photograph, printed on thick card was the first thing I picked up. Again it looked like a professional job but it had been cut in half, the person she had been standing with had been removed. I looked at her sweetly pretty face, slightly three-quarters on as if she was just turning to look at something, or someone. Her obviously fair hair was taken up off her face in a fashion of the time. She had a high neckline to her blouse, and my necklace. I looked again, yes, that was definitely my necklace, I could clearly see the shape of the opal stone and the filigree around it. Was I actually looking at the face of my great-great-grandmother, Susannah Penrose and was she dressed for a dance? I couldn't tell, it just looked like a very nice lacy blouse and a plain skirt. I turned the photograph over and scrutinised the back, tilting it against the light to see if I could see indentations or writing or embossed marks of any kind. There was nothing. I looked at her again and even without any proof felt that this must be her, but what was her story? I turned back to the papers I'd tipped out. Daisy had settled down on top of them and was dozing. I eased her solid little body over a bit and pulled the papers out from under her. The top paper was folded into four. I carefully unfolded it, already suspecting what I was holding, the marriage certificate of Susannah Penrose and Joseph Charlesworth.

The marriage took place on 25th March 1901. So she would have been at the Valentine's Day dance as Susannah Penrose. I grabbed my phone and found the calculator. If her son was born on 10th October 1901 then 280 days earlier meant that she must have conceived in January, she must have known she was pregnant when she married Joseph. But why Joseph, why not the RW pencilled in a heart on her dance programme? I thought back to that day in the graveyard, or the churchyard as the vicar preferred to call it. Joseph Charlesworth had died in December 1912, his gravestone asked God to grant him the love he deserved. My mind was racing, didn't she love him then, had she been or was she in love with someone else, the unknown RW. I was tired. I needed to work this out with someone cool headed and dispassionate and not personally involved as I was becoming. I was looking forward to seeing Liz.

By the time Liz arrived the next day I'd got all the papers arranged on the kitchen table. I'd had a fitful disturbed night on my own and slept late, woken by Daisy desperately breathing in my ear and tickling my face with her whiskers in an attempt to get me up and feed her. Liz was friendly, dressed in blue and white which suited her, looking about as she came in.

'I've never been in here, isn't it a pretty place, and what a pretty cat.' She bent down and stroked Daisy, who immediately went into cute mode. 'Do you like living here?'

'Yes I do, it feels like home,' I answered, switching the kettle on. 'Daisy likes it as well in case you were asking her.'

Liz smiled. 'Tea is good, I drink coffee in the morning but from midday I'm a tea drinker.' She took her jacket off and hung her bag over a dining chair. 'It looks as though you have found some good stuff, can I look?'

I nodded and busied myself with the tea tray, putting a few biscuits on a plate although with her figure I doubted she ate such things. I was wrong, she unwrapped a chocolate orange biscuit and ate it straight away. 'Marvellous.'

We sat down together and I started telling her what I'd been piecing together the previous night. She was fascinated and got an A4 pad out of her bag and started making notes. She was quick and practiced, leaving gaps for missing information as she sketched a family tree and pencilled a few comments or questions in a column down the side. It made them all seem real. I also recounted my brief conversation with Jay.

'So Susannah seems to have gone to a dance with someone called RW, and then she almost immediately married Joseph Charlesworth and called her first son Robert William. And she was probably already pregnant. Hmmm, curious to say the least.'

Liz was tapping her pencil against her teeth, and looking at the photograph of the lady with the locket. 'It's certainly intriguing and rather suspicious that the person she was photographed with has been cut away. Quite odd to deface something as important and significant as a photograph, they were expensive things in those days.'

'That's exactly what I thought.' I sipped my tea, tasting nothing. 'Is there any other surname beginning with a W in the parish at that time, other than Williams?'

Liz consulted some other notes she had made in a little notebook. 'No, there aren't, not in this parish.' She thought for a while. 'I could take a look at the neighbouring parishes, after all a dance like that might have attracted a few swains from foreign parts on the lookout for a pretty dance partner. Of course it was the time of year when people liked to get their affairs in order, contracts of employment organised for the year, marriages and so on. Once spring began and the farming activities took over there wasn't much time for such things again until the autumn.' She paused. 'I just had a thought, RW might have been a handsome itinerant miner, leaving no records behind.'

'Oh this is so flipping frustrating.' I drank my tea and ate another biscuit.

'Well I think it's all interesting and a bit of a mystery,' Liz said. 'But on the phone I said I'd got something that might interest you.' She was fishing about in her bag and pulled out a small parish magazine from the year 2003. 'Not very old but there's a reference to the annual amateur photography exhibition and prizes awarded, and your grandad got one.'

'Wow, I was 16 and hadn't been back here that long, it was just after my mother died.' I was squinting at a picture in the A5 magazine, trying to make out what my grandfather was standing in front of. 'Rob said he remembered seeing the exhibition. I don't think I've found his photographs yet but there are still a couple of boxes to investigate.'

I realised that Liz was looking at me, an unfathomable expression in her eyes. She was holding another magazine. 'I'm not sure about this one, it's dated 1986.'

'Oh that's before I was born, what is it?'

Liz was looking down at the magazine, now open at a slip of paper she had inserted. 'It's a picture taken at the village cricket match, I think it's your mum standing there, giving someone an award. It's a half page colour photograph.'

She handed me the magazine, my mother, slim in a floral print dress, holding a large straw hat in one hand, was handing a small trophy to the captain of the winning team with the other. The caption described Miss Tessa Charlesworth, on behalf of The Wheal Public House, awarding the trophy to Joshua H Milton. He was a golden haired young man in profile. The photograph had caught my mother's face in a moment of joy, her face turned to camera as though someone had just called her name.

'He looks a bit like Robert Redford.' Liz said.

My heart was racing.

'Do you know anything about him.' Liz asked, rather too casually.

I put the magazine down. 'Who, Robert Redford? Never even heard the name until recently.'

But I'd never heard of Joshua Milton. I paused, wondering what I had to hide and came to the conclusion there was nothing and anyway, I preferred the truth.

'Martha, Jay's mother-in-law, told me about this rumour a few weeks ago, it was the first time I'd heard it. Mum never said anything about my father and I've never heard this man's name until now.'

'Well there's nothing to be ashamed of and everything to be proud of.' Liz said firmly. 'Whatever is behind these secrets, there obviously been a lot of love in your family.'

I thought that was, in fact, rather nice of her.

Liz left before Rob returned, promising to look very hard at her parish and church records now that she had some dates and names to work on. I put some jacket potatoes on to bake in the oven and made up a salad and some homemade coleslaw. I always put a spoon of horseradish in the mayonnaise to give it a bit of a kick. I was just grating cheese when there was a knock I recognised at the back door and Rob came in with his usual call of "I'm home everyone." He'd been at the workshop all day and had obviously gone back to his place to wash and change before coming over. He folded me into his arms and held me close, smelling of soap and clean clothes.

'I've missed you. What have you been up to while I've been away?' He noticed the small pile of tidied papers on the table. 'Oh, you've made some progress. What news?'

I told him that Liz had been round and described the story I'd pieced together as we ate.

'Interesting.' Rob commented as he listened to me chatting on about what Jay had told me about their own family background. 'You've covered some ground in 24 hours, I can barely keep up.' But as usual he was paying attention.

'It's something in the water I think, makes us all gossipy when the menfolk are away toiling.' I smiled. 'But Liz is good at this, she's gone off to look at some proper records now I've given her their names. So I might get to the bottom of this story.'

'Oh good,' he stretched, 'I like bottoms.' And he reached over as I stood up to clear things, pulling me round to his side, where he proceeded to burrow under my t-shirt and blow raspberries on my stomach.

While I made us a drink he idly sorted through the documents, I could see him making connections.

'D'you think I'm on the right track?' I hadn't shown him the two parish magazines.

As I put our mugs on the table he found the cut photograph of my great-grandmother Susannah and sat very still, studying it. He pointed to the necklace. 'Is that what I think it is?'

'Yes, I think so.'

'Wow.'

I repeated some of the conversations I'd had with Liz and Jay. 'But we haven't yet tracked down who the mysterious RW was. Funny that you have the same initials.'

He hadn't moved, there was a funny look on his face. I put my mug down.

'What is it? Are you ok?' I asked him. 'Have I poisoned you?'

He didn't laugh. 'You know my cottage was a family inheritance then, and that we've been here a few generations. When I got the deed box and family papers, there was an old photograph amongst them. It's cut in half. The person he was with is missing.'

I fully understood the description of one's blood running cold. We sat staring at each other, a myriad of ideas and questions forming in the air around us, but saying nothing. I could hear someone breathing, I realised it was me.

'We need to see if the two halves match.' I looked at the kitchen clock, it was 9 p.m.

'Should we wait until tomorrow?'

'I don't think I can sleep tonight if we do.'

We took my car, leaving a few lamps on and some extra biscuits and clean water down for Daisy, who was out hunting. As I drove us down to the village Rob kept his hand on my thigh. It should have felt comforting but I could feel that he was tense. We didn't speak. I parked in the place at the back of his house and we went in, almost painfully aware of every second. Switching all the lights on he opened the door to the under stair cupboard where everything was orderly and shipshape as my grandfather would have said. He backed out holding a small black rectangular metal deed box. It was scuffed and dull and had the name Williams painted in cream letters on one side.

'Here goes.'

He put the box on the table and opened it, carefully lifting the contents out. I could see old deeds and more modern registrations of title. The photograph had been placed for safekeeping in a brown paper bag. Silently I got my half out of my bag where I'd wrapped it in a clean sheet of paper kitchen towel. With perfect choreography and in complete silence we sat down together at his little dining table and taking our respective halves, placed them together.

They were both standing, carefully positioned by the photographer, not quite facing each other. Each had a hand on the back of an ornate single chair, almost touching. There was a handsome brass pot with a tall leafy house plant, the side of a fireplace and wall panelling visible behind them. But it was the look on their faces. Her face was glowing, her expression was of a woman in love, and his, despite what must have been a long pose for the camera to work, held a look of utter tenderness. One of us gave a long sigh. I found myself brushing away a tear and glanced at Rob. His lips were compressed and there was emotion in his face. We held each other for what seemed like an age, too shaken by feelings to speak. Eventually we pulled apart and Rob poured us a stiff drink. I thought I saw his hand shaking slightly. We sat down again and studied the photograph.

'He's wearing a sort of bowler hat, and he's got a moustache.' I said.

We looked at each other.

'That photo I took at the pond - the reflection you spotted ...'

'A man wearing a bowler hat.' Rob completed my sentence.

I sat back, feeling very tired. 'Where do we go from here?' Was all I could say.

TWELVE

Despite all the emotion we slept well and long that night, spooned together in supportive, loving comfort. I'd driven us back to Orchard Cottage quite late, Rob holding the deed box on his knee as though everything in it was very precious. He'd decided with the luxury of the self-employed not to go to the workshop that day.

After breakfast we got everything out of his deed box and carefully read every scrap. Like Liz the other day, I took out an A4 pad and we worked out his family tree from what he remembered and from the names in the deeds. Working back from his own father, a successful accountant, I wrote down his grandfather, the garage owner, and his great-grandfather, the forge owner.

'Is the man in the picture your great-grandfather as a young man?' I questioned.

Rob was frowning, trying to work out dates. 'I dunno, I'm confused anyway because they owned the forge for at least two generations so I don't know who's what and where. And anyway I think it's my great-great grandfather we're looking for.' He rubbed his eyes. 'Do people actually do this stuff for a living?'

We sat scrutinising the couple again and I found a magnifying glass in the oak bureau.

'You do resemble him a bit, something about the nose and the set of the eyes. He's a good looking man.'

Rob took the magnifying glass from me and looked through it. 'I can't see it myself.' He looked at the woman. 'Maybe something of you there, it's hard to say.' He moved the glass over the photograph. 'She's got daisies in the lace on her collar.'

'What?' I took the photograph over to the window and examined it myself, using the magnifying lens. 'So she has. Little daisies, my favourite flower.'

We stopped for a break and while I was making us a sandwich Rob telephoned his sister. The conversation was brief and to the point within 20 minutes both Jay and Martha arrived. Martha made a quiet fuss of Daisy as once again I went through the story, feeling as though I was conducting an investigation.

'Maybe we need a chalked body outline and a large letter X marking the spot to help us.' I remarked at one point.

Suddenly there was a call from the open back door. 'Is there a party? I can hear voices, lots of voices, can I come in or are you up to something I shouldn't see?' It was Graham.

'Actually I'm really pleased to see you, you might be able to help.' I grabbed his arm and ushered him in.

'Oooh you all look very serious, I hope there isn't any blood, I'm not a nurse any more you know.' His sense of humour was just what we needed.

Rob made him a drink while Jay and Martha both talked at once. I found Robert William Charlesworth's birth certificate and showed it to him.

'What's this then?' Graham accepted the drink from Rob with a nod of thanks and the certificate from me with his eyebrows raised.

'My great-grandfather I think.' I told him.

Graham examined the document and looked up, his black eyes were sparkling with interest.

'Oh he was born at our place, at The Manor House. Bloody hell, did your family own it in those days then Su?'

'I've no idea, and no deeds or papers so far to even indicate that. But I do think I have a photograph of his mother, my great-great-grandmother, who lived at The Manor House.'

I laid the photograph on the table and then Rob, with a sense of theatre, matched it with his half. There was great cry from Jay as she clapped her hands to her mouth. Martha was transfixed but I was watching Graham. Observant ex-nurse that he was, he was looking very carefully at the detail as well as the couple. After a moment he looked up at me.

'Is that your great-great grandfather, Mr Somebody Charlesworth? Only his clothes although smartish for the occasion, aren't what I'd expect a toff from The Manor House to be wearing in that period. His waistcoat isn't right, or his hat. She's gorgeous though.'

Goodness, I thought, I've got to look into her background as well and find out what the Penrose family were all about. I looked at Rob, who was keeping his face neutral. Graham looked at the photograph again and smiled, taking a deep breath and choosing his words carefully.

'What's weird is, and I'm absolutely certain about this, is that this photo of this very happy couple was taken in what is now my study. I'd know that panelling and the side of that fireplace anywhere, but I really don't fancy that bloody awful houseplant.'

I felt myself flop and Rob put his arms round me.

'Quick, get the smelling salts!' Graham said excitedly.

'It's ok, I'm not having the vapours.' I gave Rob a quick hug and stepped back. 'It's just such a lot to take in.'

There was a bit of babble going on between Jay and Martha, Rob was looking thoughtful, Graham had turned his attention back to the documents.

'We need to check the deeds back at The Manor House to see if any light can be shed on this. Honestly Su, I don't recall seeing your family name, but maybe I didn't look back far enough when we got them. And it is ten or more years ago since I looked at them.'

Graham telephoned Oliver to expect a large party engaged on some sort of treasure hunt and drove off taking Martha with him. Jay drove back up to the farm to relieve Phil of his unexpected baby sitting duties and said she'd join us later. Rob put his arms around me again and held me very close.

'I don't know, this is all making me feel a bit spooked.' He said. 'Where is it all going and do we need to know?'

'I'm not sure.' I touched the side of his face, loving the feel of his skin. 'Part of me says let sleeping dogs, or in this case, secrets, lie. But I also feel as though there's a wrong to be righted, some unhappiness to be released.'

He shivered. 'Now I really am feeling spooked, but come on then, we need to see if we can find a body in the library at The Manor House.'

'You mean the study.' I shivered. 'And stay away from the candlesticks.'

I grabbed my bag and keys, locked up and again we took my car. Daisy's reproachful little face watched us go. At The Manor House there was an atmosphere of excitement, Oliver was asking questions, the dogs were barking, Martha was trying to instruct Graham in good dog management and Graham was looking in his desk cupboards and filing cabinet for the house deeds box. The cats shot out of the house, clearly having had enough. I was just advising Oliver that we could expect another interested party when Phil's landrover came through the gates containing the whole family.

Oliver wasn't concerned. 'OK, a whole new ballgame, lets go and fix drinks and some of Graham's cake and see if that will calm everybody down.'

I helped him and for a while we were occupied settling everyone in the conservatory. Luke was asleep as usual, Mabel toddled out and sat on the terrace and watched the birds on the bird feeder, Matilda wanted to see the chickens. The dogs were put outside in their enclosure and pacified with biscuits. Sanity descended and Graham, behaving sensibly, explained that he was just looking through the deeds to see if he could spot the name Charlesworth.

Oliver was doubtful, 'I don't recall ever seeing the name.'

Jay went outside to watch Mabel and Phil asked Martha what exactly was going on, occasionally firing a question at me, nobody batting an eyelid that Rob and I were sitting together, holding hands. We weren't talking and I was watching Graham scanning documents rapidly. Eventually he looked up and everyone fell silent.

'Well,' he began, 'no ownership by the Charlesworth's but if I'm reading this correctly,' he was holding a slim document with large elaborately scrolled initial characters, 'it seems that a Mr Joseph Edward Charlesworth Esquire, a gentleman of private means, rented The Manor House for about ten years in the early 1900s.'

I felt a great sigh escape me. But more questions were already forming.

'Who was he, where did he come from, what brought him here?' Everyone was asking the same things.

Oliver was looking over Graham's shoulder at the documents on the table. With a delicate finger he moved something to one side and extracted a sheet of paper which he placed in front of Graham. Again there was that rapid assimilation of facts and Graham looked up.

'Well,' he said again. 'I don't remember seeing that before.'

'What is it? Tell us.'

It was Oliver who spoke. 'Your Mr Charlesworth was a photographer, and it seems that he had established a studio here in this house judging by this advertisement.'

Rob and I looked at each other. 'Graham's study.' We both spoke.

Once more the photograph was produced and the sides matched together. Everyone fell silent, gazing at the look of expectation and happiness on their young faces, their whole future before them. There was a distinct atmosphere and it seemed as though the couple were trying to get something across to us through the decades.

I could hear distant whispering, it was Matilda asking her mother what on earth was going on with all the grown ups. Jay came in holding her daughter's hand.

'Will somebody tell me the plot please?' she demanded.

Having established that Joseph Charlesworth had obviously met Susannah by the time he photographed her standing with the elusive gentleman now known to be Rob's and Jay's relative, we were still no clearer about why she married him. The impromptu gathering split up and Phil squeezed his family, including Martha, into the landrover and went home. Jay and Martha promised to get all their deeds and documents out and have a good sort through.

'My husband's family bought the farm in the 1930s, but you never know there might be something in our documents although I haven't looked at them in thirty years.' Martha was quite excited.

Rob and I stood in Graham's study on our own for a while, just looking at the spot where the couple had stood, so in love and so hopeful. I had a lump in my throat. Rob took my hand and pulled me close to him, his arms warm and strong around me.

'I have the feeling we are meant to finish something Su.' He said, pressing his lips against my hair.

We thanked the boys for their wonderful hospitality and left, assuring them that we would tell them if anything else was discovered. Instead of going back home I drove us up onto the moor at Minions where we parked and walked, clearing our heads. A solitary buzzard circled overhead, sheep with well grown lambs and belted Galloway cattle ignored us as we walked. How many lovers had made wishes at The Hurlers, climbed up to The Cheesewring, gazed over to the sea at Plymouth from where family may have departed to the new world, or over to Dartmoor, way beyond Kit Hill and across the Tamar. The ancient landscape had seen it all and it suited our mood, it really felt as though we were carrying something important that had to be dealt with. Without putting it into so many words we both felt a bit changed by events and that made me feel anxious, unsettled. Eventually Rob, clearly on the same wavelength spoke his thoughts.

'Do you think this is right Su, looking into the past like this. In a funny sort of way it might be our own past. I mean, in a romantic way I feel as though I've known you for a very long time, but I wouldn't have said it was like, over a hundred years.'

I squeezed his hand. 'People used to talk about past lives and soulmates and all sorts of stuff in the commune, but I don't know what they really believed, or if it was just New Age talk.' I thought for a bit. 'Maybe for me it's about finding my place after years of not belonging, but I don't know, is that just daftness as well?'

Rob smiled at me. 'We'll settle on feeling faintly confused rather than terminally bewildered I think. And it would be healthy to concentrate on just being us. And right now I'm hungry.'

And this is us, and we're in our life, I thought.

The next day, with Rob back at the workshop I returned to the box room and the last unopened box. It was all looking quite empty now and quite a bit larger than I'd first thought. I wondered if it had been used as a nursery, with my various ancestors having been born here, and I felt that my own children might start their lives here too. I stared out of the window, musing things over, watching a red haired woman riding by on a bay horse.

I remembered what Liz had said when I first met her, something about finding out too much about the people who have left you behind. It was an odd feeling. I knelt on the floor, pulled the box towards me and opened it, there was an ornate old chocolate box and inside that, carefully wrapped in tissue paper were what appeared to be a series of annual photographs of a pretty woman posing with a little boy in various stages over about ten years, judging by his growth. In his young face I could see the faces of people I had known and loved. I knew I was looking at Susannah and her son. She was wearing a wedding ring and, in all the photographs, her special necklace.

My grandfather must have known all about these and, I supposed, that was where his own interest in photography sprang from. I sat on the floor for ages, lost in a kind of dream, seeing her life, so different from what she had expected and hoped for. I was glad that she had been kept safe and had been cared for but the picture still wasn't complete.

The phone rang and brought me out of my reverie. I went downstairs to answer. It was Martha, sounding excited.

'Are you sitting down Su?'

I pulled up a kitchen chair. 'I am now. What've you got?'

'I've found a ledger and some very old accounts. The family who owned the farm before us had it from the 1800s and made a good living. They'd had a cider press in one of the barns for the orchard produce and the ledger lists names and wages and annual produce. They employed quite a lot of men for work with the animals and hedging and ditching up until the first world war when their fortunes changed. They lost their youngest son in the Great War and the other to the Spanish flu epidemic. Things went downhill for them. But they had a couple of girls living at the farm, one doing dairy work and one working in the house. One of them listed in 1899 is Susannah Penrose.'

I gasped. 'She was at the farm then!'

'Yes, living in and working as a dairymaid.'

'So the Penrose family weren't wealthy then if she was a live in servant?'

'It doesn't look like it Su.'

'So she would have been the right social class and in the right place to meet a blacksmith's son.'

'Absolutely. But not the right social class to marry a gentleman of private means.'

'So why did she?'

We chatted some more and I thanked her for the information, saying I'd like to see the documents. So my great-great grandmother had worked at the farm before going to live at The Manor House. Well that was quite a change in her circumstances.

I got myself a cold drink and went back upstairs followed by Daisy, who was enjoying investigating the corners in the box room. At the bottom of the box I'd been sorting through were some very old clothes patterns which I put to one side and an old newspaper, all probably put in for padding. It was called the Cornish Gazette. Curious I looked at the date. Thursday 28th February 1901. My scalp tingled. I shuffled round so that I could lean against the wall and very carefully unfolded it. There was an article about the monarchy, Queen Victoria had died about a month before and the country was in a state of shock and full of patriotic support for the new King. There were advertisements for liver pills, tonics, embrocations and ladies shoes. There were detailed sales notes for livestock and I learned that snowfall had not been heavy that year so animals were surviving well over the winter months.

And then I found it. With a sense of dread my eyes were drawn to the heading: A Tragic Death on Bodmin Moor. I read quickly, making sense of the sombre way of reporting at the time. A young man, Robert Williams the village blacksmith's son, whilst out walking between his place of work and Moorstones Farm, thought to have been going to visit the farmer in connection with his work, had slipped on icy ground and drowned in Moorstones Pond. There wasn't a breath of scandal. His family were deeply shocked.

I sat there and cried, great tearing sobs which distressed Daisy and she stepped anxiously around me as I wiped my eyes on my sleeve. When Rob came home he found me in the kitchen red-eyed and deeply upset. I showed him the newspaper and the short article. He read it carefully.

'My mum said something awful had happened at the pond. It was him, wasn't it, it's where he died, in my pond, going over to Phil's farm. Moorstones Farm.'

Rob was cradling me in his arms, rocking back and forth, making soft noises into my hair.

'He was looking for Susannah, I know he was looking for her.' I snuffled.

'You can't be sure Su.'

'But she was pregnant, they were in love, he was looking for her, I just know it.' But I didn't know it, I was just heartbroken for their loss.

And then a piece of the jigsaw fell into place. I had a vivid picture of Joseph and Susannah talking at The Manor House. I saw her crying, holding the photograph Joseph had taken, explaining her terrible predicament.

'Joseph Charlesworth knew her because he'd photographed them, and when the news broke of Robert's death he offered to marry her to save her reputation. He was more than a gentleman, he saved her life, but she didn't love him, she couldn't love him like she'd loved Robert Williams.'

But Joseph loved her enough to allow her to name her son after his dead father.

And I'd learned from the article that Robert had a sadly bereaved brother, Richard, who was obviously Jay and Rob's ancestor. Rob had already given that some thought while I sobbed in his arms.

'I think that Susannah must have cut the photograph herself, partly to protect her son from any doubt about who he called father, and partly to give a photograph of Robert to his grieving brother, my own great-great grandfather Richard.' He squeezed me tightly. ' And that's why he named his own first son after his dead brother. It's how my name came down to me.'

We clung to each other like drowning souls.

Later that afternoon Liz rang. I told her what we had found and she confirmed much the same thing.

'But they had been going to marry,' her voice was clear on the phone line, 'because there's a betrothal notice in the church records.'

In the following days I learned from Liz that Joseph had died after eleven years of marriage, from natural causes. He was quite a lot older than Susannah and there hadn't been any other children. He had continued renting The Manor House but after his death Susannah purchased No 1 Orchard Cottages, I suspected to be near to the place where the love of her life had died, or where they had courted. They had probably walked down the farm lane and along the pond footpath while they discovered their love. In later years her descendants purchased No 2 and knocked them together, renaming their new home Orchard Cottage. I had a feeling that the pretty little old oak bureau that I liked so much had come from The Manor House with Susannah, perhaps it was a gift from Joseph.

I talked it over with Graham and Oliver one day as we walked around their house, seeing period features that Susannah might have been familiar with. It was interesting but personally I had no sense of recognition or familiarity. It was just a lovely house.

Oliver, however, had some ideas of his own. 'I reckon your Mr Charlesworth might have been gay you know. He was clearly a single gentleman of a certain age and comfortable means, with an expensive hobby but not much of a home life. Taking on Susannah in her condition would have given him both companionship and respectability as well as taking care of her situation. It was illegal to be gay and of course there was so much shame and stigma attached to having an illegitimate child. It would have suited them both.'

Graham was nodding. 'And on a practical note it saved the parish from having to pay for the upkeep of her fatherless child.'

Once we seemed to have completed their story Rob and I settled into a loving and happy relationship. We didn't feel that we were the original Susannah and Robert, we were different people, but somehow it made sense to us that we were meant to be together. At Christmas we had a quiet dinner together in the cottage. After dinner he said that he'd lost something and that I'd have to go into the sitting room to help him find it. I was giggling as he took my hand and lead me to the little Christmas tree beneath which was a slim present wrapped in plain brown paper. He presented it to me on the palms of his hands.

'What's this, what've you done?' I was smiling, we had already exchanged presents in the morning.

'Just one more thing to unwrap. I think we should start our own Christmas ritual of saving something for the evening, something special.'

I pulled the paper off and found a fire poker he'd made in slender twisted metal beaten into four sides at the top and with a curve in which nestled a finely crafted daisy. I was delighted.

'This is the prototype', Rob said, 'the use of the flower has given me the idea for a new range to make, but it can't be repeated exactly because it's unique.'

I dug him in the ribs, 'Un-i-que' I giggled.

'No really Su, it is unique, look closer.'

I looked, and found an inscription, *Robert & Susannah*. Our secret inscribed into metal, fired, shaped and cooled into something permanent and lasting. He'd used a punch to place a tiny heart either side of the names.

'Turn it and look again Su.' Rob said.

I looked at the next side, running a finger tip over the fine engraving, *Orchard Cottage.*

'And again.'

On the third side there was a date, *14th February 1901.* Tears misted my eyes. 'It's lovely Rob, I really love it. I love you so much.'

'The fourth side is empty but I can date it again if you'd like. But it has to be a significant date.' Rob pulled me down onto the sofa and then knelt in front of me. 'There's something else.'

And from his pocket he took a little pouch, and from that a small ring he'd made in twisted silver and gold.

'I want to marry you Su.'

We got married on Valentine's Day in the village church and defied current convention by walking down the aisle together hand in hand. Phil gave me away and I wore a long silky cream maxi dress of my mother's. It had full sleeves to the wrist and there were tiny daisies embroidered on the deep cuffs and around the low scooped neckline. The old ivory lace I'd found in the box room made my bridal veil and of course I wore Susannah's opal necklace, the one she had proudly worn all her life.

Matilda was my only bridesmaid, dressed in pale pink with a pale green sash round her waist and with a circlet of silk daisies on her hair. Rob and Steve had made her a shepherd's crook to carry, decorated with pink and pale green ribbons. Rob had solemnly presented it to her with a promise that we would take her out shopping.

The Reverend Ludlow also broke from tradition and before our ceremony said a few words of blessing for our namesakes, saying that love lived on beyond death and tragedy, that love was the eternal truth.

All our friends were there and afterwards we had our wedding breakfast in a heated marquee in a field at the back of The Manor House. Graham and Oliver owned the field and Graham organised the food so it was all delicious.

While the party was going on Oliver, beautifully dressed in a silver grey suit and with a stunning magenta waistcoat and matching silk handkerchief took us both aside and said they had something to show us. We followed them both to their study and he opened the door. I gasped. They had moved the furniture and set things up almost exactly like the room in the original betrothal photograph, even to 'that bloody awful plant.'

'This is where you must have your proper wedding photograph taken.' Oliver was indicating a camera on a tripod. 'I'm not that bad at photography myself.'

****

The Date Stone

Part Two of
The Lemon Juice Summer

To be honest I was getting a bit fed up with her that morning. It had been a busy month, Mike and I had burned the midnight oil for weeks preparing our pitch for a presentation at an IT games fair in Berlin and we'd made a really good sale to a Japanese company. Enough to keep us in beer and birds for a while, was Mike's usual laconic take on things. He was a good mate, we'd met at university and hit it off even though we were very different people. We'd started out by designing a few games for fun and found we worked extremely well together. One job lead to another and the sale we had just made meant more than beer money, it was going to be enough for us to continue for quite some time in the manner to which we were rapidly becoming accustomed. And we could keep paying the self employed geek who was proving more than useful to bounce new ideas off as well as babysitting a couple of our existing projects.

I glanced at her as I negotiated the Audi round the South Circular and headed for the M4. Lynn was good to look at and so she should be, she worked hard enough at it. When Mike and I were struggling newcomers in the IT world, renting a couple of rooms above a carpet shop, she was working across the road in a new glass and steel office building which had been built where a garage once stood. She described herself as an advertising executive, but her speciality was as a location finder, she could unerringly spot the prettiest place for a butter commercial or a moody location for the latest hair products preparation, shot with skinny models in soft focus. My sister hadn't been impressed, I recalled.

'She's all snake oil and smokey mirrors Daniel, I don't know what you see in her.' My darling sister Kate, with her brilliant and unrehearsed use of language.

It was Kate we were driving down to see. She had never left Cornwall. Happily married to her childhood sweetheart who had managed to land a job as a local pharmacist when he qualified, she was too busy with their new twins and their smart modern home to be bothered by the tumbledown old place our grandmother had left us.

'It's just a dank pile of cold granite Daniel. We'd never use it. We should let it go, the past doesn't belong to us, let someone else do something with it.' I could hear Kate's voice in my head. Which was the only voice I could hear because Lynn still wasn't saying much. She was busy with her tablet, her pretty little head with its short expertly cut dark hair bent forward, a dark blue scarf knotted Audrey Hepburn style around her slender neck. When she wasn't working she was usually to be found at the gym. Today she was wearing a soft dark blue leather jacket over a pale green cashmere sweater, tight dark jeans and high heeled ankle boots. I wasn't sure what her concept of dressing for the country was. She favoured silver jewellery and not all that long ago had expressed a desire for me to buy her something in platinum now that I was doing so well. I had a horrible feeling I knew what she wanted.

'I'm bloody hot.' She put her tablet away. 'Where are we?'

'Take your jacket off then.' I didn't bother to respond to the second question, she could read the road signs as well as I could.

She sighed and struggled to get out of her jacket, unfastening her seat belt to do so. The car gave a warning ping to let me know that my passenger was behaving like an idiot. Even at this time of the morning, commonly known as prat-o'clock to those of us who regularly get up far too early in order to get ahead and meet deadlines, the traffic was slow so I was able to reach over with one arm and give the jacket a bit of a tug. She wriggled out of it and threw it into the back.

'That's five hundred quid you've just thrown on the floor.' I shouldn't have said that judging by the poisonous look I received.

'I got in the sales, half price.'

'You have very good taste.' I felt the atmosphere lighten a little. She loved compliments. For someone who worked successfully in a very tough world she had a surprisingly thin skin.

Lynn put her hand on my thigh. 'Thank you.' Her fingernails were painted green and it looked quite good with her tanned skin. She twiddled with the controls on the dashboard and lowered the temperature. I didn't mind her doing that, I was wearing a thick shirt and jumper, what I didn't like was that she wanted cool air blowing on her feet when I preferred to keep the settings blowing up to the windscreen. I found it stopped the car misting up if I didn't want to use the aircon. As soon as she found something else to occupy her I switched it back and put the radio on. Someone was bleating on about an accident at junction 19 of the M4 in a cheery voice. I immediately decided to exit the M4 several sections beforehand and drop off down to the old roads heading south west. I knew I could point the car towards Honiton and take it from there. I've always loved maps and always had a good sense of direction whereas Lynn simply expected that she would arrive at her destination looking cool, unruffled, elegant and bang on time. She never made any contribution to planning a journey.

I'd helped her a lot in our early days together by showing her places outside the home counties. She loved to go on weekend breaks to country hotels because they did all the bed making and cooking, at home in the flat she wasn't much interested in those tasks. I sometimes doubted she even knew where the kitchen was in my flat. She had swooned over the golden little villages in Northamptonshire, loved the pargetting on Tudor era buildings in Essex villages and been impressed by the fine galleting on flint and clunch buildings in places like the Sussex Weald. All these things she'd been able to parrot during her location pitches, impressing people with the depth of her knowledge and her sparkling beauty. No-one ever realised that she was an overnight expert. I didn't mind, I'd just liked showing someone the sort of things I really loved about vernacular architecture. My mum always said I should have been an architect, that I had drawn buildings when I could first hold a crayon and made mud bricks as a toddler. I had dammed the stream at the bottom of our garden and my dad had gone out late at night when I was asleep to break the dam because it was just a bit too effective and the owner of the field opposite would not have been best pleased to find the bottom corner flooded.

Lynn brought me out of my reverie by asking how soon she'd be able to get a coffee. Designer coffee and Lynn were a marriage made in heaven. In the early days I used to watch out for her in the mornings from my desk above the carpet shop. I'd worked out which direction she came from and where she bought her morning coffee, and started copying her pattern until she noticed me walking along the road at the same time.

'You're a bloody stalker mate.' Mike had laughed at me. 'You could get arrested.'

After a few weeks of this I had managed to be in the right place and at the right time to carry a portfolio for her one morning, and she agreed to go out with me. I was quite smitten and eventually we became a couple. For a while it had all seemed perfect. I might be an IT wizard but I do have other interests and I was happy to go along to art exhibitions, clothing museums and whatever place Lynn's research took her to. At first it was quite stimulating but gradually I began to lose interest at the same time that my work with Mike was really making progress. It wasn't that her work was boring, there was a lot of planning and passion and determination needed to become successful in that game, but I didn't really connect with the people she socialised with as part of her job. She didn't seem to have any friends, I had realised. Lately as a couple we seemed to function mostly by either meeting at a smart opening or a launch of something, or by text or email as we worked. We always seemed to eat out. You sometimes wouldn't guess that we actually lived together. In her efficient looking-after-Lynn-way or putting-Lynn-first as Kate would have it, she'd found us a cleaner and a company who collected and did our laundry and the flat was just somewhere stylish where I kept my clothes and computer equipment. We didn't really argue because we didn't see enough of each other, but I had detected a cooling in our relationship.

I was surprised then when she announced that she was going to come down to Cornwall with me. She didn't think much of my sister or her husband and it meant travelling really early on the Friday morning because I had to meet Kate at the solicitors in Liskeard. I'd also planned to stay for the weekend. I hadn't seen much of my sister or her new babies recently and Mark, her husband, was okay in small doses. I'd known him for years obviously, but we had nothing much in common other than Kate.

Staying the weekend was the problem that had fuelled Lynn's irritation that morning. She'd got it into her head that after signing whatever documentation Kate and I had to deal with I would be on my way, and able to take her to see some pretty Cornish landscapes and fishing villages she had in mind for a project she was working on. She had also wanted to stay at a nice niche hotel where she could drink something bubbly on a terrace whilst looking out to sea. Lynn didn't do beaches, her shoes were never appropriate. Kate said bitchily that it was because she was ashamed of showing her bunions. Anyway I'd explained that I really needed to spend a bit of time with my family after gran's death. Gran had died a year after my mother, her heart broken at the loss of her daughter. It had been a rotten time for us all, only made bearable in some way by Kate having the twins. Kate had felt that she'd somehow been gifted with two new souls in place of the two we had lost. She was a devoted wife and mother and I was deeply fond of her. It was time to try a little family bonding with my niece and nephew.

'Do we really have to stay with Kate and Mark?' Lynn said again. 'I mean, isn't it an awful bother for her now that she has small children to look after?' She seemed to imply that Kate was a down at heel drudge draped in nappies, instead of a capable and well organised young woman with, to give him his due, a helpful husband and an even more helpful mother-in-law. I think what she was really trying to say was that she didn't want to stay in a house with babies in it. I was fairly ambivalent myself.

'Yes we do. It makes sense. I need to talk to her and I need to see the kids. It's too early to get to know them because they are still at the dribbling stage but they're my only family.' I was firm but kept my voice neutral, ignoring Lynn's theatrical shudder. 'The guest room has an ensuite and we're booked into a restaurant in Lostwithiel tonight. Daphne is babysitting.' Daphne was Kate's mother-in-law, she lived very close by and was mad about her grandchildren. She was a kind woman, very warm hearted and practical and she and Kate got along extremely well.

We got off the M4 and stopped at Marlborough, Lynn charmed by the handsome town. She wasn't quite so charmed by the coffee and toyed with a breakfast muffin, having refused a full English. Lynn didn't have a good relationship with food, but took loads of multi vitamins and drank strange green things she made in a blender. Since when was a muffin for breakfast and not a thing that could be eaten at tea time I wondered, as usual mystified by how marketing was changing our perception of life. Lynn had often reminded me that it was about aspirational lifestyle now. It was how she earned a good living. After my bacon sandwich I just wanted to get on.

I like driving and the traffic was kind so we made it to Liskeard in good time. Liskeard is a stannary town, it was prosperous during the tin and copper mining days and had the benefit of a decent architect who coherently designed its buildings in the nineteenth century using local granite and Delabole slate. It's fairly unspoiled by modern planning and I've always liked it. Yet it's a town waiting to be discovered. Of course I could have come down on the train from Paddington as Liskeard is on the main line to Penzance, but I hate going to the loo on a train and listening to other peoples' music. I parked and we walked to the solicitors office where I could see a familiar grinning face waiting for me outside. Kate always lifts my spirits.

'Daniel, Daniel.' Kate hugged me, she always used my full name. 'It's fab to see you. You look a bit tired love, was it a rotten drive?'

'No, it was fine.' I hugged her back. She was eighteen months older than me and we both had the same big brown eyes and thick brown hair, but hers was shoulder length and shiny. 'You look great.' I told her. I wasn't lying.

Kate turned to Lynn and they awkwardly clasped hands for a brief moment. Generous as always Kate admired Lynn's taste in clothing and told her she looked marvellous too.

'You're quite a couple to be gracing our humble streets.'

Lynn, mollified and gratified, became her most gracious and turned on the warmth and charm. I silently applauded the effortless way she did it. Gran had moved to a care home from hospital a few months before her death and I felt bad about not having been down often enough after seeing her into the place. I'd left it all on Kate's shoulders. Kate told me not to worry about it.

'She wouldn't have known you anyway Daniel and she thought I was mum. It was mum she missed.'

While Lynn went off to explore the town Kate and I sat in the solicitors office and sorted out all the business involved in a small inheritance. Gran's personal arrangements had been uncomplicated, her savings had all gone towards her upkeep in the care home and her pension had ceased with her death. Kate got all her jewellery and I got my late grandfather's tools. We jointly inherited the family house, Darleystones. The door key was quite a size.

Feeling as though I'd won a prize that might well turn out to be a booby prize we left the office and found Lynn standing in the cramped little waiting room downstairs. She looked bored but managed a bright smile.

'Well, what now?' she enquired. 'A spot of lunch perhaps Kate, we shall treat you of course. Is there anywhere decent to eat in this place that you know of?' A flick of her eyes and a curious little toss of her head indicated that she had found nothing to her liking.

Kate maintained her composure. 'I planned we'd eat at home, and I've got all sorts of goodies so don't worry about lunching out today.'

I put my hand on her shoulder. 'Shall we see you at your place then, we'll be a few minutes behind you.'

Lynn was looking like thunder as we walked back to the car. 'How can anyone live outside London?' She was complaining because one of her boots was rubbing.

I felt close to snapping at her. Kate had been right, I was tired. When you work for yourself in a highly competitive and demanding field you don't think much about rest and holidays. I'd joined the same gym as Lynn and obediently went through my repetitions and exercises, and I liked to swim, but rest it was not. Out of London I was already aware of the different pace of life and the nicer smell of the air. I was reminded of Mole in the Wind in the Willows. He'd got fed up with work and thrown the towel in and gone off with Ratty for some adventures and nice things to eat. Well, my beautiful companion was certainly ratty, I thought.

We had bought a good bunch of flowers and a decent box of chocolates when we'd stopped in Marlborough, which we gave to Kate when we got to the house. Kate had indeed provided us with nice things to eat. There were warmed samosas and delicious French baguettes with salty butter. She'd provided humous with crudités and olives and rocket and she'd made coleslaw and guacamole and got some good Cornish cheeses and some brie, with black sable grapes. It was all being set out as we arrived and she directed us upstairs to freshen up for a few minutes. The guest room was spotless in yellow and blue, with a blue and white ensuite. It was comfortable and pretty. The house was quiet.

'Where are the brats?' Lynn hissed.

'Dunno,' I responded, hanging my jacket up, 'maybe with Daphne.'

I went downstairs and found Kate opening a bottle of cold white wine. 'Screw fittings have taken the pain out of extracting corks but you can't bite them off with your teeth.' Kate smiled.

'You've been watching too many cowboy movies.' I said as I took the glasses through to the dining room. Kate liked modern things and she and Mark had good taste. There was a bit of early learning kiddie clutter about which she kicked to one side.

'Sorry about that, you learn not to step on these things eventually, they bloody hurt.'

Lynn joined us and admired the food. 'It all looks delicious Kate.'

'I didn't make any of it apart from the coleslaw and guacamole so it's bound to be nice.' Kate laughed.

We clinked glasses and helped ourselves to food. I hadn't realised how hungry I was and I didn't hang about. Lynn ate crudités and nibbled a tiny piece of cheese. Kate, like me, ate.

'It's so nice to be able to eat and drink without interruption.' She was enjoying herself.

'What have you done with Emily and Jake?' I asked, helping myself to more since Lynn clearly wasn't going to eat anything remotely like a carbohydrate and she hadn't touched the coleslaw.

'They're with Daphne, she's having them overnight. Mark and I will pop over to see them before we go out later.' She was clearly missing them.

We talked about gran and mum and old forgotten times, and I tried to include Lynn but it was hard for her to join in and enjoy what were our memories, not hers. Eventually she excused herself, explaining about an early start and the drive and so on, could she take a relaxing bath while we caught up with family news. It was gracefully done but Kate wasn't fooled for a second. She closed the dining room door behind Lynn and poured us another glass of wine.

'Why on earth are you still with her Daniel, she's such a moody cow, it's like walking over broken eggshells when she's around. And she really needs to take a battery out and calm down a bit.'

I wasn't going to indulge in one of those conversations so I steered her towards the children and Mark. She babbled on quite happily as I nodded and smiled, not taking any of it in. I was pleased to see her so involved and contented. She adored Mark, she always had, and the twins were the fulfilment of a dream. She was one of those rare people, as happy as the day is long, at home where she was born and grew up and with no wish to change a thing. I helped her clear up and she loaded the dishwasher. It was quite pleasant doing ordinary homely tasks. I had no idea how the dishwasher in the flat worked, and I'm not sure Lynn even knew where it was in the stainless steel integrated kitchen. We normally left everything for the cleaner to deal with.

Mark arrived home at what was to me the early time of 5.30 pm and I shook his hand, jokily asking if he was part time now.

'No, the great thing is I work within walking distance and I'm not doing the evening chemist duty this weekend.' He was as serious and straightforward as ever, tall and slim with an angular face and grey eyes. Mum had said that he was one of those men who was going to get better looking as he got older, and certainly a few lines and a little grey in his hair suited him.

'Blimey, I rarely get back to the flat before 9 pm.' It was certainly a different life.

I watched Mark and Kate as they dashed off, hand in hand, to spend an hour with the twins and then wandered upstairs to take a shower. Lynn was looking around upstairs.

'Hey, what are you doing?' I said. 'Should you be poking around like this?'

'I just want to see what my target audience have, get their mood, get an idea about their aspirations. I'm not being intrusive, I'm just sensing things.'

'Well don't Lynn, it's making me feel uncomfortable.' She had opened their wardrobe doors. Before I realised what I was doing I had crossed the floor from the bedroom door in a flash and grabbed her wrist, closing the wardrobe doors at the same time.

They banged shut. 'Stop it.' I was annoyed and then shocked. I'd never laid hands on her like that.

'Ow.' Lynn pulled away and make a big show of rubbing her wrist. 'You've gone all neanderthal. It must be drinking wine in the afternoon.' She pulled a face. 'Your breath smells of garlic. Maybe you should wash.'

I turned and went to our room. I think I stomped.

That evening Mark drove us down to Lostwithiel. There were toys in the car and I thought I detected a vague whiff of sick. Lynn, looking sensational in a blue sheath dress kept sniffing her wrist, inhaling her perfume in a discreet yet pointed way. She was overdressed for the occasion and Kate, pretty in a green cotton dress with a pink cardigan looked at her in awe. Mark looked at her in fear. He really couldn't stand her I realised. The evening went well enough though, the food in the small family owned restaurant was actually very nice although once again Lynn picked at her fish and vegetables, the plainest thing she could find to eat, scraping sauce off and pushing it round her plate a lot.

'You still getting away on your building jobs?' Mark asked me. Although we had little in common he was always courteous and had a superb memory for details. For several years I had unwound by going on volunteer repair and construction jobs, working on heritage buildings, stone walls, footpaths. I enjoyed experiencing the trades and learning from experts and it was completely different to my day job. Which sometimes had me up all night.

'I haven't done for a couple of years I've been so damn busy.' I told him. 'I would love to do some more, maybe get involved in building an earth ship or a straw bale house.'

'Busy making a lot of money now Daniel, judging by your car. You've done well haven't you.' Kate was smiling at me.

Lynn placed a possessive hand on my arm and gave me a sweet look. 'He's certainly going places and he is doing rather well.'

I was disconcerted by the way she referred to me, as though I was a clever but inarticulate child.

'The business is doing well and Mike and I are both working our butts off.' I said. But the funny thing was that we hadn't started out with the idea of making money, we did the work because it was fun. We loved the design and the structure and the elegance of the concepts. The thing was that what we did appealed to other people and they were prepared to pay for our original ideas. Increasingly, as we were getting known, they paid a lot. It was what mum would have called silly money, telephone number money.

'Maybe you should build your own house one day Daniel, that way you could enjoy all the things you like and get the satisfaction of making something for yourself.' Kate's eyes were shining.

I put that on the back burner. It was a nice idea.

FOURTEEN

The following morning I gave in to Lynn's increasingly urgent pleas and agreed to drive her over to a location after breakfast. She had behaved beautifully when Daphne had brought the children back early that morning and made all the right noises. The twins weren't at an age where they could employ judgement and were taken in by the pretty lady with the long dark eyelashes. To my amazement she had produced age appropriate gifts for them both and Kate and Mark were pleasantly impressed. Daphne thought she was marvellous.

We had to meet Kate at Darleystones in the afternoon so we had a few spare hours. As we drove I thanked Lynn for being so thoughtful, mentioning that although I'd thought of flowers and chocolates for Kate it hadn't occurred to me to get anything for the twins.

'I'm rubbish at this sort of stuff.' I said.

'Well the toys were left over from a job we did at the agency so I thought they may as well have them.' She was matter of fact. 'They've got everything they need really and at their age they'd be happy with the washing up bowl with pegs in it and a wooden spoon to bash them around with.'

I was surprised at the bitterness in her voice. 'Was that what you had Lynn?' I knew she'd had a tough upbringing, it was what drove her to make her life perfect.

'More or less.' She wasn't going there.

We'd looked at the location she'd had in mind from trawling the internet and she took pictures, not quite satisfied with what she was seeing. By now it was time to go back across the A30 and skirt round Bodmin Moor to my grandparent's old place. I used the small lanes and back-ways that I knew. It was early spring and there were wild flowers in the banks. Lynn gripped the sides of the seat, terrified by the narrowness of some of the lanes.

In terms of miles the house wasn't far away from a town or villages, but because the lanes were narrow and really only travelled by locals, it seemed much more remote than it really was. I'd been there quite a lot as a child but I hadn't really seen it for years. I rounded a bend and there it was, set in a gentle hillside, the moor above to one side, fields below to the other, touches of gorse in the distance and bright green crosiers of bracken in the foreground. People always think of granite as grey, but this place was golden, the granite a soft almost creamy colour contrasting with the grey slate roof. The sun glanced through scudding white clouds, highlighting the gold for a moment. I think at that moment I fell in love.

Kate hadn't arrived but I parked and got out, touching the large key in my pocket. The ground was rocky but damp in places and I got my boots out of the car. Lynn didn't get out, she was busy with her tablet again and waved a hand, not looking at me.

'You go on. I'll catch up.' She sounded peevish.

Suitably shod I went through the old farm gate and just stood looking. It was so quiet I could hear my own tinnitus. Darleystones was an L-shaped construction, with a good wide porch and a bench set to one side where it would enjoy the afternoon sun. The windows needed replacing and it looked as though the chimney needed attention but there was an extraordinary charm emanating. I walked forward and round the side, hearing the soft whinny of a horse. I knew Bodmin had wild ponies and assumed one must have got into the grounds, you couldn't call it a garden in its current state. I was wrong. A bay horse was tethered to the old iron gate set in the wall between the house and the moor. I walked a little further and saw a slim woman leaning against the side of the house. She had her back to me.

'Hello?' I called out.

She jumped, visibly startled and turned to face me, her white hands holding a small sketch pad and a pencil. She had long dark red hair in a thick plait and huge green eyes and was dressed in a tweedy greenish-red flecked riding jacket with a dark red waistcoat almost the colour of her hair. It looked a bit old fashioned but it suited her.

'Hello.' She responded. Her voice was husky. 'You startled me.'

'Yes, I noticed. I'm sorry. I'm Daniel Pencraddoc, one of the new owners.' I gestured at the house, thinking I had better announce my right to be there.

'Oh, it's sold then.' She looked disappointed.

'Not quite, it belonged to my grandmother.'

'Oh.' She said again, looking carefully at me. 'It's a lovely place, I ride this way quite a lot. I was just sketching.'

We stood looking at each other. Her gaze was level and calm and she didn't disguise herself with excessive movement or expression. She looked as though she belonged here, more so than I did.

Lynn appeared, delicately picking her high heeled way round the house.

'There you are Daniel. Oh, who are you?'

The red haired woman didn't answer. For a second I thought I detected a flash of mirth across her face but the calm look was back in place immediately. She still didn't answer. Lynn was clearly caught out.

'Don't you know this place is private.' Lynn spat, her perfect red lipstick making a hard line of her lips.

I was astounded but the red haired woman gracefully inclined her head.

'I'll be away then, and leave you to enjoy your inheritance.'

She calmly put her things away into a neat little leather bag she had over her shoulder and moved over to her horse with a gliding grace, unhooked the reins and mounted easily. She pulled on a pair of riding gloves. 'Daniel.' She spoke softly and smiled very slightly at me. Then she turned the horse through the old gate and rode off, not in a hurry. I closed the gate behind her and watched her go.   On the bay horse and in her reds and greens she disappeared into the landscape in a magical way.

Lynn was spluttering. 'What a bloody cheek. Who on earth was she?'

The relief I had felt earlier that morning when she had been so delightful with my family left me.   At that moment something broke inside me and I felt cold.   'I've absolutely no idea and I also have no idea why you were so rude to her.'

We were spared further disagreement because Kate arrived wearing a hat and scarf and pulling a quilted jacket on. 'Sorry I'm a bit late. I'm expecting it will be cold inside. Let's go and have a look then, let's do it.'

We went back to the porch, practical and graceful with granite ledges low enough to sit on. My eyes rested for a moment on the date stone above the door, 1733. I took the key out of my pocket, it was well crafted and fitted my hand beautifully. I opened the big old door and something like a soft murmur whispered past me as I stepped inside.   My feet remembered the slight dip where years of use had worn the slate floor. The hall was wide, with an old dark staircase rising to the landing. I walked forward and put my hand on the newel post, carved with acanthus leaf and worn from centuries of touch and could hear my own childish shrill voice as I ran down the stairs calling to gran, calling her to come and see, come and look at what I've found, or seen or done.

There were still a few pieces of dark wooden furniture and a worn and tired looking velour covered sofa and two chairs which had nothing to redeem them. The summer parlour, my Gran had called it, next to that the winter snug, both with open fireplaces and both with a slight smell of damp.   There was the big old kitchen with its cold pantry on the north side, and then in the smaller part of the L-shape a downstairs loo and a sizeable room which had been used as an office and library by gramps. I could remember leaning against his leg in this room as he sat in the round backed wooden chair, showing me how to open a hazelnut Cornish-style.   "You take your penknife like this Daniel and scrape the pointy end off, then careful mind, you poke the point in just here and twist and look, the nut will open. No need for a nutcracker." He had given me the penknife for my birthday, I still had it. I glanced around, there was hardly anything left in this room, mum and Kate and gran had cleared all this out after grandad died. I hadn't been at all interested at the time.

Kate was opening kitchen cupboards and examining some crockery left there. Lynn was staring in horror at some big old aluminium pans and a sizeable spider's web. I looked into the pantry, it was empty, the wooden shelves bare. I rested my hand on the old slate where Gran used to keep her cheese. It was cold to touch. We went upstairs where there were four good sized bedrooms, again mostly cleared out and an empty linen store still housing the venerable hot water immersion heater. There was a large bathroom which wasn't well planned, but bathroom planning wasn't around when indoor plumbing was installed as a necessity and not a luxury. Kate was looking a little bit sad.

'What do you think Daniel? Should we get an agent in now to see what it's worth in this condition, d'you think anyone would want to take it on?' She paused, remembering things from the past as I had. 'We had some happy times here didn't we. We could run about and shout and explore and be free.'

Mum had taken us to her family home at every opportunity and we had loved being away from the streets where we lived because it was so different. For us holidays didn't mean the seaside, they meant the moor in summertime. Looking at it now with the paraphernalia of family life stripped out I could see how unsympathetically twentieth century decoration had treated it.

Lynn stepped into the room we were standing in. 'If you sell you should get enough to buy those Italian leather sofas and Danish Designers rugs I told you about Daniel.' She spoke dismissively.

Kate's eyes widened in surprise and the cold feeling I'd had earlier returned. I'd honestly had no idea that I felt anything for the old house, it had just been there, a faded part of the warp and weft of my childhood, left behind as I'd left Cornwall and moved on. But I was faced with the increasingly sterile emotional life I was existing in with Lynn and the sudden golden warmth I'd felt on seeing the house after so many years. I turned to Kate and smiled at her, the plan enormous in my mind.

'Let's keep it and I shall do it up. I don't need to build my own house, it's already here, it just needs some repair and some love and care. It will be my personal project.'

It was Mark who was really interested as we sat at dinner that evening, dinner which Kate had made and she was a pretty good cook. I outlined my ideas, explaining that I would fund it all.

'How will you do it when you're up in London?' Kate asked. She was looking thoughtful.

'There must be builders down here who can read emails and send photographs and so on.' My mind was flying along, busily assessing the chances of linking modern technology to a house dated 1733 on the side of the moor. Even I had to acknowledge that there might be some communications difficulties.

We kicked a few ideas around and talked and laughed as people do who've known each other almost all their lives. I found myself warming to Mark, he had some interesting thoughts and ideas. I also liked the way he and Kate sparked off each other. Lynn was silent for most of the evening. Mark asked if Darleystones was listed.

'I remember having a conversation with mum after one of my "heritage weeks" as I used to call them. Mum said someone had a look at it in the 1980s and concluded it wasn't that special regarding its age or rarity. Maybe they couldn't see beyond the awful cement render outside and the horrible twentieth century improvements inside. And it's post-1700 so it's not listed automatically. I gather the place just wasn't thought important enough at the time.'

Lynn remained pretty quiet for most of the drive back to London the following day, and I thought she might have been asleep as her eyes were closed but I was so busy thinking about schedules and project management I hardly noticed her silence. That evening we went to the gym and got a salad each and were then both occupied preparing for Monday when my phone pinged a text message.

"D, r u safely back? K"

"Yes, all good here, was lovely to see you Kate xx"

"Can u talk re Darleystones?"

I had hardly replied with yes when my mobile buzzed. Kate went straight to the point.

'I don't really know how best to say this Daniel when you're so full of enthusiasm about the place, but I've slept on it and been thinking and I have to sort this out.' She sounded a bit breathless.

'Go on,' I said, 'what's the problem?'

'Well it sounds a bit money grabbing but Darleystones is half mine - and I know you said you would fund the build and stuff but, well, the thing is I'd sort of been expecting to sell it and get my half of the money soon. The thing is,' she said again, 'I was hoping to pay some of our mortgage off and put something aside for the twins. I guess I'm being protective. Are you cross?'

'No I'm not cross. And you are being sensible.' It was true, I wasn't cross and my ever active mind had flicked over the possibility of buying her out the minute I had stepped over the threshold. I just hadn't acknowledged it.

'Kate.' I said decisively. 'Kate, get it valued and let me know. We'll take it from there.'

'And sell it?' She wasn't keeping up with me.

'No Kate, you can sell your half to me.'

The next few weeks were busy, situation normal. I felt pretty fired up and optimistic about everything and when Mike asked me what substances I was taking I told him a bit about my plans for Darleystones.

'I don't know at this stage whether it's going to be a holiday home for me or a project to do and then sell. I just know I really want to do it.'

Mike, who knew all about my short breaks into building and conservation over the years took it all in his long lanky stride. 'Sounds like a plan mate. What does the gorgeous Miss Milton Keynes think of it?' He took the piss out of Lynn quite regularly, although not to her face. I was beginning to realise that nobody really seemed to like her.

'I haven't explored Lynn's views on the matter.' I said, not rising to any dig at her.

Mike didn't pursue the conversation. He was far more interested in alternative reality anyway. I don't think he'd ever had a serious girlfriend. I thought about asking him and then thought the better of it.

Kate got three valuations which were all pretty close and I thanked her as we talked on Face Time one day.

'Being a mother hasn't completely coddled my brain stem you know. Daniel it means you will have to come down again to do the transfer paperwork. When can you come?'

I consulted my spreadsheet and gave her a couple of possible dates.

'Okay I'll fix one with the solicitor and let you know. Will Lynn be leaving her bat cave to come down with you? I know she'd love to see the twins.'

I snorted. 'Don't be nasty Kate, it doesn't suit you. I'll get back to you on that.'

It's great being your own boss. I got everything sorted out with Mike and the geek, who answered to the name of Radio, I had discovered. He and Mike were clearly made from the same mould, I thought, looking at them one day. Then I texted Lynn.

"Got to go down to Cornwall to sign the papers off Friday. Same as before. Are you coming down with me. X" I hated text speak and never used it.

Her answer was brief. *"We hve a date at UK cheese prod launch that nite."*

There had been a recent government initiative to advertise buying British produce which was proving lucrative to the agency she worked for.

"That a No then?" I responded.

Lynn did not reply.

I felt pretty cheerful as I packed my weekend bag on the Thursday night. I was looking forward to the Cornish Project as I thought of it. Lynn had gone straight to the gym from work. It wasn't that we weren't talking, we seemed to have nothing special to talk about. Again I left early on the Friday morning, kissing her cheek before I left as she was barely awake. Since she would be working late she was having a lie in.

'Hope it all goes well tonight. I'll text you.'

I didn't get much of a response.

This time I channel-flicked on the car radio to my hearts content and played music that I like, occasionally singing along. Mike and I played music at work and it never seemed to distract me when I was thinking. In fact my subconscious often seemed to bubble away and let ideas float to the surface quite efficiently when I wasn't concentrating. It was a fine clear day as I drove into Liskeard and found a parking place, and once again there was Kate, this time with a double buggy.

'I don't know what I was thinking about, it will never go through Humbert & Richardson's door.'

Somehow I dismantled the thing while she held an armful of twins, and we decanted everything into the waiting room, managing to knock a leaflet stand over. The receptionist came to investigate and righted everything. 'Don't worry, nobody ever looks at these anyway.' Half an hour later we decanted everything back outside and I was one hundred and thirty-five grand poorer. Kate looked like she'd won the lottery. I escorted her to her people carrier and again we went through the tedious procedure of

143

dealing with the equipment needed to ferry two small human maggots about.

'Can't you just sling them round your neck in a pouch or something?' I commented. Then I pecked her on the cheek and said I'd be at her place in time for dinner. I had to go and see Darleystones and I had arranged to meet a builder Mark had recommended.

I got there with an hour to spare. It was peaceful, there were a few sheep grazing round the side of the wall and a buzzard sweeping through the sky overhead. I walked round the outside and realised I was looking for a bay horse and a rider. I still didn't know who she was and when I'd mentioned it to Kate she didn't know either.

Eventually the builder and another guy turned up. They were both Northern lads, they told me they had come down to help with a job for a friend and liked the climate and the girls so much they had stayed. They made a few cautious jokes to sound me out, being a bit unsure about the London connection they told me much later, but I gave as good as I got. We went over the house, inside and out, and made notes. I was reassured by the way the builder, Andy, and the chippy, Steve, talked. Steve was all over the staircase with a look of real pleasure on his face and Andy had a way of placing his hand on a stone which I found intriguing. His father had been a professional stonemason he told me, and that was where his own interest had begun.

'I mean bricks are okay, on handmade bricks you come across paw prints, bird prints and hand prints which are amazing, but I do like a bit of faced stone and lime mortar.'

We agreed that the cement render all had to come off. It was the worst thing that could be applied to stone, I already knew this from my building conservation experience. We made lists and exchanged contact details and discussed dates. It was clear to me that I'd be working with these guys.

Back at Kate's house I held my nephew on my knee and made some baby noises. Jake wasn't impressed. So I asked him what he thought about the state of the government today and whether being post-Brexit had completely fucked his future. To my surprise he broke into delighted gurgles and then farted. We all collapsed laughing. Kate and Mark were relaxed and I observed baby bath time, more interested in the looks on the parents' faces than in the babies. Mark asked me how I felt about being an uncle.

'I'm a Nuncle?' I said in mock amazement. Then I was honest. 'It's a bit weird really, I mean I know I'm related to your delightful offspring, but I'm not sure what I feel yet, they're the first maggots I've met and I'm not sure what their function is at this point.'

'You always were a bit of an odd fish Daniel.' Kate was teasing me. 'The black fish of the family in fact.'

There was more laughter at her strangulation of English and Mark said he used to write down the things she said. The light mood continued all evening. I realised they were both relieved to have extra money in the bank but not having Lynn there possibly contributed to the happy atmosphere. After a few glasses of wine Kate asked me, not for the first time, whether I really could afford to buy her out.

'I can. Right now I'm loaded.' I wasn't joking. Putting some spare cash into a property actually made good financial sense.

Mark was working the next day, it being his weekend on duty, so again I took myself off to Darleystones. It was a tranquil day. I had a very satisfactory pee against the garden wall and then walked round and round the place, trying to work out where to begin. I hadn't a clue. My grandad hadn't allowed anything to be planted against the walls, preferring to maintain a path all the way around. He'd been practical about being able to get at windows and gutters, talking about *clearing he and cleaning he* and *keeping atop of they tasks* in his broad Cornish accent. You didn't really hear that accent now.

I found myself studying the windows and the lintels and the stonework around them. The builder Andy had asked me about double glazing and said he could recommend a man who would make bespoke hardwood frames and stick to the design of the original casements, there was a harmony in the design and how they fitted with the house. As I was looking I noticed a shape scratched into the stone at one side of a window upstairs. I went inside and climbed the stairs. It was at the front of the house. I found my hanky and rubbed the pane clean because the window itself wouldn't open. There, I could see it, a mark like two letter V's, one inverted so it made a small diamond shape in the middle. This had been my grandparent's bedroom so I hadn't spent much time in here as a child. I was gazing at this when movement below caught my eye. A bay horse with a rider was coming along up the track towards me.

FIFTEEN

I hurried downstairs and went outside. I could hear her singing as the horse walked, swinging along in a comfortable rolling stride. She was sitting easily with the reins quite loose, dressed as before but with no riding hat. She saw me and stopped. I don't know how she did it because she didn't pull on the reins, it was as though the horse was aware of her mind.

'Daniel. We meet again.' That low slightly husky voice.

If I had been wearing a cap I would have doffed it. As it was I just stood there and said the first thing that came into my mind.

'Hello. The red lady.' Wow wasn't I an utter prat.

She considered that, looking serious for a moment, then she smiled. 'I like it. Better the red than the green.'

I hadn't a clue what she was talking about, but she spoke again.

'I'm Fiona Rose Frazer. Is your wife with you today?' She was direct.

'Who?'

She was looking at me, taking everything in. 'Your wife, the person who was here with you when we last met. There were two ladies, I assumed one must be your wife.'

'Oh no,' I blustered, 'my sister and my girlfriend.' I'd never been able to say, "my partner", that was Mike, not Lynn.

Fiona was now looking at the house where the door stood open. 'She's not here.' She stated.

I assumed she meant Lynn. 'No, I'm here alone.'

'Then I will visit.'

And with that she dismounted and led the horse in through the farm gate. Off the horse she was slender and graceful. I was pleased that she was looking about with interest. I had the urge to show her around and ask her opinion about things. She took the horse round to the back gate again, clearly knowing her way about. I followed them. She looped the reins around the granite gatepost and stroked the horse, which huffed at her in a friendly way.

'Water here for you Bel, remember this.' There was a deep long stone trough at the side of the gate. I remember one summer lying in it as a child, full length. Gran had not been very pleased. Fiona was looking at me.

'You are cloaked in memories.' She said. 'Will I intrude?'

There was something about her use of words and intonation and the way she phrased things which intrigued me. She accepted my silence gracefully.

'I have a sandwich which you can share with me.' She indicated a small flat leather bag she was wearing over one shoulder and under the other arm. 'I always carry a few things when Bel takes me out.'

I got it. 'You're Scottish.'

Again there was that old worldly inclination of the head. 'You have the half of it right, and my name is confirmation. But my mother was Cornish so the blood of the Celts runs in me.'

She lead the way back to the front porch and sat on the old bench to the side. There was no fussy inspection of the bench, no flicking away of imaginary dust or rubbish, no whining or complaining. She had a sizeable sandwich packed in her little bag, along with the small sketch pad she carried. I found my tongue and my manners.

'I'll get a plate, hang on.' I went inside and found the crockery Kate had been looking at a few weeks ago. From the middle of the stack, not so dusty I thought, I took a plate. I had the penknife grandad had given me twenty years earlier in my pocket. I took the plate and gave it to her, then went over to my car and opened the passenger door side. I'd got a bag of crisps and an apple in there, and a bottle of fizzy water. I walked back to her and sat down, not too close. We placed everything on the bench between us and, fishing the penknife out of my pocket I cut the apple into quarters, carefully wiping the blade clean on the bottom of my jeans. I said nothing, deciding to play her at her own game. She had watched everything I'd done with an expression of lively interest. Her eyes were very green.

'You move nicely.' She commented.

I didn't know how to respond to that, so I inclined my head. She gave a gurgle of laughter. 'You are an observer too Daniel.'

This was getting beyond me so I asked her what was in the sandwich. She opened the wrapping and placed in on the plate, already cut into four triangles, making a pattern with it and the apple. I responded by opening the bag of crisps.

'A feast. A picnic. An unexpected picnic, always the very best.' She looked pleased.

The sandwich was delicious, brown nutty bread with a flavour I couldn't place, hard boiled egg with a little bit of heat from some rocket and soft freshness from shredded lettuce, a little bit of salt added and mayonnaise to bind it. I ate and tasted and crunched and sniffed at the bread and finally finished off with apple and licked my fingers. Even the fizzy water was good. All the time there wasn't a word from her, not a whiff of criticism or a comment about the calories. It was great.

'That was fantastic Fiona.' I told her. 'Food eaten outdoors is always good. Where's the bread from?'

'I made it. I saw you sniffing.' She smiled at me. 'I mix spelt and rye into the flour with sesame seeds and sunflower seeds, it's healthy and adds flavour.'

Blimey. This girl knew her way into a kitchen. I drank some more water from the bottle and then fished in my pocket for a hanky. I wiped the neck of the bottle and handed it to her. 'It's okay, the hanky is clean.'

'There, you have a gentleman's manners.' She drank deeply and I observed her long neck as she swallowed, her skin pale and fine with a colour like Devonshire cream. So very different to Lynn with her spray-on permatan. Then she surprised me, it was as if she knew what I was thinking.

'Your girlfriend was unhappy I think. Not with me Daniel,' she added, 'but with her situation. I was just an excuse for the expression of it.'

I thought about it for a moment. That was quite a conversation killer for me. I don't like discussing other people but there was actually some kindness in Fiona's words and I had to acknowledge the truth to myself.

'Lynn isn't a happy person at the moment. I don't think she knows what she wants, and when she gets things she's not satisfied.'

Fiona considered me and what I had said. 'Perhaps she doesn't yet know who she is beneath the make up, and happiness comes only from within, not from without.'

I was silent. Fiona spoke again. 'On that day you were a man in a waking dream who had found something important, there was revelation and self knowledge in your face. I thought about you as Bel took me home.'

That statement warmed me. Blimey, apart from Kate asking how I was every time we spoke or met, who on earth ever said anything about noticing how I was feeling. It touched something inside me that felt undernourished. Frankly, it scared me a bit. I changed the subject.

'You said your mother was Cornish?'

'Is Cornish.' Fiona corrected me. 'My parents met down here, he was in the RAF. It was love at first sight.'

'But your accent is, very softly, Scottish.'

'Boarding school and living with the grandparents when my parents were overseas, and then art college has made that so.'

'I like it.'

'Thank you.'

We sat on the bench in companionable silence but I was very aware of her. She sat with her hands quiet in her lap. I noticed she wore no nail varnish and no jewellery. The edge of her riding jacket was a little worn. A strand of her dark red hair curled down over one arm, her profile was neat and a little bit proud, she had a slight bump in her nose. I was about to suggest showing her round when the horse whinnied.

'Bel wants to go now Daniel.' She folded up the sandwich wrapping and the crisp packet and put them into her little leather bag.

'But I wanted to show you over Darleystones. I thought you might be interested.' I was disappointed.

'You shall, next time. We've shared food now so it's inevitable that I shall see you here again.' Before I could ask her what she meant she was on her feet and her intention to leave was clear, but she turned to me and said, 'Please don't throw the plates away.'

'What?' I followed her back to her horse and watched as she mounted so easily. 'What do you mean about the plates?' I asked again.

'They are pretty.' She spoke over her shoulder as she turned the horse around. They paused and I found myself looking into the dark wise eye of the horse. And then I obediently opened the gate onto the moor. I swear the horse asked me to do that.

'We thank you Daniel.' Again that graceful nod and they went through the gate.

Till next time, I thought it but didn't say it, looking after her. She didn't look back but she raised her arm in not quite a wave, not quite a salute. I realised I was smiling, broadly.

Fiona was right, the plates were pretty. I hadn't really noticed, they were white and a bit square, or not quite round, edged with tiny blue flowers amongst little traces of green stalks and tiny leaves. My gran must have used them for decades for Sunday tea time I guessed. Well, they would stay then.

Feeling invigorated I went round the house, the sofa and chairs were definitely going, the rooms were going to be gutted, tanked and plastered inside and the lime mortar repaired outside. There was an old dresser which suited the kitchen but which was going to have to go into store when all the work started and old stick chair which always sat by the range. I was keeping that as well, there was nothing wrong with it and it had memories. I didn't know if the range worked, I wouldn't have a clue how to work it anyway, but somehow it belonged with the house. We would have to work round that one regarding cooking arrangements. I had an image of Fiona in here, knowing how the range worked, filling the kitchen with the smell of freshly baked bread. I had to shake my head to clear the feeling that evoked in me. I looked at the kitchen floor, it undulated a little, it probably had no insulation underneath and doubtless would have to come up and be relaid to modern standards. I knew I wanted to re-use the existing floor slates as much as possible to retain the integrity of the building. I realised, looking around downstairs, that the house had no skirting boards. On closer inspection of the bottom of the walls below the windows I thought I knew why, there were signs of damp. Skirting boards would eventually just rot.

That evening I talked these things over with Kate and Mark. I'd bought a couple of good bottles of wine and then on impulse I'd also bought some expensive champagne. We had to toast the future of Darleystones. Mark knew of a place for furniture storage.

'They will collect and pack things too if you're keeping gran's crockery.' Kate was excited. 'But be sure to mention the lane is narrow so they don't bring a huge lorry.'

I was fired up and into full planning mode, I loved it when I could feel data streams rushing through my head, making patterns, linking and looping together. I knew I wouldn't sleep until I'd got some of them down on my notebook. I was thinking in colours, which was a good sign.

Kate was pondering my description of the state of the downstairs floors. 'Funny how I never noticed that, but I suppose we were there in the summers when the doors and windows were always open. Will you be putting underground heating in then?'

Mark and I were convulsed with laughter. Kate didn't mind. She liked people to be happy.

When I got back to London on Sunday afternoon Lynn's case was in the hall with her jacket and work bags ready next to it. She was in the, what should I call it exactly, the place where we could sit on a sofa when we weren't at the place we sat to eat. The flat was large and mostly open plan, very lifestyle and desirable probably because of the view of the Thames. She was watching a film. I sat down next to her, remembering Fiona and her calm presence. Lynn seemed tense and almost a stranger. I realised I didn't like the sofa, the back was too low so you couldn't rest your head comfortably like you could in Kate's sitting room. I had another epiphany, I liked separate rooms, they could be personal, different.

'You're going away.' I said to her by way of a greeting, leaning over to kiss her but she moved away and flicked the sound off.

'I have to go up to Norfolk. We're away for a couple of days.' I assumed the *we* she was referring to was her team of fixers and doers.

'Are you okay?' I asked her.

The slightly poisonous look was flashed my way. 'You didn't text me once.'

Bloody hell. I hadn't thought about her at all, apart from that brief moment when Fiona had mentioned her apparent unhappiness. I tried to explain and apologise, the driving, the solicitors, meeting the builders, celebrating with a glass too many of bubbly. I paced around realising I was on a losing wicket. She had to have the last word at every point and it was a bitter and nasty exchange. We ended up looking at each other from opposite sides of the room, fighters circling each other. I took a deep breath.

'Look, why don't we calm down and go out to get something to eat.' I said. 'You can tell me all about the launch you had on Friday night.'

'You can do what you like.' Was her response. 'I'm getting picked up in, oh about now actually. We're travelling tonight for an early start.' She was looking at her large flashy wristwatch.

It was like a TV farce. The door buzzer rang almost immediately and she invited someone into the building, checked her lipstick in the hall mirror and swung the door open as the lift pinged. Her face was flushed from our argument I thought. A man I'd never seen before was standing there. He saw me and looked a bit surprised. Normally I would have stepped forward and said hello, introduced myself, offered a handshake. But something held me back. He was tall and dark and very well dressed, not in the usual smart trainers and casual stuff worn by people who were lugging equipment about. Lynn was all smiles and falsely relaxed.

'If you can manage my case Giles, I'll bring these.' She glanced back at me defiantly as she put her designer label jacket on. She was in a dress as well, with high heels, not her usual travelling gear of well cut trousers and top. 'Bye, I'm sure you can get something from the Tesco express.' I would have to. There was nothing apart from tea and coffee in the cavernous stainless steel thing described as a kitchen.

While Lynn was away I used every spare minute to work out plans and schedules. We didn't text each other. I was in what we referred to as the planning den before Mike in the morning and Mike had to throw me out at night when he was ready to leave. We ate together on the Wednesday night and I told him about everything, apart from Fiona. I was totally fired by the renovations and plans for Darleystones. Mike was great.

'Look,' he said, 'our contracts are all in great shape, Radio is totally cool and more than useful. Neither of us have had a real break for a couple of years. Why don't you stay down there for a month to do whatever is it you need to do, you can do work stuff if there's electricity available down there, at any time of the day or night. Whatever suits.'

I was thinking fast. I didn't really want to stay with Kate and Mark, there was a limit to being with family. A hotel? For a month? Not appealing. Mike was watching me over his beer, as usual on the same wavelength.

'You want to use my campervan mate.' It wasn't a question.

'How the hell am I going to explain this to Lynn.'

'Wear a flack jacket.' Mike advised.

154

Lynn returned sometime on the Thursday. I'd gone back to the flat quite early for me and her stuff was on the bed, of her there was no sign. It looked like she'd been having a sort out which wasn't unusual. She was at the gym I guessed. I checked my wardrobe, jeans, boots and shirts which were all very smart but I decided it was all too much of a London wardrobe. I would have to buy some working gear. I left the flat and used the Satnav to go over to Mike's address. I'd never been there before, we hadn't ever socialised outside our work, why would we, we spent most of our days together. So I was pleasantly surprised when I found he'd got a swanky mews property painted cobalt blue and with two huge red pots holding white flowers outside.

'Christ, I hadn't realised we were doing so well.' I greeted him when he opened the door.

'I own about this much of it.' He grinned and indicated a level of about a metre.

Inside it was beautiful. I had no idea that this lanky old mate of mine had such taste. Everything was simple but good, a few nice pieces of modern furniture, a deep long sofa and a swivel chair in matching fabric with a footstool. He liked to lounge about. Mike made tea while I poked about, noticing books and a stock of old vinyl records.

'I didn't know you could read.' I shouted. 'Where's all your geek stuff?'

'Upstairs, a whole floor of it. But this is where I come to relax'.

I went into his kitchen it was long but well organised in galley style. I opened a few cupboards. They had food in them, so did his American fridge. And it was clean, spotlessly clean. There were French doors open at the end so I stuck my nose out. 'Bloody hell, you've got a garden. There's a tree and green things out here.' It was a small paved private space with a couple of teak sunloungers and a dark blue table with four chairs. He clearly liked to barbecue. The green things were pots of various herbs and lavender but there were red flowers as well. I looked at the tree.

'It's a very old myrtle.' Mike spoke behind me.

'How do you know?' I quizzed.

'I know stuff that you don't mate.'

'Seriously, did the estate agent tell you that?'

'Nope. I told her.' Mike smiled, not in the least self conscious. 'Your way of unwinding is buildings and repairing them. I like gardens. When we retire in about ten years time I'm having a place where I can grow stuff. You can come and do my hard landscaping.'

I had no idea that Mike had plans. I indicated the red flowers.

'Penstemon and Geum. They last for months and they are perennial.'

'Wow.'

We drank our tea and then walked out down the mews to a decent cobblestoned parking and garage area. Mike's campervan was there. He rented an unused outside parking space off a neighbour. Wow again. It was a smart small modern thing, not the rickety bald tyres and gaffer tape construction I'd somehow been expecting. My mate was full of surprises and I now realised he'd changed a lot in ten years. He was clean and his clothes fitted for a start. Funny how familiarity stops you noticing things.

'I don't think I actually know you at all do I.' I said as he opened the van.

It had everything I needed, well it was designed that way. It was perfect. He talked a bit about ventilation and showed me how to deal with the toilet and fill up the water tanks.

'But I'd suggest you go outside as much as you can if the place is that remote, and take a shower at your sister's place, or use the leisure centre if there is one.'

I drove back to the flat, my mind buzzing with ideas. Before I went in I shopped in the local deli, choosing things I liked to eat, even carbohydrates. I let myself into the flat and found Lynn waiting. After Mike's place it seemed characterless and empty. I realised I'd put nothing of myself into it, Lynn had chosen the cool grey colourless sofa. She wore colour but didn't live in it. There was a peculiar atmosphere. I put the bags down in the kitchen thing and spoke. 'I've brought us some eats.'

'I'm not staying'. Lynn said.

I raised my eyebrows. 'What's up?'

'I'm leaving you. I moved all my stuff out today.' She gestured around the flat.

No wonder it had all seemed characterless, there were no ornaments and I realised a few pictures were missing. Funny how you stop noticing things when you have them. I didn't know what to say so I said nothing.

'Aren't you going to say something!' She was taking refuge in anger.

'Good luck and cheerio then?' She took a step forward and I thought she was going to slap me. 'Sorry,' I said quickly, 'that was pathetic of me. I guess we both knew that this was going nowhere didn't we.'

'Well it's too late to have this conversation, but yes, it's been over for ages. In case you are interested, which I don't think you are, I've been seeing Giles for two months now. And I think I love him.' She'd started striding about, holding one arm across her front, hand clasping the other elbow. All she needed was a cigarette in a long holder, she was doing the elegant distracted femme fatale act, I know because I'd seen in it the movies she liked to watch.

'Okay, er, well I'm happy for you.' I said lamely. What the hell was I supposed to say, she'd got everything arranged and sorted out to her own satisfaction, I'm surprised she'd stayed to tell me and not just left a note. I thought quickly, very quickly. 'I do want you to be happy Lynn, you deserve it.'

She stopped walking about and looked at me. Before she could say anything I told her I was just a geeky IT freak, and probably not in touch with my emotions. I wasn't going to give her a chance to repeat what she'd said many times before. She sighed and put her hand out. 'Shake.'

Well that was weird, but I shook her hand. 'Goodbye Lynn.' And she was gone from my life. Maybe she got a cab or maybe that handsome clotheshorse Giles was waiting downstairs for her. I washed my hands, not just symbolically and tore open the deli packages, I was starving.

SIXTEEN

A couple of days later I was on my way. There'd been huge amounts of emails, phone calls and arrangements made. I'd bought some cheap jeans and working shirts and some manly gloves because I had soft girly IT hands. Also I knew, borne of previous heritage works experience, that handling stone and tools could take your skin off. These days health and safety kit was quite sexy too. I'd told the cleaner I didn't need her for a month but I gave her a decent cash tip and promised I'd call her when I got back. There was no milk to cancel. I set off for Cornwall, the Audi safely garaged in the subterranean parking slot at my flat and Mike waved me off. I'd given him the set of keys Lynn had left behind. He was going to call in at the flat once a week if he remembered to.

'Ditch the junk mail and don't forget to water the plants darling.' I'd said to him. There were no plants.

'Don't forget to write honey.' Mike had blown a kiss.

The journey down was a lot slower in the campervan and I stopped a couple of times, just breathing in the unexpected freedom. There was novelty in having a packed refrigerator with me. For a while I toyed with the appealing idea of just going awol and driving all over England and beyond. The attraction of travelling this way had never occurred to me.

I had explained to Kate that I would be camping at Darleystones and that I would not be a pain to have around. She'd been quite excited, but she always was a positive girl.

'You can get provisions at the farm shop in the village, and the food at the pub they have there isn't bad. But I'll pop up and see you and bring you condiments.'

'You mean comestibles I think Kate.'

'I know exactly what I mean.'

Kate had already overseen the removal of the things I was keeping. Andy and Steve were on site when I arrived. Darleystones looked empty without curtains at the windows and kind of deflated, as though its essence had seeped away. It was going to look even sadder when the windows came out but I knew that things had to get much worse before they could get better. The scaffolding they had erected made it look like a sick person on life support. There was cement on the ground because Andy had experimentally removed some from the two external walls coated with the stuff. I greeted them and they were interested in the campervan. I told them it was borrowed.

'Good that you're on site though mate. Keeps things safer when a place is occupied. Tools and stuff.' Andy said.

I unlocked the door and they quickly established a place for storage. They had method and a plan and were happy to use me as their labourer. We worked for an hour and decided that everything was set for the following day. They would be on site at 08.00 sharp.

'And we wont be bringing you a coffee and your morning paper guv'nor.' Andy said.

'Be better if you have the kettle on ready for when we get here.' Steve stated.

That first week was solid hard slog stripping cement and plaster and I was glad I'd spent all that time at the gym over the past few years. I started filling potholes on my part of the lane with cement rubble, the old plaster went into a skip.

'It's a mental way of earning a living sometimes.' Andy was talking to me. 'You never see an old builder.'

After they had gone on the Friday I cleaned myself up and washed and decided to try the pub. It went by the name of The Wheal. It was quite busy but the barman said that if I didn't mind eating at the side of the bar he could accommodate me. I had a bitter shandy and ate and idly watched two couples at a table across the room. One of them was Steve but he didn't notice me at all. They all seemed to like each other very much, there was a woman with silvery hair and a tawny haired woman with her back to me. I thought about my red lady. There had been no sign of her. I finished my meal and left, having asked Kate if I could call in and plug into their internet.

Mark was on a late shift. I left the campervan in the street rather than park on the drive, vaguely thinking about not waking the twins. I needn't have bothered, they were awake and grizzling when I got there. Daphne was in attendance and both she and Kate were looking tired. I was greeted with one word, teething. There wasn't much more to be said and I thanked my lucky stars that Mike had loaned me the van to sleep in. A couple of hours whizzed by, as it does with IT, but I quickly caught up with things. I kissed Kate and left, driving off into the dusk with something like guilty pleasure. It was so peaceful at Darleystones on my own.

I sat outside late into the night and watched shooting stars. On a whim I'd made a chunky rubble circle one evening and now I had a fire going outside, burning some bits of rubbish. I'd also collected some broken dead gorse, which I'd quickly learned you had to wear gloves for. It burned well.

Steve had said there would be a lot more to burn as he was going to make several new doors. We had found woodworm upstairs in doors and floorboards and I had plans for built in wardrobes, all of which needed his attention. The boards were chemically treatable he thought, but I had a feeling that a lot was going to have to be taken out. We hadn't found any dry rot so far but it was going to be an expensive job and no doubt work would have to be done on the roof and the rafters.

The next day, Saturday, I was awake early. With the physical work and fresh air I was sleeping, not like Kate's babies obviously, but I was sleeping like I hadn't in years. I felt amazing. I had a fry up on the little stove I'd bought for outdoor use, not liking to mess up Mike's clean hob. The farm shop was providing decent essentials and I was eating well. I made everything tidy and used the loo in the house. We'd had no need to disconnect the water at this stage of the works and I'd had the septic tank emptied. Then I walked around the place again, outside and inside, touching the stones, mentally reassuring the house that all would be well. I looked at the mason's mark on the window reveal upstairs, Andy had smiled when he'd seen that.

'We'll look out for some more, wouldn't surprise me with a place this age. But it might be a ritual mark scratched by the home owner. Two V's like that are for good luck or to ward off bad luck. In my trade we know them as the Virgin of Virgins. It's for the Virgin Mary.'

Musing over his words I decided to do a bit of work upstairs, there was more plaster to knock off and a nasty bit of old partition to remove where the ugly bathroom had been put in when the place was modernised. It was too large and the plan was to split it to incorporate a small ensuite as all the waste pipes and services were conveniently located on the same side of the house. I kitted up and worked for a couple of hours until my safety glasses got too dusty and I got fed up with wearing the face mask. I decided to go and make a mug of tea. We'd made a tea station in the old kitchen which we could use until the wiring all had to be stripped out. Andy had said it looked bloody dangerous and had already set up an electrician he was used to working with. I was gazing through the window when the bay horse came into view. I was outside in a flash with a huge smile of welcome on my face.

Once again the horse stopped seemingly of its own accord. 'Hello Bel, good to see you.' I put a hand on its long nose. The head went up and down and it huffed at me.

'Bel is wondering about the van and all the mess.' Fiona said. 'It looks and smells different, she's very aware of changes.' There was that lovely husky voice again.

'It's all okay Bel. Nothing to be worried out.' I made myself calm and gentle.

Fiona was watching me, her expression bright. 'It's a happy man I see. And you have had help here. Is the spirit still at the place?'

I didn't know what to say to that so I retreated into reassuring builder talk and said something about sympathetic restoration and renovation.

'Grand words.' Fiona responded. 'Will I take a look then?'

'Will you take tea with me?' I echoed her speech.

'I will.' She dismounted and lead Bel round the back of the garden wall to the old gate rather than have her step over rubble. I followed and together we made the horse safe, her access to the old water trough unimpeded.

Fiona stood for a few minutes looking at the scaffolded building before walking round to the door.

'Have you found anything old here?' She asked me.

I mentioned the mason's mark.

'Show me please.'

She hesitated behind me at the threshold as I lead the way inside. Her eyes lighted on the carved newel post with pleasure and then looked up the stairs where dust motes were heavy in the sunlight streaming through from the doorless and empty rooms.

'Not just yet then.' She sounded apologetic, still not setting foot inside the house.

I agreed and told her she could probably see it from the outside, so I guided her round to the front and pointed it out. She seemed relieved and interested.

'Oh yes, it's a mark in their old language. That's a good thing to have. Sometimes there are marks against witches.' She shivered slightly.

My offer of tea was accepted and she agreed it would be nice to sit in the little folding chairs I had over at the van. From there we could look at the house and there was a lovely view. I went back inside and came out carrying two mugs.

'I didn't ask if you wanted sugar.'

'Honey sometimes Daniel, but no, I don't take white sugar.'

I offered her builder biscuits but she declined. I decided to be ordinary with this extraordinary girl so I asked her how she was today and got an old-fashioned look in return.

'You're making polite talk today Daniel.' She sipped her tea thoughtfully.

I decided to be honest. 'I'm pleased to see you, I've been here a week and I have thought about you.'

'I'm glad about that. I've thought about you. I've talked to Bel about you. She took me a different way on our last ride out. She likes to see the stones up on the moor.'

'What stones are those?'

'They are known as The Pipers, The Hurlers and The Cheesewring. Silly names for ancient stones. There are carvings and marks up there too. I'll show you if you're interested.'

I had seen them all in my childhood but it would be good to see them with her and I said so. She was looking about, there were dozens of tiny yellow flowers staring the sheep nibbled grass. She pointed her foot. 'D'you know the name of these Daniel?'

I hadn't a clue, I wasn't Mike. I shook my head.

'Tormentil. Funny how the sheep don't eat them.'

I couldn't stand it any more. 'Fiona,' I asked, 'I hardly know anything about you other than you're half Scottish and half Cornish. You're a great rider and you sketch and make bread and you've just identified a flower I'd not even noticed although I can now see them everywhere.'

'You know quite a lot about me already then.' She carried on sipping her tea, then turned to me and smiled. 'And I know that you don't live here but you're Cornish and have inherited a lovely house and have a sister and a girlfriend. And you make a decent pot of tea.' She raised her mug as though toasting me.

Fair enough. I put the odd stuff to the back of my mind; the way she and the horse were together, the referral to better the red than the green, asking about the spirit of the place and so on. I drained my mug and sat back, it was a nice day.

'What do you want to know? Ask me anything.' I slipped into control, deliberately using open body language, nothing crossed, arms relaxed and palms open and upward on my thighs. I didn't look fully at her but kept her in my line of vision so that I could assess her reaction. Over the past week I'd mentally rehearsed conversations with her as I toiled, I knew that the first thing I wanted to tell her was that I unattached. I glanced at her hands again, definitely no rings. She hadn't moved, she had such a quality of inner stillness and calm it made her quite unique. I was accustomed to busy, expressive, competitive women.

'Will you be staying here then Daniel.'

'Another 3 weeks then I have to go back to London. My work is there.' I paused, a deeply unappealing vision of an empty soulless flat in my mind and Mike saying I could easily do work from here if they had electricity in Cornwall. I realised that Fiona was looking at me, a deep, searching, knowing and compassionate look.

'Your heart isn't in London though.'

'My heart is single and I'm lonely.' The truth shocked me and my heart started beating as if for the first time, hard and steady and loud. I was looking into her green eyes and I wanted to tell her everything about me. I wanted to show her all over Darleystones and ask her opinion and make things nice for her. It was an amazing and almost immediate revelation, the knowledge fully fledged in my very core. I couldn't speak and all I could do was hold out my hand. She put her hand in mine and we just sat there, looking at each other.

Fiona told me she had an older brother, who had followed in his father's footsteps, also joining the RAF and marrying a Cornish girl just as he had. Her brother and his wife were presently posted overseas and she was living at their house in the village for a couple of years.

'It's all very normal. I am an art teacher three days a week, funding cuts being what they are these days. But it gives me four days a week to draw and paint and ride Bel. I like it very much down here, in a way it's not unlike the Scottish Borders where my father comes from. My parents live in Kelso. We're lucky, we can all get the best of both worlds having a base in the Celtic borderlands both north and south.'

'Aren't you a bit lonely, living in the house on your own?' I asked her, dying to know exactly where it was.

'Not really, I lose track of time when I'm in the studio and right now I'm preparing to put a few paintings into an exhibition at Tavistock and I'm taking part in the arts trail this summer, and then there's work time and Bel time. And I go to a yoga class.'

I told her I understood, time meant nothing when I was working on an idea with Mike. Our planning den had a couple of loungers which we had sometimes slept on when work had taken us deep into the night and it wasn't worth going home. It had got a bit smelly I recalled, nothing like the world of virtual reality. Perhaps scratch and sniff would be available on the games consoles one day. I asked her about art college.

'Glasgow School of Art. It was a wonderful time in a great city. It's a magnificent and inspiring place to learn. I didn't really want to be a teacher, but commercial art isn't in me, so I teach and I like encouraging the children to express themselves just by making marks on paper. Sometimes they are afraid but I just tell them they can do it. And I have a studio of sorts and sometimes I sell a bit. It's a satisfactory way of life just now.'

I could just listen to her talk. We had stopped holding hands but part of my mind was still dwelling on the specialness of that moment. It had been a moment of mutual recognition. On impulse I said, 'Will there be Darleystones time now?' I felt like a prat immediately, it was the soppiest thing I'd ever said.

Fiona was quiet and thoughtful. Eventually she answered. 'It might be so, if we are truthful.'

Once again I was struck by her phraseology. 'You're a poet Fiona. Tell me what that really means to you, to us.'

'Just that you're The Hanged Man. It can be a very good thing.'

I was absolutely none the wiser.

Once again it was Bel who let us know that she was ready to move on. This time I took Fiona's hand as we walked to the horse. I'd got three weeks left to get to know her.

'I would very much like to see you Fiona. I went to the village pub last night, the food was good. Can I take you there perhaps? Or is there something else you would like to do. And I want to talk to you about Darleystones, with your eye you might have some good ideas about what the house needs.' It needs Fiona Rose Frazer in it, was what I was secretly thinking.

That caught her attention. 'I'd like that, the house has a lot of love in it, I've looked through the windows in past weeks and felt it. You don't want to lose something like that.' She paused, letting go of my hand and taking Bel's reins off the post. This time I had an apple for Bel which managed to delay her a little longer.

'And what about a meal out. Food is better shared.' I said, remembering that first lunch on the bench.

'Yes, I'd like that as well Daniel.'

We agreed to meet outside The Wheal on Tuesday evening. Cornish pubs never do food on a Monday I had learned. I heard her singing as she rode away.

Energy was coursing through me after she'd gone. I felt fresh and optimistic. I had an imaginary conversation with Mike. He would say I'd been defragged. I cleared and wheelbarrowed muck and rubble about, I swept and carried buckets of stuff downstairs. In a weird way I was clearing out all the emotional crap that Lynn had left me with. I worked until my shoulders ached and then cleaned myself up a bit. I was using the sort of sense I'd gained on my heritage conservation trips years ago, strip off outdoors, put your work clothes into bin liners, try not to mess up the place you sleep or eat in. There was no one about to see me nipping from the house to the van in my underwear but as I did so I found myself laughing loudly, would I be described as the beast of Bodmin? Man flashes to van would be the headlines. I had a quick wash and drove the van to the leisure centre. A few lengths in the swimming pool was a great way to get really clean.

Kate drove up to Darleystones the next day. She brought me some home cooked food and put in into the little refrigerator with instructions that it must be eaten that night. She decided I was looking pretty well, and I explained that I'd had company with Andy and Steve, eaten at the pub and that I was going there again on Tuesday evening. I asked her if she remembered Fiona.

'The red haired woman on the horse that Lynn was rude too.' Kate remembered.

I just had to talk to someone about Fiona and Kate was a good listener. I'd already told her that Lynn and I had split up.

'Taken herself off with the handsome clothes peg.' Was how Kate remembered it.

I told her a bit about the unusual way Fiona sometimes spoke and mentioned her preference of the red rather than the green, and that she had said something about me being a hanged man. Kate looked at me over her mug of coffee, she didn't like tea.

'And that means nothing to you because you're a stupid gizmo-geek.' Kate had qualified to teach English and was, she often said, much better educated than me. 'Have you never read the Narnia books Daniel, we had them at home, I've still got them and the twins will read them one day.'

I shook my head. 'Anything to do with fairies never floated my boat.'

'Oh you're hopeless, it's nothing like that, there's a much deeper meaning. It's about sacrifice and wisdom and eternal truths. It's very special and written by a profoundly clever man.'

'I'm still not with you.'

'Fiona might be referring to the lady in the green kirtle, she was an evil witch, a green serpent who had enslaved the prince. They rode on horseback together in the woods, her in her peculiar green dress and him in his armour, never speaking. Oh you're not getting this at all are you.'

I shook my head. 'Perhaps I should read the book.' I said.

'Books.' My clever sister corrected me. 'Yes, if you're going to be a decent uncle you should get to know a bit more. I want my children to be stimulated.'

I laughed. 'I'll be doing transformers with Jake when he's old enough. But what about the hanged man that she referred to.'

'That's not up my canal.' Kate replied. 'I paddle my canoe away from that sort of thing.'

Blimey none of the women in my life made any sense these days.

Kate left kindly taking my washing with her, nothing really needed ironing and we agreed that the washing machine and the tumble drier would be doing the work, not her. I made a mental note to get her more flowers and then I did a bit of work offline for Mike. I'd have to send it via Kate.

Then I walked round the house again. It always gave me a thrill, it had a timeless beauty, it had been here for a little under three hundred years. It looked hurt and scared where the external cement was being carefully removed from the West walls. I found myself promising the house that everything was going to get better. I wondered why someone had decided to build out here, there was a good fresh water supply and I supposed there were sheep and cattle to live off, but the mines were over the other side of the moor. Perhaps the people who lived here made a living out of supplying the miners with meat and with milk.

I looked at the land enclosed by the wall which went right round the house. It was a large area, south facing, slightly sloping. A couple of fields below were also part of the plot. Sheep had clearly been getting in and keeping the grass down which I didn't mind at all. There was a tumbledown granite outbuilding where I think there had once been pigsties and a small store, overlooked by a gnarled and twisted crab apple tree. Kate, of course, called it the crap apple tree. Grandad had kept half a dozen chickens but in a wooden coop, long since gone. They used to roam around freely I remembered. Over the centuries people had patiently moved all but the very largest of the stones and boulders, using them to build the walls and probably part of the house as there were huge stones in the base of the external walls. I knew there was a quarry or two up on the moor, Waterloo Bridge in London was built from granite from there. I'd always felt a connection with Cornwall when I'd crossed it. There used to be fenced vegetable beds between the house and the pigsties, nothing was wasted in the old days and my grandad had made compost that recycled everything from the wood ash in the fireplace to the tea leaves and the chicken dung.

I went inside again, having left the big old front door open all day. The dust had settled and I was pleased I had made some progress for Andy and Steve to see. My hand almost caressed the dark bannister as I went upstairs and viewed the space where the bathroom was, assessing again the space needed for creating an ensuite to the master bedroom and where fitted wardrobes could be built on internal, dry walls. The huge old chimney came up between the master bedroom and the bathroom, it doubly served the parlour and the snug on the ground floor. I thought it slightly odd that there were no fireplaces upstairs. I was looking at the construction where I had removed most of the old partition and some of the ceiling when I realised there was a tiny cupboard up at the side of the chimney breast. I fetched a ladder and went up three rungs and peered at it. Why it was up there and concealed and what on earth it was for I didn't know. It was covered in grey dust from the work I had been doing but I reached up and took hold of the knob. The little door opened. There was something inside. I fetched a torch.

There was something in a bag, which felt rough to touch. I hoped it wasn't a dead animal. Carefully I pulled it out and got down off the ladder. I was holding what might be a hessian bag or small sack, with a very rough weave. I'd once bought an expensive pair of walking boots which came with a little sack like that. They were the most uncomfortable boots I had ever owned. I stood for a moment holding the bag in one hand and then crouched down, placing it on the floor before I opened it.

Nothing smelled unpleasant, there was just an odour of old plaster and dust. Inside was a pair of leather shoes, slightly pointed, with a deep tongue and eyes for laces and a small heel. I studied them, they were more like ankle boots really, thinking of the things Lynn used to wear. But these were narrow, for a small foot and they had been well worn. I looked inside the bag and then went up the ladder and shone the torch into the cupboard. There was nothing else there. I went up a step and reaching forward put my hand in and felt about, something metal moved under my fingertips. It was a coin, dated 1812 with the words *Success to Cornish Mines* round the face. It had the value of one penny.

SEVENTEEN

I showed Andy and Steve what I'd found when they turned up to work bright and early. They were interested and curiously respectful. Steve didn't touch the shoes, preferring to look. Andy suggested calling the local museum. I'd already used my phone to look on the internet and been surprised to see that things like these were turning up in old house renovations all the time. Shoes, mummified cats, money, jewellery, newspapers, caches of old letters, recipe books, all life was there. I told Andy and Steve this as we had our first coffee of the day.

'Pity it wasn't a load of old jewellery.' Steve said. 'That would have been like winning the lottery. You'll be finding the smugglers' hoard next, barrels of brandy and bales of tobacco for everyone.' He was particularly interested in the old coin.

Andy had given the position of the cupboard some thought. 'I reckon it used to be an access point for riddling the soot out, before the extending brush system was designed for chimney sweeping. Once it was redundant someone closed it up and made a secret storage place for valuables. You had to keep your cash someplace safe in a remote place like this. Heard of this sort of thing in Northumberland and North Yorkshire.' That, for Andy, was a quite a speech.

We got on with the work and I enjoyed myself labouring, humping and dumping stuff about and generally keeping the site tidy. I cannot stand working in disorganised mess. The next day there was a delivery of lime mortar needed to start making the external walls both weatherproof and stronger. Andy said he'd be getting a lad into help as Steve was a carpenter and had far more important tasks to carry out for the house down at his workshop. I spoke to Steve about the doors he was thinking of for the rooms upstairs. He quickly sketched an idea, involving plain boards ledged and braced and with wooden latches. I liked the idea but thought the wooden latches were a bit too plain. He said he knew a very good artist blacksmith who could probably make some unusual door furniture.

'I had a meal with him and his girlfriend in the pub on Friday night.'

'I saw you, I was at the bar. Who was the amazing girl with the silver hair and Norwegian eyes.'

'That's Liz, my wife. You should've come over, I could have introduced you.'

We knocked off at five and I hosed myself down using the outside tap. It was bloody freezing. No wonder I was feeling so good though, the personal trainer at the gym had once said that cold water improved the white blood cell count which contributed to good health and a spanking immune system. It worked for the Swedes, how fantastic do they look if you think about it. All that rolling about naked in the snow. I finished off in the little shower cubicle in the campervan, at least I could shampoo my hair and shave. I was singing to something on the radio when I drove out to meet Fiona.

I parked up at The Wheal and sat on the wall outside to wait for her. It was a fine evening and peaceful. With my ears no longer assailed by London traffic and sirens I was surprised at how much I actually could hear. There was a blackbird, or maybe a thrush, singing its heart out in a tree almost opposite the pub. My heart lifted when I saw Fiona walking down the road towards me. She was wearing cream sandals and cream jeans, with a dark green long sleeved t-shirt and a blonde suede jacket slung over one arm. With her long red hair she looked a picture and I said so, taking her hands and kissing her on one cheek. She was a little flushed and I noticed she had a tiny smudge of blue paint on her cheekbone.

'I was nearly late, I was painting and I forgot the time.'

We went inside and settled ourselves into a small table near the unlit wood stove. I got myself a shandy, since I was driving, and she had a spicy tomato juice. I asked what she was painting.

'A bit of the pond and the sword.' She said, then noticing my baffled look said by way of explanation, 'Dozmary Pond and Excalibur.'

Okay, Kate was right, I needed to educate myself. I filed that away for future reference and asked what she'd been sketching at the house the first time we had met.

'Oh I've filled a whole sketchbook with the house. On that day I was seeing what it was like when the early folk lived there, growing their vegetables, keeping a few animals and so on. That's why I didn't hear you and your girlfriend arrive, I was a long way out. What I can't understand is how it has such a grand porch and staircase for all that it's out on its own.'

I'd had the same thoughts myself. We ordered food, she had the vegetarian moussaka and I had beer battered fish and chips. It was superb. She asked for a chip and dipped it into her dish. Apart from Kate I'd not seen a girl who enjoyed her food so much. She didn't leave a scrap and was really appreciative, identifying ingredients and enjoying flavours. After we had eaten I told her about finding the shoes in the chimney cupboard. Her green eyes grew wide.

'Something old. I'd like to see them. You are keeping them inside the house aren't you.'

'Well, I haven't taken them outside.'

'You must not. They have power against bad luck, they were left there to protect the house and the people in it.'

'Come as soon as you can, I'm there all day every day, the guys are there until 5 pm.'

'I could come after school tomorrow.' She was smiling her secret smile.

'We could have a picnic round the camp fire in the evening if you'd like.' I suggested.

'Should I bring a few things Daniel?'

'Anything you like, we can be like Mole and Ratty.'

'Oh they had the best picnics didn't they.' She was laughing now. Thank god I'd read something other than Geek Weekly and science fiction when I was a kid.

With the meal clearly over I asked if I could take her home. She agreed and hopped up into the van, looking around, fascinated. I'd kept it pretty neat thankfully. Her brother's house was two minutes up the road, one of a few detached cottages set back in a cluster from the road, accessed by a short private track to the rear of a set of four terraced houses. They were once miner's cottages I guessed. Fiona had the door key in her hand, she lived in a separate granny annexe constructed from an old store and workshop. It was charming outside. I could smell horse and sure enough Bel's stable wasn't far away round the back, with a paddock beyond that.

'Come and look at what I'm painting.'

It was a good ice breaker. These first moments were excruciating. I wasn't going to behave like a plonker though, my hands were in my jeans pockets. Her studio was at the back in a sort of greenhouse.

'It's not ideal, I freeze or I fug, but at least the paint stays in here and doesn't mess up the annexe.'

I followed her through and stopped in my tracks. Her work was amazing. The first thing I saw was a large painting in delicate hues in a sort of misty abstract style with a small overlay of unfurling bracken against a stone wall, the botanical detail perfect, the side of a house all dreamy and insubstantial and Bel, burnished in bronze and black and gold standing three quarters on with her reins over a granite post. The painting had a waiting quality. It was, she explained, mixed media using watercolours and pen and ink. There were a dozen or more in a similar style, showing standing stones, stone troughs, a view to Dartmoor with Kit Hill in the foreground. She didn't paint to the edge of the canvas. There was the one she had spoken about of Dozmary Pool with a hand and an elaborate sword. There were sketches, different but as beautiful in their way. Bel featured in several.

Fiona was standing watching me, her slender figure outlined against the windows. I looked at her and swallowed hard.

'This is outstanding stuff. But the sword picture is very different, I mean it's your style but it doesn't fit with the integrity of this other work.'

She smiled. 'I'm glad you can see that Daniel. It's something that has been requested by a colleague who has a legend crazy musician in the family. I don't like to do commercial art but he wants a cover for his Cornish folk songs. I won't charge them much.'

'What would you charge for the picture of Darleystones and Bel?'

'I don't know, it's a special moment. I painted it straight from the heart.'

'It belongs in the house, it should be the focus of one of the rooms there. It's something that I want to see every day.' I felt absolutely passionate about it. 'Fiona, I'm not a man who wants to own or possess stuff, I'm not a collector, but I know when something is beautiful and true and it was a special moment. I recognised it too.' Phew, I thought, where did *that* come from. I realised I was actually trembling.

'Then you should have it. Money isn't the issue here.'

I took her hand and for some reason lifted it to my lips and kissed it. There was something medieval about this proud and unusual woman and she deserved proper round table chivalry.

'You have me at a disadvantage Fiona. I shall accept it, I can't refuse, but I shall do something for you in return.'

And then I kissed her a lot, gently, and for a very long time. She seemed to like it, winding her arms round my neck. It was heaven, it was ages since I'd been so close to a woman who seemed to like me.

The next morning I was back at Darleystones early but not before the guys. Not that they were concerned. I just said I'd gone to the farm shop for provisions. I was keeping us in milk and tea and biscuits, and I'd found a few things for the picnic that evening. I was thinking about Fiona all the time, remembering how lovely and how passionate she'd been last night.

I had an idea that her creativity could be used to effect in the house, I needed window furniture and door latches and hooks and I wondered if she could design and sketch something that the blacksmith friend of Steve's could make. I needed to meet him and I asked Steve to set up an introduction, either at their workshops or at the house, whichever suited.

Fiona drove over as promised. She had an old VW Golf, tired in body but strong in heart and she kept it clean, as a struggling teacher should she had informed me. I don't know how she had found the time but she had made cheese straws, using three cheeses and a hint of paprika, she had also brought some bread rolls, again of her own making and some sweet cherry tomatoes. I'd got olives and lettuce and some Cornish cheeses and red grapes and we put a decent feast together. It was a novelty making a meal with a woman who liked eating. She didn't drink much in the way of alcohol and I had bought some healthy juice concoctions and a vegetable juice drink. I liked this sort of stuff anyway. I kept kissing her while we were working in the tiny space in the van, she tasted salty from eating olives. I told her she was pretty wonderful.

'Thank you Daniel.'

I liked the way she simply accepted a compliment and didn't try to say anything equivalent. After we'd eaten and finished with a few grapes, I suggested that we should take ourselves and our bursting stomachs over to the house.

'It's safe and cleaner in there than it was the other day. The little shoes are downstairs.'

This time she didn't hesitate but walked in with me, holding my hand. It felt like a homecoming and I pulled her into my arms and kissed her just inside the door before leading her to the old kitchen. Her eyes were everywhere, her expressions of interest sincere.

'It's bigger than I thought, I love it, the views, oh the fireplaces, that range, the floors oh Daniel no wonder you couldn't let it go.'

I showed her the little bag which I had placed inside one of the old kitchen cupboards. She opened it very carefully and looked in at the shoes, folding the hessian down around them and making a kind of nest. Like Steve the day before, she did not touch the shoes but looked at them from all angles.

'I am not entitled to touch them, only the owner should do that.'

'Andy touched them.'

'He's sympathetic to what you are doing here, and he's a maker, hands-on, so that may be alright.'

I had an idea. 'Could you draw them.'

'Yes. Easily. Just as they are.'

To my surprise she had a small camera in her bag, for some reason I'd thought that technology of any sort had passed her by, but she snapped away proficiently until she was satisfied. Then she held her hand palm down just above the shoes and whispered 'Sorry.' She wanted to see where they had lain all these years so I took her upstairs, again by the hand. She was fascinated. But I'd forgotten the coin, it was tucked inside my wallet.

'A token, used by the miners I think, to spend locally.'

We put the shoes away and went back outside where the evening was fading.

'Daniel, I can't stay. I'm working tomorrow to get everything ready for the arts trail visitors, if I get any and anyway we both need some sleep.' Her eyes were bright and affectionate. It was so long since a woman other than my sister or my mother had looked at me like that, with affection and with pleasure that I was content just to hold her hands and stand there looking at her. She was lovely to look at with her green eyes and mahogany coloured hair.

'Okay.' To be honest I felt that being in the van was cramped and somehow, not sordid exactly but disrespectful to her, to myself and to Mike.

I asked if we could meet on the Friday but then remembered I was seeing Kate and Mark that evening.

'Unless you'd like to come and meet them. It's just a meal together, Kate doesn't do dinner parties.'

'Your sister. Will she mind? It's so soon.'

'I'll call her. Just come and meet her. She's lovely. I'll pick you up at six-thirty on Friday evening.'

Time flew by and I laboured and shovelled and could feel my gym muscles toning in different ways. Andy complained, jokingly, that he couldn't keep up with me. He was as fit as a flea. I'd rung Kate and asked if I could bring Fiona round.

'You'll like her I think, she's an art teacher and as honest and natural as the day is long.'

'Not a skinny latte bubblehead in a leotard and leggings with a spray-on tan then?'

'Nope. And they call it lycra and don't wear leggings these days.'

'Can't wait, bring her round.'

'Kate, I don't think she's much of a meat eater.'

'Okay, I'll think of something.'

I picked Fiona up as planned. She wasn't the sort of woman who dressed up to look pretty. Her look, with her fine eyes and amazing hair was quite strong and she knew it. She dressed very simply and in plain colours. This time she was in a teal coloured blouse with a grey wrap, like a cardigan but without buttons, grey jeans and little black shoes. She wore a red belt with her jeans and had pinned a few strands of hair up so that they fell around her face. She wore no make up and no jewellery.

'Will I do? I didn't ask if they had dogs?'

'Yes very much. No, they haven't. You look lovely and I've missed you.' I really meant it.

Mark let us in, reliable, straightforward no-nonsense Mark. He took one look at Fiona and gave her a huge smile. 'It's so very nice to meet you.'

I could see he meant it and she was charmed by his welcome. He had never greeted Lynn like that. I was pleased. We handed over wine and chocolates and kept our voices down. Mark pointed up the stairs and mouthed that the twins were asleep as he ushered us through into the sitting room. Kate joined us almost immediately, with her lively brown eyes and shiny hair she was pretty in pink and cream and grinned up at me.

'Have you cooked anything decent and have you done my washing?' I demanded and gave her a hug.

Kate laughed at me and spontaneously took Fiona's hand. 'Don't ever let him treat you like that Fiona. He's a wretch. I've never actually liked him.'

'I thought it was the fairies did his washing.' Fiona was straight in.

We had a fantastic evening. They loved her. They made teacher talk, art talk and baby talk. I don't think I could have felt any happier. Kate had made a hearty mushroom and chestnut bourguignonne heavy with herbs, burgundy wine sauce and small whole onions. There was crusty olive bread to tear up and mop up the sauce and cheese and fruit afterwards. Kate wasn't doing puddings, as she was still tackling the baby weight. Mark and I did our useful manly bit and cleared the table and Fiona asked if she could look in at the twins. Mark and I retired to the sitting room.

'What a lovely girl Dan, you suit each other.' Mark was the only person who called me Dan.

'There's certainly no walking over broken glass with her.' I agreed.

Kate came downstairs alone, Fiona had gone to the bathroom. 'Daniel she's just lovely, her brother has small children, she misses them. And she got that lovely wrap in a charity shop. I can talk to her without feeling she's assessing the price of everything I'm wearing or measuring the size of my thighs.' She sat down next to Mark who put a hand on one of her thighs and squeezed it.

'I love your thighs Kate, always have, always will.' He said it quite unselfconsciously.

We talked about Darleystones and I outlined some of the ideas I was having. I wanted to incorporate some green technology since it had a south facing roof, I also intended using the tried and tested Cornish system of slate hanging the exposed west facing walls where the horrible cement render had been applied decades ago.

'I shall still get Andy to repair and lime mortar all the walls externally and he's going to tank the insides before replastering. I'm going for the full belt and braces to make the house weatherproof and warm.'

'That's going to be very expensive I expect.' Mark said.

'It's worth it, cold wet walls are no good, you know what granite is like. People think it's waterproof somehow, but they couldn't be more wrong. And I don't want to lose the integrity of the internal walls by putting in block work.'

We didn't stay too long, parents tire early and anyway I wanted to be alone with Fiona. I drove us back over to her place, she was entertained by the view as the seats in the van were higher than in a car. She could see over hedges and into windows.

'In Glasgow I used to love seeing into buildings and houses at night. It's like looking into doll's houses, all those lives you can make stories up about.'

I parked up and we went indoors. Since I was driving I wasn't drinking, but being stone cold sober suited me, I've never been a boozer. Fiona made some peppermint tea for us both. We sat down in the tiny sitting room, the two seater sofa just right. I put my arm round her and kissed the top of her head, ouch, I kissed a hairpin. I started removing them and putting them one by one into her hand. Then I folded her hand over them and kissed it.

'I've got just over two weeks Fiona Rose and then I have to get back to London. Mike will want his campervan back. I can stay at Kate's at weekends when I come down but I'd rather be here with you. Is that presumptuous of me?'

She didn't think it was. I was very, very thankful.

EIGHTEEN

I stayed at Fiona's place until Sunday evening and it was great. We both had things to do, she took Bel out for a few hours and I found I had a proper connection for all my work stuff so I did a lot of catching up. Mike would be pleased. I was also full of ideas. While Fiona was out I went into the studio and photographed everything I possibly could without disturbing anything. Then I worked on an idea for a game involving characters finding spooky things in a house and having to fight evil beings which could turn into green snakes and fire venom. You had to find and use special tokens for protection and to enable you to get from room to room. It had a clever horse in it who could save people and gallop them away to a safe place with turrets where a very good and powerful red haired witch lived. I named her the Rose Queen. There was also a nasty witch with short black hair, a forked tongue and a long green dress who lurked behind things, she was bit of a shape shifter and could fly. I called her the Green Crow. It was all to do with hidden cupboards, smugglers hoards, secret passageways and so on, not my usual kind of thing but I had an outline and shared it Mike.

Fiona was, I was realising, a capable woman. She certainly knew her way around the kitchen and was brilliant with flavour combinations. I watched her smell and taste her way through making even simple things and listened to her explaining why ingredients worked together. She was the only woman I knew who had pots of herbs and actually used them and she praised Kate's cooking. She said her Scottish grandmother was a good plain cook and she'd taught Fiona from an early age how to do things. I asked her if she knew how to make a good Cornish pasty and got water flicked at me. I retaliated by flicking the tea towel at her and she ended up in my arms, her green eyes sparkling.

'So who taught you how to make those things.' I asked that evening. We were cuddling on the sofa and I pointed at the basket in the hearth.   There was a small wood stove all laid for the autumn, and in the basket was dry kindling and oddly twisted newspaper.

'The paper firelighters?'   She smiled.   'My Scottish great-grandmother was in service in a big house and apparently the housekeeper was a Yorkshire woman.   She instructed her how to make them.   We've kept the knack of it in the family, it connects with me with her although she was dead long before I was born.' She paused.   'It was the days when you couldn't show an ankle and they covered up the table legs with long covers.'

I looked at her slim ankles, they were rather fine I thought. 'Show me how you do it.'

Fiona laughed and found a sheet of newspaper.   Using both hands she proceeded to roll it into a tube and then she bent it in half and rapidly folded it, length over length, finally tucking the shortest remaining end in and leaving the remaining part of the tube as the piece to light.   I had a go and produced something floppy but she made me unwrap it and do it again, and again until I got the hang of it.   I got a lot of kisses for that.

The weather stayed kind and I worked like a slave, enjoying every minute of it.   I got the best suntan from the waist up that I'd had in years.   During bait one day, as Andy and his taciturn young labourer whom I had privately named The Grunt called the lunch break, I was looking at the OS map for the area and as usual pouring over the area around Darleystones. As I studied the topography I realised that running over the moor above the house was an old mineral line.   It was in the direction that Bel always took so I grabbed the map and an apple and quickly walked the quarter mile up onto the moor.   The sheep nibbled turf clearly showed a fairly narrow levelled and curving track and I walked a little way east. It was laid at regular intervals with short granite sleepers although some were missing.   I had a feeling that some of them were down at Darleystones in the garden wall.

Back down at the house there was a van I didn't recognise and a fit young man talking to Andy. Both had mugs in their hands.

'Here's the guv'nor.' Andy said.

The other guy put his hand out for a shake. 'I'm Rob Williams, my mate Steve Bradley asked me to pop over and talk to you about door and window furniture. He's making your new doors.' His grip was strong. This guy was used to squeezing hammers or something.

I took him into the house and showed him around and pointing at the existing cobwebby window furniture said that I wanted nothing like that on the new windows.

'You may think I'm weird but this is a chance to have something not just bespoke but actually designed to compliment the house.' I said. 'My grandparents lived here and I think a few generations of my grandmother's before that. I'm looking for something that reflects the setting and I'm going to ask my girlfriend if she can design something. She's an art teacher.'

Rob stared out of the dusty window, deep in thought, his fingers drumming on the window ledge.

'Sorry if I sound like a prat.' I interrupted his thoughts.

'No you don't. I make stuff that's different. If I can make a curve, a twist, a flower head or an animal or something abstract that suggests a living shape then that's what I will do.' He was still looking out of the window. 'There's a woman on a horse outside.'

I dashed downstairs but then slowed up respectfully in order not to upset Bel. Their arrival had caused a flutter of interest so I didn't hug Fiona but I did take her hand. 'There's someone here I'd like you to meet.'

I introduced her to Rob, saying rather awkwardly, 'Fiona, you're an artist, this is Rob, an artistic blacksmith.'

They looked at each other and smiled. 'We've already met, several times.' Fiona said.

I must have looked startled and I certainly felt uncomfortable, he wasn't a bad looking bloke.

Fiona was smiling at me, still holding my hand. 'Rob is my next door neighbour. He knows my brother and his wife.'

Then Rob spoke to me. 'I saw you at the bar in the pub one night. I was with Steve and his wife and my girlfriend Su.'

Oh, well maybe that wasn't so bad then. I relaxed, feeling relieved. I explained to Fiona what I'd been saying to Rob and she was intrigued but also considerate to Rob's own skills.

'I've seen Rob's sketches, he can draw, he's a good designer.' She turned to Rob. 'But it would be a fine thing to find out what the house would like and to make it. Did Daniel show you the shoes?'

Once again I found myself showing someone the shoes and the coin.

'Wow.' He studied them, again not touching. 'How long did you say your family had lived here?'

'I'm not sure, but generations plural.'

'You should check your deeds if you have them, they could shed some light on the history. Su, my girlfriend is doing that sort of thing on her grandad's cottage at the moment. It's proving all rather interesting and a bit surprising.'

Well that was a thought. The deeds were lodged with the solicitor though, for a fee. But I thought I might look into that when I had the time.

Rob went off to take some measurements and to have a bit of a think. Fiona, with her usual sensitivity had read my mind.

'He's completely in love with his girl, I've seen them together. They glow.'

I remembered the two young couples in the pub that night as I'd propped up the bar, I'd been lonely and alone that night. I looked at Fiona, into her wide green eyes and at her calm smiling lovely face.

'You make me glow you lovely unusual woman.'

She laughed with delight. 'Oh I am having such a nice time. Shall there be tea for me now?'

Another week of hard work passed quickly, I was loving it but dreading it ending. I'd made contact with a company who could fit solar panels and give me hot water, and Andy was capable of doing underfloor heating downstairs once all the necessary internal floor excavations and associated improvements had been done. He also recommended a business who could do the ground source heat pump for my green heating system which was in addition to the wood stoves I intended to have installed. I'd photographed and recorded the slate floors so that they could be reassembled as near to the original as possible. I was especially concerned about the worn and dipped part of the floor just inside the front door. A lot of this was obviously going to take place while I was back in London. The very thought frustrated me.

I spoke to Mike on Face Time. He told me that Radio was running with my game idea and developing it further. The other projects were fine. I asked if I could have a bit more time.

'I've got shedloads to sort out down here, and I've met someone rather special.'

'How are the van springs bearing up?' Mike wasn't usually crude.

'Pristine and untouched mate, and anyway it's the potholes which do most damage down here.'

We agreed that I could tack on another week. We were our own bosses, it wasn't as though we had HR breathing down our necks. But he needed the van for a trip of his own later in the month.

Kate and Mark drove up one day for a look at progress. Kate was shocked at how the house had been gutted and stripped out and couldn't visualise how it would look. Andy and The Grunt were busy removing the last of the cement render from the exterior stonework on the wall of the room grandad had used as an office, just across from the entrance porch and what I now privately thought of as the picnic bench. We sat on the folding chairs over at the campervan and talked.

'Give me my bright warm modern house any day.' Kate said. 'I loved visiting here in the summer, but I've never wanted to live here. Mum used to tell us tales of getting cut off in winter and making toast on an open fire, although we don't seem to get snow much any more down here.'

'Have you any idea how long our family has lived here Kate?' I asked her.

'Not really,' she replied. 'Grandad said generations but I don't really know.'

'You should look at the house deeds.' Mark was rocking the buggy with one foot, his long legs stretched out. 'It would be interesting for these two to know a bit of your side of the family history. My lot are all Durham-Irish steelworkers and miners as far as I know.' Mark's father had been an optician, the first of his family to go to university. He'd met a girl from Plymouth and settled just over the River Tamar in Cornwall.

Suddenly there was a yell from Andy. 'Come and look at this!' He had his visor up and sounded excited.

Kate and I hurried down and through the gate, carefully negotiating rubble. Andy had got down from his ladder and fetched a brush. He swept over a stone in the wall, revealed by the removal of the render. There were three initials and a date. Andy brushed again. 'Good job the drill didn't go in too far, it's not damaged.'

'What does it say?' Kate was trying to make it out.

'I can see the letters DPP, and the date underneath is 1812.' I said.

Andy was back up the ladder tracing the letters with his fingers. 'It's DPF. The last letter is an F.'

The middle letter P was raised slightly above the D and the F either side. I thought that whoever had carved it had sunk a few pints too many that day.

'Is that P for Pencraddoc, our name?' Kate was excited.

Mark had joined us. 'Can't be, that's your dad's name, it's your mum's family we're looking at.'

'Kate, Mark is right, we are going to have to take a close look at the deeds. He's not the first person to tell me that.' I was thinking of the coin in my wallet, the mining token with the date 1812 on it.

Andy was even more excited than us. 'This house keeps on giving doesn't it. I've been all over it and I reckon this bit was added at a later date, the stonework I'm uncovering has been patched into the side of the main house quite nicely but it's a different hand to the one that originally built the house and porch.'

'Wow,' Kate was wide eyed, 'about two hundred years ago someone was standing here right where we are admiring their modern extension. It's amazing.'

Even I got goosebumps. Later that day I emailed the museum in Liskeard and sent them a photograph of the dated stone and another of the shoes. When everyone had gone I just stood looking at it. Call me soppy and sentimental but I couldn't help thinking it was an omen.

Rob Williams sent me a message via Andy about some design ideas. He asked if I could stop by his house that evening. It was a day of site meetings. I'd found an architect because I wanted to build a separate double garage with a wood store to one side in a way that didn't detract from the house. I was also having ideas about putting a studio in the garage roof and there were discussions to be had about conservation grade roof lights. Andy joined us and made practical suggestions about a water supply at the garage. The architect suggested that the place was likely to get listed now in view of the date stones and the initial plans had to be amended and resubmitted to the planning department. After the architect had gone I made us all tea while I caught up with my notes. There was so much to decide and plan.

'I take my hat off to you guys,' I said to Andy, 'I make my living by designing software and that's quite complicated, but what you do is almost doing my head in.'

'I said it was a mental way of making a living.' Andy agreed. 'Reading plans, or sometimes there's no plans and I have to read the client's mind, and then there's the measuring, calculating, ordering, looking for the services, finding things on site you don't expect like mine shafts or huge hidden granite boulders right where a trench should run. And that's before you deal with planners, building control officers, conservation issues, angry neighbours, deliveries that get lost or don't turn up.' He paused and gulped his tea. 'Then the client changes his mind, that's outside, and her mind, that's indoors. It goes on and on mate, how long have you got?'

It was a nice moment of blokes bonding. I make a joke about them adding a fee to their bills for therapy. I could see that they were enjoying my sympathy. Then The Grunt spoke up.

'And everyone thinks you should just take a month to build them an extension, and can't understand why it takes six. Always think of a time, double it and then add your inside leg measurement that's what I always say.'

Andy and I fell about laughing, it was the longest speech I've ever heard The Grunt make.

That evening I called in to see Rob. Fiona came with me. He lived at the end of the four terraced houses just across from the driveway into her brother's house. Again I had that weird sense of how lacking in style I was, his place was entirely different to Mike's but once again it was a nicely done and welcoming place. There was dark grey and cream and some really good framed surfing prints, all splashes of primary colour. I was beginning to realise that I wasn't cut out for loft living, it just didn't inspire me. I accepted a beer from Rob as he was having one, and Fiona had a glass of orange juice, then we looked at his sketches. The one I liked the best was of slender curving window fittings with a crozier like curl at the end, reminiscent of the bracken on the moors. The crozier shape made nice handles and looked beautiful and practical. He'd done a similar thing for the door latches.

'What do you think?' he asked me.

'Beautiful. Simply beautiful.' I looked at Fiona, she was nodding in agreement.

'I said he could design. This is wholly sympathetic.'

Rob was smiling, looking pleased and a bit relieved. 'It's a strong house with a lot of history, but this is what I could see outside the window.'

Then he pulled some other sheets of paper out of a folder. He'd sketched an idea for some fire irons similar to the window and door furniture and a weathervane consisting of a little shoe with a heel, the laces curling back behind to make a graceful not quite circular shape.

'You need something to help catch the wind so I extended the idea of the laces. Dunno if you need a weathervane but after seeing those shoes that day it just came to me.'

I was charmed, I could already see it on the top of the studio I was secretly planning. Fiona was delighted, so that really did it for me. I asked him to price the work and we all sat chatting for a bit, Fiona leafing through a portfolio of photographs he'd taken of his finished work. There were some beautiful gates and other stuff he'd made for clients, like house signs. There was no doubt, this guy was hugely talented.

We left him to it and strolled back to the annexe. I mentioned to Fiona that I was becoming conscious that interior design had passed me by.

'My flat in London is a soulless cavern and I haven't got much colour in my life. It's not that I'm not interested, I just don't seem to have got round to doing anything about it.'

She smiled and squeezed my hand. 'Colour is sometimes a reflection of your state of mind Daniel.' She said.

NINETEEN

Rob sent the quotes through and I thought he was being very reasonable. I rang him to agree and promised to confirm my order via email.

'Thanks for the design work Rob, but shouldn't I be paying you for the ideas and the concept as well as for the work once they're made?' I was thinking along the lines Mike and I had developed over ten or so years. Rob, however, didn't seem to think that way.

'I'm not in the business of ripping folk off Daniel, and anyway you're Cornish mate, we look after our own down here. But while you're on the phone do you mind me asking you a personal question.'

'Depends what it is.' I was mystified.

'Well, your house is going to take months to get to the point where it's liveable, and Fiona told me you've only got the temporary use of a mate's campervan. Thing is, I think I'm going to be moving into my girlfriend's place permanently and I wondered if you might need a place to rent for a while once the winter sets in. One with internet access.'

Well, that was worth thinking about.

I went round to pick Kate up and mentioned Rob's proposal. She thought it was a great idea. We were on our way to the solicitor's offices once again, this time to sit in a quiet room and have a really good look at the house deeds. The secretary offered us a cup of tea but Kate opted for coffee of course. She was quite excited.

'I can't remember when I last used my brain cells,' she giggled. 'These days I mostly have crazy foam between my ears.'

'Especially with the twins teething.' I remembered.

We settled ourselves at a table and opened the deeds box which the secretary had brought us. She was quite interested.

'It's rare to have documents surviving this far back. Treat them gently.'

A dusty, musty smell wafted out, the smell of history and other lives. There were old documents strangely sized to the modern eye, on very thick important looking paper and folded three or four times. Kate had come prepared with a writing pad and coloured pens.

'Typical teacher,' I teased her. 'Different colours for different subjects, just like when you were doing exam revision.'

'It helps me think, and it helps me remember things. Some words do have a special colour of their own you know.'

I think I understood, when I was having really good ideas I saw them in colour.

We started looking at the same document together, a hand written account in cursive script describing the ancient ownership of a piece of land separated from the moor for farming, with a two-roomed dwelling on it. There were words like appurtenances which my living dictionary Kate had to explain. There was also an account of commoners' rights for moorland grazing, which the owner of Darleystones had a right to do. We deciphered the name Dowrlegh, but didn't know if that was a surname or a place name. Then we decided to take a document each, because as Kate said, we'd be there all night. I found it all a bit dull at first, there were old fashioned legal words I simply didn't understand so I started skimming through for words I recognised. Then I looked at a document dated 1809 and found the name David Penive. I concentrated hard on the writing, tracing the words with my finger like a kid learning to read. As far as I could make out he owned a sizeable piece of land under which someone had discovered a lot of mineral wealth. I knew from school that the Bronze Age meant there had been mineral excavation in Cornwall since, well, the Bronze Age. I sat back and rubbed my eyes.

'Kate, when was the Bronze Age?'

'Oh, I'm only an English teacher, but if my memory hasn't entirely gone gaga I think it was from around 2000 to 700 or so years BC.'

I stared at her in amazement. 'How do you know that?'

'Mark likes history, before the kids or the era known as BK in our household, we used to go to museums and digs and watch Time Team repeats on telly. It kind of sunk in. Why?'

'Because there's a man here called David Penive who owned the land and in 1809 someone has assessed a value due to the amount of mineral wealth estimated to be underneath it. It must have been like the gold rush round here in those days.'

Kate looked at me. 'That's three years before the stone with the initials on it that Andy uncovered.'

'DP, David Penive.'   We spoke together, like siblings sometimes do.

'He must have come into money and done his house up a bit, maybe bought a new horse and cart and a pig and a bonnet for the wife.' Kate was giggling.

'Or been able to afford to get a wife.' I added. And with the first initial F, I thought.

We didn't find a document with a woman's name on it until the 1900s. Kate said it wasn't surprising since women weren't usually allowed to own anything and anything they did own became their husband's property on marriage. It seemed that the Penive family had owned Darleystones for several generations.   Finally we worked out that in 1919 the sole surviving owner of the property was a young woman named Gwenne Penive who married Owen Isaac Pencraddoc. And the rest, as they say, is history. I sat back, feeling knackered.

'So we are descended from the original Penive family, and our relationship with that piece of land goes back over 200 years, maybe even more since the original date stone over the porch is 1733.'   Kate had been making careful and colourful notes. 'Goodness, I feel very small.'

My phone beeped and I looked at it.   There was a message from Liskeard Museum, someone introducing herself as Sally Evans wanted to come out and see the house and meet me, tomorrow at 2pm if that was possible. I replied saying yes, please do come along.

That evening the four of us met at the pub since Daphne was having the twins for the night. We told Fiona and Mark what we had discovered and Mark thought that it should all be written up in a chronological properly sequenced family booklet. Fiona thought she could illustrate something like that and then we were all off into the mad realms of fantasy, imagining our ancestors discovering Piskey hoards of wealth below Darleystones and marrying fairy princesses who wore tiny shoes and hid coins in chimneys.

'You may laugh but I make a very decent living from imagining stuff like this and turning it into computer games. I'm having a ker-ching moment.' I mimed money falling from a one armed games machine.

Fiona picked up her bag and took a small package out of it. 'Thinking of things I do for a living, I made you both a little present to say thank you for the dinner and being so welcoming that first night we met.' She handed the package to Kate.

Kate glanced questioningly at Mark and he nodded, as though to say open it. I'd observed this type of wordless communication between them before. Kate undid the wrapping and took a small picture out. She gasped and looked at Fiona, who was smiling at her.

'Is it right do you think?' Fiona asked.

Mark was looking at the picture, an expression of pride and tenderness on his face.

'Yes, it's very right. It's quite the most lovely thing to be given. Thank you. We shall never part with it.' And he leaned over the corner of the table and kissed Fiona on the cheek.

'May I see what has turned my brother-in-law into a gentleman and my sister into a quivering jelly please?'

Kate handed me the picture, wiping tears from her eyes. Fiona had done a small and perfect pen and ink drawing of the twins asleep together, with a delicate colour wash tinting their faces and their clothes. It was exquisite, you could see the downy softness of their skin, a touch of moisture on their eyelids and lips. I was so proud of her I couldn't speak. I just reached for her hand and squeezed it. She squeezed back.

'I hope you don't mind,' she said to Mark and Kate. 'When you left me alone upstairs that night I took a couple of photographs of them. You can look through my camera to see what I took if you like.'

'So they can have some prints as well?' I asked.

Fiona looked at me. 'I'm a teacher, to be around children you have to have CRB clearance these days. This is for my protection as well as theirs.'

Mark sighed. 'It's sad but true Daniel. It's an odd world we live in now.'

The following day Sally from the museum turned up just a few minutes after the appointed time. I'd put the kettle on to be hospitable and made us both a mug of tea.

'Satnav was a bit unsure but I'd already looked at the OS map and worked out where you were. This is a lovely spot isn't it, fantastic views and not a wind turbine in sight.'

'That's the benefit, or curse depending how you feel, about living in a World Heritage Site and an AONB.' I said, pleased that I'd paid attention to Kate in recent discussions.

We rather awkwardly shook hands and Sally accepted the tea, not pursuing the conversation any further. It was just an ice breaker. She was tall and angular with dark eyes and crinkly dark hair pulled back off her face. She was also a mine of information about date stones and marriage stones and stuff hidden in old houses. I mentioned my trawls on the internet. She nodded.

'Yes, it's a wonderful resource, but there's nothing like actually seeing the real thing, close up and personal.'

Sally looked at the stone for quite a while and took a lot of photographs. 'I think it's simply a date stone, the significant thing being the building of this extension by the people whose initials are there. A marriage stone usually has a heart on it, I know of three such stones on a farm not all that far away. Nevertheless it must have meant a lot to them to go to this trouble.'

'I did a bit of research into the house deeds yesterday with my sister.' I told her. 'I think that DP stands for David Penive, a distant ancestor of ours, who came into some money when he sold the mineral rights under his land.'

'Oh, he became a Mineral Lord did he. He should be traceable in County Archives then.'

I could feel her speaking with capital letters, academics always did this in my experience. I asked her if she knew anything about the mineral line running on the side of the moor out of sight of the house.

'The actual Caradon to Liskeard railway was built somewhere around the mid 1800s but I'm a bit hazy about records for the branch lines. I guess they were put in as and when needed and doubtless some of them were speculative and eventually proved useless. I think that's perhaps why the granite setts used for laying railway sleepers onto were robbed out. They could be used elsewhere in buildings or on more profitable lines.'

But it was the shoes she really wanted to see. Once again I watched someone look at them for the first time, noticing that first moment as though trying to pick up a faint signal, there was something in people's eyes and an expression as though they were listening. Sally didn't touch them either but asked my permission to take photographs.

'Be my guest, everyone does it.'

Sally clicked away and talked as she photographed.

'It's thought that shoes were hidden in houses, often near fireplaces and windows and staircases as protection against evil spirits. They're certainly considered to be a symbol of good luck. Think about tying shoes to the back of the newlyweds car or drinking champagne from the shoe of the woman you love.'

She pulled a face at this point and we both laughed at the mental image.

'Then there's the old nursery rhyme about the old woman who lived in a shoe and had so many children - obviously a reference to fertility. Shoes are found in all sorts of places where votive offerings have been placed, but only if the conditions are right for preservation. I'm sure there could be a book on the subject.'

'Perhaps you should write one Sally.' I found her interesting and liked her enthusiasm.

Then with my help she made a rough plan of the house and a description of the location of the little cupboard I had revealed. I showed her the coin. She was happy to hold that for a while, turning it over in her fingers, thinking.

'Same date on the date stone outside. I think that Cornish Mining did your ancestor a favour that year.'

'Yes, somewhere between 1809 and 1812 he was granted a windfall that improved his life and expectations. Lucky chap. I still don't know who F was on the stone. Is there any way I can find out?'

Sally thought for a moment. 'Births marriages and deaths started being recorded properly in 1837,' she said. 'But the parish, church and chapel records might still be available if you're thinking it might refer to Mr Penive's marriage. You could go and see the local vicar or check out the local history society. I'm sure I've got some contact details back at the museum. I'll email you if you like.'

I thanked her and said I'd like that very much. But I was thinking that might be a job for my sleuth Kate, since it was almost time for me to return to London. I was not feeling very happy about that. After she'd gone I fastened the shoes up with a plastic bag over the hessian and put them back up in the original cupboard for safety. I didn't want them to go missing or get horribly dusty with all the work going on and I was conscious that Fiona had said they mustn't leave the house. I don't know why but I trusted her judgement.

In those last few days I was kept very busy making all sorts of arrangements and decisions and keeping Andy up to speed with everything. I took Kate a huge bunch of flowers and sent them a crate of assorted wine from my favourite supplier. I contacted Rob and said that I'd love to rent his place once his personal arrangements were sorted out, and I spent every moment possible with Fiona.

We went for a walk on the moor and strolled widdershins, as she called it, from the car park at Minions up to The Cheesewring on Stowes Hill and then down and round to The Hurlers. We held hands most of the time and I felt the pressure of decisions and of potential changes in my life heavy on my shoulders. Fiona didn't ask me any questions but she too was deep in thought. I knew she had the art exhibition in Tavistock that next week, nothing much really, she'd told me, dozens of other artists are exhibiting in the same place. She was also getting ready for the start of the new term. Eventually we stopped walking and stood right in the middle of The Hurlers.

'I feel like crap.' I gave myself no prizes for erudition. 'I can't bear the thought of being so far away all week. It's like walking into a brick wall. I mean we can Skype or Face Time and text and email but it's not the same.'

'Daniel.' She said my name and sighed. 'Daniel, I don't do those things. I don't even like using the telephone, and I don't do twitterbook either.'

Blimey, she sounded like Kate. But I was shocked.

'What?' I began. 'Then how are we to keep in touch? By carrier pigeon?'

'Can you not write a word?' She asked me.

'Snail mail? You mean letters?' I was gobsmacked. I was a twenty-first century IT wizard, not bloody Shakespeare.

'A card, a note will do, it needn't be a letter. Just let me know you are there.'

'I shall be here with you every Friday night if you can bear it.' I wanted to hug her hard but she had that other worldly fey look on her face.

She looked into my eyes and I had a sensation of falling into a deep green ocean.

'Well we are facing time. And you are The Hanged Man.'

TWENTY

So that was it. I was packed. I hosed the campervan down and then washed it as best I could. At Fiona's I borrowed her vacuum cleaner and cleaned the inside. She came out with the painting of Darleystones and Bel carefully wrapped and we put in into the back of the van. Fiona had made us a light lunch but I couldn't taste a damn thing. I made a big effort not to be a moody sod, I could hear my mum's voice telling me to count my blessings. I was my own boss, doing work I enjoyed and making a good living. I had the enormous good fortunate to own one currently unliveable house, and I had a small mortgage on an impressive if unlovely London flat. It was Sunday now and I'd be back here on Friday night. I could feel that there were changes happening in my life, but I was beginning to realise that some enormous decisions were going to be made over the next few months. I could sense Fiona's awareness and I took her hand across the table.

'Twice now you've told me that I'm a hanged man. I haven't a clue what that means. Unless I'm putting my head into a noose regarding the situation here with Darleystones and with you. Fiona I have to ask, is there something you haven't told me?'

'It's just the feeling I have Daniel. I'm not sure if I can explain but I'll try. At University I shared a house with three other girls and one of them was a girl from the highlands, with a deep interest in the Tarot. I never had a reading, but I used to watch her read the cards. Someone once drew The Hanged Man and I thought it must be a terrible portent but she said it was quite the opposite. She said it meant that the person was at a crossroads facing life changing options. She said it was a chance to gain enlightenment, to let go and to release yourself from people who were controlling or to make a significant decision about the way you were going to go and live your life. It's how I see you.'

I released a huge breath, letting go some pent up emotion. 'Wow,' I said, 'that's it more or less. That's how I am feeling.'

She squeezed my hand. 'It's how I saw you that first day, a man in a dream, taking his first steps into a different place. You had a look of awakening on your face. I was privileged to see it.'

I didn't know what to say, everything had been so full on this past five weeks, I already knew my life had changed a lot. Was Fiona the key to changing things even further. I hoped so.

I drove back to London in a more optimistic mood and parked up outside the flats. Mike was meeting me at my place for a beer and something to eat. I'd just got my stuff indoors when he turned up.

'Darling have you missed me.' His voice squawked through the intercom.

I buzzed him in and surprised him with a quick manly embrace. I'd never done that before.

'Bloody hell Daniel, you've got in touch with your emotions down there, and if you squeeze any harder you'll break my bloody ribs.'

Mike was grinning. I let him go and we shook hands. 'All gone pretty well then.' He wasn't asking me a question.

I popped a couple of cans and we went out onto the balcony into the late sunshine. I couldn't believe the noise. I talked pretty much non stop for the first hour, then we went down to look over the van and he thanked me for taking good care of it. I'd filled up the tank as well.

'That's pukka mate. Appreciate it.' Mike said.

We went round to local restaurant and we talked about work. Radio had a few things to show me tomorrow and Mike had appreciated the work I'd done from Cornwall.

'I've been thinking. We could live anywhere we like and still do this work together.'

'I know, the thought has crossed my mind.'

I told him about Fiona. 'It's early days yet but I can't see her living in London. For her it's either Cornwall or the Scottish Borders, and I think with her brother married to a Cornish girl and buying a house in the village that's where they might end up. It would suit me what with the house and Kate and the kids locally.'

'Have you proposed then?' Mike asked.

'Blimey no. It's weird, I can see us being together but the idea of a wedding, I can't get my head round that. Anyway, it's early days yet.'

I can't say I settled down into my usual routine although I did go to the gym. The trainer was impressed with my physique and my tan. He touched my biceps caressingly.

'Five weeks on a building site? I thought you'd been away on holiday or sick or something, we don't seem to have seen Lynn either.'

I didn't bother to explain.

I did go into an art supplies shop and with the help of the assistant I ordered quality paper, watercolours and inks, remembering some of the things Fiona had shown me that she used. It was whole new world to me but I had the lot sent down to her. I also bought a card in a medieval style of a red haired lady looking out of a tower down to a knight on a black horse crossing a bridge. I thought I was beginning to get the hang of the way she saw things. I wrote inside it, "better the red than the green", but didn't sign it or write anything soppy. I was starting to enjoy this.

I also hung her painting in the sitting area in the flat. Remembering what I'd seen at Rob's house and Mike's place I went to Heals where I bought a big blue and green rug and some similarly coloured cushions to put on the grey sofa. The sales assistant pointed out a few appropriate accessories, one of which was a large grey pot with a swirly speckled blue-green pattern splashed and sprayed across it and with a slash of scarlet. I thought what the hell and bought that as well. I was quite shocked by the difference it made to the flat. It was more like a home, but more importantly I kept thinking what would Fiona see and would she like it if she came to visit. On that thought I phoned the cleaner. There's a limit to what a bloke can do.

Meanwhile I put in extra hours at the planning den, which seemed a lot tidier and better organised than when I'd last seen it. I noticed a pot plant and asked Mike what it was. Apparently Radio had brought it in and they had named it Archie. For some reason unknown to me it caused them considerable mirth. It was Mike who had found Radio on an exhibition stand at a computer games trade show. They'd hit it off when they recognised each other's Bristol accents. It was interesting to see how Radio had developed my initial idea and we sat and tweaked that for a couple of days. He was a good bloke, tall, fair and kind of gentle and with some really mental ideas about fantasy weapons for my game characters.

I got a couple of emails from Andy and one from Steve with a photograph showing progress on the doors. I approved the style and the design. There was nothing from Fiona so I wondered how things would be when I got there on the Friday evening. I packed some clothes and a couple of bottles of wine, but I didn't have any good ideas about what to take her personally. Unlike Kate she wasn't much of a chocolate eater and I didn't know if she liked cut flowers. Lynn had always wanted a particular kind of perfume or a new designer label scarf. I was looking in a jewellers window after going to the local deli to get a few nice things to take down with me when I saw a lovely little bronze horse, standing saddled up like Bel in the painting. It was perfect in detail, tiny, not ostentatious and I bought it.

After the campervan it was great driving the Audi again and I set off mid afternoon, devouring the miles between London and Cornwall. I thought about how my life was changing as I drove and sang along to a few songs. When I saw the great hump of Dartmoor appearing my spirits lifted and I took the Tavistock turning, following the back roads to the edge of Bodmin Moor. I swear I could actually feel Fiona driving this same route. It was a lovely evening as I turned into the little track and I parked up behind the annexe next to Fiona's car where I sat for a few moments with the engine off and the car door open. Apart from the ticking noise as the engine started cooling it was peaceful, a dog barked a couple of times somewhere and something twittered in the hedge. Then I heard the sound of hooves and I knew it was Bel clopping up the short track. I got out of the car just as she came in through the gateway and I saw the look on Fiona's face. She swung a leg forwards over Bel's head and slipped off the horse straight into my arms where she kissed me and hugged me quite fiercely and all my fears and worries disappeared. I didn't even try to keep the grin off my face, this was my world and all was well within it.

After a lot of cuddling Fiona thanked me for sending the art materials and then I took my stuff indoors while she saw to Bel. I made myself useful with the purchases from the deli a few hours earlier. It seemed unreal as I looked into cupboards for plates and bowls, that I'd been in London just now. This was much more like home and as open plan living went this was cute, not like the cavernous thing I lived in. Fiona came in, her brows raised as she looked at what I was doing and sniffed the air.

'This is thoughtful Daniel, and rather exotic. It smells wonderful, but shall I wash first as I don't think Bel compliments this fine food.'

I kissed her forehead and turned her round, smacking her on her firm round bottom as I did so. 'Go and wash then woman and then present yourself to me naked for examination before we eat.'

She gurgled with laughter as I made as though to chase her to the bathroom. I got the feeling she hadn't had much teasing in her life and she responded well to it.

While she was freshening up I stepped into the studio, there were fewer paintings on view but there was a new drawing she was working on, a study of the shoes. It was interesting to see something that wasn't a landscape. She'd drawn the shoes in the nest she had made of the hessian and photographed that day. I loved it, managing to take some photographs before she came in, smelling of soap and shampoo, her long hair and combed and damp. She'd dressed in a pair of black cord jeans and a green t-shirt.

'I thought I'd better make an effort since you are so finely dressed Daniel.'

I looked down at myself, of course I was wearing London gear, chinos with loafers and a rather nice shirt with dark blue and tan stripes and a bit of a red and blue paisley pattern over one shoulder. She'd never seen me dressed like this before. I felt pretty good about myself and put my hands either side of her slim waist and kissed her several times.

'I'm famished. Come and eat something and tell me about every minute you've spent here without me. And don't miss anything out.'

I took her hand and led her back to the little table. Fiona was quite animated, a bit like she'd been that first evening with Mark and Kate and it was a pleasure to watch her as she described the art show, the camaraderie and the help with humping and dumping and hanging pictures. It seems she'd met a nice bunch of people and had a drink with several of them one evening. Then of course she'd had to do a day there manning the sales desk. People made income from selling cards and prints of their work, as well as selling originals. Some even went as far as having their designs on mugs, calendars and tea towels. She'd learned a lot, and I took it all in.

We celebrated her selling four paintings in four days, all of local moorland views with the famous stones and the incredible touches of botanical detail she put in. Apart from occasionally including Bel or the unmistakable shape of a buzzard she didn't seem to bother with the sheep and ponies and cattle all of which were integral to the landscape. Afterwards, to get London out of my lungs we strolled down the track and through the village. The pub was busy and I saw Rob and Steve in there with their ladies. I asked Fiona if she wanted to go in.

'Not really if you don't mind.' She wrinkled her nose with its attractive bump. 'When it's quiet I like it, but a Friday night with the elevated laughter and beery bonhomie makes me feel uncomfortable.'

I didn't mind at all. I wanted her all to myself.

TWENTY ONE

Obviously I had to go and look at Darleystones and I asked Fiona to come with me after we'd had breakfast.

'It will be my pleasure Daniel.'   My medieval red lady was back.

We cleared up the breakfast things together in a harmonious and happy atmosphere.   I found a pan in the refrigerator and investigated the contents, it was a rich tomato and herb sauce with little bits of onion and mushroom in it.   'Smells good.'   I commented, putting it back.

'That was for last night, I was expecting us to eat pasta but you came with goods from the city. We can have it tonight.'

The fact that she'd been expecting me, thought about what we might eat and actually made something for us to share made lights go off in my head. And she'd had a busy week. It made up for my pang of anxiety when she'd mentioned having a drink with all those artists. As soon as I thought that, I told myself off for being a fool.   For all she knew I might have half a dozen fabulous women hanging around me in London. I had to learn to trust and anyway, it was my card standing on the little table at her side of the bed.

She had taken a long look at the car and then smiled at me.

'My brother and my father would both love you for having a beast like this. Pilots always go for this kind of thing.'

'But what about you?' I paused, surely I wasn't going to ask her if she would love me because of the car. I thought very fast. 'Are you interested in cars Fiona?'

I got that old fashioned look. 'That's polite talk Daniel. I do like good design though, although what goes on beneath the bonnet is not really of interest to me.'

'What about the colour, does that matter to you.'

To my amusement she made a noise. I started laughing. 'You just blew a raspberry.'

As we drove over to Darleystones Radio 3 was playing something from The Tallis Scholars. I knew this but not just because the clever radio was telling me so. Fiona stretched back and sighed with pleasure.

'Oh I get the goosebumps when I hear Tudor music.'

'You'd get on with my partner Mike, he plays Tallis in the planning den.' Mike actually played a lot of different stuff, he was interested in the structure of music. He'd taught me a lot in our years of working together.

'I play it sometimes when I'm painting.'

'What else do you like?' I asked her.

'Sinatra singing, his phrasing is wonderful. Annie Lennox, Dire Straits. Anything but jazz, I'm a bit old fashioned, living with my grandparents is the cause of it.'

I had much to learn about her that was for sure. I made a mental note to take her shopping for something to store her personal playlist.

As we approached Darleystones I became concerned. 'What the hell?' There was a battered old van there and someone sitting outside using a camping stove. I parked up and strode across in a get the hell off my land attitude. I was about to speak when the person turned and saw me and grinned. It was The Grunt. I stopped in my tracks.

'Alright Guv? Thought I'd move in and keep an eye on things and stuff after you'd gone. Andy thought it would be okay. Want a sausage?'

I was so relieved that I returned his grin just as Fiona joined me. The Grunt raised his hand in a curious salute to her and nodded. Fiona inclined her head in greeting.

'Fiona this is.' I had no idea of his name. 'Sorry, brain fade, I've forgotten your name mate.'

'Simon.' Fiona was speaking.

Bloody hell, did she know everyone round here.

'Of course, Simon.' I blagged it. 'How's it going?'

Simon was still waving a sausage on a fork. 'Brilliant.'

I turned to Fiona. 'And you already know Simon.'

She was looking over at the house, still clad in scaffolding. 'Oh yes, I ran some drawing classes for a few weeks at the village hall before my teaching job started. Simon came along. He has good technical skills. But we first met because Simon looks after my brother's garden one day a week.'

Simon got up, rubbing his hands on his grubby trousers. 'Miss Frazer is a really good teacher, she gave me lots of encouragement. I've carried on Miss. I reckon I might go for a tech drawing course.'

Fiona gave him her attention. I loved that cool green gaze with all the layers of thought and expression it encompassed. 'You should do that Simon. I will help you with the application.'

He actually blushed so to spare him any embarrassment I suggested he get on with his breakfast and we went on down to the house.

Progress seemed painfully slow but I could see where Andy had been cleaning and working on the external walls. The awful cement render had gone and there was an area of fresh lime mortar between the old stones. Funny how solid it made that bit of the wall look. We walked around and stopped at the date stone. Fiona hadn't seen it until now and as she made out the letters she drew her breath in sharply. I watched her closely. She looked a bit shocked.

'I think I know how you feel.' I said as I put my arm around her shoulders and felt her tremble. 'I had the strange feeling that I'd been here before when I first saw it.' She didn't speak so I went on. 'I think it's David Penive, a distant ancestor of mine and Kate's. But I don't know what the letter F stands for.'

'His fair lady.'

Fiona was in a daze so I pulled her round and cuddled her for a moment. 'And you are my red lady. Hey, what's up?' She had tears in her eyes.

'It's the beauty of it. All that passion and intention so many years ago.'

I couldn't follow that with anything sensible so I walked her inside, kissing her at the threshold as I liked to do. I really wanted to say something like "Welcome Home" but I thought that might be a bit heavy in the circumstances. Only the slate flagstones of the hall were still intact, Simon The Grunt had finished the job we started together and all the flagstones in the rooms had been lifted and moved outside so that the floors could be dug out, levelled and insulated and made ready for the underfloor heating system. It was a colossal job. There was nothing I could do and anyway I wasn't dressed for it. It all looked forlorn downstairs and Fiona gave a deep sigh. I smiled at her.

'Don't worry, it all has to get a lot worse before it can get better, but believe me it will and it will be restored. It's going to be very lovely, I know it.'

We went back outside and over to The Grunt. I'd got to start thinking of him as Simon. He was actually quite personable. He'd got a pot of tea and asked if we'd like some, and asked after Bel so we made some pleasant small talk and sat with him. I assured him that I was fine with him being here, in fact it was a very good idea. He also told me that Steve had been back doing measurements upstairs for the wardrobes.

'He can't make a start until the tanking and plastering has been done, and that's not for a while, but he needs to get on with ordering the wood and getting stuff sorted. And he was all over that staircase. He reckons it's older than the house. Must have come from somewhere else.'

We chatted for a bit about information Andy had sent through to me. Steels were going to be inserted to stabilise the roof once the walls were done. Andy was getting a roofer in to help with the work and to do roofing repairs. It was going to be many months before I could move in.

Later on we called round at Kate's for a quick hello and I updated her on things. Fiona sat happily cuddling Emily. She was a natural with the kids, fluttering her eyelashes on Emily's wrist and tickling her face with what she called butterfly kisses. Emily gurgled and giggled and waved her fat fists in the air. Kate had being doing some local research of her own.

'I've been talking to your man Steve's wife at the village library, the girl with the platinum blonde hair and very blue eyes. She only does half a day a week there but she put her hands straight onto a history article from the paper a few years ago and it mentions a Mrs Penive who used to pick snowdrops to send up to London. Of course she might not have been from Darleystones, I don't think snowdrops grow there, but it's obviously a relative from way back when. Funny but there aren't any Penive's listed in the phone book.'

'Interesting.' I said. 'Maybe she's the person to give us some guidance on finding family details, did you mention that we were interested?'

Kate gave me a look. 'Yes, I managed to string enough words together beyond goo goo and gaga to ask her about that, and she can help up to a point. I've decided I'm going to pursue that since you've got enough on your platter with the build, and London and travelling and working. It worries me a bit Daniel.'

'Don't worry sweetie, I have a cunning plan, it will take a few months to sort out but sort it out I will.' I said.

We left Kate and I drove us back to the annexe. Fiona went and checked on Bel who was out in the paddock behind her brother's house. There were a couple of other horses in the field beyond and Fiona was happy that Bel had her own kind to talk to. I poured us a glass of red wine. When Fiona came back in she was thoughtful.

'Penny for them.' I raised my glass to her.

'Oh.' She leaned forward and picked her glass up but she didn't drink. 'All the talk about your family history has made me think I must talk with my own parents about their origins when I see them at Christmas. My mother comes from a village further down Cornwall where the RAF station was. My father of course is Scottish through and through. I take after him in many ways.'

'In what ways?' I was interested.

'In looks, my colouring. I'm all Frazer. He likes the truth too.'

I had to ask the question. 'What's your favourite place then, Scotland or Cornwall?'

'They both have their merits Daniel. I've lived most of my life in the Scottish borders, sometimes I only saw my parents for holidays because they were posted abroad so much. But I do like it round here. I do love riding Bel on the moor.'

And then I realised what she'd said. 'You're seeing your parents at Christmas then.' I'd been thinking of inviting her up to London.

'Yes, my brother and his wife and the children will be home for Christmas so they are coming down to stay. It will be grand to have everyone together.'

Bugger, how was I going to fit in with that. I supposed I could stay at Kate's. Fiona was watching the look on my face, her green eyes dancing.

'Daniel, we will work something out. It's three months away.'

I stopped thinking about it and drew her close to me, kissing the top of her head and the side of her neck. She wriggled away giggling and had a sip of her wine and then went to put the pasta on. It was absolutely delicious and, later on, so was she.

Weeks went by like that. I worked my butt off in London and flew to Munich to an IT games fair with Mike where we sold the game I'd come up with in Cornwall to the same Japanese client we'd dealt with earlier in the year. I went down to Cornwall at weekends, remembering to find something to send to Fiona every week. She reciprocated by hiding small drawings in my weekend case so that I'd find them when I unpacked in London. I started having them framed, tiny perfect drawings or watercolours of places where we had walked, the shoes, Rob's fern-like window furniture with a bit of a view beyond, a bottle of wine with two half full glasses and the spine of a book of hers that I'd been looking at. Each one had a memory attached. Each one went up at the flat until I had a wall with a series of these on display.

I'd had to leave the house key with Andy but as he said, weighing it in his hand, he wouldn't be able to get a duplicate made. Andy did a fantastic job on the exterior walls at Darleystones and helped the roofer and his team to get the chimney fixed and the roof repaired, safely supported and watertight. Winter on the moors, I knew from experience, could get nasty. They'd had to get a crane up there to move the steels into place, I wished I'd seen it but Simon The Grunt had filmed it on his phone and sent it to me. I was grateful. The new hardwood double glazed windows, with Rob's window furniture, were all fitted in and the place was dry and secure which was a weight off my mind. The Grunt had only camped there for a few weeks and was back home in the warm with his mum in the village. It was a good job I was earning good money because I paid out shedloads for this first few months' work.

Meanwhile I'd given a memory stick with the photographs of Fiona's paintings and sketches to a woman who lived in one of the flats below me. Frances had a gallery on the South Bank and was always on the lookout for new talent. She was happily and openly gay and liked to showcase female artists. One Sunday night there was a handwritten note in my mailbox asking if I could drop in for a drink at the gallery on Thursday night. It was only a short walk from the flat but it was a lousy evening with rain drenching down, so I got soaked. Despite the weather the gallery was packed with late shoppers looking for new stuff to decorate their expensive homes, or simply to be seen at an opening. Frances seemed to know the names of most of them and greeted me as though I was family.

'Daniel my darling you look half drowned, did you swim here tonight.' From somewhere she produced a cherry red hand towel and patted me down as though I was a wet dog, at the same time pressing a glass of white wine into my hand while people looked on. 'There are nibbles over there, I'm having a little party to introduce a few new talents. Speaking of talent, where did you find Fiona Frazer, I adore her already. Wonderfully individual abstract composition and with those little bits of perfect detail overlaid like lace on a designer frock. Quite gorgeous.'

Frances was tall and had a mane of streaky coffee coloured hair which she wore over one shoulder, together with lots of make up, bronze nail varnish and a slinky gold and cream dress. She was wearing enormous lumps of amber coloured resin jewellery and under the glitz and bling she was a fine businesswoman. I'd got to know her through Lynn and as if on queue Frances took my arm.

'I haven't seen the lovely Lynn around lately,' she murmured confidentially. 'Have you split up darling?'

I confirmed that we had. 'No regrets on either side Frances.' I was not going to have a discussion about my personal life. I explained that Fiona was a Glasgow School of Art Graduate, teaching near my home down in Cornwall. 'I've seen her studio and she sold four paintings at an art fair in Tavistock in the summer.' I paused, remembering the look of pride on Fiona's face and the pleasure at her sudden windfall. It had all been spent on Bel's welfare.

'Four you say. Hmm, rather provincial though darling. How long was the art fair?'

I said it was on for five days as far as I remembered.

'Darling I would like to see some real examples of her work, can you get any here? Your flat would be convenient I suppose since it's just upstairs from me. If it's as good as it looks in the photographs I'd like some in the gallery before Christmas but I'd need to meet her and discuss terms and so on. Can that be arranged my sweet?'

I told her that it could be. I also told her that I'd got an original hanging in my flat already.

'Oh she's that special. Well I don't mind darling. But let's wait until I see about half a dozen. Call me as soon as you can.'

Frances popped a business card into my top pocket and wandered off to make a fuss of someone else. It was her way of doing business. As soon as I could I slipped away and squelched back to the flat. I had to call Fiona.

Fiona answered the telephone after the third time I'd rung the number at the annexe. She apologised, explaining that she'd been in the studio. I told her I'd got a confession to make, a good confession I hoped and told her all about photographing her work and the gallery owner's request to see some of the real thing.

'Frances wouldn't ask to see more unless she liked it. She was making positive noises and your work is good.'

'My goodness Daniel. I'm overwhelmed I think. That you have done something like this for me. And now I'm afraid, how on earth will I get them to London?'

'Let me arrange that. I'm sure I can organise a specialist courier. But it will mean that you'll have to come up on a week day.' I knew that her teaching was part time and that she had Tuesdays and Wednesdays free. I was going to be busy, but I was always busy. I liked it that way.

After the phone call, the first ever with her, I made a sandwich and spent a few hours emailing art couriers. I love the internet and the twenty-four-seven society. The next morning I had three replies and had everything fixed before I left the planning den to drive down to Cornwall at midday. I felt like the spider in a children's story I'd once read. I had my hands on so many ideas and projects and was pulling Fiona into my world and up to London for a night or two. I was thrilled simply because I would see her for a few extra nights, that's what made it special. As I drove down I phoned Mike.

'I'm a bum hole Mike.' I began.

'So what's new about that. Are you in trouble, you've only just left here.'

I explained that Fiona had to be in London on Tuesday for a meeting. 'She's a poor struggling art teacher mate, it would be better if I drove her up on Monday night, so if it's ok with you and

Radio I'll not be in the office until Tuesday. After that I promise to be good.'

Mike laughed. 'You keep throwing me and Radio together, but I guess we'll cope. There might be favours to be called in at some point though.'

'Understood.'

Then I rang the cleaner because she did my place on Fridays and asked her if she would mind buying some stuff from the deli.

'Fill the fridge up please, if you can find it in the kitchen. I left some money in the empty fruit bowl but leave the receipt on the worktop and I'll settle up any difference.'

I found Fiona in the studio sorting through her paintings and sketches. She was quite excited, her face a bit flushed and she kissed me passionately.

'It's meant to happen.' I told her, gazing into her green eyes. 'I got lucky with a courier who was doing a run down to St Ives, they hate to have an empty van. They'll be here on Monday morning at ten to load up and will deliver everything to my place on Tuesday morning.'

'But I'm at work on Monday, and how will I get to London in time. And the cost Daniel, I can't afford it.'

'Madam,' I said, twirling her round like a dancer under my hand, 'everything is arranged. I shall be here to deal with it. You will come up to London with me on Monday night and be there at my flat for the delivery on Tuesday while I'm at work. Frances is coming round on Tuesday evening, and I will take you to Paddington to get the train back here on Wednesday. And in between all that we might have a nice meal together and celebrate.'

Fiona was breathless. 'Daniel this is wonderful, but I hope there shall be something to celebrate. She might not like my work.' She paused in our mock dance. 'And Bel, what about Bel?'

Oh rats, I thought, and there was me ridiculously pleased that I'd got everything sorted. I stared at her, not knowing what to say and was just wondering if Kate knew how to feed a horse when Fiona snapped her fingers, the smile back on her face.

'Of course, I can ask Simon. He loves Bel and always brings her a carrot when he's gardening. I'll call him.'

She went off to make the call and I sat down on a chair in the studio, letting out a huge sigh of relief. I'd make the job worth it for The Grunt.

The weekend was fabulous, we sorted and wrapped a selection of her work but I asked her not to include the one of the shoes. Fiona agreed with me, it was another special and personal piece. We talked, ate, made love and visited Darleystones where there was nothing I could do. Woodworm treatment had been done, but meanwhile there were ceilings to be replaced, insulation to be fitted, plastering to be done and green technology to be put in place. It was going to take months before the place could be decorated and furnished but it didn't stop me thinking and making plans.

It was odd in a nice way seeing her off to work on Monday morning, it made me feel like we were a proper couple. The art courier's van turned up as arranged. He had to reverse up the little track and I complimented him on his driving.

'Happens all the time mate, usually at the places I go to deliver, galleries always have inaccessible back entrances and so on. If you can't reverse you can't do the job.'

I told him it was like that driving in the narrow lanes around Cornwall, if you can't reverse you're in trouble. Many a holidaymaker reversed into a Cornish hedge to let traffic get by only to find that it contained a solid wall.

After he'd gone I made myself useful round the annexe and then went over to see Kate for an hour. I gave her a quick update and helped her while she was juggling the twins doing some complicated mummy stuff. It was all rather smelly. To take her mind off the ghastly task she was doing I told her that Fiona's family were all descending en masse at Christmas.

'I'm not sure how a strongly Presbyterian Scot will view my apparent familiarity with his only daughter. He's an ex-RAF officer so he's maybe not a trained killer, like ex-Army, but I don't want to upset the bloke, so would it be okay if I was here with you and Mark for a couple of days?'

'A proper family Christmas with you playing uncle?' Kate said.

I had a sudden lightbulb moment. 'Will it spoil your first Christmas together as a family?' I couldn't ever recall having had such sensitive feelings before. Even Kate was taken aback but we were both getting light headed. I had to open the back doors and windows to let the pong out. At that point she was glad to be able to breathe and relieved enough to agree to anything.

TWENTY TWO

I stopped off in Liskeard and drew some cash out and filled up the car at the supermarket before going back to the annexe where I logged into work for a bit. It was a cool autumn day so I called up the flat's Nest program and instructed it to switch the lights and heating on at seven that evening. When Fiona got in I had a bowl of tomato and basil soup ready with a cheese and onion sandwich, all courtesy of the supermarket, but at least I'd made the effort. She's the sort of girl who noticed things and she commented on the filled wood baskets and the stove all laid ready for her getting back on Wednesday. I'd even put the rubbish out. I'd never known myself so domesticated.

'What do you charge per hour?' she teased me. 'I could get used to this sort of help.'

'You couldn't afford me if I told you.' I wasn't joking. I noticed a slight frown but she didn't pursue it. We sorted Bel's evening arrangements together and I left an envelope where Simon could find it with a tip in it and a note thanking him for being so helpful recently. I'd signed it from us both but I didn't tell Fiona I'd done it. Then I made her laugh telling her about helping Kate to change the twins.

'Do you think you have changed these last few months Daniel?'

She was right on target as usual.

'Yeah I think I have. I think it's the house you know, the feeling of all that time it's seen, lives coming and going. I feel that things matter a lot more now. I feel more connected.'

It was all true, I wasn't pretending. I was noticing all sorts of stuff, even Mike had commented and asked me what vitamins I was taking. Finally I got our bags into the car, there was a slight delay while Fiona put a few more sketches into a portfolio and away we went. She was excited.

'I haven't been out of Cornwall since I came down to start the job last Christmas. That's nearly eleven months.'

'Okay country mouse, prepare yourself for the bright lights and the noise.' We crossed the toll bridge at Saltash and let the car do its stuff.

We were both pretty knackered by the time I pulled into my secure underground parking space. We took our bags over to the lift and waited for it to arrive. Fiona was thoughtful.

'You do this journey every weekend Daniel.'

'Where there's a will there's a way.' I responded lightly but my head was aching from the relentless stop-start Sunday evening traffic.

The flat seemed quite welcoming and her first comment was that it was so big. It was, the annexe and the studio would fit into the living area, not including the kitchen and the bedrooms. She walked about, seeing her painting in the living area, liking the rug, trailing her fingers over the big pot. Her expression at the fully integrated kitchen area was one of utter disbelief.

'Is it a space ship? All this brushed stainless steel, it feels so cold. How on earth do you find things and do you know how to use this thing?' She was looking in amazement at the oven with all its touch pad equipment panel.

'I haven't a clue. It's never been used.' I didn't laugh.

'Then why did you buy it?' Fiona was genuinely mystified.

'It came with the flat. It's a concept in lifestyle. Like the lighting and heating which you can operate remotely.'

'Oh'. Was all she said.

The contents of the fridge were greeted with interest. 'It's all fresh and unopened. Is there someone who does your shopping?'

I said that I'd had a little help. I remembered the joke she'd made the night she met Kate, saying she thought the fairies did my washing. I felt as though I was at the wrong end of the telescope, seeing a bloke who paid people he didn't know to do his laundry, wash his dishes, clean his flat, do his shopping, change his bed. Oh god, I thought, I've even thrown money at The Grunt and she's probably already made a payment that she can afford and that he feels is acceptable. I'm a dolt, I thought,

I'm an absolute oaf. I saw that other person I'd been earlier today, taking simple pleasure from actually doing things for her and for Kate. At that point I could have thrown myself on the ground and shouted hallelujah praise the Lord because I knew what Fiona meant by the hanged man. I was at a crossroads, deciding what sort of person I wanted to be.

Fiona continued to look around, accepting my silence and not saying much. It didn't seem to going how I'd pictured it. I'd thought she'd be knocked out, I'd seen myself pouring champagne, there was some ready in the wine fridge, lifting her off her feet and showing her a different life. Instead I was beginning to feel embarrassed. Through her eyes I was seeing a huge and stupidly ostentatious monster of soulless aspirational living. I wasn't beaten though. I took her outside to the long balcony.

'I think this is what it's all about.' I said.

There was a fantastic view of the Thames at night, lights reflecting in the silent powerful body of moving water. She looked and sighed, holding onto the balcony rail and rocking a bit on her feet.

'Yes, that is quite amazing.'

It was cold so we went back inside and she asked for a cup of tea and to be shown the bathroom. I didn't explain that there were two, each bedroom was ensuite with a large walk-in wardrobe and dressing area. Neither did I tell her she could have any sort of music she wanted playing and that she could have a light show while she was in the wet room. Fortunately I had got the sort of tea she liked and when she came back into the living area she was smiling.

'I've just seen all the little pictures I put in your bag over the weeks, you've been having them framed.'

I'd got them all on a wall in my dressing area by the walk-in wardrobe. 'They're what I see every morning Fiona. I love seeing them.' I was quite proud of the way they looked as a group, in differently coloured frames, black, blue, red, yellow, depending on the mood the picture invoked. And they all had non reflective glass so I could see them from any angle.

'I like how you've treated them Daniel, it's sensitive and appropriate. I'm impressed.'

I must have looked relieved because she leaned over and kissed me.

'That's the Daniel I see, that's how you are inside. This place,' she gestured with one hand, 'this place is where you hang your clothes at the moment.'

Despite the initial awkwardness over the flat we slept well, cuddled together in quiet comfort. I didn't try to make love to her, it didn't seem right and anyway I really was tired. Her only comment was that she missed the smell of fresh air coming through the window. The flat was a sealed unit, adjusting itself continuously to what should be the optimum in living comfort. Okay for a robot, but not really for a human being, the air was dead. No wonder I slept so well in Cornwall, the windows were almost always open.

I had to get off to work but I explained all the buzzers and gizmos and access codes she needed to know about and set off after kissing her. She seemed a bit distracted but I guessed she was nervous about meeting Frances that evening. I'd be there to help, so I wasn't worried. Obviously I didn't use my car, no one who lives in London does. Mike and Radio were already in when I got there. Mike was looking concerned.

'What's up?' I asked him. 'Plant died or something?'

'Radio thinks there's been an attempt at hacking our systems.'

Shit. Not good news then. It was heads down for the rest of the day and I didn't have time to call Fiona at the flat. I felt a bit bad having to leave them to it but I had to get back to the flat in time for Frances calling at seven that night. When I got there the place was in darkness but there were a couple of bin liners full of packaging and bubble wrap. The pictures had been delivered okay then. I put all the lights on and looked around. There wasn't a sign of Fiona or the pictures but there was a note on the kitchen worktop. I had a really bad feeling.

Daniel, your friend Frances came up with the delivery and we spent the morning together, she has taken everything to the gallery. Simon phoned my mobile, he couldn't believe what you'd left him, neither could I. I know you mean to be kind and considerate but all this has taken me somewhat out of my depth. I've gone back to Cornwall because I need to be able to think. I need a little time to be on my own. F.

I think I actually cried out. I certainly swore. I'd been right about the feelings I'd picked up last night then. Most women would adore all the stuff money can bring, but not Fiona. I'd gone over the top. I kept re-reading her note and then I phoned Frances. She answered on the third ring.

'Daniel darling, how are you and how is the lovely and talented Fiona?'

'I'm fine Frances thanks.' Nothing could be further from the truth. 'Fiona has just popped out, how did it all go then, she says you took everything.'

'Oh I did, her work is stunning, most impressive. I think sales will make it a nice Christmas for us. But she was a little startled when I quoted her my ideas on prices. Of course people forget there are the gallery running costs and I have to make a living too. I did explain that if this goes as well as I think it will, and my intuition doesn't usually fail me, then I'd want to take her work on an exclusive basis for a period. I can also represent her at a couple of other galleries I co-operate with.' She paused. 'They do tell them all this at art college these days don't they.'

I thanked her and ended the conversation as soon as I could and started pacing round the flat. I'd been going to take Fiona to a nice little restaurant on the South Bank, toast her success and her future. I'd been intending to give her the little bronze horse I'd bought weeks ago as a memento of a special day. Then I'd been going to surprise her with a first class ticket back down to Liskeard. Several times I picked the phone up to call her and put it down again, she wanted some space. I went to the fridge, nothing had been opened. I swore quite a lot.

I hardly slept and when I got into the planning den I realised that neither had Mike and Radio. I'd bought three coffees on my way in and some bacon baps. At least I'd done something right by the way they fell on them. By lunchtime it seemed that we'd got everything sorted and safe although almost everything had been shut down for a period. I told them to bugger off and get some rest and a shower. Mike clapped a hand on my shoulder.

'Thanks. You can babysit now. Start bringing things back up. I've got to sleep. And I've got to pack.'

I'd clean forgotten that Mike was taking a break. As the day progressed it became quite clear to me that I would not be going anywhere for several days. Fiona was going to get her personal space whether she wanted it or not.

Two weeks went by before I could even think of returning to Cornwall. Mike deserved his break and Radio had other commitments since he was self employed. I was on my own quite a lot which was both a curse and a blessing. Andy was still keeping me up to date on progress and I'd agreed that he should take on the project management as well as the build. He was more than capable and what he was earning from me was going to take him and his family on a warm holiday at Christmas.

Eventually I telephoned Kate and told her the whole story. She was patient and listened carefully.

'You really do like this girl don't you Daniel.' I could hear the twins gurgling in the background.

'From the minute I set eyes on her. She's special. I really don't know how to deal with this bloody situation Kate, I thought I was helping her, I don't want to control her or take over. She's got fantastic talent and I don't think the teaching job is secure. What the hell do I do?'

'Stop it this minute you naughty boy.' Kate sounded cross.

'I'm sorry?' There was a pause in the conversation and I could hear Kate breathing.

'That's better. Now leave her alone.'

'What?'

'Sorry Daniel, Jake was trying to poke Emily's eye out. I've just separated them. Now, about Fiona. Have you told her what you've told me?'

'Not really, I sent her a card.'

'What sort of card, was it a get well card or an I'm thinking of you type of card?'

I didn't bother to comment on her irony. Actually it had been the one of Klimt's lovers kissing. Lots of gold. I think it's beautiful.

'Oh just a nice arty card, I did say there was a crisis at the planning den and that we were working all day and all night to fix the problem.'

'Ye gods was that all you said, has she replied?' Kate thought the snail mail routine was weird but then she's a thoroughly modern girl.

'No.'

'Oh why am I not surprised? Daniel you are a prize plonker. She'll just think that's an excuse not to contact her. Get your quill out and tell her everything, and do it now, before it's too late.'

'Write her a letter?'

'Yes Daniel. Write her a letter.'

Well honestly, there are books on writing wedding speeches and how-to manuals for just about everything. But whoever writes a book on how to apologise to your girlfriend in writing should make a bloody mint. It took me hours and my hand ached. It was easier labouring under a hot sun pushing a wheelbarrow about, at least the blisters were on my hands then, not my heart.

Mike came back looking relaxed. He'd been up to the Lake District to visit a friend and then down to see his folks near Bristol. He had something on his mind, I could always tell. With

226

things running smoothly at the planning den he suggested we should take a long lunch and have a proper catch up over a meal.

'You look slightly rough round the edges mate. Since we've had no more unwelcome visitors fiddling around with our knobs and switches in the night do I deduce your love life has hit a bump in the road?'

'Yeah a bit, I'm not sure if the wheels are off the cart yet, but a touch of the plonker on my part has had to be apologised for.' I tried to sound unconcerned but failed.

Mike looked up from the menu he was studying. 'Son,' he said, 'never apologise, never explain.'

'You try arguing with Kate.'

'Ah.' He nodded. 'I see.' Mike had met Kate. He said she was a lot like his mum only much, much prettier. He adored his mum.

'So, how's the folks then?' I thought it best to turn the conversation to his family rather than discuss my problems in gory detail.

It turned out that Mike's folks were fancying a change and had decided to move to a quieter area.

'Dad's got a bit of a dicky ticker, he's changed his eating habits and can now bore for Bristol about the mediterranean diet. He's also keen on his golf since he's retired and wants to move. I've told him he's just coffin dodging and that they shouldn't leave their friends but they've seen a place in Somerset near a golf course and reckon it's just what they need.'

I just nodded and made a decision about steak versus chicken.

Mike ordered us a large glass of wine each. He was having fish and wanted white so I opted for the chicken and had the same. The very pretty waitress gave us a complimentary dish of olives and toasted almonds. I noticed she had red hair, rather curly, and dimples. Mike kicked me under the table.

'I went down with them to a look at a place. I found myself explaining to the owner that I didn't live with my mum and dad and wasn't interested in looking an ensuite bedroom for myself.'

The waitress brought the wine. I said a well behaved thank you and focussed on Mike.

'Why are you telling me this?' I thought of Fiona. 'You're making polite talk Mike.'

Mike took rather a large swig of his wine and put his paper napkin to his lips.

'Forgot it wasn't beer.' His eyes were watering.

I remained silent. I'd learned a bit from Fiona, I thought fondly.

'Thing is Daniel, it's lovely over there. I had a look round on my own, and there's a country house I fancy buying. Not a wreck like your dump obviously. It's got views and a lovely garden and a small converted old building that the owner uses as a needlework quilting-thingy studio. But it's big enough for my gear. It's even got a loo so it would make a great office. And there's a double garage and good parking. It's got potential.'

'Did you propose to the estate agent?' I was enjoying this.

'Twat. He was rather good looking though.' Mike wasn't laughing.

I looked at my friend. I remembered saying to him a few months ago that after all this time I didn't really know him at all. I took in the nice clothes which suited his long frame, the long fine hands, the bony face with its ready smile and hazel eyes. He looked back at me with a steady gaze.

'Bloody hell, you've had a decent haircut and you're pretty smart these days Mike. Have you met someone at last?'

'Yes. I have. His name is James. You know him as Radio. We're going to move in together.' And Mike exhaled very slowly.

Was I surprised? Not really. I'd never known him serious about a woman and our private lives had remained private, partly because I'd been with Lynn for ages and partly because we liked it that way. I realised he was waiting for my reaction. For some reason I stuck my hand out across the table and we had a silly moment resulting in a handshake.

'Mike, I'm really pleased for you. I really am. Radio's a great bloke. Can I come to the housewarming when it happens?'

Mike's pleasure and relief were huge. We talked for ages about houses and life and a bit about interior decorating. I described Rob's house and what he'd done there. Then we got round to Mike's own family. It seems his parents had known he was gay from the year dot but that his older brother was tense about it. Mike said he didn't much like his brother's wife and wasn't too bothered. Finally we got talking about our business.

'It was when you borrowed my van I realised that we could do this work from anywhere. I mentioned it to James and he said he was thinking about leaving London and moving back west anyway because it's cheaper and the cider is better. If you do want to move back to Cornwall and we move to Somerset we can meet and work together and there's at least two handy airports if we need to go to market to sell our wares.'

With his Bristol accent he was sounding more like Uncle Tom Cobley and all. Eventually we realised that the restaurant would quite like to see the back of us and we walked back to the planning den. I was feeling more positive than I had done for ages. I was really pleased for Mike, if things could work out for him then they could work out for me as well. I felt as though I was giving myself permission to make changes in my life as well. I looked around as we walked, the familiar views and accessibility to so much of interest, yet London was massively indifferent. We both decided to call it a day and I thought I'd go and swim rather than go to the gym. As I walked past the gallery I saw Frances and on impulse went in.

Frances was looking stylish as usual, in her favourite creams and golds and wearing a very wide brown belt with laces instead of a buckle. She was wearing front laced boots as well. She saw me looking.

'It's not bondage darling, it's based on a stomacher, like a basque or a bodice worn over the clothes in Restoration England.'

'Oh, Merry Monarch stuff. Nell Gwynne and all that. Very nice Frances.' I made a kissing noise somewhere near her left cheek. Before I could say anything else she gestured towards a wall at the end of the gallery.

'I was about to make a call to your darling Fiona Frazer. We've sold a large watercolour and a small pen and ink today. I think she's going to be pleased. Would you like to call her instead and give her the good news?'

'No, I think it will be exciting, and professional, for her to hear it from you Frances.' I was not going to interfere any more.

We walked over to the wall together. For a moment my chest felt tight. Fiona'a displayed work, properly lit, was lovely. It drew you in and whispered to you of other places and quiet ancient memories. There was a good head and shoulders photograph of her taken outside against the railings overlooking the Thames, not looking into the camera, her red hair whipping around her head in a breeze, a heather and olive green coloured scarf wound around her neck against the chill of the day. I stood and gazed at it, Fiona, my lovely clever and unusual Fiona.

'Maeve took that. Rather good isn't it. She's a very handsome girl.' Frances was standing quietly at my side. Despite her huge personality she had the ability to withdraw whilst not moving. It was a neat trick because it gave buyers a few moments to make up their minds without feeling physically pressured. Maeve was her long term partner, a slim severe looking Irish woman who kept the gallery organised. She had a smile that would frighten horses and small children and she loved Frances.

'It's all lovely Frances. Really, very lovely.' I just wanted to stand and stare and be with my own memories. I realised that Frances had moved away and was walking back to her lair, it wasn't a desk, it had all her working paraphernalia but incorporated a sofa with a trendy coffee table and some spindly chairs.

Fiona, her light touch, her attention to detail, her warmth and care, her passion and integrity. I stood there and almost bathed in her presence, the feelings invoked by her paintings and drawings were so powerful. My reverie was interrupted by Frances speaking on the phone.

'Yes my darling, that's right, another two sold just today. Wonderful isn't it. The pen and ink is going to America. I would have phoned earlier but you're out at work. And guess who is standing right here, it's Daniel, he's just popped in having neglected me lately. Do you want a word?' And she handed me her phone.

TWENTY THREE

There was silence. I took the phone and turned away from Frances. All I could say was her name. 'Fiona.'

'Daniel.' She responded in her slightly husky voice. It gave me goosebumps. 'Daniel, I got your letter. Thank you, I'm sorry I haven't replied, I've been a little bit unwell.'

I was immediately concerned. 'What's wrong, what can I do?'

'If you can come down to Cornwall at the weekend that would be nice. I'm alright now, I was just a bit sick. I think I might have had the Norovirus bug, it goes around schools you know, they call it winter vomiting virus. Except people can get it all year round apparently.'

I thought she sounded tired.

'Yes I can, and I will. We're all fixed and sorted out and Mike and I had a good talk about things today. I'm ready to get out of London in more ways than one, but it's all good news, nothing to worry about. And I've missed you.'

Conscious that Frances was within earshot I congratulated Fiona on her sales and asked her to *please* phone my mobile if anything was wrong.

'I know you don't like talking on the phone but I hate to think of you feeling ill and being alone. I'll be there as soon as I can.'

I was full of energy again so I swam ten lengths, showered off and got a healthy salad with lots of avocado and prawns. My fitness club described itself as a wellness experience and provided shopping opportunities for its members. I could buy the latest in exercise gear and use the very good cafe. It also had wifi so I thought damn it and explored the possibilities of having food and flowers delivered to Fiona. I eventually registered with a well known supermarket and picked a delivery slot on her day off, ordering a variety of designer soup and healthy smoothies and some flowers. I also got a card included and wrote, "Hope this helps, get well and please take care of yourself". I'm sure Kate would have snorted but it was the best I could do.

London had been aware that it was nearly Christmas since October and I'd cynically ignored it. I don't know anybody who enjoys mince pies at bonfire night or that relentlessly awful music. But as I walked back to the flat I actually enjoyed the window displays and the lights. I wondered what Fiona might like as a present, I'd got to get beyond art materials and food.

The week seemed to go slowly and I was frustrated that I'd heard nothing from her. Once again I began to doubt that the passion and feelings I'd got for her were reciprocated. Mike took pity on me and told me to shove off on Friday morning. Actually I think it was because Radio James was in and they wanted to be alone to discuss their move. That was on my mind as I drove. It looked at though they might be leaving London before I did at this rate. I reckoned that we'd be closing the planning den and relocating by Easter, so I needed to speak to Rob Williams.

I saw his van in the parking space when I turned on to the track so I pulled up alongside and got out. He came to the door and smiled when he saw that it was me. We shook hands and he invited me in. His girlfriend Su was with him. I'd seen her around but we'd never been properly introduced. Like Fiona she wasn't covered in make up, her tawny hair and lovely blue green eyes didn't need any enhancement and she was a very pretty girl.

'Good to meet you at last Daniel. I see Fiona at the yoga class I've joined but she wasn't there last week, I was going to pop round.'

'She's been a bit poorly, norovirus she thinks. But she's on the mend now.'

'Poor Fiona. That's a rotten bug.' Su said she knew all about these things from her previous life.

'I'm going to be moving into Su's place soon Daniel so this house will be free if that fits in with your plans. I'll let you know dates as soon as possible.' Rob said.

I congratulated them and said that suited my own plans perfectly. I didn't want to crowd Fiona and anyway I needed space for my work equipment, none of which would fit into the annexe. I asked him if he was leaving the place furnished and he said that it would be since Su's place was fully kitted out. Su offered me a hot drink or a beer but I declined as I wanted to see Fiona. Rob told me he was working on the weathervane and showed me a couple of shots he'd got on his phone saying he liked to record progress as new pieces developed. It was looking good.

'There's no rush to make it though Rob, the garage and studio won't be started until well after the New Year, and I haven't told Fiona about the studio idea, it's going to be a surprise.'

Rob nodded. 'You know though don't you, when you've met someone right. I met Su when I was eighteen and it's taken us twelve years to get together, but she was always at the back of my mind.'

Blimey, I hoped it wasn't going to take that long to get things sorted out between me and Fiona. Before I left I suggested we should all get together for a pre-Christmas drink and Su said we should both go to Orchard Cottage. I took the car round to the annexe. Fiona came to the door before I could knock and her arms were round my neck before we said anything. Then I realised she was emotional. Women crying can be utterly tedious and some of them do it a lot, but it seemed very out of character for her and I cradled her very gently kissing the top of her head several times. I really wanted to make it stop. I made shushing noises like those I'd heard Kate make to the twins.

'What is it sweetheart, what's wrong?' I heard myself speaking into her hair. Where the hell did the word "sweetheart" come from? It wasn't a normal part of my vocabulary.

She drew me inside and wiped her eyes on a balled up bit of kitchen towel.

'Sorry Daniel, I've been a fool and I don't usually cry. I just feel so rotten.'

That was a lot to take in. I accepted the apology, said she wasn't a fool and I was glad that she didn't cry much. But why was she feeling so bad? Was it bad about walking out on me, bad for not contacting me or bad because she felt ill. Women can be so complicated but she explained that it was all of those things which was quite a relief. I felt as though I was in control of the situation.

I made us some green tea with lemon while she washed her face and calmed down. I could see that she was feeling peaky and I really was concerned. We sat on the sofa and I pulled her feet up over my legs, that way I could see her face and cuddle her a bit. It was intimate but unthreatening and I saw her relax. We drank the tea and talked about everything. She wouldn't accept any more apologies from me, apparently I'd explained myself and my motives well enough in my letter. It was a good talk, we covered a lot of ground and found we were both on the same side. I was so relieved, I felt as though I was back on oxygen. A bit later I heated some soup - that had been a good idea, and I told her all about Mike and his plans and hopes for his future with James. I said that it was good to see him so happy. She was delighted even though she'd never met them.

'So it's the intention of all of you to leave London sometime next year.'

'Absolutely. I don't know how I shall get wifi and all the IT connections I need, maybe I'll have to rent an office if Darleystones remains in the dark ages. But come what may Mike and I shall continue our working relationship. Meanwhile I shall be renting Rob William's house soon so I shall be your neighbour. Can you stand that?' It was nice to see her laugh. Her colour had improved too. 'Oh and we have our first invitation as a couple.' I told her about getting together with Rob and Su one evening.

'Yes, I think I might enjoy that. And what about your flat Daniel?'

'I don't know at this point. It could be useful to keep a London base, or maybe I'll rent it out. I really haven't got to that point yet.' I didn't mention the gallery or the possibility of her needing to stay in London if she had to see Frances.

We checked on Bel together and I heaved a bale of straw to the field shelter. It was quite chilly outside and there was a bit of wind getting up. Bel stamped her foot.

'Bel doesn't like the wind.' Fiona was soothing her, giving the horse some food, her hands kind and sure on the horse's neck. It had been quite a day, I breathed deeply, smelling the sweet horse and hay combination, watching Fiona. My world felt much better.

We had a quiet weekend, full of the sort of tenderness you have when you've had your first row and made up. We did a bit of shopping together and she taught me how to make an omelette, saying she didn't fancy much else. I couldn't believe how easy it seemed, trying different fillings like sliced chestnut mushrooms and red onion cooked together in a knob of butter with black pepper, and poached asparagus with a little grated cheese. Over one of these meals I told her that Kate had said I could stay at their place for Christmas.

'I don't want to upset your folks before they know me Fiona. They might not take kindly to finding me under their roof.'

Fiona's green eyes flashed. 'They left me with my grandparents and at boarding school for many years Daniel and they know I have made my own way and my own life.' She paused, her breathing slightly elevated I noticed. 'But you're right, perhaps that is more considerate to my brother and his wife, after all it's their house and I do love them.'

'When do they all arrive here?' I asked.

'My brother and his family will be here on the 15th, they're on extended leave. Our parents will be arriving on the 20th.'

'Extended leave? When do they go back then?'

'They're all here until the middle of January.'

I thought I detected a little bit of tension and didn't pursue the conversation. Anyway I was thinking bloody hell, I've only got her to myself for one more weekend then.

I turned up at Kate's for Christmas with a car full of presents, including a pretty decent hamper of goodies from London's most popular distributor of tasty goods to the wealthy. It was very well received. Daphne was spending Christmas Day with us but Fiona had invited the three of us to join her family on Christmas Eve for drinks between five and seven in the evening. Kate thought it sounded a bit stuck up but Mark said not to worry, the RAF do things that way. I was just glad to be able to see Fiona but secretly I was pleased that my family would also be there to dilute any awkwardness.

I drove us over and we arrived bang on time. There was some serious metal in the driveway and Fiona's old battered VW looked out of place. As we were getting out of the car Fiona appeared, wearing a well fitting long sleeved dress I'd never seen. It was a very fine dark blue velvety cord with emerald green ribbon round a low neck and she'd put her hair up. She looked pale and quite beautiful. I saw Kate looking at her very closely. Kate had lost most of the baby weight and was looking pretty in an appropriate afternoon ensemble of mid length skirt and a blouse with a sleeveless top. She'd said it was from a catalogue which sold Scottish clothing. Fiona kissed all of us and took my hand.

'Come in and meet the family.'

We'd never been inside the main cottage before and it was a colourful friendly place with some good bits of furniture and decent rugs. There were a couple of paintings on the wall and I recognised Fiona's work, including drawings of the children. A small dark haired girl came shyly forward and took Fiona's hand, they clearly liked each other and took refuge from the noisy family in each other's company. Her name was Verity. Then we were into the main room and everybody was speaking at once, making introductions and laughing a bit too loud.

Fiona's mother came forward and held my hand briefly, she was dark and slim and introduced herself as Hannah. She was leaning on a stick.

'I am delighted to meet you Daniel. I gather you've helped Fiona with an opening at a London gallery.' Her voice was kind.

'Her talent speaks for her Mrs Frazer, I've hardly done anything.' I responded. 'But they've sold five of her paintings now which is brilliant.' The gallery wanted some more.

'She's a very clever girl and no mistake.'

A deep Scottish voice was speaking at my side but with no great warmth. I turned and put my hand out.

'You must be Fiona's father.' I realised I was about to say, 'Sir'. How the hell did you speak to a retired Group Captain when you weren't in the RAF? 'I'm Daniel.'

'I am Alexander Eildon Frazer'. I could see where Fiona got her looks and her proud appearance. I had a sudden flashback to the way she'd introduced herself to me; "I am Fiona Rose Frazer." He was a fit looking commanding man, mahogany hair flecked with grey, shrewd green eyes assessing me. We were the same height and eyeball to eyeball. 'Please call me Don.'

He shook my hand a little too strongly and then turned to his wife, carefully shepherding her to a chair, indicating that I should join them. No way was I going to address him as Don. It felt like a test that I had no intention of failing. He was clearly not a man to mess with. Predictably I got the inquisition. I answered questions about my parents, which Hannah delicately did not pursue when I explained that they were both dead. Hannah craftily asked me if I had any dependents to which I said that I'd never been married and had no children of my own. I felt like saying okay you can stop shining the light in my eyes now, I've got nothing to hide and no baggage. There was some enquiry about how I came to own the cottage that I was doing up and the Group Captain was interested that I was paying to have most of it done and not actually working on it by myself. He'd got a bit confused about the story Fiona had told him of me living in a campervan and labouring on site. I could see him looking at my shoes and my clothes and he'd seen my car. I briefly considered letting him stew then thought what's the point, he's Fiona's father and I might have to see him occasionally so I casually explained that I'd done mathematics and computer sciences at university, where I'd met my business partner and we'd got involved in designing computer games. I explained how we'd got lucky, that our ideas had been taken up by German and Swedish and Japanese clients, and that the immediate future looked set fair. They were politely interested but clearly didn't have a handle on the computer games world. Maybe they would when their grandson got a little older.

Then Fiona came over with Mark and asked her parents to stop monopolising me. Mark asked Hannah about her hip and started talking drugs and medications in his "trust me I'm a pharmacist" voice. Fiona's brother Tom said he was interested in my car. I noticed he was wearing a good old Rolex. I took Tom, a squadron leader and his little boy Alex out to the car where Alex sat pressing buttons. Tom looked more like his mother but had his father's nose with the bump in it.

'Don't worry about the old man, his bite is a lot worse than his bark but the trick is not to get bitten in the first place.' Tom said helpfully.

Back indoors Kate and Tom's wife Elaine had slipped into animated discussions about children and motherly stuff, Fiona was still keeping company with Verity and the Group Captain was keeping a close eye on me. I drank some fruity non alcoholic Christmas punch, which seemed a bit pointless really, and then it was all over before I'd had any chance to talk to Fiona properly. While coats were being found I managed to grab her hand and pull her to one side.

'I have a little gift for you, open it tomorrow, on your own, and think of me for a moment.' I put the little wrapped box containing the bronze horse into her hand and she slipped it into a pocket before reaching up with both hands and pulling my face down to hers for a fierce quick kiss on the lips.

'I have a gift for you Daniel.' There was a small wrapped package on a table in the hall. She put it into my hand. 'Likewise, tomorrow, alone.'

I drove the three of us back and listened while Kate and Mark discussed what they'd said and who they'd spoken too.

'They seem like a very nice family Daniel, Elaine is lovely.' Kate said from where she was squeezed into the back of the car.

'Hard to tell at first meeting.' Mark was thoughtful. 'Mostly normal I'd say but the Group Captain looked as though he might have been more comfortable in the freezer.'

On Christmas Day I took part in all the fun with the twins, laughing at the way Kate pantomimed with their presents, taking photographs of the happy little family. After lunch Daphne went home for a rest and I decided to go over to look at Darleystones on my own. The moor was completely quiet, the air still and cool under a surprisingly clear sky. The house seemed to be waiting. I walked around imagining that next Christmas it would be full of colour and laughter and the smell of good food and sweet woodsmoke. I wanted it so much that I could see the pictures in my head. Mostly I saw Fiona; I could see her turning to me in the kitchen, holding a dish of something steaming and delicious, I could see her standing in the hall welcoming guests and admiring the decorations weaving up the old staircase. Then I could see her sitting by the fire waiting for me to join her with glasses of something fine for us to drink and making a Christmas toast. I almost groaned with longing, I was having a virtual reality moment. Then I took the package she'd given me the evening before and held it for a while, turning it over in my hands. It was slim and flat, about the size of a paperback. I opened it carefully. I was surprised and then amazed, perfect in detail it was a small wood carving in relief of the shoes, to one side the initials as they appeared on the date stone, DPF with the letter P slightly raised, and to the other a strange flat sided symbol a bit like a letter D but with the top and bottom of the D forming a bit of a tail. There was a handwritten note in brown ink on thick deckle edged speckled paper.

I carved this on lime wood. My cipher is FF but with the F for Frazer reversed. I realised that, when placed on its side, it looks like the letter D. Maybe it's just my imagination but I feel that it connects us in some way. Happy Christmas Daniel, I love you. Fiona Rose Frazer.

I held it to my chest where I could feel my heart thumping. My throat felt tight. I wondered if she could tell what I was feeling right now and I wondered when she had opened her present. I had tied a tiny label around the horse's neck and on it I had written these words;

Fiona, I have loved you since the day we met. Happy Christmas, Daniel.

The rest of Christmas Day went by in a dream. I ate and drank and watched some crap TV with the family, enlivened by Mark's sarcastic comments. One thing I did know, the more time I spent in Mark's company the more I liked him, in some ways he reminded me of Mike. It was an effort to stay calm and behave normally when all I wanted to do was see Fiona and hear her say the words she had written. I couldn't get off to sleep that night, I'd had too much food and one of the twins was grizzling a bit. I lay in bed with my hands clasped behind my neck deciding whether or not to drive over to the village and walk up the lane to the annexe and tap on her bedroom window. That eventually got me to sleep but I awoke after a horrible dream where the Group Captain had burst in upon us and accused me of violating his daughter. He'd been wearing a kilt and brandishing a knobbly club which he fully intended to brain me with. I didn't think that the concept would make a good computer game.

There was a knock at the door and Kate came in with a mug of tea for me. She was in her dressing gown with her dark hair tousled. 'Room service, please adjust your dress and make yourself decent.' She put the mug down on the bedside table and perched on the side of the bed. 'So things are all well between you and Fiona now. What's the plan if there is one?'

'I dunno yet Kate, but we have declared our feelings for each other. And since I'm going to rent Rob's house I'll be seeing a lot of her from Valentine's Day. I think I'm going to be moving back to Cornwall.'

Just as Kate was expressing her delight there was the sound of a car outside. Kate got up and looked out of the window, wondering aloud who was out so early on Boxing Day.

'Better get your dressing gown on Daniel, you can begin seeing a lot of Fiona starting right now.'

Kate was a darling. She ushered Fiona upstairs to my bedroom where I had just managed to clean my teeth and left us alone. Fiona came into my arms and we just stood there cuddling and giving each other little kisses and saying silly things like "Did you really mean it?" and "I've got it in writing so it must be true". And at last I could look into her eyes and say it.

'I love you Fiona Rose Frazer.'

Eventually she went downstairs while I had a quick shower and by the time I joined her the family were at the breakfast table and Fiona was helping to feed the twins. She was very good at it. Mark was pleased because it meant he could eat his toast in peace. Fiona had a plan, she thought it would be a good idea to show Darleystones to her family.

'We have the traditional Boxing Day walk before lunch, not mum obviously, but we can go up onto the moor from the house and Alex and Verity can run around and let off steam.'

We arranged to meet there late morning. Fiona would bring the children and Tom could bring Elaine and his father. Kate and Mark declined the offer of joining us.

'It's your privilege and honour to have Fiona's family to yourself Dan. Be a man my son and rise to it.' Mark was hugely amused by his own wit.

As Fiona left the house Kate rummaged in the hamper and amongst the various provisions she had laid in and emerged with a tin of shortbread biscuits with one of those dreadful Scottish scenes on the lid, a small bottle of whisky, a selection of mixers and a packet of small plastic beakers. 'Maybe you should offer them a toast or something for luck, just a nip. Drivers and the children can have a mixer. At least have it there as an ice breaker.'

'You're a cunning and scheming woman Kate and I'm glad that you're on my side.'

I went and found a jumper and my jacket and after another mug of tea drove over to Darleystones. There was no one there and I let myself in, looking around critically and seeing it through new eyes. I was proud of this house and wanted them to see what I was seeing. Eventually I heard cars and went outside to greet them. Everyone piled out and came over, picking their way around the rubble and mess of the building site. It was another quiet still winter's day and Elaine was complimentary.

'What a truly beautiful spot Daniel, the views are simply wonderful.'

Fiona walked straight to me and took my arm. I kissed her briefly on the forehead, watched by the Group Captain. Then he too looked around and was taken in by the beauty of the setting.

'Ay, it is lovely. I do like the moors. And so this is the house?'

He stood looking up at it and I pointed out the mason's mark at the front and then the date stone that had been uncovered. The significance of the letter F was lost on none of them although nothing was said. Elaine looked from me to Fiona and back again and smiled, and I put a protective arm around Fiona's shoulders. She was on my territory now, this was my place and I was in control.

We all went inside and the Group Captain ran his hand over the newel post.

'Fine work. Wonderful old skills here.'

He was similarly complimentary about Rob's work and I warmed to him a fraction. The kids ran about after Tom checked that they weren't going to fall through a hole in a floor and then I showed them all the shoes and the coin. By now I'd got a spiel rehearsed and was able to talk dates and history quite knowledgeably, saying how long my mother's family had lived here and how things were fitting together as they were discovered. I could feel Fiona's father taking it all in and being suitably impressed by my research. Then I offered them a toast and a shortbread biscuit. It was all accepted with grace and good humour and I silently blessed Kate. Fiona turned her nose up at the whisky saying it smelled funny to her, but she was driving anyway so she accepted an orange juice mixer and nibbled a biscuit. The Group Captain had another generous nip from the bottle and got right into the spirit of things, describing some ancient rite of blessing a new hearth by throwing a tot of the hard stuff into the fireplace. It sounded mad to me and I was glad there wasn't a fire lit. But I went along with it and let him have the honour. It put him in a fine good humour. Then we all trooped up onto the moor so that the kids could run and jump. Fiona walked with me, holding my hand and not saying much. She was smiling. Tom and Elaine walked ahead and I could see that they liked each other. The Group Captain was good with the children and with his guard down I could see a different man. Fiona was watching him.

'If only he had been like that with me.' She said in her husky voice.

While we were walking I voiced the idea I'd been kicking about.

'Fiona, with all the family here for the next three weeks we've got no time alone together. Would you like to come up to London for the New Year with me, if your family could see to Bel? The view of the fireworks from the flats are pretty good.'

She didn't hesitate. 'Yes, that would be grand and we could maybe shoehorn in a couple of small paintings for Frances.' She squeezed my hand and we made plans. I agreed to call round to the annexe to see her the next morning on the pretext of choosing a few paintings to take back to London.

I waved them all off and laughed to myself about the strange rituals we put ourselves through in order to be accepted by another tribe, or clan in their case. Alex hadn't wanted to go back in Fiona's old car, he was just like his dad and Don, he liked metal and lots of knobs and buttons. I was already rehearsing the story for Kate and Mark and of course for Mike and James. I wondered how Mike's Christmas was faring and sent him a text.

"Over for another year, she loves me! Relatives friendly, how's yours been?"

"Survived and bearing up, James coped, bring on the New Year!" Mike responded.

On an impulse I suggested they join us for the fireworks. I was going to have a little celebration.

I was at the annexe by ten in the morning and Fiona was alone. The family had all gone to Plymouth for shopping and entertainment. There was a film for the children that the adults could doze through. I breathed a sigh of relief and pulled Fiona to me as I sat on the edge of the sofa.

'It's good to have you to myself again. Not that your family are awful, but I like it best when it's just us together. I'm not really ready to share you.' I was babbling a bit as I rubbed my hands up and down her thighs and over her bottom. She was wearing an old loose pair of yoga pants and a paint stained green sweatshirt, ready to mess about in the studio.

'Yes, you forget how tiring people can be when you spend so much time on your own.'

I stopped fooling about and looked at her. She was smiling at me but I thought she looked tired.

'Fiona, are you feeling okay? I'm not sure you're entirely over that vomiting bug you had. It knocked you for six didn't it.'

'I think I'm quite well now Daniel, but all the Christmas food hasn't agreed with me. Normally I would eat everything but this year it didn't appeal, and both mum and Elaine are good cooks.'

She was looking thoughtful so I went and made us some weak Darjeeling tea. She'd gone off her usual green tea saying it smelled like compost. I had no idea what compost smelled like but took her word for it. I took it into the studio and we spent a happy couple of hours sorting through her work and trying to work out what Frances would be charging. Fiona had received a healthy payment for the pieces sold. Finally we had four replacements selected and wrapped which I could fit into my car, just, with room for my bag and her weekend bag. We were finishing a bowl of soup with toast when the family came home. Fiona waved through the window and Verity came in, smiling shyly at me and going straight to Fiona. They made quite a picture having a little cuddle while Fiona asked about the shopping and the film, Verity's dark hair against Fiona's dark red head. There was a tap at the door and "call me Don" and Hannah appeared. He was wearing a rather alarming hairy tweedy jacket. I vacated my place so that Hannah could sit. She thanked me.

'I've had a good day Daniel. I managed all the walking though I'm still a bit useless when it comes to stairs, fortunately the cinema had a little lift. I have to move about though or the physiotherapist will know I haven't been doing my exercises.'

I hadn't asked about her limp and her stick, preferring people to tell me, if they must, what was wrong with them. Mark of course had had the full story about the hip replacement. I nodded and made appropriate noises, I didn't know her well enough to actually care very much but she was being friendly. I could hear my own mum saying that manners cost nothing and gained you everything. I suddenly realised I missed my mum.

Fiona was saying something to her father about the wrapped pictures and having to go up to London for New Year. I could see that he was quite animated.

'New Year, in London, it must be quite an event now that the English have almost got the hang of a proper celebration. I hear that the fireworks are something to be seen. Will you be seeing them?'

I couldn't help boasting a bit. 'You can see them easily from my flat overlooking the Thames.'

'We love the fireworks, Hannah and myself. That would be a sight to remember.'

Me and my big mouth. I was looking from Fiona to her parents' expectant faces. Oh crap, I knew what I was going to have to say even though I hated saying it.

'I have a guest room with its own bathroom it you'd like to come up as well.'

So that was that, plans all shot although at least Fiona and I would have a room to retreat into at night and since it was my place I had some territorial control and Don and Hannah would have to be on their best behaviour. We drove off to London the next day which at least gave us two days together before her parents arrived on New Year's Eve. We took the paintings into the gallery which Frances kept open over the main shopping period. There was much kissing and congratulations all round.

Once again I raided the contents of the local deli who were doing a roaring trade, but this time Fiona was with me and there was a reason to shop so that we could feed Mike and James as well as her parents. Mike had taken the news that he would be meeting Fiona for the first time as well as her parents pretty well. His voice was calm over the phone.

'Can't be any weirder than my brother and the folks meeting James for the first time. I've learned to keep the drinks flowing and to develop a deaf side depending on what I don't want to hear. I've developed temporary blindness as well. It's great as a coping strategy.'

I wasn't bothered that the flat had no decorations, Christmas was over and anyway I had the light show to play with in the flat if the fireworks weren't enough. Fiona had different ideas though and picked up a couple of huge poinsettias and a big bunch of twiggy stuff sprayed gold which she put into the large grey pot. It all looked rather good. We made up the spare room and just enjoyed being together, doing ordinary things. By the time the entry box squawked and her parents drove through into the visitor parking bays I was well chilled. I went down and helped with the overnight bags and we had a couple of hours while they freshened up and admired the flat. Just like Fiona previously, Hannah stared at the kitchen in horror.

'Yes, it's awful isn't it.' I said. 'I bought the flat because of the views, and in London I mostly eat out especially because I work odd hours.' I don't know why I was trying to justify the place, but somehow it seemed to keep things sane. 'The Darleystones kitchen will be conventional I promise you.' I added.

"Call me Don" joined us. He'd had an odd experience in the bathroom when he'd managed to turn the light show on when using the shower.

'It was quite entertaining and unusual Daniel, but I suppose it amuses the young and rich.'

I resisted the impulse to tell him that at least I hadn't bought the flat with the Japanese toilet which gave you a rather surprising wash and a blow dry in the nether regions whether you wanted it or not. Better than a bidet was how the estate agent had described it, perfectly seriously.

We made some small talk and Fiona and I set out the buffet. She had managed to work out how the grill operated and heated up some small savoury things. By the time Mike and James arrived the flat smelled welcoming and we had drinks ready and some soft background music on. I introduced them as my partners from the planning den. Don didn't seem concerned that we all hugged each other. It was obviously normal behaviour for people in civvy street doing the sort of work we did. Then I introduced Fiona. She'd put her hair up again and was looking lovely in the soft light in a longish silky dress with a simple gold chain I'd insisted on buying for her the day before. Mike kissed her hand and James said he'd like to use her looks for a 3D animation he was designing. Everyone helped themselves to food and we had a relaxed few hours eating, taking property and learning about the many places Don and Hannah had been posted to. I noticed Fiona was quiet and at first I thought she might be a little bored by her father banging on about his postings when her memories of those times were mostly about boarding school and living with her grandparents. Then I noticed she hadn't drunk her wine or eaten much. I raised my eyebrows and she caught my look, smiled and shook her head slightly.

Finally it was time to put the TV on and see what other countries had provided to mark the beginning of a new year. I got Mike to help me open the champagne and we charged the glasses while people got their coats in readiness for going out onto the balcony. I helped Fiona with her coat and a scarf. Her hands were very cold and I offered her a pair of my gloves but she just stuck her hands in her pockets.

We all went outside and the night was perfect. It was cold and clear and there was just a hint of frost in the air. We could hear the chanting and almost taste the anticipation from the thousands of people gathered for the start of the fireworks. It was wonderful and we ahh'd and ooh'd in proper admiration for the spectacle. I gulped some champagne and grabbed an opened bottle to top up glasses. Don had started singing Auld Lang Syne in a good voice and Hannah joined in. She'd had years of practice and wasn't too bad either. Mike and James were arm in arm and singing dah dah dah quite happily. They were quite pissed. I put an arm round Fiona's shoulders and held her close, it wasn't such a bad night after all. I wanted to clink my glass against hers and kiss her and as the last of the fireworks burst in the sky I loosened my arm and turned to her. She fell against me, went down onto her knees and backwards onto her bottom in a sort of comedy fall and it was only by grabbing her coat that I stopped her head crashing to the floor. I heard the sound of her champagne glass smashing somewhere way below outside the flats.

Hannah gasped and I heard Don say, 'What the hell!'

I crouched down and held Fiona's head off the ground, saying her name. Then I looked up to see Hannah staring at me in confusion and Don staring at Mike and James, who were locked in a deep embrace.

I developed temporary blindness and went deaf on one side. It helped a lot.

To be fair Don was a man well trained to cope in a crisis and he didn't lose his head. Together we lifted Fiona's light weight and by the time we got her indoors to the couch she was regaining consciousness. She was groggy but her parents were a good team and made her stay lying down on her side while I saw Mike and James off the premises.

'Never apologise and never explain, but I'm really sorry if we've fucked up mate.' Mike giggled as he and James wobbled off together into the night.

I went back into the flat. Don fixed me with a stare but I wasn't in the mood for masculine stomping and went straight to Fiona. She was sitting up now.

'Sweetie you're not well.' The words were my mother's when we'd been poorly as children. 'Do I need to take you to hospital?' Not a great idea on New Year's Eve I thought.

Fiona shook her head. 'No Daniel, I'm not ill, there's nothing to worry about.'

'Then what caused you to faint. I realised you weren't eating much and you hardly drink alcohol anyway so what's wrong, do you know?'

'I think I might know what it is.' Hannah was speaking. 'Tell us darling.' She was sitting next to Fiona and she took her hand.

Fiona looked at her mother. 'I think I'm pregnant.'

I waited to hear the proverbial pin drop.

'Well this has been a night I shall never forget.' Don actually started laughing.

The anger and parental confrontation I'd somehow expected never happened. Fiona went to bed and after Hannah had checked that she was physically okay she came back and made us all tea. Don had put the kettle on while I was sitting on the sofa in a state of shock. I realised that Hannah was asking me if I was alright. I sat up and pulled myself together. This was not a time to prevaricate.

'Yes, I'm okay, just a bit stunned. I hadn't a clue.' Even in my shocked state I realised that this probably wasn't what Fiona's parents wanted to hear from the bloke who had got their daughter knocked up.

'We obviously need to talk about it in the morning, as a couple.' I went on, conscious that I was now sounding like a relationships text book. I took a deep breath. 'The thing is, we love each other and I know we'll be able to er, adjust to this. Unexpected event.'

Hannah did a great job clearing away what little was left of the buffet while Don tidied up bottles and glasses. This was a couple who had given many a drinks party during his career. Then they went to bed and left me to myself. I sat back and looked around the flat, it had an atmosphere for a change. There were the plants and the curly gold twigs that Fiona had placed. Her painting was on the wall. The cushion at the end of the couch still bore the indentation of her head. She was in my bedroom pregnant with my child. Her parents hadn't killed me. The shock had melted away and I sat there in a reverie, picturing the future, our future.

A small voice spoke in the quiet room. 'Daniel, are you cross?'

I looked up, Fiona was standing there barefoot in her plain dark blue cotton dressing gown, shivering slightly. I stood up and went to her with my hands held out and she took them in hers.

'Anything but cross. Surprised, a bit scared, but mostly delighted I think.' I had tears in my eyes.

Fiona gazed at me with that searching cool green look I knew so well. She always needed the truth.

'That's it Fiona Rose. That's the truth.' Her hands were cold in mine. 'Back to bed with you madam. You need to rest in your condition.'

At least that got a giggle.

TWENTY FIVE

I helped Don with the bags after breakfast the next morning. Fiona was going back with them and I was staying on in London. I thought I knew what was coming as Don arranged the luggage in the boot and then straightened up, fixing me with his gimlet green stare.

'Daniel I'm not sure if I can actually thank you for this unusual New Year, but Hannah and I had a good talk last night and we want you to know that you both have all our support.'

That wasn't what I had expected and it was a nice way of putting it. He clearly wasn't going to throw his daughter out or thump me. I cleared my throat and wondered what to say, but he continued.

'I love my daughter very much. She doesn't always appreciate that. Hannah says she's coping with feelings of rejection over her school years when I was posted overseas, but you know, we thought we were doing the right thing by giving her stability in one school rather than moving her about. It's hard being a parent, as you might find out.'

I got it immediately. 'Thanks for that er, Don. I fully intend to find out what it's like to be a parent. As I said last night I love Fiona, but at the moment we need to take it one day at a time.'

As we stood there sizing each other up I caught a look in his eye. He spoke again.

'She needs a man she can trust and respect. Perhaps that's your role Daniel. I wish the both of you luck and much happiness.'

Wow this guy was a constant source of surprise to me. We shook hands as though sealing some sort of agreement and went back up to the flat where the women were talking. Fiona was looking better, more relaxed and she'd eaten some breakfast. Whilst Don and Hannah stepped out onto the balcony for a few minutes I took Fiona in my arms.

'I love you Fiona Rose Frazer. Go and see the doctor. And for god's sake use the bloody telephone and call me the minute you need me. I shall certainly be phoning you every day now so bloody get used to it. Do you understand?'

She smiled and nodded. 'Yes Daniel, after all it's not just about me now is it.'

The next few weeks passed in a blur. The game we'd sold in the autumn was so hot it had practically melted the shelves in the shops over Christmas and the business made a mint. Magazines started badgering Mike and me for interviews. It felt a bit strange seeing articles about ourselves but it also made relocating the business somehow easier.

Tom and Elaine said I could store some of my things at their place since they were vacating it again so I was able to move personal stuff down ready to move it across the lane into Rob's house. We had dinner at Orchard Cottage one night and Rob had looked at us in amazement when I said that Fiona was pregnant.

'Blimey, you two don't hang around do you.'

I told him that we hadn't discussed it, but that it had just happened.

'Nobody ever told me about the birds and the bees.' I laughed. I'd discovered there was a bloke thing about proving your potency. It felt good. Woman claimed, child fathered, chest thumping sort of stuff.

'Oh well, new house new baby is how the old saying goes.' Su said. 'I'm really happy for you.'

Rob and Su were quite into family research I'd learned. I mentioned that Liz Bradley was looking into mine. Rob looked at Su who nodded at him.

'Daniel you said your mother's family had been at Darleystones for about two hundred years, is that right?'

I nodded.

'And their family name was Penive?'

Again I nodded.

'Then we're probably related. The first of my Williams ancestors to arrive here from Wales bagged himself a local lovely by the name of Jenifry Penive. Which means you are also related to Su because she and I also share a common ancestor.'

'Yikes is that healthy?' I couldn't help myself.

'Oh we're all far enough removed for it not to matter.' Su said.

'So just how far are we removed Cousin Rob?' I asked. We both grinned.

'Well, we're not close enough to be kissing cousins, but there is a slight similarity in looks, Su thinks.'

Fiona was interested. 'Looking at the two of you standing together I think there might be although Rob has a different nose. Her name was Jenifry did you say Rob, that's unusual.'

'Isn't that where Dr Who comes from?' I was hugely amused.

Rob started laughing. 'You mean Gallifrey. But perhaps Dr Who was originally Cornish!'

'Or the Cornish are from another planet more likely!'

It was Su who replied. 'I think it's Cornish for Guinevere, you know, the King Alfred and Tintagel legends. Or is it Cornish for Winifred. I can't remember.'

'It could be Cornish for cake for all I know.' I laughed but I had an inkling that Fiona was thinking about names for our child. It gave me an odd feeling and I said so.

'Something between the collywobbles and the jitters.' Was how I described it.

Fiona started giggling, saying she'd never heard the term collywobbles.

'Sounds like something you suffer after eating a bad prawn.' Rob said.

'That's exactly right, it's an old name for a tummy upset or so I learned when I was working in the lab. Sorry, I sound like a textbook don't I.' Su said, pulling a face at Rob

It was obviously an old joke between them.

Fiona was on my arm in the church the day Rob and Su got married and straight after Valentine's Day I moved into Rob's place. Thankfully Fiona recovered from the first early weeks of nausea and as my mum would have said, lost her own appetite and found a donkey's. She ate almost all the time and glowed with health and carried on riding Bel even though I said it wasn't fair on Bel to be carrying two people. She didn't take any medication and even if anything had been prescribed she wouldn't have taken it because, as she explained, she was so focussed on the health of the child.

Kate was thrilled that the twins were going to have a cousin.

'Do you know what flavour it is yet?' She asked Fiona one day, making us all laugh.

'No, we've decided to wait and see. But it feels as though it's been playing computer games so I'm thinking it's a boy at the moment.' Fiona said.

I looked at the twins. They were toddling about a bit now and making almost sensible sounding noises. I reckoned they were talking proper Cornish. Mark welcomed me to parenting as he dashed across the room trying not to shout "*Nooo*" as Jake starting pressing buttons on something of Mark's.

'Keeps you fit and alert Daniel. No need to go to the gym. Just get a toddler or two, you can borrow these any time if you want a workout.'

Kate claimed that she had guessed that Fiona was pregnant on Christmas Eve.

'Something about the eyes of a pregnant woman Daniel, the egg whites kind of shine.' Of course Kate would say something like that. But she was a diamond; with the only two other women in Fiona's family who'd had kids either away in Scotland or living abroad it was Kate who stepped in and did all the helpful and reassuring pregnancy talk.

They all came out to Darleystones with me one day. It was looking like a proper house outside and the first fix was just about finished inside. I had promised Fiona there'd be no weird London stuff unless she wanted it, everything would be conventional. Kate viewed a mountain of second hand granite cobbles I'd bought from a reclamation yard near Plymouth.

'Are they for some hard landscraping?' Kate asked, finding a new word to strangle.

'Oh well done Kate.' Mark smiled at her.

I confirmed that they were indeed for landscaping, explaining my plans.

'They'll make a sympathetic surface for driving in and parking.' I said, waving my arms about and visualising the long low building of a double garage incorporating a generous tool store and wood store at either end and with a room in the roof divided into an office and a studio. I could see the north end gable all glassed, with wonderful views to inspire Fiona. It was going to be fantastic and it was time to share all this with her. The cobbles would link the house to the garage area. And I also had plans, which I didn't mention, for a new date stone of our own on the new building.

'It sounds wonderful Daniel, but there's also Bel as well as the baby. We have a lot to discuss.' Fiona said.

I turned to face Fiona and put my arms around her. 'It's all about us Fiona. We'll discuss every step and aspect of it. I can't do any of it without you at my side. I mean that.'

I took her hand and walked with her into the house where I kissed her at the threshold. It was becoming a private little ritual of ours. Kate and Mark had wandered off to see Steve who was upstairs finishing off the wardrobes. He'd put his own little touches to the doors with the router, echoing the shapes made by Rob's metalwork. He had also done some work tidying up the little cupboard in the master bedroom. At my request he had made a little box to fit inside and the centre panel of the hinged lid now held Fiona's lime wood carving. Inside the old shoes nestled in acid free tissue. He had done a lovely job for us and Kate was thrilled, seeing it for the first time.

'Something old, something new…and a silver six pence in her shoe.' Fiona murmured. 'It's an old bridal poem but I can't remember it properly.'

Steve smiled at her. 'I wonder if we'll ever know who this Cinderella was, hiding her shoes in the chimney.'

I wondered the same thing. I was enjoying watching not just Darleystones take shape.   It was going to be an interesting summer.

****

Facing Time

Part Three of
The Lemon Juice Summer

TWENTY SIX

As the Skybus climbed into the clear sky above Perth I settled back in my Business Class seat and stretched. I'd spent a lot of time in the air in my career but in nothing as large or as luxurious as this. I took a quick look around at my neighbouring passengers wondering if I was the only person travelling alone. You couldn't see much the way the individual pods were staggered in their rows, but I knew they were the usual mixture of business folk, already tapping away at their gadgets, couples going home suntanned after a month or more down under visiting their families and then there were travellers like me going somewhere for a special reason.

I closed my eyes. I wasn't tired, I just liked to think with my eyes shut. I'd almost nineteen hours in the air to look forward to and about nine thousand miles to travel, and I was going back in time as well, sixty or so years. I had a mental image of myself moving backwards in a capsule around the earth, faster and faster and getting smaller and smaller to a time when I wasn't sure who I was and I certainly had no idea of what I was going to do with my life.

My first memories played behind my closed eyelids. I was running on the endless beach at Saunton Sands in North Devon, sliding down the huge dunes with my older sister Pamela, getting sand in our clothes, eating ice cream cones and hating the way my dad always used to break the bottom off the cone. He would dig the broken piece into the ice cream and present me with two ice creams to eat, thinking it would amuse me, but I disliked the way the melting ice cream would run out of the bottom of the broken cone and down my arm. I could never eat the bigger cone fast enough to stop it happening. Why on earth had I never said anything I wondered. But you didn't question your parents in those days.

There was a memory of the dogs we had, beautiful little brindled whippets, Cassie and Clip. There were no issues about

260

taking dogs to the beaches in those days. I had loved those dogs, I certainly got more attention and affection from them than I did from my parents.

My parents were long gone now. They'd been good people in their way, struggling as folk did in England after the war and they did their best for us but theirs was not a happy marriage and it affected Pam probably more than it affected me.

Pamela had gone on to teach and like me had used her qualifications to go abroad. Somehow she'd got herself attached to the MoD, after all wherever there were postings overseas there were married quarters and that meant children. It had given her a good life I think, seeing the world and sailing and horse riding a lot in her youth.

"I shall never get married." Pam had confided once. "I love children so I shall teach, but I'm never going to become a domestic drudge to a man I can barely tolerate."

I could still see her passionate face with her blue eyes sparkling defiantly and her auburn hair waving around her shoulders. She'd been an attractive girl and very sociable but had never settled with anyone as far as I knew. And now she was dead.

Extracting a soft drink from the supply provided at my pod I took out my notepad, turning to the page headed Pam. I was the only person using pen and paper apart from someone doing a crossword. As her surviving relative I was going to have to say something meaningful at her funeral and I guessed it was going to be a pretty small affair. Pam had moved back to our old home town of Bristol about five years previously and I knew she'd joined the library and started a book group in the retirement apartments she'd moved into, but I didn't think she'd kept up with many friends from her years abroad. Everyone was, as she once described it, "Distributed around the country and a bit of a faff to keep in touch with." Pam had always lived in the present, never in the past.

The words "a rolling stone gathers no moss" occurred to me and I wrote them down. Would Pam mind being compared to a rolling stone I wondered. I sighed and drank some orange juice. I'd seen plenty of bereavements in my time and often thought that it should be mandatory for people to fill out a form stating their favourite music and poem and what they wanted doing with their body once they had no further use for it. A sort of an addendum to a Will. It would save a lot of trouble and anxiety for the living left behind.

Thank god Nick was in the UK and would be at my side for the funeral. We'd had a good talk on Skype when I'd learned I would be flying to the UK. My son Nick, so like his mother, a warm and friendly guy with her lovely grey eyes and dark hair and a string of broken hearted girlfriends behind him. Nick was on a post graduate course at Bristol, my old university. He'd opted to do a year in the UK and he'd stayed with Pam for several weeks when he'd first arrived. When I told him that his auntie Pam had passed away he was surprised.

'But I only saw her a month ago dad, what happened?'

'A massive stroke. I doubt she'd have known much about it bless her. So I'll be coming straight over to do the honours.'

'Is mum coming as well?' Nick adored his mum.

'No, she's got a schedule she can't break unless it's me that croaks.' I said.

My wife was a well known musician and much in demand for the Winter Season. She had some solo performances that she'd worked hard on and I didn't want her to miss her moments of glory.

We'd caught up on family news and made some tentative arrangements. I needed to be in Bristol for about a week and Nick would be with me at the funeral. He would join me for a break a little later for a week or so while I looked up some old family stuff in Cornwall for his mother. I told Nick to be grateful that Pam had always been a tidy and thoughtful woman and died just before he broke for the holidays. I'd promised him some surfing time down there so he was well pleased, but surprised when I said I'd booked a holiday cottage for a month in a village on Bodmin Moor.

'Dad, can't you read a map, that's miles from the beach.'

'It's where I want to be Nick, I can do a bit of family research there for your mum while you get up at dick o'clock and bugger off to the beach on your own. Besides, this late in the season I was lucky to find anywhere to stay.'

Nick wasn't that worried, but then nothing bothered him much anyway.

The journey was what I'd expected, long and tiring for me although the comforts of Business Class helped a lot. I always felt that sleeping on an aircraft was like coming out of anaesthetic, everything ached including your ears. I telephoned home and left a message that I'd arrived safety and then crashed out for a night in a hotel at Gatwick. The next day I collected my hire car and drove to Bristol where I was staying in a hotel. The Satnav was useful, I hadn't driven in the UK for a couple of decades and everything looked different to me. And so bloody green.

It felt weird going into Pam's flat. It was neat and anonymous and as I'd suspected her personal arrangements were very simple. She'd labelled things in envelopes in her desk, knowing with the foresight of a person who has lived on their own all their life that someone else would have to sort things out one day. The deal was that the flat had to be sold back to the company who owned the retirement complex so I had nothing to do except dispose of her stuff and a local charity had a warehouse which was geared to all that.

Finally all I had left of her were a few photographs, some personal papers and a bit of plain but good quality jewellery. And a pot containing her ashes. I was relieved to find that she'd made her wishes clear. Her earthly remains were to be put into the sea and there was a number to phone for the Maritime Volunteer Service. The guy from the MVS had asked if we wanted a conventional ceremony or something that wasn't religious. Nick and I opted for the non-religious as neither Pam nor us were church goers, so a few days later on a cool day in late June he read John Masefield's poem Sea Fever while we carried out a private little ceremony at sea. It was beautifully done with quiet efficiency and dignity. I was quite moved and even Nick was affected. I'm a methodical man and well used to both welcoming new life and seeing people at the end and I respected the way Pam had organised things, but even I felt saddened with the way a life can be rolled up and put away.

I was in a thoughtful frame of mind then when I left Bristol and headed down through the counties of the South West and into Cornwall. I was a medical student when I'd first done that journey by train, off to do a summer shadowing at a GP practice, a short placement offered by one of the doctors to his old medical school to enable a student to get a little experience.

The doctor had lived in The Manor House, a handsome old place in the centre of the village where he held his surgery. He and his wife had no children of their own and they had put me up in a couple of rooms in the attic, I guess where the maid had once lived. For a very small fee I'd received bed, board and training. It was incredibly generous of them and I wondered if I'd been suitably grateful. Somehow I doubted it.

It had been a hot Cornish summer and I remembered how the house martins used to skim along the quiet road outside shrieking with excitement as they hunted flies from dawn to dusk. There was much more that I remembered about that summer, that bitter sweet summer.

I got to the village just after lunchtime and it was almost how I remembered it, although a bit tidier. Houses had been done up with new windows and looked better cared for and there were a few new properties built where there had once been large productive gardens. I noticed stone troughs and hanging baskets, the telltale signs of gentrification.

The arrangement was to go into the pub, The Wheal, and ask for Sarah. The pub entrance hadn't changed although the interior had and I stood for a moment looking about. The barman appeared and greeted me in a friendly way, apologising saying that I was too late for a proper lunch, but that they could do me a salad with some chips if I was hungry. I accepted and asked if he knew Sarah.

'That's my wife, I reckon you're at the holiday cottage across from the church then.'

As I nodded he went to a door at the back of the bar and yelled her name. Sarah appeared, a curvy little brunette just a little bit annoyed about the way she had been summoned. I waited patiently as she told her husband off. His name was Tim and he was teflon coated where her criticism was concerned. Then she turned to me and took a bunch of keys from her apron pocket.

'Everything is ready for you Dr Milton. There's bread, milk, eggs, tea, coffee and sugar and I've put a home made fruit cake in. You might want to nip up to the farm shop for provisions especially since you're here for a month. I'll come in on Fridays and change the beds and the towels and take any rubbish, but there's a washing machine and all mod cons for you to make yourself at home. There are two of you aren't there. And I'm right here, so ask if you need help with anything. And we don't serve food on Mondays.' It was a well practised speech and she was efficient but bossy. She was looking over my shoulder for the missing second person.

'My son is joining me but he won't be along till next week.' I explained.

'Well, I hope you will like it. It's our first season. I'm quite excited.'

I enjoyed a half of bitter and a decent cold chicken salad with chips. We didn't possess a deep fat fryer at home so the chips were a novelty. It was also a novelty to be eating in the pub, they hadn't served food back then, only packets of crisps.

The place was quiet and I sat looking out of the window at a scene that had been etched on my mind thirty years earlier. There was a tatty village hall with a small flat field to one side, today it had a children's playground in it but back then it had been a place to kick a ball around or have a cricket match. It didn't look as though ball games were played there any more.

Shaking my head in an effort to clear the memories I got up and put my empty plate and glass on the bar.

'Thanks, I appreciated that.'

Tim the barman nodded to me. 'You're welcome.'

He knew a good source of income when he saw one, a lone traveller staying for a month would surely be a regular visitor.

'You've come a long way if your accent is anything to go by.'

I saw no reason not to be polite. 'Yes, I'm British by birth but thirty years in Oz has had an effect on my vowels I think.'

'Well, have a good stay, see you around I expect.'

I was dismissed. I went out to the car and drove the hundred yards to the cottage opposite the church, not needing any directions. I carried my bags inside and unpacked some shopping I'd brought with me. It was a comfortable little place, nicely done out in what my wife would call polite colours and I poked about a bit with that moment of interest you have in a new place noting the well used paperbacks and scruffy board games of a different era. It was odd being alone but I privately acknowledged that coming over to England on my own was, in a funny sort of way, giving me some personal space and time. For years I'd been responsible for other people, as a doctor, a husband and a father so this was an opportunity to get in touch with myself and just have a breather. There was also a piece of unresolved business I wanted to lay to rest if possible.

My wife Marianne had been casting about for things to keep me occupied in the way that a busy woman does. She didn't see my usual habits of swimming and riding as a useful way to spend my retirement, and had all sorts of plans for me including sorting out my man cave stuff and getting more involved in crafts like woodworking. To be fair I had gone along to a local group over the years and done a bit of making and whittling and the company was quite enjoyable, mostly old blokes getting out on their own but they had some skill and talent and better still, good stories to tell. And I enjoyed learning from people who knew how to do things.

With a cup of tea on the little garden table out back I unfolded a map of the South West and focussed on Bodmin Moor, tracing the route to the village of Altarnun with my index finger. Marianne's family had left that place when her own father was a toddler and headed for the new life down under. Although she had never visited England she'd grown up hearing stories of the village and of Cornish folklore. Now that our own kids were making their way in life she'd become curious about her origins and whether there was anything she, or in this case, I, could put together as a family record.

I thought it was a neat idea, these days you could make your own book via the internet, using photographs and a bit of text and it would make good Christmas presents for our two. I think my wife was hoping for grandchildren and this was a way of setting the seed for a new family tree in the mind of our recently married daughter. I sat back and smiled at the thought of anyone telling our daughter what to do. Anna worked in fashion and retail and had very clear ideas of her own. She was a young soul and I always felt she needed to do some living and get experience beyond the latest lipstick colours. But she was clever and determined and would no doubt be successful at whatever she turned her mind to.

I pottered about until bedtime and went up to bed with one of the paperbacks. It was a whodunit, not my usual sort of choice but I like to keep an open mind. I read a couple of pages when the peace and quiet and fresh air coming through the open window knocked me clean out. It was the best sleep I'd had in a week.

In the morning I cooked myself a very good breakfast and ate lots of toast with English marmite before deciding what to do with myself. I wanted to share the trip over to Altarnun with Nick, partly because when you're hunting around gravestones two pairs of eyes are better than one. I'd also got the location of the place where my wife's family had lived and I thought that two guys asking if they could take photographs for the family history book would seem less pervy than one bloke taking snaps.

It was a nice day outside so I decided to go for a walk down memory lane. There was nothing particularly remarkable about the village, it wasn't a tourist place and the people who had lived there when I spent my brief summer at The Manor House had been mostly involved in farming or in small local businesses. In those days it hadn't attracted wealthy city types whose wives were hankering after the elusive country cottage idyll.

The Manor House was just a short distance and I stood in the road gazing at it. Very well cared for, there was a gravelled drive and small lawned turning circle that hadn't been there when I stayed, and it looked at though the little coach house to one side had been turned into a garage with a room above. There was masses of lavender in the old flower beds under the windows and two Lutyens benches and it was so quintessentially modern English that I smiled. There were also a couple of nice cars parked outside so I didn't linger too long.

I walked all the way down one side of the road fascinated by the difference with what I'd become so accustomed to in Australia. The houses here were so small in comparison but I recalled I'd been in several of them that summer, helping to dress a wound or visit someone sick, learning practical stuff about dealing with people that the textbooks and lectures couldn't teach. I could still hear the old doctor saying, "Listen Mr Milton, first listen and then look". He'd constantly repeated that mantra. Listen to what the patient says, listen to their story, listen to the breathing, listen to the patient's voice, is it strong or is it weak? That was the sort of thing that had settled in my mind as I completed my medical training. I knew I didn't want to become a consultant, to be honest I thought that some of them at the hospital had a problem with attitude and arrogance that sat uncomfortably with the Hippocratic Oath. I'd known I wanted to work right out there with people who needed immediate help. These days the opportunities for that sort of work are wider, but when I was first qualified and wanted a fresh new start the Royal Flying Doctor Service in South West Australia offered me everything I needed. It had been wonderful.

Retracing my steps I wandered back along the other side of the road. Only two cars and a van had driven past in thirty minutes. I ignored the church, I have no particular faith and the church hadn't featured in my distant summer so I went along to the pub and stood looking over at the little playground. Making up my mind I walked over the road, unlatched the gate and walked in. There was nobody about as I crossed the empty playground with its brightly coloured swings and seesaw and some odd animal shaped thing designed to encourage children to climb. On the other side of the field there was a stone stile, just as I remembered it. Cornish hedges are all made out of stone. I remembered the advice given to me by the old gardener Dr Webster had employed, always knock the hedge wall with a stick if you're going to climb over because that frightens away the vipers.

Climbing the stile into the next field I noticed there were beasts grazing. Pausing for a moment to check that it was just bullocks and not cows with calves I started to follow a path around the field and up to a little copse at the top. The sun was high and all was quiet with a sort of shimmer in the air, then I had the sense of slipping sideways out of my body and walking alongside a young couple. They were holding hands and talking. He was slim and upright with tawny gold hair shining in the sun. His face was unlined and his eyes were so blue as he looked down at the girl he walked with. She was vibrant, with long streaky toffee blonde hair and beautiful hazel eyes, her bare arms were slightly tanned as were her bare legs and she wore a flower sprigged green and white cotton dress with buttons up the front.

The memory was so strong that I think I gasped. A few bullocks lifted their heads and regarded me indifferently and then returned to their grazing. I proceeded on to the little copse and counted one, two three, four. The fourth tree had smooth bark, oddly bent and sloping by growing on a windy exposed part of the field. I gazed at it for a long while and then put my hand up on to the trunk and caressed a set of initials. JM + TC. Someone had carved a heart at the side. My fingertips touched the scared marks, the initials had healed and spread in the bark over the years but left a clearly visible lighter surface that was easy to read. There was nothing else carved there, no dates, no messages, nothing to indicate that anyone knew what had taken place here. I leaned against the tree and let the memory flood over me, hearing her whispering to me, feeling her softness against me, remembering that explosion of release and love and amazement that anything or anyone could be so beautiful. I murmured her name aloud. Tessa.

It was ages later that I pulled myself together and realised I was focussing on an abandoned drinks can. Slightly annoyed I picked it up, it was desecration of a special place. As I walked slowly back across the field I toyed with the idea of looking for her but then decided that was a stupid idea. I was a happily married old man and a father and it wouldn't be fair. I could see myself now, grey haired and slightly stooping with lines and marks on my face that spoke of a little too much time in the sunshine. There was nothing wrong with memories, they make us who we are and of course everyone remembers their first time. But it was more than that, it wasn't an adolescent fumble behind the chemistry block, it had been an extraordinary joining of two young people who found absolute joy in each other.

Back at the playground I put the can into a waste bin and walked back to the holiday cottage. The church tower, square like most in this part of Cornwall cast a shadow over the road. I remembered commenting on the lack of church spires around here and Tessa had said that the four pinnacled corners were Matthew, Mark, Luke and John all looking over the village. I don't know if she was right, I just remembered the things she used to say. And the way she used to look.

As I reached the cottage gate I saw a horse coming down the road. It was a fine bay mare with classic white socks and a white star on her head moving at a steady swinging pace. A young red haired woman was riding. I noticed she had a light touch and a good seat. I've done a lot of riding and could appreciate the harmony between a sympathetic rider and a happy well schooled horse. She saw me watching and inclined her head rather gracefully. I was charmed, she was a picture and I raised my hand in a salute. I could see that she was very pregnant. I couldn't help myself and called out to her.

'That's a great look the two of you have.'

The horse stopped and they both regarded me with an intelligent gaze.

'Thank you.' The woman had a nice voice, rather husky and with a slight accent. Her dark red hair was in a thick plait over one shoulder.

'My wife rode until two weeks before giving birth to our son. Just a gentle hack but she hated being away from the saddle.'

'I understand how she felt. Bel helps me to be myself and it does us both good to get out onto the moor.' She looked over my head to the cottage and spoke again. 'You are taking a holiday?'

'A trip down memory lane, I'm here with my son, I stayed here one summer a long time ago. A very long time ago.' Why was I telling her this I wondered, perhaps after recent emotions I just wanted to speak to someone.

She looked at me with close attention and nodded. 'A life well lived I think. And your wife, is she no longer with you?'

I was surprised by her directness. 'She's at home, she's a pianist and has concert bookings. She couldn't get away.' I said.

We smiled at each other and the horse nodded her head up and down, huffing a bit through her nostrils. She wanted to move on. I raised my hand in farewell and got the graceful inclination of the head again and watched as they went along and turned into a bumpy unmade track behind a terrace of houses. I made a mental note to find out if there were stables locally, I enjoyed riding. Perhaps I should have asked the red haired lady.

Indoors I made tea and a sandwich and sat outside at the back. Hours had passed, a whole lifetime had passed and I felt tired but somehow grateful. It's funny, I thought as I ate. We think we're in control of our lives and that we make things happen but looking back it seemed that I'd just reacted to chances and opportunities. The only decisions I'd made were to train as a doctor and to go to Australia, everything else had just happened. That made me resolve not to go looking for Tessa. The decisions I'd failed to take as a young man couldn't be laid at the door of whatever woman she'd become now. The past was the past, and better left there.

TWENTY SEVEN

I slept quite late and woke the following morning to texts on my phone. My wife wanted to know what I was up to and if I was okay and I decided it would be best to call her a bit later. There was also one from Nick advising that he'd be travelling down on Friday and that I should get the bacon and the tinnies in. He liked a beer or a lager and loved bacon sandwiches. I think he lived on them.

After busying myself with the domestics I walked out and found the farm shop. I'd driven past it the other day, surprised to see it because I recalled a run down little garage on that spot when I was first in the village. The shop was quite big and very well stocked and the staff were friendly. I bought more than I had planned to and struggled back to the cottage. I wasn't used to carrying shopping very far.

I checked the clock and UK versus Oz times, they were several hours ahead at home and I reckoned it would be evening there so I should be able to get Marianne if I rang now. She answered on the third ring.

'Marianne Milton.'

'Hey love it's me, Josh.' I could picture her sitting in the den in her favourite chair with her legs tucked up at one side.

'Hey stranger, say something nice, I'm feeling a bit lonely tonight and it's frighteningly quiet around here without you.'

'I miss you. Are you in the den? I can see you sitting there. It's a nice picture in my head. How's practice going?'

We chatted as people do who've been together a long time and still like each other an awful lot. She established that I was okay and that Nick was joining me the following day and that I had plans in place for visiting Altarnun. I asked if Anna had been in touch and was glad to hear that she had, and that she'd wished her mum good luck and to break a leg at Saturday night's performance.

'She won't be there?' I asked.

'No, she's flying to Sydney to put on a fashion show. Well, she's taking part but in her mind she's in charge and it can't possibly happen without her.'

I laughed. 'Our girl will go far that's for sure. Marianne, have you found a little gift I left for you?' Whenever I went away for more than a few nights I always left her something. This time it was a box of chocolates I'd put in the fruit bowl.

'I did you naughty boy, how will I fit into my dress on Saturday night?'

I could tell she was pleased though by the sound of her voice. She'd always kept herself trim and fit. Her beach body she called it. We were an active family.

'There might be something else but it's calorie free so it won't be in the kitchen. You'll have to check the bedroom. That's the only clue you're getting.' I had got her a little bottle of rather expensive perfume, one she liked and I'd hidden it in her wardrobe together with a card.

'I think I found that too. It's really lovely. Did you find mine Josh?'

'I did. Thank you.' There had been a couple of pairs of rather jazzy new socks in my case, practical if a little mundane, but what did a guy want at my time of life. The best thing was to be cared about and needed sometimes.

We talked a bit more and I told her that I'd be thinking about her sometime on Saturday.

'I shall check the reviews online. But I know you're going to do well Marianne.'

It was good hearing her voice. I told her that I loved her and missed her. It was true.

I had to find a supermarket selling petrol so that I could fill up the car. Nick was driving down in his battered student-mobile but if we were going out I'd rather use the cleaner and more comfortable hire car. I backed out of the parking space and drove off in the direction of Liskeard, finding everything I needed in that handsome little town. Then, as it was a nice afternoon I decided to explore a bit and drive to the coast. After checking the road map and then the OS map I headed east and ended up at Rame Head which had great views but I couldn't see where Nick could get any surfing. I spent an hour or so wending my way down the coast towards Looe and thanked my lucky stars it wasn't the school holidays because the roads were frightening to a guy used to lots of space. I found myself holding my breath as oncoming traffic negotiated the narrow lanes with me. Several times I thought the hire car was going to get badly scratched and eventually at the point of screaming in terror I called it a day and found a decent road back to Liskeard and to the village.

My head was aching and I felt tired so I made a big sandwich and ate a hunk of the rather good fruit cake Sarah had left me and hit the sack early. I needed to be ready for an active few days with Nick.

Nick arrived in time for lunch and brought the sun with him. He was always tanned and while he lost no time in changing into shorts and flip-flops I grilled bacon and buttered bread. We sat in the sunny back garden and ate appreciatively, watching a robin taking an enthusiastic bath in an old stone trough. Nick had a lager and I had a cup of tea. I really like what they call builder's tea, it's refreshing and satisfying and dances on the tongue when matched with salty bacon and fresh crusty brown bread. I threw some crumbs to the robin who was keeping a close eye on us.

'One thing the Brits can really do dad is bacon. What did you miss most when you emigrated?'

I thought for moment. 'Probably sweetbreads and brisket I think.'

Nick thought for a second and snorted with laughter. The benefit of having a smart son with a doctor for a father was that he knew that I was referring to the thymus gland of an animal and a rather gristly thing my mother used to keep between two plates with a house brick on the top and served sliced in gravy made from a little brown cube. I hated it. We used to play these silly games as family. Marianne was a good cook and would serve up something delicious and imaginative and the kids would try to guess the ingredients. It used to get quite daft and I smiled, remembering the laughter.

'Seriously, didn't people used to eat sweetbreads like two centuries or so ago?' Nick spoke with a mouthful of sandwich.

'Seriously yes, and not so long ago. But I think that when the hamburger was invented people found that they preferred those. No accounting for taste really is there.'

We fooled about like this for a while. I love Nick's company and I think he was born laughing although Marianne always said she didn't remember that. Nick slapped some sunscreen on and thoughtfully dabbed a bit on my nose and the tops of my ears.

'You get an okay colour dad but it takes you a while.' He was thoughtful. 'I'm glad I've got mum's colouring, it'll be interesting to find out what her folks place was like tomorrow. But I've never asked, where did your guys come from?'

Nick had never met my parents. By the time I'd settled down with an Australian wife my own parents were dead. With both Pam and I living abroad and without family closeness they just kind of gave up and stopped living.

'My dad's people were originally from Ireland, hence my gilded colouring in my youth.' I answered him.

'Yeah, ginger,' Nick sniggered. 'So how come we're not called O'Milton.'

I ignored him. 'Mum's surname was Davies so I guess her folk were Welsh originally, she grew up in Monmouthshire. Her dad, your grandad, ran a hardware shop in Monmouth.'

'I've been through there, it's very pretty, very rural.' Nick opened another can.

I was quiet, wondering if my son was going to settle in England. I was surprised at the pang it gave me, thinking of him all those thousands of miles away from us but he was his own man and had to make his choices. At least my little family loved each other.

'So I'm a combination of Cornish, Irish and Welsh?' Nick was still thinking about family origins.

'Yep. Celtic right through I suppose.' I said.

'Wow. I might do one of those DNA tests. Could be interesting.'

'Maybe.' I said. 'But I reckon you're mostly made out of bacon and beer.'

Nick made as though to throw his drink at my head.

We caught the local news on TV and there was a useful weather report at the end giving surfing conditions and a few place names. Nick, it turned out, had already done his research and established that he should be heading for the North coast. I'd been driving along the South East coast which was very pretty and great for walking but not as good for surfing.

I'd decided we should eat at the pub that night and already had a reservation so we splashed our faces and dressed and strolled over. It was quite busy and there was a nice smell of good cooking in the air as we went in. Tim acknowledged me and nodded at Nick and a dark haired young waitress showed us to a small table in a corner.

'Quite the local dad, they know you already.' Nick was looking over at the specials board.

'I think he's my landlord actually. And your tidy bed is thanks to his wife not me.'

We chose our food and while Nick got the drinks in I looked around. I'd drunk in here regularly when I'd stayed in the village that summer. In those days it had smelled of cigarettes and beer, damp dogs, old men's jackets and young men's aftershave. We'd been laughed at for our long hair and for wearing coloured shirts and jeans. Now almost everyone was wearing jeans and looked pretty smart. Nick came back to the table and put our drinks down.

'Blimey dad there are some lookers in here tonight. I like redheads and a dirty blonde. Were they always like that round here?'

Nick knew I'd spent a summer working in this part of Cornwall, but his attention was on a stunning girl with long platinum blonde hair. She was clearly taken, judging by the very fit looking guy standing with her, that and the wedding band on her finger. I watched Nick watching her and saw myself in this very place, mesmerised by a streaky blonde beauty pulling pints behind the bar. Absently I took a pull at my beer and it went down the wrong way, causing mild consternation for a few moments.

'No worries everyone.' Nick had grabbed me a few paper napkins and was patting me dry. 'Dad thought he might like to inhale his beer instead of swallow it.'

There was some laughter and a few interested looks in our direction, probably due to Nick's accent. Nick was handsome young man, I noticed the waitress checking him out from her station by the kitchen door. I also noticed that Nick had noticed her.

'Do you mind sitting with an old fart who has spluttered his beer down his shirt and looks as though he's wet himself or am I cramping your style?' I asked him, wheezing a bit.

'Oh you're still good looking enough to pull dad.'

I wasn't really in the mood, I never had been the sort of charmer my son clearly was.

The food arrived and it was good, with plenty of vegetables nicely cooked. We talked a bit about his course as we ate. He was studying maxillofacial surgery. He'd originally studied in dentistry but he was becoming very interested in helping victims of illness or accident that had affected or damaged facial bones. He talked a bit about the research and developments into 3D tissue printing. It was fascinating stuff. Under the banter and the good looks and the surfing dude attitude there was a very clever, very kind man and I was sometimes in awe of him. I asked him briefly about his exams and decided I should cut him some slack because of course he'd recently sat some and was waiting for the results. That's the thing with the medical professions, it takes forever to qualify and then you never stop having to learn new stuff.

We cleared our plates and decided to indulge in a pudding. While Nick went off to the gents I glanced through the menu and then turned slightly in my chair to look up to the specials board just in case anything else was listed. There was a grey haired rather handsome lady at the bar waiting for her drink and she was looking right at me. Our gaze locked for a moment but I had no idea who she was and she broke eye contact. When I looked again she'd gone and was sitting with a group of people which included the young woman with the silver hair. I glanced at her a couple of times but gave up, I guessed she was older than me, small and slim and a bit county set in her get up. She could certainly have been around when I was first here, but I didn't remember her.

Nick and I made our choices, both avoiding cream, and ate far too much. My belt was tight against my belly and I groaned as I paid the bill. I couldn't keep this level of calorie intake up for a week that was for sure.

TWENTY EIGHT

The next day we made an early start to Altarnun, negotiating our way over the busy A30 and into the narrow back lanes of time gone by. It was gorgeous, there were a few new houses amongst the old but it was all so well kept and well presented that I was enchanted. Nick laughed a bit at the signpost names like Camelford and Polyphant, imagining a strange animal until I reminded him that back home we had some pretty peculiar names like Yangebup, Coogee and Beeliar although our home was in Dalkeith.

I parked up in a turning directly below the church and we got out to hear the sound of fast running water. I walked over to the lovely two arched bridge and leaned over. The water was low and noisy as it rushed on its way. A fat blackbird and a robin were scratching about by the water's edge. Nick joined me and we leant on the wall for a bit, the water was too shallow and too rocky for pooh sticks. We strolled round to a little sort of meadow where some thoughtful persons had placed a couple of benches and picnic tables. They were all deserted, probably because there wasn't a pub or a tea room there. I stopped to admire a little sundial with zodiac symbols round the edge and noticed a plaque in the ground where the local Brownies group had placed a time capsule to be opened in the year 2100. There was a sense of time passing and time still to come and I waited on a bench for a moment while Nick walked round the meadow. A black cat joined me and we sat in mutual contemplation until he joined us.

'I'm not feeling any ancestral connection yet dad. So what is it exactly that mum wants us to do here?' Nick asked.

'She'd like some up to date photographs of the area for her family history album. Her dad's family left here when he was just two years old but she remembers her grandparents talking about it and has done a fair bit of family research via the ancestry websites, so she has names but very few pictures.' I explained.

'So our task is to take a few photos here, but mostly of you since you carry her family genes.'

'Darn it, I forgot to bring my dressing up box. D'you think I could find a funny hat to wear and piece of straw to chew?' Nick was smiling.

We had a lot of work to do. My wife's family had lived somewhere between Altarnun and Fivelanes where cattle fairs were held, stage coaches had once stopped and John Wesley had preached. She knew her dad had been christened in Altarnun church and she had a feeling she might have an ancestor buried there so it was our job to look around and find things, if things were to be found.

As we walked towards the church Nick's attention was caught by some marks on a top stone of the wall above the river. Someone must have repaired the wall and replaced the stone the wrong way round because the words and dates were all upside down. We made out two dates, 1901 and 1906, but nothing else significant. It gave Nick a shiver though.

'One of my ancestors might have scratched that date while he was waiting for a girl.'

'Your ancestors would have been waiting in the local tavern if they were anything like you mate.' I smiled at him though, he was getting the vibes.

We spent ages in the little churchyard. I was entranced by the quality of the mid nineteenth century carvings on the gravestones. I smiled when I saw someone had a middle name of Mutton, and wondered about another stone which recorded the burial place of a faithful servant of fifty years. Neither of us spotted any relatives. Inside the church was still and quiet, with a lovely ceiling. I photographed the old Norman font where you could still see traces of the colours it had been painted with centuries ago. We were both amazed by the pew ends, all carved nearly five hundred years ago from oak, they showed people, birds, fish and dragons. I bought a little booklet to study later and then we left for a walk though the village.

At the church gate I stopped. A red haired woman was getting out of an old car, it was the lady on the horse I'd spoken to in the village a few days earlier.

'Hello, we meet again. Lovely day.' I greeted her.

She regarded me for a few moments with her fine green eyes and then smiled warmly.

'Then there must be some meaning or significance to our meeting at this time.' She stepped forward and held out her hand to me. 'I'm Fiona Rose Frazer.'

I was mystified by what she'd said but I took her hand anyway and introduced myself. 'And this is my son Nick.'

Nick beamed down at her. 'We're here doing some family research Fiona.'

His Australian accent was quite strong. It made her smile again.

'I know a few people locally who are doing that, it's very popular.' She said. 'Are you both Australian?'

'Nick is, but I'm only Australian by marriage.' I told her.

'Would you mind taking a photograph of me and dad with the church behind us, it's for mum you see. If you can do it on my phone I'll send it to her so she can see what the doctor and the dentist are doing in their spare time. Not playing golf or surfing that is.'

Nick spoke with disarming honesty and took his phone out and set it up but I felt like a tourist. She considered him quietly and then looked at me. I liked the quality of stillness about her, it was quite rare.

'Josh and Nick.' She took Nick's phone but looked around us and then at us. 'I think you should stand just over there, I need to be able to include the background and get some context. And relax, talk to each other for a moment and don't look at me.'

She continued giving us simple instructions and I realised we were in the hands of an accomplished professional as she took photographs.

'I'm not used to this instrument but if you have a camera with you I could probably do better.' She said after using the phone.

I handed her my camera and she clicked away, making us move a little, zooming in and out, taking shots from a few different angles. I was fascinated simply watching her. She handed the camera back to me.

'I've done my best Josh, I'm not terribly supple at the moment as you can see or I would have knelt down to get a better effect.'

I thanked her. 'I'm sure you've done a great job, you can certainly handle a camera Fiona, is that your profession?'

'I am an artist and a teacher, soon to become a mother for the first time.' Her voice was husky.

'Pretty soon I'd say if my medical experience is anything to go by.' I replied.

'Then you are the doctor and not the dentist.'

'And you are Scottish and not a local.' I said.

'Touché'. She had a lovely laugh. 'Now I shall go and study some carving, I have ideas for something I am making for the child's new bedroom. I hope your research goes well, Josh and Nick.' She inclined her head and walked carefully up the steps towards the church.

Nick watched her go and was silent until she was out of earshot. 'Wow. What an amazing woman. I can see her mounted on a horse wearing a breastplate and wielding a sword. She's magnificent.'

I nearly said that he'd been reading too many comics but refrained, he'd got a point, she was an attractive girl.

We walked up and down the short street admiring the cottages for a little while and guessing the original uses of some of the old outbuildings, then considered the narrow road ahead of us leading to the next settlement of Fivelanes. Although it was only a short distance there were no safe places to walk and the locals drove like lunatics so we went back to the car and I drove, very slowly, while Nick looked to see if he could spot what Marianne had described we should be looking for. Eventually I parked at

Fivelanes near the pub and we walked back a bit, distracted by the noise of cars on the A30 which was concealed by hedging.

'It would have been easier using Google earth.' Nick commented. 'Either mum's sense of direction is up the creek or the place has been pulled down with that road development.'

A woman with a dog on a lead, a retriever with a plumy tail, was walking towards us.

'Are you needing directions?' She said as soon as she got close enough.

I explained what we were doing and asked her if she knew of a place called Rosemary Cottage once lived in by a man called John Henry.

'Oh yes the cottage is still there but I've never heard of the other name. It's on the other side of the road set back a little. I know the couple who live there, they're friends of mine, shall we go and see if they are in?' She had a no nonsense attitude and we obediently followed her. A few minutes later we were standing outside a long white painted cottage, set quite well back down a narrow drive and sideways on to the road behind a hedge so it was hard to spot from a passing car. We were introduced to the owners and our quest explained, upon which the owners, who we now knew to be Jeremy and Kath, invited us in like old friends. The lady with the dog didn't hang about but left to continue her walk.

The owners told us they were retired teachers and that they were both very interested in family research. Nick lost no time in telling them that he was new to the game but that he had genuine Celtic ancestry.

'I was thinking about it last night dad, how the Celts, that is the Irish, Welsh, Scots and Cornish have all been really good at making new lives abroad.'

'And the English only went abroad if they were deported or if there was an opportunity to colonise and exploit.' Jeremy responded.

I told them what little I knew about my wife's family background. In return they told us that the cottage was once several simple dwellings and had been lived in by agricultural labourers and a blacksmith's family. Jeremy found some old photographs for us to look at which had been left behind by the previous owner and Kath provided us all with tea and a freshly baked lemon sponge cake.

Later on we poked around the outside of the house and Kath said she thought Marianne's family would have lived in the part of the cottage at the far end because there were some useful old granite outbuildings, one of which had definitely been a small stable. Nick and I stood there and sniffed deeply but there was no smell to suggest smithing and no signs of a forge. Jeremy said that previous owners had demolished and rebuilt part of the outbuilding when they had turned it into a garage.

'People didn't used to be so bothered about keeping any past identity. There's a lot more sympathy now and the planners are interested in what sort of building materials are used.' He was looking at a red brick wall with some distaste. 'Look at that, they took an original granite wall down and replaced it with that.'

'And used the spare granite to build a fake well in the garden.' Kath added.

I took a few photographs anyway and suggested I should send them copies but they declined my offer.

'But I might be a burglar prospecting the place and noting where the family silver is.' I said.

There was much laughter and Jeremy said that if I spotted any silver would I please let him know because on a teacher's pension he could do with something to sell. We talked history and Kath returned to the fact that Marianne's great-grandfather had worked as a farrier in the village. She thought it was tragic that he'd gone off to war with the lads from the village and never come back to his young family.

'However did they cope in those days?' Nick was thoughtful.

'Extended families, parish relief, the Workhouse. Children were taken into care, told they were orphans and sent abroad to places like Canada and Australia. Social history tells us some frightening tales. They certainly weren't the good old days.' Jeremy said.

'I'm going to tell you something now,' Kath said, 'but please don't laugh. When I'm out in the garden, on my knees weeding, I often smell what I would describe as horse liniment. At first I thought it was a plant with an odd medicinal smell and I spent ages rubbing leaves between my fingers and sniffing. But eventually I decided I was being kept company by a ghost. After hearing your story about your wife's ancestor who worked with horses and didn't come back from the great war I wonder if it's him in my garden.'

I didn't laugh. 'It's a nice story. People used to self medicate, if it was good enough for a precious animal then it was good enough for an aching man. I've come across it time and time again in the outback in my early days with the RFDS.'

'And they often made their own recipes which were kept secret from competitors.' Kath replied. 'I think I might have something your wife would like.'

She left the room for a minute and came back with a small horseshoe.

'We found this in the outbuildings when we moved in. It had been placed high up on a rafter out of sight and we found it when were exploring with a view to converting the building. Perhaps your wife's ancestor made this. Perhaps her family put it there before they left. She should have it for luck.'

I was really touched by the gesture. People round here were so friendly. Jeremy meanwhile had selected some of the old photos we'd been looking at and scanned them onto a couple of pages. He handed me an A4 envelope.

'Take these as well, it might be nice for her to see them. I've written our names and email on the envelope. If we can help please get in touch.'

I realised we'd taken up a couple of hours of their time so I eased the meeting to an end and thanked them for their extraordinary hospitality. I was smiling as we walked back to the car.

'Well that's something to show your mum and it's been fun.' I said as I clicked the seatbelt on.

Nick was busy sending Marianne an email with a photo of us outside the church.

'I don't think she'll be disappointed with today when she sees what you've got. I'm just sending her a good luck note for tonight.'

Before we spent the evening playing a board game I made sure I sent her one as well.

The next day was glorious so we decided to go to the North coast early and find a beach in time for high tide. Because all Nick's surfing paraphernalia was in the student-mobile I even agreed to let Nick drive me though it meant I had to map read because the car didn't have Satnav. He'd chosen to go to Porthtowan and it was a great choice. We found a carpark with satisfactory facilities and the beach was good and clean. Nick surfed and I swam, we both love the water. It was a day out without a care in the world for either of us, just the sensations of warm sun, cool sea, the taste of salt and the tingle of muscles after a good workout. We found a place to eat and enjoyed the freshest ever fish and chips and drank tea. Afterwards I dozed in the sun and Nick went back to the water, I could see him making friends, he had that easy ability with people. When we packed up Nick asked if I'd mind him coming back the following day. He wanted to surf with his new friends and I said I didn't mind at all, one day in a cool sea was enough for me.

Back at the cottage we showered off and changed and I made us both a bacon salad sandwich before we strolled over to the pub for a convivial pint. The place wasn't very busy but there were a couple of smart looking blokes chatting to the landlord. Tim greeted me pleasantly.

'Are you having a good time Dr Milton?' He nodded at Nick.

'Sun, sand, sea and surfing,' Nick replied. 'What more can a man want.'

One of the blokes was looking at Nick appraisingly. 'All those words beginning with "s" makes me ask if you play skittles? Tim's got an alley in the back room and we were hoping to have a game but none of the regulars are around.'

'That's because it's Sunday night Graham and they all go back to work tomorrow, that or they've all got their barbecues out.' Tim said.

'We'd have a game wouldn't we dad?' Nick was always friendly.

'Sure why not?' I'd played there before in the distant past but I didn't let on.

'Ooh good, I'm Graham, this is my partner Oliver.' He looked at me enquiringly.

'I'm Josh Milton, Nick's dad.' I said.

He raised his eyebrows but the significance was lost on me. We took our drinks into the back and Graham busied himself switching lights on and getting everything organised. He clearly knew what he was doing and where everything was and moved about quickly and efficiently, setting up the nine pins at the end of the alley. Nick kindly got another round of drinks lined up which I paid for and then we agreed on a best of five games. Graham slaughtered us in the first two rounds although we fought back once we realised how serious he was. Nick was pretty competitive anyway. They were nice guys, Graham was funny with black twinkling eyes, he moved lightly and gracefully. We won a round.

It was my turn. 'Okay the holiday cottage versus the locals.' I took aim and bowled. It was a good shot, skittles everywhere.

'Awesome dad! And again, knock 'em dead.' Nick was encouraging.

We won the next round so it was a dead heat, two all.

'Will we humble village folk sleep unvanquished at The Manor House tonight?' It was Oliver speaking as he pretended to polish the old wooden ball and blew it a kiss. His first roll resulted in a full strike. We knew we were going to be beaten but did our best.

Oliver insisted on buying us another drink since they were, as he put it, gracious winners and I accepted a half pint. Nick said they owed us anyway since they were used to the game and we weren't. I was pretty relaxed and in a good mood.

'Speak for yourself Nick, I've played this game before, in this very room, long before you were even thought of.'

The guys were immediately interested as they ushered us over to their favourite table.

'So Josh, did you live round here, you said you'd played here before, when was that?' Graham was looking at me attentively, clearly very curious.

I explained, briefly, that I'd been a medical student and spent a summer in the village before going back to Bristol and then eventually moving to Australia. They both seemed very quiet and I thought that I might be boring them.

'You mentioned The Manor House while we were playing.' I looked at Oliver and he nodded. 'I lived in the attic there for twelve weeks, two rooms to myself and the use of the bathroom on a Sunday, so I had a bath once a week whether I needed it or not.'

Oliver and Graham exchanged a look.

Nick pulled a face. 'Gross.'

Graham sat forward, his attention focussed on me. 'Oh then you must come over and have a look round, we've changed it a lot since we bought it fourteen years ago, there are three bathrooms now plus an extra loo and shower downstairs. I use the shower for the dogs.'

'We had all the deeds out fairly recently for someone's family history research. Who owned it when you were here?' Oliver asked.

Graham answered before I could. 'It was a doctor, I remember that because being a nurse myself I was interested that there were medical vibes in the old place.'

'They'll have been good vibes then,' I said. 'It was Dr Webster, he had his surgery at the front and a little pharmacy in the room behind that. He was a kind and considerate man and his wife was charming in spite of her antiquated views on personal hygiene.' I took a pull on my half pint. 'When did he sell it to you?'

'Oh someone else had it between the doctor and us.' Graham was thoughtful. 'I remember we had to get rid of a vile yellow bathroom suite and a lot of brown and cream paint and some really horrible wallpaper. Oliver's an artist so he knows a thing or two about colour.'

I told them I'd met another artist, the red haired lady, Fiona.

'Oh the fair Fiona, we know her.' Oliver said. 'I gather she's had some success in a London gallery recently.   She teaches locally, or did, I think she's quit with it being nearly the end of term and her baby due very soon.'

'And not married,' Graham said. 'Not that it matters a jot these days. And her chap is very much in the picture.'

I wasn't one for gossip, especially about people I didn't know, and we'd had a long day. I explained that Nick was off early to surf again the next day and that I was ready for the sack.   I thanked them for an enjoyable evening.

'How long have you got here Josh? We'd really like to show you over the house for old times sake. Can you come over for lunch, say twelve thirty on Wednesday?' Graham asked.

I really fancied a look at the house and said so.   'And lunch would be great if it's not too much trouble.'

Oliver wrote their phone number on a beermat and gave it to me. 'Let us know if there's a problem.'

In the morning Nick was gone before I woke up.   I had a feeling I wouldn't be seeing him until bedtime so I had to decide what to do with myself. Eventually I made up my mind to drive down to Truro and explore a bit.   It was both Marianne's and Anna's birthdays in October and I thought I might find some small gifts there.   I'd visited Truro once before in that long ago summer and remembered a handsome town.   It didn't disappoint. I strolled about fascinated by the granite pavements and the rainwater gullies around the old central square.   There were some smart shops, a good bookshop and decent places to eat so I kept myself busy and happily occupied for most of the day. After finding a couple of suitably English presents I even treated myself to a new shirt before stocking up on groceries from Marks and Spencer and driving back towards Liskeard on the A30.

Deliberately turning off at Jamaica Inn I drove several miles over a narrow back road across the moor.   It was ancient land, damp looking and a bit scrubby but people had been making a living from it for a long time.   There were plenty of sheep with half grown lambs, some stocky Belted Galloway cattle and a few ponies about.   It was all very picturesque.

There was no traffic so I drove slowly with the window down, looking about and trying to remember where Tessa had lived with her father.   There was a new looking sign to Moorstones Farm and a pretty cottage almost at the side of the road.   I recognised the house name, Orchard Cottage, and felt my breath catch in my throat.   Stopping briefly and leaning forward I saw there was window open upstairs.   I reversed a bit to get a better view and could see the edge of some scaffolding at the back, a small extension was being put on.   I guessed that like The Manor House it had been sold long ago and that this was the latest change.   I listened, it was all quiet.   With a sigh I put the car into gear and drove on.

After negotiating the road over the top of the moor beyond the tiny hamlet of Minions I stopped in a free car park and sat in the car looking towards Dartmoor.   It was a stunning view and I had once walked up here hand in hand with a wonderful girl.   What would my life have been like if I'd stayed in England, I asked myself.   Would I have married Tessa and been a country GP in the

South West? Would I have swum in a cold English sea and gone riding on the moor? Would I have had children with different names? They were stupid questions. I'd had a great life with fantastic opportunities, married a lovely and talented woman and got two lovely kids. I didn't feel I'd missed out on anything, I'd been so bloody lucky, so why did I carry this odd hard little wound in my heart. I remembered telling my kids not to pick at a scab because the wound wouldn't get better. I started the car and slowly eased out of the rutted stoney carpark. Time to take your own advice old man, I told myself.

I took myself back to the holiday cottage and sorted out the domestics. Nick was here until Friday and then he was joining some friends in Snowdonia in North Wales. Once he'd gone I had a week left on my own. I was beginning to wonder what the hell I was going to do with myself. I'd given Nick all the necessary legal powers to sign documents at the solicitors on my behalf once Pam's place had sold, so there was no need for me to go back to Bristol. I picked up the beermat and checked the number, then dialled The Manor House.

'Wednesday would be great for me if that's okay, but I can't confirm whether my son will be with me.' I told Oliver. 'He's found some surfing friends.'

I was told it wasn't a problem. 'We'll be having another friend in for lunch and it's just as easy for Graham to cook for five as it is for four. I'm looking forward to hearing your stories about the attic and the village, so will our friend, she's lived here all her life.'

As I'd expected Nick had got back late and slept late the following day. The weather was continuing fine and sunny so I worked out how to use the washing machine and then went into the back garden with a book and a pot of tea once I'd had my breakfast. After a while the book didn't appeal so I got my phone and composed an email to Marianne. Her first recital of the season had gone very well and she'd got good reviews because I'd checked the Perth newspapers online. The State Theatre Centre was holding a Beethoven season and presenting a selection of sonatas with guest performers. Marianne was up there with some pretty famous names from Europe and America and I was proud of her.

There was still no sign of Nick, even the washing machine whining on the spin cycle hadn't woken him. I made more tea and took a mug up to him. He grunted when I opened the door.

'Don't expect this service too often mate, but I think you should be showing a leg now. It's nearly lunchtime.' I pulled the curtains open and left him to it.

He appeared after I'd pegged the washing out and looked around in a slightly bemused state, holding his empty mug. 'Any more tea?'

I pointed to the teapot on the garden table. 'Hard night?' I asked him. 'Were you on the sauce Nick?' I hoped not since he was driving.

'Nope. I stayed on the soft stuff. It was a hard day's surfing, those guys were dead keen, they're in training for some championship and taught me a thing or two even though I've been at it for years.'

He poured himself another mug of tea and offered me one. I shook my head.

'They invited me back to their holiday cottage and we put a barbecue on. Just blokes but it was good fun. Every part of me aches today. In a good way.' He rubbed one of his shoulders. 'I need to get my kit out and swill the salt off.'

While Nick busied himself washing the salt off his stuff at an outside tap I picked the book up again, it was tedious so I went inside and put it back. Nick hadn't eaten so I contemplated the stores and thought about lunch, settling on samosas, humous and a bag of ready made salad with some garlic bread that just needed heating. I added some cherry tomatoes and there was cheese and fruit as well so I made us a decent spread which was well received by Nick.

'Thanks dad, mum would be impressed. I know I am.'

'Thank the boffins that made it, I just assembled it.'

'Yeah but with such panache dad. You're a culinary diva.'

As usual we joked and laughed while we ate outside.

'D'you miss living in England? I mean, with weather like this and the food and the people, it's pretty decent all round.' Nick always saw the rosy side of life.

'To be honest I'm not sure I can answer that. I didn't have a particularly happy home life and Australia provided me with a life and a marriage that's been amazing. I love the place. And samosas and humous weren't available here when I was in my twenties.'

'Did they still have rationing then?'

I looked at my son, he wasn't joking. 'Son, you're a decade out, what did they teach you at school?'

'Can't remember, I'm a sciences man, history and the arts never interested me.'

I smiled to myself, Nick was a more rounded man than he was letting on. You don't grow up with a brilliant pianist as a mother and not learn a thing or two about the arts.

Nick had a thought. 'We've looked up mum's ancestral pile, do you want to revisit where you grew up.'

I shuddered, the idea didn't appeal. 'No, thanks for the offer, but it's a no to that.'

After our leisurely lunch I decided to go for a stroll while Nick rested his aching muscles on a sun lounger. I put my camera in my pocket to give me something to do and mooched off around the village. I didn't want to go to the copse again, the memories were too strong and I'd take a few pictures at The Manor House tomorrow. I walked up to the pub and took a few photos of the front and the pub sign and then walked up one side of the road and back, feeling a bit aimless. There were cottages I remembered going in when I was learning how to visit the sick and infirm. One of them had been on the little track where Fiona had ridden and I wondered if she lived in it, so I walked up.

The track was behind a terrace of old houses, miners cottages in the past I suspected. Funny how I didn't remember learning about the mining history when I was here, but Dr Webster must have talked about it as he took me round on his house visits. At the end of the terrace a superb car was parked. Nick would call it a muscle car and I was pretty sure he would indulge that passion once he started earning. The track ended at gates into a private driveway and I thought I could smell horse. I stood there for a moment when a husky voice called my name. Fiona was coming out of the place where the swanky car was parked.

'Hello again Josh. Did you find what you were searching for at the altar of Nonna?'

I knew from reading the little booklet I'd bought that she was referring to the saint the church at Altarnun was named for.

'Not really, she kept her secrets although I did photograph the font my wife's family were baptised in. And we did find the old family house which the current owners let us look at. They were very helpful.'

Fiona seemed interested and she invited me take a look at some drawings she'd done of the font.

'They're in my studio at the back of the annexe just up here.'

As we walked up the private drive she explained that this was her brother's house.

'I live in the annexe as caretaker while he's away, and I dwell across the way in the house my man is renting while his steading is being rebuilt.'

There was a weird sense of the medieval about this woman when she spoke.

She showed me into the small studio. I'm not an artist and I've always left interior design to Marianne but I liked Fiona's work, there were a variety of paintings and drawings and even I could see that she had used different media. We talked for a bit about the different properties of watercolour and pen and ink while she found the drawings she'd made of the font at Altarnun.

'It's the heads that fascinate and inspire me,' she said. 'They are so commanding, almost fierce and yet calmly stern. I want to make a carving for the lid of a toy box.'

'Typical Vikings. It's the original Norse font isn't it. I bought the booklet and read about it.' I looked at her as I spoke, I thought I could see the same proud strength of a northern warrior race in her face. 'Don't make the box lid too scary if it's for toys. Is it a boy you are carrying?'

'I have no wish to know Josh, I won't find out until the baby arrives, which would be right now if I could wish it, but there's still two weeks to go if the counted days are correct.'

'It'll come when it's ready. My wife was late with the first and early with the second. You can't always be sure when conception took place.'

'Conception. Yes, the subtle connection of the cells beneath a woman's heart.' She smiled. 'All creation is alchemy don't you think Josh?'

I shrugged and made a noise. 'You're probably right there.' I said.

She showed me another idea she was working on. It was a beautiful pen and ink drawing of an ancient twisted apple tree with very fine detail, but as well as a few fruit it had names beautifully scripted in gaps in the branches. Either side of the tree two people stood clasping hands across the trunk, I could see that it was Fiona and Daniel but dressed in simple clothes hinting at something timeless. It was clever and lovely and I said so.

'This is to be my child's family tree. I might give it a little colour wash and then it will be framed for the bedroom, but I think it's something I could do for other people. I like the apple tree's ancient roots in the mythology of creation and of joining people. Did you know that if you planted the pips from one apple you would get different trees? They will not be true to the parent plant. Just like people.'

I watched her as she spoke and almost envied the way she had of viewing her world. She could see and feel things that were missed by the rest of us. I realised that I liked her very much.

'Well you're a fine artist and must have been a wonderful teacher Fiona. Your baby's going to have a lucky start in life.'

We stepped back outside and again I could smell horse. 'How's your mare today?' I asked her.

Fiona frowned slightly. 'Bel is confused I think, I haven't been able to ride her for two days and I should really take her out but it is getting difficult for me. I groomed her this morning and Daniel, that's my man, got me a mounting block made but he's not happy about me riding now.' She indicated a sturdy set of steps at the side of the tack room.

'I could take her out if you like, I've ridden almost every week for thirty years. Tell me where to go and I'll give her a bit of exercise.'

Fiona was delighted. She called to Bel and to my surprise the horse actually walked across the paddock and stood at the fence next to us. Her reward was a carrot. I stoked her neck and over her withers with the flat of my hand and Fiona nodded approvingly.

'Bel doesn't like to be patted. To a horse it's like a slap would be to us. Horses nuzzle each other and their touch is more like a stroke with their muzzles. I can see you like horses.'

I helped with the tack, lifting the saddle and smiling as Bel looked round at me twitching her ears, her intelligent eye taking me in and assessing my intentions. I talked to the horse as I would talk to a patient, a little bit of information about what I was doing and why. Bel was relaxed and so was Fiona. I wondered about borrowing a riding hat but Fiona was already ahead of me.

'This is my brother's, try it for size.'

I mounted up and Fiona walked at our side as far as the house with the car while she told me where to go.

'But Bel knows the way, she will show you.'

It was good to be on a horse. We didn't own horses back home but went to a livery yard every week and sometimes when I was working in the outback I'd get a ride. That way I'd ridden all sorts of horses and got a fair bit of experience. Bel was an angel, she had a smooth gait, lovely responses and a nice personality. We walked and warmed up, found the way onto the moor and I could feel her moving the gears up a notch. Finally at a long grassy sheep cropped stretch I gave Bel her head and she took off with a long floating stride. It was a great ride and I felt invigorated. I was back within ninety minutes and Fiona and her man were waiting on a bench outside the annexe. He had a protective arm around her shoulders and she was leaning against him, they looked comfortable together. She introduced me to Daniel and I dismounted and shook his hand.

'You don't ride Daniel?'

'Bel and Fiona are giving me lessons, but I don't go out of the paddock yet. I envy you.'

'Bel's superb. Well schooled and responsive. She's a lovely horse.' I said.

I insisted on cleaning Bel down and I checked her hooves since Fiona couldn't. Daniel helped and as we worked he advised that he was on maintenance duties.

'It's not just riding lessons,' he said. 'I have to poo pick the paddock, try saying that after a few drinks, and clean the tack as well.' He was smiling at Fiona and there was a soft look of mutual understanding between them.

I said I'd better be getting back to the holiday cottage and that Nick would be wondering if I'd broken a leg or something.

'I'm here for another week Fiona, if you like I'll take her out again, she's a fine horse.'

Fiona said that she'd like that and I suggested Friday afternoon, since Nick was going that day and it would fill in a loose end for me. As the three of us walked out of the private drive together I looked at the end of terrace house Daniel was renting.

'I think I remember visiting an old couple there. It looks a bit different now.'

'That will have been Mr and Mrs Williams, the house is still in the same family but the current owner got married in February and has moved to his wife's place just outside the village. When I move out I think they'll run it as a holiday cottage.'

It was all change and time moves on. I went back to find Nick. I needed a shower.

THIRTY

I woke in a happy frame of mind but aching slightly. Nick and I laughed at each other over a light breakfast of toast and yogurt. He was still sore from the surfing and I hadn't ridden for three weeks so a few muscles were complaining. We compared mobility and practised a stooping walk, fooling about and joking.

The previous evening he'd been interested to learn about Fiona's paintings and about Bel.

'So you went out riding, on a dark horse eh dad?'

He was even more interested in Fiona but I told him I'd met her man.

'She's spoken for Nick. His name's Daniel and he's got one helluva car. I wonder who you'll find one day.'

He didn't appear too concerned. 'All in good time dad, I guess I'll know it when it happens.'

'Your mum is hoping for grandchildren before too long.'

'Anna had better get busy then. I'm still a penniless student.'

Odd but I couldn't see Anna as a mother, she was a passionate career girl. I reminded him that we were invited to lunch at The Manor House and explained that I'd left it open since I wasn't sure of his movements.

'Oh I wondered why we were on half rations for breakfast. That'll be nice. Anyway I'm curious about your old garrett. And I won't have to cook tonight if we eat out.'

Nick had made us a hearty mushroom omelette served with the remains of the salad leaves and tomatoes the night before.

We smartened ourselves up and I put on a pair of the jazzy socks Marianne had packed for me. There was a note tucked inside; "*Hope there's an occasion to wear these and knock 'em dead cowboy!*" It made me smile.

Nick found a bottle of wine to take with us. It was only a short walk in glorious sunshine and our arrival was announced by two large labradors contained in a gated area, barking in a frustrated sort of way. They sounded friendly rather than aggressive.

Before I could lift the door knocker the door was opened by Oliver.

'Welcome back to The Manor House Josh. Nice you to see you again Nick.'

I stood back for a moment. 'It's a lot prettier outside than it used to be, the turning circle works, it only used to have a straight drive in and a lawn with flowerbeds full of dahlias and roses.' I didn't much like dahlias.

'We've made a few changes, come on in and I'll give you the official guided tour if you can bear it.'

I remembered the feel of the house, the flagged passageway used to be covered by a long runner but I guess with dogs hard floors are easier to clean. The surgery was now a pleasant light room with bookcases and comfortable chairs with side tables and lamps. There were magazines in a pile and framed prints of country activities on the walls. It was very much a gentleman's room. Oliver explained that this was now the morning room, hence no television.

'It gets good morning light so we like to have coffee and the newspapers in here.'

The pharmacy was now a study, with lovely panelling revealed and with a nice fireplace which I didn't remember ever seeing, probably because the place used to be stacked with stuff. We said hello to Graham in the kitchen and he twiddled a few dials on the range cooker and came upstairs with us.

'The house is much more graceful than I remember.' I said. 'And it doesn't smell of boiled cabbage and gammon.'

'Really? God that must have been awful. Come and see what you think of your attic now.' Graham replied.

I remembered the little flight of steps from the top landing and the low door, but what was once two adjoining rooms was now one long room and had been turned into a lovely guest room. I described my single iron framed bed with the thin hard mattress and the lumpy flock pillow. There had been a wardrobe with a door which always used to stick and a small chest of drawers with a funny smell. A bowl and mirror were provided for shaving and Mrs Webster used to carry a jug of hot water up the stairs for me which she always left outside the door. The floorboards creaked no more and the room was thickly carpeted. The small paned windows in the dormers were double glazed replacements. Oliver said that they were hardwood, made locally.

'The place is listed so conservation is an issue. No plastic allowed.'

'You've done a terrific job. I don't recognise it, except for the view.' Up there on the top floor you could see for miles up to the moors where I had once walked with Tessa.

We admired the new bathrooms and I made them laugh when I described Mrs Webster's pride in the fact that they actually had an indoor bathroom, and that on weekdays I could use the basin to, as she put it, "Wash up as far as possible and down as far as possible", using individual flannels which she used to boil clean in a saucepan on the stove every couple of days. Graham got quite hysterical at the thought of what one did with the "possible" and then we had quite a sober discussion about how indoor plumbing had made huge improvements in hygiene and dealing with disease.

By this time we were all back downstairs cluttering up the kitchen and Oliver was pouring us all a glass of wine. The conversation then switched to Australian wines and the wonderful stuff coming out of our part of Western Australia. As we were talking I heard the door knocker and then a female voice calling out 'Coo-eee'.

'That'll be Martha,' Oliver said and he called out. 'In here Martha, we're in the kitchen.'

A small slim elderly woman came in carrying a plastic shopping bag with a picture of kittens gracing it.

'Four men in a kitchen, that's quite unusual unless you're all chefs.' She greeted us all, glancing at Nick and me briefly before kissing Graham and Oliver and delving into her bag. 'Graham,

I've brought you some preserved berries for your next pie. I only hope I get to taste them.'

There was the normal sort of domestic flutter and thanks and then the lady turned to us. She was pretty fit for her age. Oliver made the introductions.

'Martha, this is Josh and his son Nick, from Australia. They put up a good fight at skittles on Sunday night but we held on to the village cup.'

Martha shook hands with Nick and made some comment about liking his distinctive accent, then she turned to me.

'Joshua, how nice to see you again.'

She held my hand quite firmly in a warm dry grip and looked right into my eyes. I knew I'd seen her before, she was the lady at the bar in the pub on our first night. But why did she call me Joshua, no-one had called me that in decades. Graham and Oliver were looking intrigued but I responded calmly.

'It's nice to meet you as well, I saw you in the pub the other night didn't I, when I choked on my beer.'

'Beer not cold enough for you I suppose.' Graham laughed.

There was no further discussion as Oliver ushered us all into a fabulous conservatory to give Graham space in the kitchen. I looked around with interest, remembering a small kitchen garden in the old days, all gone now. Martha engaged Nick in conversation and very quickly learned that he was spending a year in Bristol at my old university. I watched her nodding and using appropriate body language to draw him out, although he was an easy enough conversationalist anyway. Sure enough Oliver joined in and the story about my living here in the house years ago one summer was the next topic. For Oliver and Nick it was all new and interesting, but I could see that it was all just confirmation for what Martha already knew. I sipped my wine and smiled and kept quiet, she obviously knew me but I just couldn't place her and I didn't want to seem rude.

We were summoned to eat in the dining room. Graham apologised for the formality but said that the table in the conservatory was too small for five to eat comfortably. I could see what he meant by the amount of food he produced. There was a tureen of chicken soup served with chopped fresh herbs, bread rolls and salty butter, followed by a dish of monkfish tails cooked in a sticky savoury glaze with mediterranean vegetables fragrant with just a touch of garlic and then a mixed fruit pie and ice cream. There was no doubt about it this man could cook, even the bread rolls were home made. I complimented him.

'The restaurant trade's loss was obviously nursing's gain, that was marvellous, and without a doubt the best lunch I've ever had. In England.' I added with a smile.

We talked about food and cooking for a bit and I confessed I was okay in charge of a barbecue but that was as far as cooking went with me. Then we all moved into the conservatory for a coffee and I made a bit of small talk with Martha, learning that she was a widow, a farmer's wife and that she still lived on the farm with her youngest son and his family. I was wondering if I should ask where the farm was when Nick asked her about their animals and she got talking about rare breeds and hens and was interesting to listen to.

The talk moved on to what the guys had done with their lives, old stories I guessed but always refreshing to tell them to new ears. Nick left the room to find the bathroom, Graham calling after him that they had four toilets, which meant Monday to Thursday were catered for and that for the next three days they went outside. I think he'd had a bit too much wine judging by the way that Oliver was frowning at him.

There was one of those lulls in the conversation that tell you that a gathering is coming to an end when a few notes of music came rippling through from the next room. Nick had found a piano.

Oliver sat up, a look of pleasure on his face. 'Is that your son?'

I nodded. 'I hope you don't mind, my wife is a pianist and both our kids have grown up with music.'

We all trooped through to the sitting room and watched Nick for a several minutes. Nick was a competent player but Oliver was passionate, he got the same look on his face that I'd seen so many times on Marianne's.

Martha turned to me. 'You've had a good life in Australia Joshua, a talented wife and clever children as well as a satisfying career.'

She spoke quietly, again with that disconcerting use of my name. I had the feeling that she was dying to talk to me but I wasn't sure if I was detecting aggression or something like sorrow, so all I did was nod my head and smile, deciding she'd made a statement and not asked a direct question and using the fact that Nick was playing as an excuse not to speak.

And so the very long lunch came to an end. I asked the guys if I could take a few photographs of the front of the house with them in it and they were happy about it, pulling Nick in to join them. Martha said she'd be on her way and climbed into a muddy landrover which farted a diesel cloud as she drove off.

Graham coughed and waved his hand in front of his face. 'Oh I do wish she wouldn't do that.'

The next day we dozed in the sun at the holiday cottage and Nick spent a few hours sorting out his stuff. I helped by cleaning the inside of his car, I drew the line at washing it.

Really we both wanted a change now even though as father and son we got on very well. There's a saying isn't there, "After three days fish and family stink". We'd had the best part of a week in each other's company, but I could tell that Nick was ready to go and join his friends in North Wales.

We shared the household chores and I went off to the farm shop for more provisions and a newspaper before it closed. Then I emailed home telling Marianne a bit about what we'd been up to.

While I read the local paper and watched television Nick occupied his evening with emailing his friends and packing. In the bathroom he'd found the complimentary male grooming kit I'd been given on the Business Class flight.

'Can I take this dad?' He interrupted my reading. 'I've never seen one of these handy kits before. I didn't get one when I flew over.'

'That's because as an economically invalid person flying cattle class you didn't deserve one. But take it my son, take it. Accept it as a gift. Your friends will think you're loaded when they see it.'

He made as though to throw it at me.

THIRTY ONE

Friday started even warmer, the summer heat gaining that ominous pressure which heralds a storm. You can feel the electricity in the air. In the morning we had an early breakfast and then he was at the door with his car keys in his hand.

'Okay dad I'll be heading off then, will you be alright on your own for a week?'

'Sure I will, I'm riding Fiona's horse this afternoon so that will pass a bit of time, there's the pub and no doubt I shall do a bit more exploring. Before I know it I'll be queuing up for the big silver bird to go home.'

I bunged him a clip of spending money and we hugged and patted each other on the back a bit, and then he was gone. I just hoped the old wreck would make it to Snowdonia intact. With true fatherly concern I had checked the oil and the brakes and they were fine and the tyres had plenty of tread on them.

I left the cottage in Sarah's busy hands. She had a fat girl with her who'd come to help with the hoovering and dusting and she was really enjoying giving her orders. I walked round to find Fiona to see if she was still happy for me to ride Bel. Fiona was in her studio having a good tidy up and looking very restless in a dark blue smock over some stretchy leggings. Her thick mahogany hair was pulled up quite high in a ponytail with a few strands falling around her face and neck. The effect was attractive. I greeted her.

'Having a chuck out I see.'

'Sort of.' She acknowledged me but I could see her mind was far away as she moved about restlessly picking things up and putting them down again.

'There are some things worth putting aside for an exhibition in due course, some is work in progress and I need to be able to see it better and I am terrible at throwing out empty containers or packaging in case I need it. It's got to the point where I don't have enough space to move around.'

I watched her, there was enough space, the space she needed was in her mind and her body. I'd seen this activity before in my own wife, in women and in animals out on the farms, this sudden flow of slightly tense energy in a female preparing to give birth.

'Is Daniel around?' I asked. I didn't want her to be on her own.

'Oh yes, he's in the house working on a project. He loses track of time at a certain point and I've known him forget to eat. He's a very creative man and his work takes a lot of precision and planning. I don't pretend to understand it, but I do sympathise with the process.'

I'd learned that Daniel was something in IT and ran his own business, pretty successfully if that car of his was anything to go by. Somehow I couldn't see it filled with baby paraphernalia and idly wondered if he'd be changing it. Fiona was looking at me and as she straightened up she smiled, one hand absently rubbing the small of her back.

'I've already got Bel at the post by the tack room, but you'll have to do all the rest Josh.'

'No worries, I can do all that, you carry on here with your sorting.'

Bel considered me and flicked her tail a few times, raising a back leg a bit irritably.

'I know old girl, you can feel the weather can't you. Come on then, a bit of a ride out and a canter and you'll be safe home and scoffing carrots before you know it.'

Bel snorted at me. I thought it sounded a bit derisive. I saddled up, found the bone dome as we called protective hats of any kind in my profession, and rode out. I didn't see Fiona and there was no sign of Daniel. Bel was in a funny mood but she understood that I was in charge and we had an hour alone out on the moor. The sheep were all bunched together and facing one way as though looking expectantly for something. There were large black birds falling sideways through the sky like bits of torn burnt paper above a bonfire. I think they were jackdaws by the way they called out to each other. It was an eerie sight and I was beginning to dislike the look of the sky to the South so I wheeled Bel round and we made it back to the village in spanking good time. Bel was positively turbo charged I thought.

I called out a hello as I passed the annexe but there was no reply so I saw to Bel and spent a while sorting her out and making everything tidy before going to look for Fiona to tell her everything was okay and that I was going. I looked in at the studio window but couldn't see her so I went round to the annexe door and knocked. There was no response. I stood there for a moment, listening hard but all was quiet. Remembering that she'd said Daniel was deeply engaged in a project and probably wouldn't want to be disturbed at the house I knocked again and then tried the handle. The door wasn't locked so I opened it and called her name.

'Fiona, are you there, hello, it's Josh.'

There was nothing. I was about to go when I thought I heard a faint sound but there was a sudden mean gust of wind. I stood still and listened, focussing hard with my senses. There it was again, a faint moan and what I realised was rhythmic panting. Experience made me react and I went into the annexe, there was an open plan kitchen, dining and living area with a closed door at the back. That's where the sound was coming from. I crossed the room and knocked on the door.

'Fiona, are you in there, it's Josh, are you alright Fiona, can you hear me?'

Reckoning I'd given her enough time to be decent if my instincts were wrong I opened the door slightly and called her name again. This time I got a response.

'I'm in the bathroom Josh. It hurts, the baby hurts.' And there was a long low moan.

She was standing in the bathroom with her legs apart bending over slightly and holding the towel rail so hard her knuckles were white. Her leggings and pants were on the floor and I could see that they were stained where her waters had broken. There was a sudden flash of sheet lightning and a distant rumble of thunder.

The bathroom went very dark and the atmosphere was poised with expectation.

'Hey, let's get you both into a more comfortable place sweetheart. It's okay, I'm right with you and I've attended more deliveries than I can count.'

What I didn't tell her was that I'd never attended one totally on my own. She moaned again, I could see the sweat on her face, this was a baby in a hurry to appear. I grabbed the hand towel and twisted it into a rope.

'Hang on to this Fiona, you can squeeze it and bite it if you need to, I'm going to support you over to the bed. Everything's okay, I'm not leaving you, come on pet, come on.'

I got her to the bed but she dropped to her knees at the side of it on the rug with just her face and arms on the cover. She was panting and shuddering.

There was a telephone in the main room and I dialled triple nine, rapidly going through the procedure for the ambulance. The questions were efficient and straightforward and the operator sounded very kind. I explained the situation.

'No, I'm not the husband, I'm a neighbour. I'm a retired doctor. She's very dilated and I found her alone. I have nothing to aid the delivery. I'm doing what I can. Get here quickly please.'

I dashed back into the bathroom and stripped my t-shirt off and washed my hands and arms as thoroughly as possible. There was a big bath towel and some others folded neatly on a shelf. I grabbed the lot, one to protect her from me since I was covered in the fresh aroma of horse. There was another flash of lightning and this time a rumble of thunder overhead. I heard Fiona crying out. I wasn't leaving her and there was no way to call Daniel, I didn't have the house number and anyway I couldn't know whether he'd be a help or a hindrance. There was a tremendous crash of thunder overhead and I swear things shook. I went back to Fiona and did everything I could to help her. It didn't take long.

The room was dark and still, the only sound was rain drumming hard on the windows and the small sound of new breath. Fiona was still on the floor by the bed and I was on my knees at her side. I'd got her lying propped up on pillows and cushions and towels. Her eyes were closed and tears of exertion were seeping from below her eyelashes. I'd cleaned the baby's face and airways and wrapped the little thing in a towel, the cord wasn't cut yet and there was still a lot to take care of but both were breathing and conscious and I was making encouraging comments. At that point I became aware of lights and voices and all the people I needed came through the door at once. I love paramedics and emergency response teams, I love the efficient harmony and skill of these people. I surrendered my patient to them and stood back, my bit of the job done. Daniel was with them and straight down onto the floor at Fiona's head.

'I saw the lightning and heard the thunder and then the electricity went off. I thought you might be scared and I'd just got to the door when the ambulance came up the track and they were shouting to me asking if I knew where you lived. Oh my god Fiona, my dear darling, are you okay?'

Fiona waved a weak hand and spoke. 'Josh was here in time. He helped me.'

The medics wanted to see to Fiona and the baby so he got up and we moved out of the way. I glanced down at the state of me and went into the bathroom to wash again and put my t-shirt back on. When I went back in Daniel was standing wide eyed in the kitchen area and in a state of mild shock.

'This wasn't the way it was supposed to happen,' he said. 'I was supposed to be at the birth, with her in hospital. She had her case packed and everything.'

I smiled at him. 'Life's like that Daniel. But hey, you're a proud father now.'

There was a slow look of comprehension on his face and then a flash of emotion tore across it. I thought he was going to cry but he pretended to cough and pulled himself together and walked back to the bedroom door to look in at Fiona and the baby. They were still surrounded by people all doing their stuff. He came back to me and took a deep breath.

'Are they okay, is Fiona going to be okay?'

'I think so, she's a fit healthy girl and in good hands now and the baby is a good colour under all that goo.'

He couldn't help himself, the poor guy shed a few tears of relief and joy and I slapped him on the back.

'Come on mate,' I said. 'I don't know my way around this place but I think the electricity is back on so let's have a brew up.'

I got him busy and took another look into the bedroom. All was going well and I wasn't needed so I went back out to Daniel. He still needed help so I suggested he might start by calling Fiona's family to give them the good news, and asked if he had anyone locally who might be able to help.

'Kate, my sister, she's just a few miles away. Yes, I'll call her first and tell her, and, er is it a boy or a girl?'

While he was on the phone the health visitor arrived right at the end of her shift and like a real trooper spent a while with Fiona. I kept company with Daniel. He'd called Fiona's folks up in Scotland and I gathered they'd had things packed and were now already on their way down. It was going to be a long drive through the night for them. Then his sister Kate turned up and took over organising him.

'She's so small, and she's pretty.' Daniel was sitting by Fiona who was dozing in bed now, just gazing at them both like a man besotted, as he surely was. Kate wanted to hear the story minute by minute and gave us more tea and some rather nice biscuits she'd brought with her. I was beginning to realise I was a bit hungry and ate several. After going through it all again I sat back and watched the two of them starting to weave a new family legend, it was all rather enjoyable. They were very alike, similar in looks and dark colouring and I wondered if Nick and Anna would ever share a moment like this. It was very special.

Daniel's phone started burbling and he moved away to take the call when my stomach rumbled alarmingly.

'Sorry Kate, my stomach thinks my throat has been cut. I'll be off now I think and find something to put in it.'

'I guess Daniel hasn't eaten either has he. Would you eat a few slices of pizza doctor, it won't take long.' She'd come prepared. 'It's just a quick easy snack, proper food will happen tomorrow.'

I thanked her. 'I'd like that if I'm not in the way. And please call me Josh, we don't do formal where I live, and anyway I'm retired now.'

'In the way? Silly man, you're the evening star tonight, shining brittle clear.'

Goodness, I thought, the women around these parts did have a nice way of talking.

I checked on Fiona and the baby. The baby was in a soft sort of carryall on the bed next to her and one of Fiona's hands was holding the side. Daniel was right, the baby was a pretty little thing, I've seen plenty of long thin red angry ones and short fat snuffling porky ones but this one was a delicate creature with nice features. Daniel came in quietly and stood next to me. He started getting emotional again.

'I can't thank you enough Josh.' He whispered.

I answered quietly. 'Hey, Fiona did all the work, I just hung around and encouraged her.' A thought crossed my mind. 'So are you letting on what the little mite will be called?'

He nodded and leaned over the bed and touched the baby's face with one finger.

'Yes, she's part of an old story, she's brought her name with her. This is Flora Rose.'

While we ate pizza the best way, using our hands, Kate and Daniel told me the story of their old family home, a place a couple of miles away over the moor called Darleystones. I learned all about hidden things and about an initialled date stone their builder had uncovered. Bits of research had eventually come together and they'd discovered the name of an ancestor called

David Penive and his wife, Flora. Daniel said he was having another date stone made for a garage and studio extension he was having built. It would have the same initials but a new date. It was all very interesting but I was flagging.

'Guys it's been a very long day and I'm going to go now and get a shower and some shut eye. Shall I drop by tomorrow afternoon to see Fiona and Flora?'

Daniel grinned from ear to ear and said that was a good idea. He shook my hand firmly and thanked me again and I walked back to the cottage in the twilight. The air was fresh and there was that sweet smell you get after rain in England. The cottage was all tidy after Sarah's ministrations and it felt a bit strange without Nick's things there, but it had been an odd sort of day. I stripped off and shoved everything into the washing machine and went and had a very long hot shower. After sending Marianne another email I could feel myself fading I was so tired. Clean sheets welcomed me and I crashed out.

THIRTY TWO

In the morning I woke late and by the time I was up and dressed it was nearly lunch time so I downed a cup of instant coffee and went over to the pub to see if they could fit me in. It was already quite busy and several heads turned as I went in. Tim shouted a greeting.

'Here he is, the man of the moment everybody, ladies and gentlemen I give you Doctor Milton!'

And to my amusement everybody started clapping. I burst out laughing as a few hands slapped me on the back.

'I know news travels fast in villages but how on earth did you find out?' I asked as Tim handed me a pint.

'Let's see,' Tim was holding out some fingers which he proceeded to bend closed with the other hand. 'First there was the ambulance, then there was the health visitor, then you were spotted walking back to the cottage, but the real clincher was that Mr Pencraddoc's sister met Sarah at the farm shop this morning and told her all about it. Quite a story.'

There was a bit of a buzz in the place and I felt slightly embarrassed so I took a few sips of my pint.

'Do you have space for one for lunch Tim?'

'If I didn't I'd throw some of them out for you. Anything you want off the menu, or off the specials boards. It's on the house for you today doctor.'

He was speaking a little too loud I thought as he handed me a menu. I guessed it was for the benefit of the other customers. I protested but Tim insisted, so I ate a fine steak with grilled cherry tomatoes and chips and salad. I didn't want anything else but I let them force a coffee on me, although I've always felt that following beer with coffee was just wrong.

It was mid afternoon before I judged it appropriate to call over to the annexe. There were a couple of cars parked up the drive and I guessed Fiona was holding court. The annexe door was open and I called a hello and knocked, Kate appeared and pulled me in by the hand.

'Everyone, here's the doctor who helped Fiona. This is Dr Joshua Milton.'

There were some murmurs of greeting and a swirl of smiling faces. I asked them to call me Josh.

'Where I live and work we're pretty informal and anyway I retired a couple of months ago.' I had the feeling I was repeating myself and that it was falling on deaf ears. The English do seem to like things kept in a categorised and formal way.

Kate kissed my cheek, an older rather handsome lady who was Fiona's mother also kissed me. A proud and commanding Scotsman who was so obviously Fiona's father shook my hand a little too hard and Daniel gave me a warm hug which I thought was very New Age and relaxed. There was a tall young man who I learned was Kate's husband and who was shepherding two toddlers, and most importantly, in the bedroom was Fiona with little Flora. It was them I went through to. She held out her hand and I took it and perched on the side of the bed.

'Well well, you clever girl, how are you today and how's Miss Flora Rose?'

'We are here together and very happy, thanks to you Josh. It's where she first came into being and where I preferred to be to give birth to her if the truth is to be told.'

We talked a bit about what had happened and the storm coming over. Fiona was very taken with the strength of the elements and the power of giving birth. It all fitted together for her way of thinking.

'Daniel was sure we were having a son, but Flora was the name in my mind. It was her initial on the 1812 date stone at Darleystones we think. This baby was meant to be here.'

'Nice how things can come round again.' I said agreeably.

Fiona nodded. 'Some souls belong in a given place.'

I changed the subject, asking if anyone had seen to Bel. Apparently some chap I'd never heard of had taken care of her, a gardener or something and now that Fiona's mother was "over her hip" she would ride her while they stayed. There was nothing more for me to do for Fiona but her family all wanted to hear the story yet again so chairs were carried into the bedroom and prompted by Kate we spent a couple of hours talking and laughing. It was a privilege to be included. The women folk couldn't get over the fact that Fiona had given birth without pain relief and Fiona's father was bursting with pride.

'Hannah and I have three grandchildren now, and all with a Scots name. My darling little Flora, she's already stolen my heart. I'm not ashamed to say it. And I think she already has the family hair.'

I decided that Fiona should have some peace and some quiet time with her mum and Kate and said that I'd be off. As I was leaving Daniel walked out with me saying he needed to get something from the house.

'We'd like to keep in touch with you Josh if you don't mind. I've written all my personal and private contact details down for you.' He handed me an envelope. 'Also, if you come back to England for anything I have a flat in London you can use, it's right on the Thames and pretty handy for the sights. I gather your wife might enjoy the cultural scene if you'd like a holiday. You can stay as long as you like as my guest.'

'Hey that's very kind Daniel but you don't need to go to all this trouble, I was just in the right place at the right time.' But I was touched and said so.

'Fiona said that meeting you had some meaning or reason. I love her but I don't always get what she's on about. My business partner Mike says she's a bit fey, she does know about things in a funny way. Maybe it's because she's an artist, I don't know.' He paused thoughtfully and then went on. 'Mike describes fey as being something like radio reception. Our business is all about communication and alternative reality, about what people see and perceive and respond to in computer games. Some people get it and some don't. Fiona sometimes seemed tuned in to things I don't perceive. Her personal reception receives things that I miss.'

'Sounds like a female perception thing.' I said. I thought he'd explained it quite well but fell back on tried and tested words, a bit corny but with an element of truth in them. 'She's going to be a lovely mother I do know that. Take good care of her and of your daughter. Speaking as a father I can tell you the best is to come Daniel.'

We shook hands again and I walked back to the cottage feeling a tiny bit weary. I'd got just four days left before travelling back to London on Thursday for my flight at dick-o'clock on Friday. After all the events of the past few weeks and the excitement of the last twenty-four hours I was ready for a bit of peace and quiet myself. As I rounded the corner of the track and onto the road I saw a muddy landrover parked outside the cottage and had a funny feeling that peace and quiet was going to evade me.

She was sitting in the landrover, waiting for me with the window down. I raised a hand in greeting and smiled at her.

'Martha, it is you. How are you today?' I've always found that a pleasant approach disarms most people with a mission.

'Joshua, I wondered if I might have a word. And thank you, I'm very well.' She was courteous but a little nervous I thought.

I invited her in and offered her tea or coffee. She opted for tea without sugar and stood looking about, a petite little figure in taupe coloured trousers and a dark blue blouse. She was wearing a single string of pearls and I had the impression she'd dressed for the occasion.

'What a pretty place this is. Sarah and Tim have done a nice job in here.' She turned to look at me as I put the kettle on in the little kitchen. 'Did you visit the sick in here do you remember?'

I wondered what she was getting at. Was there some malpractice somewhere in the past, some oversight perhaps. I was honest with her. 'Not here I don't think. I was never out of

Dr Webster's sight when I was working. And yes, this is a lovely little cottage.'

I put things onto a tray and asked if she'd like to sit outside. Outside was good. I fetched us a couple of seat cushions and decided to give her some encouragement.

'Martha, I've been a doctor for a very long time and I'm fairly good at reading people. I think you have something you want to share with me. Is there anything you want to tell me or is there something I can do to help you?' My mind flashed a graphic picture of helping Fiona last night, at least Martha wasn't going to give birth. I smiled at the memory and poured our tea, feeling calm and in control. Martha remained quiet, thinking.

'I can never remember the correct way to do milk and tea in England,' I said conversationally, to put her at her ease. 'My mum always put the milk in first, but from my student days I've been a slob and put the milk in last.'

Martha absently traced a finger over the cup. She had short clean fingernails and the veins stood out on the backs of her hands.

'It depends on the receptacle doesn't it Joshua. I think it's milk first for delicate porcelain, so the thermal shock is lessened from the hot tea, and the other way round for thicker things like mugs.' She frowned. 'I think that's how it goes but now I'm not sure. Porcelain is surprisingly tough for such a fine thing.'

A nervous laugh followed this explanation but I couldn't help thinking that this small slim person was as tough as porcelain in her own way. I smiled at her, feeling more sure of my ground.

'Well, it's good tea. Shall we talk about the weather now Martha?' I sat back and crossed one leg comfortably over my knee.

'Don't be silly. Actually, I've come to ask you a favour Joshua,' Martha said. 'Will you walk across to the church with me?'

That was the last thing I was expecting her to say.

'To the church?' I was confused but then had a sudden insight. 'Oh, of course, we were talking about family research at Graham and Oliver's the other day. But I don't think my wife's family had any connections with this village, or is there something you've found?'

I was watching her face as I spoke and could see that I was off track.

'I'm thinking aloud here,' I said quickly. 'It's something else isn't it.'

'Yes, it's something else.' Martha's voice was firm but she didn't look me in the eye.

I finished my tea and stood up. 'Excuse me, I'm going to go up to the bathroom and then we'll go over when you're ready.'

I went indoors and upstairs feeling just a little bit baffled. What on earth was all this about? Was Dr Webster buried there, was that it? Why couldn't she be straightforward?

Martha was waiting in the house, leaning on the side of the little sofa.

I picked up the keys. 'Shall we then?' I indicated the door.

Martha nodded and smiled in a tense false way and we went outside into the still warm air, so pleasant now after the storm last night. We crossed the road without speaking and I stood back to let her go up the steps from the road and onto the church path. It was a fairly well kept churchyard, quite tidy, peaceful and dappled with sunlight. She walked slightly ahead of me up the path with a very determined set to her shoulders. Round to one side I could see there were some newish headstones, very different to the old carved traceries with eloquent descriptions in Alternun.

She stopped and looked at me and made a curious gesture at once both apologetic and defiant.

'Do you see anyone you might recognise here Joshua?'
'What?'

I looked at her in bewilderment and then looked at the headstones. I didn't know what she was going on about and for a moment was quite blind, then I saw it.

George Charlesworth. His wife Christina Charlesworth. Daughter Tessa Charlesworth. Together United Forever.

I felt the breath knocked right out of my body. I know I gasped and put my hand to my mouth. Tessa. Tessa. I said her name out loud and something squeezed my chest hard. I stumbled forward and put both my hands on the headstone and leaned over it, still catching my breath and trying to breathe deeply. Martha was at my side and put a warm dry hand over mine.

'Oh Joshua, I'm so terribly sorry, you didn't know did you.' It wasn't a question.

I shook my head, unable to speak.

'Joshua I've been an utter fool. I'm angry with myself and embarrassed. There's a bench just over here, can you get to it and sit down?'

I allowed myself to be taken to the bench and I sat with her. She produced some paper tissues and handed them to me.

'I'm so terribly sorry Joshua, I really am. Please forgive me.'

I don't know how long it took to pull myself together. Eventually I spoke.

'That was unexpected.'

It was a typically British understatement and I made that stupid sound Englishmen make when they're out of their depth and unsure about what to do next. It's between a laugh and a cough and expresses our national failure to deal with emotion.

'I don't know what to say Martha. You clearly know something and I'm clearly deeply affected. Would you mind coming back to the cottage with me and telling me all about it please.'

She nodded. 'I think I owe you that.'

We walked back together in silence and I went upstairs to splash my face. I felt as though the world had changed somehow. It wasn't as happy. Back downstairs Martha had got the kettle on and was rooting around in the empty cupboards.

'I wondered if you had any biscuits Joshua.'

'No biscuits but there's a bit of Sarah's cake left in that tin.'

'Good, that girl's talents lie in baking and cleaning, if not much else.' Martha sounded a bit sharp.

We shared the cake and drank tea, the atmosphere not so tense now. I could feel Martha's compassion but I felt bruised. Once she was sure that I was calm she spoke.

'I'll start at the beginning shall I?'

'Yes please.'

'The night I saw you in the pub, I was at the bar, I knew I'd seen you before. You're quite distinctive looking, that summer we all thought you looked a bit like Robert Redford, the actor if you know to whom I'm referring.'

I nodded, people had said that before when I was younger. Personally I thought I looked more like the Australian actor Paul Hogan but it really wasn't a point worth discussing.

'Well you still do, I mean you're older obviously and people do change, your hair is grey now but your eyes and your profile are still the young man I remember.'

Martha paused and thought a bit, then went on.

'Tessa was my neighbour's daughter, I live at Moorstones Farm and she lived with her father, my friend George Charlesworth. Their cottage was, is, at the end of my lane. Her mother Christina died when Tessa was about eleven or twelve I think, and I tried to help George with her. She was a lovely girl and I'd got two strapping little boys but no daughter. My youngest son Phil wasn't born then, he was what you call a late crocus.' She smiled a bit. 'Tessa used to confide in me, she was always welcome at the farm house and she and George would sometimes eat with us.'

Martha stopped and I could see her eyes were glistening.

'Your turn for the tissues I think.' I handed her several.

She dabbed her eyes and wiped her nose.

'Oh this is all very emotional isn't it. I thought I was over the crying, but even now I miss my husband and the old days.'

I nodded and we both blew our noses.

'Anyway,' she went on. 'I was quite cross when I saw you in the pub. I thought you'd got a bloody nerve coming back, but when I met you at Graham and Oliver's and talked with Nick I began to suspect you didn't know about Tessa.'

I shook my head. 'I'm still in the dark here Martha.'

'I think I'm right in saying that you and Tessa had a bit of a thing going that summer.'

I actually snorted. 'A bit of a thing. Is that what you'd call it? I was crazy about her and at the time I was pretty sure she felt the same way about me.'

Martha looked at me and smiled. 'You do say that with absolute conviction, and I'm pleased to hear it.'

I remained silent. I could see Tessa's face, her pretty face and her toffee coloured streaky hair shining in the sun as she turned to me and laughed at something I'd said or done. We were always laughing together. I found Martha's eyes fixed on me.

'You were remembering her weren't you.'

'I've never forgotten her.'

'So why didn't you come back for her then?'

'I hated going back to Bristol after that summer. I wrote to her.'

'You wrote to Tessa?' Martha was surprised. 'She didn't tell me that.'

'What did she tell you Martha? She was nineteen, wanting to leave home and I asked her to come to Bristol to be with me. I was a poor student with a few more years to go until I qualified and hadn't anything to offer her but I optimistically thought we'd work something out. I was wrong, obviously, because she never replied and never came.' I paused, the memories coming fast. 'And remember, those were the days before mobile phones and the internet. Letters and telephone calls were all we had then.'

I sat there recalling a long ago moment of offended embarrassment. 'I telephoned the cottage once and her father told me not to call again. I don't know why. I thought he was bloody rude.' I was breathing quite hard I noticed. Curious how angry I felt remembering this stuff.

'George was over protective, he'd lost his wife and now he was seeing his daughter breaking her heart. He didn't know what to do for the best. George was a good kind man Joshua, but I think he made a mistake there, possibly because he wasn't in full possession of all the facts.'

'So why was she breaking her heart when I'd asked her to join me? What happened to Tessa, she obviously made some sort of a life for herself, even if it was shockingly short. What happened to her, tell me please.'

Martha took a deep breath. 'Tessa went away, ran away really. She was gone for over a year. When she came back she had her baby daughter with her.'

There was a long pause while I tried to take this is in. Martha's eyes were looking into mine and I could see that she trying to communicate something. I was trying to do calculations in my head.

Martha spoke again. 'She looks an awful lot like you Joshua.'

For the second time that day my heart nearly stopped and I gasped.

'What on earth are you saying? Are you telling me that Tessa had my child?'

My voice sounded loud in my ears and I got up and started pacing about.

'I can't believe it. Oh Christ!'

I was picking things up and putting them down, it's called displacement behaviour in the profession. It happens when people are upset or shocked or simply don't want to deal with a situation. In a mild form it's when you find yourself cleaning your bathroom rather than revise for exams. I forced myself to get a grip and sat down but almost immediately stood up again.

'I have another daughter?' I couldn't believe it. 'Jesus Christ.'

'There's really no need to use His name.'

'What? Oh I'm sorry. It's just an expression. I'm sorry Martha, I don't know what to say. But why on earth didn't Tessa let me know? I wouldn't have abandoned her.'

'I can see that now,' Martha said. 'But I don't know the answers Joshua, I'm so sorry.'

She went into the kitchen and made another pot of tea. I didn't want any more blasted tea. I was sick of tea and shocked to my core. I was suddenly reminded of Daniel last night, trying to get his head round the fact that he was a father. I'd been detached but caring in a smugly professional way I realised. I remembered the way I'd felt when Nick and Anna had been born. The rug goes right out from beneath your feet and you're bobbing about on cloud nine one minute and shaking with terror the next.

'Hang on, did you say she looks like me, this daughter, Tessa's child, my daughter?' I was gibbering now.

Martha nodded and smiled.

'Can I find her, is she far away?'

'She lives at Orchard Cottage right at the end of my lane. With her new husband. She was in the pub with us all that night when you choked on your beer. She was sitting about ten feet away from you.'

The information was too much and I had to sit down. So I now had two recently married daughters. I had a ridiculous moment of stupid hilarity because I'd only had to pay for one wedding. I started to say this but gave up. Martha was looking at me expectantly and I tried hard to get a grip.

'And what does she know about me, does she know that I'm here?' I asked her.

'She hardly knows anything. It seems that Tessa told her nothing but she learned about you for the first time, a little bit anyway, last summer. She knows your name and that you're a doctor but she doesn't know you are here, although the way word is spreading about your delivery of Fiona's baby last night she very soon will. In the circumstances I think it would be best for you to meet her as soon as possible.'

'What's her name?'

Shit, I thought, my mind racing. I'd only got a few days left in England. What the hell was Marianne going to say, and Anna, and Nick? I realised I was raking my hands through my hair.

'I can't keep her a secret,' I was thinking out loud again. 'I shall have to tell the family.'

'Her name is Susannah, Tessa named her after her great-great-grandmother. She calls herself Su, that's without an 'e' on the end. She's a lovely girl.' Martha said.

'And you said she, Su, has recently married?'

'Yes, on St Valentine's Day this year, here in the village church just across the road. It was a very happy wedding. Su and Rob are very much in love, their's is a real love story.' Martha said.

I realised my eyes were watering again and couldn't speak. I was overwhelmed by it all and wondered whether I was actually capable of meeting my daughter and holding myself together. Martha was watching me compassionately and she spoke kindly.

'Joshua I should speak to Su as soon as possible I think. Before she hears it from someone in the village. It's already Saturday night and you've only got a couple of days left I know.'

'Yes, no, oh I don't know. I wish there was more time to prepare myself. What the hell am I going to say to her? Hello I'm your dad and I've been holidaying here for a few weeks and I didn't even know you existed until an hour ago. It's a joke. Will she even want to meet me?'

'I don't see why not Joshua, Su is a mature and thoughtful young woman and she has a very kind nature. And as far as I know Tessa, although she didn't tell Su about you, never said anything unkind about why you weren't around.'

I was thinking fast. I couldn't back off, I'd always been a man who accepted his responsibilities.

'Okay, go and talk to her. Tell her I'd love to meet her if she feels able. Tell her I'm here until Wednesday late morning. And tell her I'm bloody terrified.'

THIRTY THREE

I hardly noticed Martha leaving. My mind was whirling around, Susannah, Marianne, Anna. Funny how the names seemed to be linked by pronunciation. I felt rather than heard myself moan, it was a hell of a big ask for Marianne to learn and accept that I had another daughter. It wasn't as though I'd been unfaithful, and I certainly hadn't lied to her, we'd both talked about our first loves but it had all been so innocent back then. Somehow the fact that I had a daughter I'd known nothing about seemed in a weird way like a betrayal. I guess the betrayal was to Tessa in the first place. But why hadn't she told me she was pregnant, did she think I would have rejected her? It just didn't make sense to me. I felt terrible as I thought of her going through her pregnancy alone. Then I got angry and paced around the room again, dammit did she have someone else, did another man take my place? But she hadn't married, the name on the gravestone was her maiden name. And then I had to ask myself, was Su really my daughter? Martha seemed to think so but she had no proof.

Several times I thought about picking the phone up and calling home but I realised I couldn't dump all this on my wife without seeing her face to face. There was nobody I could speak to. In desperation I got my notebook out and started a new page. I wrote the heading, just one word. Susannah. What was I going to tell her?

I was facing time down the years and sat there lost in memories. It was all so long ago. I was Nick's age or maybe a bit younger when I'd arrived in the village with a head full of theory and a keen desire to learn. The best thing had been not being at home that summer since my relationship with my father had deteriorated even further. It had been practical to stay living with my parents in Bristol since I was studying in the city, but my father seemed resentful that I wasn't earning a proper crust as he put it. He always had problems with anger and I was planning on joining my student friends in digs. Looking back I suspected that my mum had suffered from depression, not really recognised as an illness then.   Dad and I had never been close, I never had worked out why.

Dr Webster had been an old school country GP, a competent and caring man although a little dated in his outlook and I thought a bit too fond of his place in society. But he and his wife were kind to me although I may not have appreciated it at the time and I smiled, remembering sitting through lunchtime meals with them. You knew what day of the week it was by what Mrs Webster served up. She operated the old routine of a roast on Sunday, cold cuts on Monday and rissoles on Tuesday made up from everything that was left.   On Wednesday it would be boiled gammon with mashed potatoes both of which I loathed, then thinly sliced ham with unadorned boiled potatoes and a plain salad of lettuce and tomatoes, which I could tolerate and of course white fish in a parsley sauce on Fridays which was pretty nauseating. Vegetables were always overcooked and very plain. For the life of me I couldn't remember what we ate on Saturdays but there was nothing spicy apart from the mustard which came with the sliced ham.   No Asian food, no pizza, no speciality breads and any cheese was always either Stilton or cheddar. Food in those days was something to be endured, not enjoyed. I shook my head in disbelief. No wonder people were slimmer in those days.

Outside the practice I'd tried at first to get out and about by borrowing an old bicycle and exploring the lanes and villages but I'd been lonely. Dr Webster's abiding passion was cricket and he'd got a team together over the years and invited me to join in a few games. I'd played at school and wasn't too shabby so I agreed, the company of the village boys and men was better than nothing. We played on the field opposite the pub, which the local junior school had also used as a playing field.   There was no pavilion and no changing rooms but the pub landlord at the time was a member and let us use the skittles room to change and store our stuff. It was all really a big fool about with a bunch of blokes having a laugh. Cricket wasn't all that big in Cornwall although the neighbouring parish had a team and there was much joking about the Cornish preferring to dance about waving flowers and lighting bonfires. In fact the village skittles games had a bigger following so Dr Webster decided that the cricket team and the skittles team should take turns at playing each other. It was all just silliness, an excuse to spend time at the pub and mess around. We made up our own rules and the landlord proposed that a trophy should be awarded to the team with the best scores at the end of the summer. I was made captain of the cricket team, I don't remember who was captain of the skittles team.

With the focus of activity on the village pub the landlord, who looking back I realised was a canny businessman, employed a pretty barmaid on Friday nights and Saturdays when the games were being played. I first set eyes on Tessa through a haze of cigarette smoke and I guess my first words to her would have been a request for half a bitter. I wasn't a cider drinker.

She was beautiful with her long wavy toffee coloured hair and expressive hazel eyes and right from the start we were easy in each other's company. I don't recall her being flirty or coquettish, she was intelligent and curious about life outside Cornwall and interested in everything I had to say about life in a city, and I was interested in everything about her. I lost no time in asking her what there was to do in the evenings and she'd said that there was nothing, expressing her frustration with the difficulty in even getting to the cinema, a bus ride away.

'You can get there alright if you get the tea time bus, but it's the getting back that's a trial.' She had said to me, bemoaning the fact that she also lived just outside the village which made travelling more difficult. And I recalled that her father had been unhappy about her being out on her own, something to do with her mother having died when she was a child.

We went on a few bike rides up to the moor where we walked and talked for hours in the summer evenings and on Sunday afternoons. Tessa had sometimes made us simple picnics, home made Cornish pasties and with plums from the orchard. That had been the food of the gods, eating with her up on the moors in the sunshine and that was where we had our first kiss, in a pretty secluded place by an old quarry pond called the Gold Diggings. She'd reached over to brush a pastry crumb from the corner of my mouth and I'd grabbed her wrist and kissed the palm of her hand and pretended to bite her fingers, then pulled her over to me and kissed her. She tasted of plums. Time seemed to last forever when I was with Tessa.

When I woke unrefreshed and late on Sunday morning I still didn't know what I was going to say to Susannah and I hadn't written a thing down. What would I want to know if I was in her place I wondered. Had we loved each other? Was it a one night stand after a village dance? Where was I conceived? I wasn't sure about the last question and my stomach was rumbling. There wasn't much in the cottage to eat so I grabbed my jacket and walked up to the farm shop, thankful that it stayed open all hours.

There were some tubs of cut flowers outside the door with a handwritten sign saying that they were locally grown. There were sweet peas and some orange and yellow things I didn't recognise. Acting on an impulse I took the sweet peas and made a few other purchases and walked back to the cottage. Dumping the bag indoors I went straight back out and crossed the road to the church.

The shadows were quite long where she lay and I stood there in sorrow and disbelief for a very long time, just wishing I could have seen her again if only once to say I'd never forgotten that summer. I murmured her name into the silence.

'If there's any sort of afterlife Tessa you'll know what has always been in my heart. I'll carry it to my own grave. It's never left me.'

I stooped and placed the sweet peas on the grave, they did smell lovely. A breeze, cold in the shadows whispered past my face and briefly I shivered. As I turned to go back to the cottage I heard my name called. It was Graham out with one of the labradors, taking a short cut through the churchyard.

'Chilly when you're not in the sun isn't it? How are you Josh, I hear you're quite the man of the moment regarding Fiona's baby.' Graham shook my hand while his labrador goosed me and waved its tail. I could smell the dog's breath and it wasn't pleasant. Graham's black eyes were assessing me. 'You look done in, are you feeling okay?' He asked.

'Been quite a day, quite a few days actually.' I didn't say why.

'Do you need company? I'm on my own. Oliver's away in London visiting family, I'd be happy to share a glass of something, cheer us both up I think.'

'I wouldn't mind that.' The thought of being in the cottage on my own didn't appeal. 'But I haven't eaten yet Graham. I was just going to make myself something.'

'Oh I can oblige, I was just going to have some cold chicken, there's enough for two. Be my guest please or I'll have to feed it to the dogs and they are plenty fat enough already.'

Graham glanced at where I'd been standing and I knew that he'd noticed the flowers.

'Did you know the Charlesworth's back in the day?'

'I met him once or twice, I knew Tessa briefly.'

'Odd life she had by all accounts. Tragically short.' Graham was looking at me curiously.

I nodded but didn't reply. I didn't trust myself to discuss her with a stranger especially as I didn't know what sort of a life she'd had. We started walking down the path to the road together and I changed the subject to dogs. Graham was sensitive enough to follow my lead. He didn't mention the flowers. We spent a companionable few hours eating and talking over a chicken salad and a good bottle of Chilean white. We followed that with a slice of lemon tart and coffee. Graham was an entertaining host and brilliant at taking my mind off my troubles. We got onto common ground, talking about medical stuff, eventually roaring with laughter over the crazy silly things that people got up to. Graham had done a stint in A&E and I was able to top some of his tales with tales of my own about the mad things lonely people got up to in the outback that only a caring and professional doctor could understand. It was like telling tales from the confessional.

Eventually I decided I'd outstayed my welcome. I was grateful for Graham's company and said so as I thanked him for an unexpectedly pleasant time.

'That's okay Josh, glad to have helped. This is a small village and secrets have been shared between friends in recent months. I hope you can find some answers before you go home.'

He gave me a long look. I half expected him to put one finger alongside his nose and wink but he wasn't that crass.

'Thanks again Graham. Cheers.'

I strolled back to the cottage thinking a bit about the time I had lived in Graham's house. Time that still mattered to me even though it no longer existed. It was early evening and the air was very still. A cat crossed the road ahead of me, intent on hunting. Taking the key with its large fob I unlocked the door and went in. As I turned to close it the draught moved something on the door mat. It flipped over and settled, a piece of paper folded in half with my name written on it.

Hello. I called to see you. Can we meet tomorrow please? Any time will suit me. Su.

She'd already been to see me. It was a note from Susannah. I sat on the edge of the sofa looking at it for a long time, my senses picking up the recent presence of my daughter. I thought I could detect a fragrance and I sniffed the note.

There was a telephone number. The handwriting was strong, clear and forward sloping, and placed centrally on the paper. The writing of a balanced and happy sort of person I thought and straightforward, like her mother. And Su had been strong enough and determined enough to come to meet me, or to confront me, I wasn't sure which.

I was tempted to phone her there and then but I bottled out. I showered and cleaned my teeth and fell into an early bed with the lamp on. I was exhausted but I couldn't relax so I just lay there propped against a couple of pillows holding Su's note and trying to think about what I would say to her. The words just wouldn't come. When I woke up the drawn was breaking, the lamp was still on and I was still holding her note.

After breakfast I picked up my phone and went outside. I was as nervous as hell but I put the number in and made the call. It was answered on the second ring and there was a slight pause before a low female voice spoke.

'Hello.'

'Hello, is that Su?' I realised that my palms were sweating and I rubbed one hand on my jeans. 'This is Josh Milton speaking.'

I heard a ragged intake of breath and felt sudden compassion for her. Why was I so nervous when she was probably feeling much the same.

'Yes, hello, this is Su.'

'Su I'm so sorry I wasn't here yesterday, I didn't imagine you'd call by. I was over at The Manor House quite unexpectedly for a few hours. I guess I should've given Martha my phone number but it didn't cross my mind. There's been a lot to take in the last day or so. I just wasn't thinking.' I spoke in a rush and then dwindled to a halt.

'That's okay. I was a bit impulsive. I was on my own for a bit, my husband was out spinning with Martha.' She sounded tired.

I had a couple of weird mental images. I could see Martha using a spinning wheel and then thought of spinning at the gym.

'They were taking a class at the gym?' I said, grasping at something normal to say to my new daughter.

'No, spinning honey, he helps Martha in her back kitchen. They always do the bees together. Sunday was a good day for it.'

Okay so that cleared that up then.

'Interesting, but look Su, there's a lot I want to say, let's not do it over the phone. Shall I come to you or do you want to come here, or should we meet someplace neutral? Or do you want to have someone with you? I don't really know how to play this situation, it's not one I've ever been in!'

I gave a shaky laugh. I was walking up and down the small garden, hardly aware of anything except how hard I was gripping the phone.

'I think I shall come down to you if that's alright. It's only a few minutes in the car. Should I come now? Have you had breakfast?'

'Yes. Come as soon as you are ready. I'll put the kettle on.'

I heard her say okay and she rang off. I was taking great breaths and exhaling loudly. I was indoors and putting the kettle on to boil before I realised it. What was this predilection the British had for hot drinks in times of crisis I wondered. I dashed upstairs and checked my appearance and thought that for an old guy in a state of shock and anxiety I didn't look too bad but I washed my hands and for some reason brushed my teeth again. I didn't want to have a clammy handshake and bad breath. Then I wondered if I should put a nicer shirt on so I went into the bedroom and changed and used a bit of talc so I had to wash my hands again.

I heard a car pull up outside and was momentarily thankful that the little Cornish villages off the tourist track didn't have problems with double yellow lines and parking restrictions. I was downstairs and opening the door just as she raised her hand to knock.

It was like being hit with kryptonite. It was like seeing Tessa through a veil but with hair the colour mine used to be, tawny gold Irish hair. It was her eyes though which startled me, not my dark blue eyes and not Tessa's hazel eyes but unusual green blue flecked eyes with long eyelashes. She was wearing an opal pendant necklace.

334

'I've seen that before.' Were the first words I said as she stood there. At least it stopped me gaping at her but my throat had gone dry and I thought I sounded a bit odd.

Her hand went to the necklace and I could see that she was trembling slightly.

'It belonged to my great-great-grandmother. My mother gave it to me.'

She had a nice voice and there wasn't a Cornish accent. We stood there on the threshold looking at each other for a few moments. Time had just spun away from me and I wasn't really conscious of anything except this girl's face.

'Should I come in then?' Su asked me.

I stepped back to let her in. 'Yes of course, come on in, I'm sorry, I guess I'm a bit shocked by all this.'

We went into the little sitting room and I looked about feeling helpless. It wasn't a feeling I was used to.

'I think I remember switching the kettle on. Do you want to be in here Su or should we sit at the kitchen table, or outside, it's a nice day.' I was fussing like a stupid old git.

She glanced at me and looked around.

'I just need to sit down. I don't care where.' She followed me into the kitchen. 'This is nice and bright, let's sit in here shall we. And I drink tea if you have it, I don't like coffee.'

'Tea it is.' I sounded hearty and false and told myself not to behave like a prat. Su was looking at me, her expression serious. 'Can I be honest Su, if I sound like a prat it's because I'm nervous.'

'Makes two of us then. Except the part about being a prat.'

'No, you don't look as though you've ever done a prattish thing in your life.' It was like talking to Nick.

'Oh I have, but hasn't everybody.' She was much more relaxed than me.

I couldn't help it. 'You look like your mother.' And I made a noise between a cough and choke. 'You'll have to help me out here Su. This is a pretty emotional thing for me.'

She got up and took my hand and sat me down at the table. Before I knew it there was a glass of water in front of me and she'd fished a box of tissues out of her bag. Then she put the teapot and two mugs down on the table and found milk in the fridge. I was suitably grateful.

'Martha told me everything you said yesterday. I gather she came here to confront you, she can be quite a force but her heart is good. She's been kind to me.'

We sat and looked at each other.

'Are you okay with this Su?' I asked her.

She nodded, saying nothing.

'Su you have me at a disadvantage. You know more about me than I know about you. Let's start at the beginning. Tell me why you don't have a Cornish accent for starters.'

I wish I'd had a tape recorder or put my phone onto record as I listened to her speaking. I learned about her early life, how unconventional and questing Tessa had been. I heard about what a loving mother she had been and about her skills as a teacher to the little kids, although untrained she'd schooled the kids at the commune. The tea went cold so I made a fresh pot. I would have preferred something stronger.

'I have to ask Su, did your mum meet anyone else?'

'It's funny but I've thought about that a lot since I started doing family research. And others have asked the same question, but I don't ever remember anyone special in our lives that way. In the commune people weren't necessarily monogamous, the adults had quite strong views about roles in relationships and how they fucked you up. But I honestly don't remember anybody being described as special to mum in that way.'

She didn't apologise for the expletive and didn't need too, it was appropriately expressive.

'So your accent could have been Welsh since you spent so much time there.' I lightened the moment.

Su shook her head. 'We were a group of people from all over the British Isles. Geordie, Brummie, Cockney, Irish and West

Country. They wanted to change the world in a small way. What I do remember is the laughter and how helpful and capable people were. They had skills or developed them and the odd loser or weirdo was weeded out and sent packing. There was quite a strong moral code about living in community and understanding the consequences of your actions. It was all pre-Gaia and wasn't an environmental movement but looking back they were quite an enlightened bunch, I often wonder what happened to them all.'

'Are they still on the site?' I asked.

'No, it was all disbanded years ago. I drove there as soon as I was able to drive and had a car. It's now a proper smallholding with a single family living on it. The guy who started the commune on his family home died and the place was sold.'

There was a moment of quiet between us and I sat watching her. I was fascinated by Su, I could see glimpses of my face in hers and glimpses of Tessa but she was a personality separate and apart, thoughtful, considerate and I thought, kind.

'Su I'm wishing I had been part of your life, but you probably wouldn't be the extraordinary woman you are today if I had been around. Tessa obviously did her best in difficult circumstances but I still can't understand why, for the life of me, she didn't get in touch and tell me she was pregnant. Or why she didn't tell you about me.'

Those questioning opal eyes were turned on me.

'Perhaps mum thought I was too young to know about you. I don't really know. You really are my father?'

The question surprised me. 'Su look at us, I think there's no doubt I'm your father. We're physically alike and Martha could see the similarity and ...' I stopped, struck by something Graham had said. 'I think other people know don't they? Graham said something at The Manor House yesterday about secrets being recently shared.'

'Yes, Graham and Oliver were part of the revealing. It's how I think of it.' She said in response to my questioning look. 'They have both been wonderful, they came into my life at my lowest time. I've been very lucky.'

I sat enthralled as she talked about her family history, the love story between Susannah Penrose and Robert Williams, her great-great grandparents, and the tragedy that followed. Then she explained about the Charlesworth connection and at the mention of The Manor House I sat bolt upright.

'But I lived in The Manor House for nearly four months that summer, the summer I met your mother. It's weird that love in your family should have that house as a central focus.'

Su thought for a moment. 'But it was lost love in both cases wasn't it. My great-great grandmother had lost the man she loved, who had fathered her unborn child, and my own mother somehow managed to lose you.'

There were tears in her eyes and I reached over the table and took her hands in mine.

'I'm so sorry love. I don't know what else I can say.'

'You can tell me about my mother, tell me what happened. Tell me your story.' She said. She didn't call me Josh and she certainly didn't call me dad.

THIRTY FOUR

'Where do I begin?' I let go of her hands and stood up. 'I need a change of scenery and a bit of fresh air. Let's take ourselves outside shall we?'

Su nodded and followed me into the pretty garden. I got the cushions and we sat opposite each other again at the little table on the sunny patio. Neither of us wanted another cup of tea. All the thoughts and memories that had been sparked off in the recent weeks back in England enveloped me in a kind of a buzzing cloud. It was a separate, golden time in my mind, nothing to do with and nothing like the thirty happy years I'd had as a husband and father in my life with Marianne.

For some reason it was Marianne's face I could see now, as clearly as if she was sitting right by me. I could see the focus in her grey eyes, the dark thick straight hair framing her calm face. I realised that one of the things I loved about her was her ability to be straightforward, measured and kind. She wasn't a fussy tricky woman. Tessa had had a similar quality. I found it was Marianne I wanted to tell the story to but I also wanted some sort of forgiveness from all my women.

The robin I'd thrown crumbs to when Nick was here appeared at the edge of the patio and flew up onto the fence, bobbing and flirting his tail. It was so quiet here. I waited for my thoughts to settle and for the words to come. I heard a voice asking me to be truthful. How much do you tell someone and how much should remain private, and do we remember accurately all those moments which lead to something special and momentous, can we even do them justice. I sighed.

Su spoke quietly. 'Is this too painful for you?'

'No. Well yes, it is painful, but it's important that I get the words right. Saying things like "we were both young and it was a beautiful summer and we were thrown together and in the circumstances the almost inevitable happened" doesn't really describe it.' I took a deep breath and spread my hands on the table. My training recognised it as an unconscious gesture of honesty and the professional part of me acknowledged it. I consciously dropped my shoulders and began.

I started with the easy bits and told her all about my upbringing, about my older sister Pamela, the uncomfortable relationship we had with our parents, about wanting to be a doctor from about the age of twelve. I talked about riding and swimming and about studying hard for years, so hard that a personal life, especially when you are still living at home as I was then, was virtually impossible. I told her about the sense of relief and freedom I'd felt when I came down to Cornwall that summer to stay with the Webster's at The Manor House. About how good it had been to learn things in a practical way from an experienced practitioner who simply expected the best of me.

Su was nodding and she gave me a few moments break while she recounted a story of her own training in microbiology. That was a whole other discussion to have with her. I was amazingly proud that she'd pursued that profession and told her about Nick, her half brother, training as a dentist.

'I have a half brother and a half sister. I'm not alone am I. I've got family.' She was moved by the idea and it was my turn to give her a break.

'I met Tessa for the first time here in The Wheal. All the matches and games were played from there and I joined in to keep Dr Webster happy and to give me something to do in the evenings and at weekends. She was pulling pints and doing bar work and I couldn't take my eyes off her. She kind of glowed and when I spoke to her something clicked into place. I just wanted to spend my time with her. She was lovely, beautiful and bright. We made each other laugh and it was like I'd always known her we got along so well.'

Su was nodding. 'I felt like that with Rob.'

I hardly heard her speak. It was like watching home cinema footage in my head. The human brain is truly the most amazing thing.

'I borrowed a bicycle and she took me for bike rides so I could explore the area a bit. I told the Webster's that we were going to look at churches but we went for walks and picnics instead. Anything we could do to prolong our time together we did and do you know I don't remember a drop of rain that summer. Whenever I wasn't working with Dr Webster or doing some studying I was outdoors with Tessa or at the pub playing games and waiting for Tessa to finish work. After the pub we'd walk back along the lanes to Orchard Cottage with our bicycles and I'd kiss her goodnight at the copse by the bend in the road before you get to the cottage. Her dad used to lean over the front gate waiting for her to get home so she had to get on her bike and pretend to be a bit puffed out as she cycled the last fifty yards. I often used to stand and wait until they had gone in and then I would cycle past and go up the lane, turn around and cycle back to the village. If I could get a glimpse of her face through a window I felt as though I'd won something.'

The feelings and the memories were rolling through me. It was quite cathartic letting all this out.

'I'd never had feelings for anyone before. I mean I knew I loved my sister but that's a different kind of love. And although a couple of the female students at university were attractive and flirtatious I'd never fallen in love. I really had no idea what it meant until I met her. With Tessa I could imagine a whole future of happiness and possibilities of a life together. I felt so right with her. She was precious and special and everything about her mattered to me.'

I paused for a minute. Su was motionless, absorbed in what I was saying.

'We talked about what she wanted to do with her life. I know she wanted to get away from the village and live a bit, and she wanted to go to a city. She was hungry for culture, the arts and theatre. She'd not had any career advice, in those days unless you had vocational leanings like in medicine, music or maths we were always told to go into the civil service. Women were invited to try female occupations like nursing or teaching. Joining the armed forces was another option if you wanted to get away from home. But Tessa was a bit of a free spirit who needed to fly for a bit. I wanted to help her do that. I suggested she should get up to Bristol where I was and I was sure I'd be able to find some way for us to be together. I desperately wanted to leave home as well. The only question was how to do it when I was on a student grant. Of course she said she'd get full time work in a pub or a restaurant to begin with and she was all ready to get work to support me. She was amazing. She really was amazing.'

I stopped speaking, lost in my thoughts and memories. Our ideas and hopes had been so strong, how on earth had she slipped through my fingers and disappeared. It didn't make sense to me. I felt drained and sat back in my chair, shaking my head.

Su was looking at me sympathetically. 'I suggest we make a sandwich and take a comfort stop. Our blood sugar must be falling and this is all pretty intense.'

I was surprised to see that a couple of hours had passed. As we buttered bread and assembled things to eat together I felt a subtle shift in our very new relationship. There was something very special about sharing food together. When we sat down outside to eat I asked her if she'd ever thought about who her father was. She nodded with her mouth full, making an impatient gesture with her hand as she chewed and swallowed.

'Yes I did, I used to look at the men in the commune and wonder if one of them was my father. But after mum died and I came back here to live with grandfather I really began to wonder why my life was different and how I came to be. But I never said anything to him because he was pretty cut up about mum dying so young, and I started at a proper school and was fully engaged in learning how to deal with conventional teenagers. It was a pretty tough time. Grandfather used to do his best to keep us occupied, he took me swimming and riding and sailing just as he'd done with my mum when her mother died. We were busy surviving and time passed. Then I went away to study and never really came back. It must have been so hard on him. And then he was dead and it was too late to ask questions. It was only because of a chance conversation with Martha last year that I learned that you existed and that they'd guessed you were my father. Then a friend in the village did a bit of digging, she does a voluntary stint in the library on cataloguing local information. That's how I learned your name.'

I ate my sandwich as I considered her story.

'So when I phoned from Bristol to speak to Tessa and your grandfather answered the phone, why did he tell me never to call or to bother them again?'

Su had no idea. 'I'm as bewildered as you. Martha told me you wrote to my mother as well.'

'I did. It was the only way of communicating in those days.'

'What address did you use?' She asked me.

'I wrote from home, my parent's home. I told her that I was looking for digs and that I had student friends who would let her use their sofa while we got ourselves sorted out.'

Su's eyes widened and she put her sandwich down. 'So mum was intending to come up to Bristol to join you and to get work to support you both and then she found she was pregnant and knew that she wasn't going to be able to work for long.'

The penny dropped. 'And she thought she would have been a burden on a penniless student and she didn't see how we would cope.' I finished Su's sentence for her. 'Is that what happened, was that the reason she didn't come, she didn't want to be a burden or to trap me into marriage or something? Oh Jesus Christ.'

Unlike Martha, Su didn't admonish me for using His name. I got up and walked up and down a bit, always my habit when thinking.

'I'm trying not to tear my hair out here.' I said, absently raking my fingers through my hair, another of my habits which always amused Marianne. 'But I would have married her, dammit I loved her. Ye gods there would have been ways of getting support and help for a couple of years until I qualified. Oh god, my poor silly proud Tessa!'

I sat down again, too gobsmacked to speak. The thought of Tessa struggling along on her own with a small baby horrified me. Those were the good old days, when doctors didn't like to prescribe the pill to a girl unless she had a ring on her finger, when society was still censorious about unmarried mothers. This was a double kryptonite day as Nick would have put it.

Su was looking at me, taking it all in and thinking.

'When I was little I remember going to Bristol. I'd never seen a real city before so the memory stuck, especially because we caught a taxi. It was the most exciting thing I'd ever done, we'd been on a train and in a car. I thought it was a holiday. Mum was looking for a house on a road that sounded like a flower. I remember a green hedge and a semi-detached house with a red door. Mum spoke to a woman who didn't know who she was looking for. I think she let us use their toilet and then we left. Mum was upset but I didn't know why.'

My blood ran cold. 'My folks lived at Coronation Road. Maybe you heard it as carnation, like the flower. It was a semi, but they left not very long after I moved out and went to a retirement bungalow in another part of Bristol. Tessa went to look for me didn't she. My poor darling Tessa.'

We both had tears. It was emotionally exhausting.

'So you loved each other and it was all just a stupid misunderstanding.' Su was shaking her head and rocking backwards and forwards on her chair with her arms crossed in front of her and her hands squeezing her upper arms. 'It's so sad.'

We sat there in the sunshine with a box of tissues between us like two recently bereaved souls. But, I thought, there has to be some healing in all this. At least we'd found each other.

'Su I came back here to this village quite deliberately as you must realise. It was for purely selfish reasons, I had no idea of your existence. I just wanted to find out in a low key kind of way what had happened to Tessa Charlesworth and to lay the past to rest if possible. I've never been able to forget her but that makes me feel horribly disloyal to my wife Marianne, because I love her too, very much. I don't know what I'm going to say to her when I get back home, but I have to ask your permission to tell her about you. And then I have to tell my kids. How do you feel about that? You said earlier that you felt you weren't alone and that you had a family now. And that's very important but.' I stopped talking. I didn't really know how to go on.

'But I'm the cuckoo in the nest.' Su said.

'No. Please don't say that.' I felt awful.

'We need to talk more. A lot more'. Su said, looking at her watch. 'Would you like to come over to the cottage tonight for dinner. It's nothing posh. You'll meet Rob, my husband. He's no fool, and another head might help us sort something out don't you think?'

I agreed. It was a great idea. We decided I should be there about half past six.

THIRTY FIVE

That gave me about three hours. I went upstairs and crashed out after setting the alarm on my phone for just after five. Despite my head whirling I slept without moving for a couple of hours and woke up to the alarm beeping. Once again there was the ritual of shower, shave and dress and this time I drove up to the farm shop and bagged another bunch of flowers and a bottle of Australian red. The girls in the shop were giggling.

'More flowers for Fiona and the baby? Aren't they lucky.'

I was noncommittal and let them enjoy making two plus two into five. I checked my appearance in the driver's mirror and drove slowly to Orchard Cottage, accompanied by a lovely girl on a bicycle. At the copse by the bend in the road she drew back and waved me on, smiling. I blew her a kiss.

There was a car I recognised as belonging to Su and an unmarked silver van which I guessed belonged to her husband. Bloody hell, I thought, I'm about to meet another son-in-law. I squeezed the hire car into a gap and got out. Su was already walking to the side gate to greet me. I liked the thought that she'd been looking out for me. She looked a lot more relaxed and confident on her own ground.

'You made it,' Su was smiling at me. 'I thought you might have fallen asleep or got cold feet.'

'I did fall asleep. This is all very tiring for an old guy like me. I bought you these flowers. I don't know if you like cut flowers.' I said, taking in the pretty garden.

'Yes I do, that's lovely of you. Come through.' She unlatched the gate and I stepped in, observing the scaffolding to one side.

Su followed my gaze. 'Rob is putting a garden room onto the side, he has all sorts of plans for the old place.'

'It will look good. He's a tidy worker   I'd forgotten how pretty old English cottages are after decades in Oz.'

'And how small.' A man's voice spoke.

I turned and looked straight into Rob's face, we were the same height. I was used to looking up to my son who was a couple of inches taller than me.

'I'm Rob, Su's husband.'

'That makes you my son-in-law sort of, I guess. Well I'm honoured believe me Rob. I'm Josh Milton.'

We shook hands and I offered him the bottle of red. 'I don't know if this is appropriate?'

He took it and smiled broadly. This guy Rob was a good looking man with a slightly aquiline nose and a slim strong muscular physique.

'Su's already told you about my many weaknesses has she? Red wine, cats and salty caramel chocolate.'

I laughed, he had the same sort of social ease that Nick had.

'I shall bear the chocolate in mind for next time and no, she didn't mention the thing with the cats.' In fact I didn't really know a thing about him.

At that moment a cute little tortoiseshell cat came weaving through the garden making little inquisitive yipping noises, her tail up straight and curved over at the top. I knew it was a female because torties always are, just as ginger cats are almost always male. One of those weird facts I'd picked up at a pub quiz or something.

'Meet Daisy Fur Pants, the female in charge of this establishment.' Rob said.

I bent down and offered her my hand which she sniffed delicately and then before I could stroke her she took the side of my forefinger in her teeth and gave me a gentle nip.

'Oh that's different.' I said, standing up again. 'What with dogs goosing me and cats nipping me and Fiona's horse with her own equine opinions on how things should be done.'

'Like I said, she's in charge and that's her being really friendly,' Rob said. 'A bit peculiar maybe but she fits in ok.'

We went into the cottage and Su indicated a downstairs cloakroom. 'You can wash your hands in there, wash the Daisy lick off.' She still didn't use my name.

I did as she suggested and joined them in the kitchen where something smelled nice. I could detect garlic and herbs. Su was putting the flowers I'd bought into a vase and Rob was already pouring red wine, a different bottle I noticed, into glasses. He turned to me and handed me a glass.

'I'd already got this one warmed if that's okay with you Josh.'

We stood there in the kitchen and raised our glasses in a slightly awkward way, the Brits don't have a deeply embedded cultural habit with wine and it shows. We're not relaxed until we've had a glass or two.

'To family.' I said, almost without thinking.

'To family.' They echoed, Su turning slightly pink.

'Su said you knew where to find Orchard Cottage.'

'Yes, but until this moment I have never set foot inside. It's very pretty.' I said.

'Mum was born here, and so was grandfather.' Su told me.

'I don't think I knew that.' I said, looking around and liking its dimensions and layout. 'Did you do all this?' I asked Rob indicating the hand built kitchen units. 'It's a nice design.'

'No.' Rob shook his head. 'All made and fitted years ago by Su's grandfather. He was ahead of his time and a skilled man for someone who made a living in sales. We wouldn't change it.'

As Su busied herself quietly at the stove Rob chatted about making things. I mentioned I'd got a bit of an interest in woodwork and more particularly in wood carving. Our talk moved onto the church bench ends in Altarnun and I mentioned Fiona's drawings for a toy box lid. He picked up a folder from a stack and opened it.

'I've had some input from Fiona about some metalwork I've been doing for their house.'

I was looking at beautiful drawings for window casements and fire irons.

'Wow they're very nice. Is that her work?'

'No it's mine, but she had some creative suggestions.' Rob said.

I was looking at him with respect. I heard Su giggle.

'He's too clever by half, he surprises me even now.'

'What, after five months of marriage you're still surprised by me?' Rob laughed and went over and kissed her on the forehead.

I watched this little unrehearsed cameo of affection with a slight pang. Here they were, very happy together in the house where Tessa had lived. She had known this room, her hands had touched some of these things. I wished for an intense moment that she could see what I was seeing, our beautiful happy daughter. I took another sip of my wine. It was deep and fruity and rather good. Rob was looking at me and I got the impression he hadn't missed a thing.

'The wine is even nicer with food, especially the things Su cooks.' He said.

We sat down to a home made lasagne that I could only describe as succulent, followed by a small light salad which cleansed the palate and then fresh fruit with a decent selection of cheeses. It was simple, tasty and elegant and I complimented her.

'I've always liked cooking, and Graham at The Manor House has been giving me lessons. So has Martha.' She said.

'I've experience of Graham's cooking,' I said. 'He's awesome.'

'He organised our wedding reception and did quite a lot of the catering himself.' Rob said.

I looked at Su. 'Of course, you married quite recently, I didn't know but there's a lot I don't know. Where was the reception held?' And who gave you away I wondered.

'It was actually at The Manor House. The boys put a marquee in the field just behind the door in the walled garden at the back. It was the driest February in living memory so we got lucky, especially as we walked to the church together from Rob's house in the village.'

'Williams, of course.' The penny dropped. 'The house Daniel is renting.' I said, vaguely aware of having made a house visit to an old couple there a long time ago, my mind running along several levels at once. It made a connection.

'So celebrating your marriage from The Manor House laid a few ghosts to rest then?'

Su nodded and got up. 'On balance I think it's a happy ending. Come into the sitting room, I can show you a couple of photographs.'

I followed her through while Rob stayed behind to clear up. It was a comfortable and graceful room done out in soft greens and blues and with a wood stove at the far end. The flowers I had brought were on a built-in bookcase. Su pointed to a little oak bureau holding some framed photographs of her wedding day so I picked up a photo frame and studied the picture as she looked over my shoulder.

'I'm wearing an old dress that belonged to my mother, do you recognise it?'

I shook my head. 'I have to say I don't. I only ever saw her in day dresses or jeans. But you do look lovely Su.'

There were a couple of pictures showing them with a group of people, Rob's family apparently. She named a few of them.

'Rob's sister Jay, and his brother-in-law Phil, Martha's son. Phil gave me away.'

Well that answered my earlier unspoken question I thought, as I looked at the photo, looking at a stocky man with good if somewhat blunt features and posing a little stiffly for the photographer.

'It's a pity I haven't any with you.' Su voiced my own thoughts.

'I was thinking the same.' I smiled at her. 'But maybe we can fix that.'

'I have one of you and mum together.'

'What? You do. I don't remember any being taken. How come?' To say I was surprised was an understatement.

Su opened the bureau and reached inside. 'I think I mentioned that my friend in the village does some family research locally and she found this in an archive the village is putting together for everyone to use.'

She was holding a small parish magazine and opened it to the centrefold. I got my reading glasses out of my shirt pocket and put them on as she handed it to me. Once again I had that dizzying sensation of the years falling away and I was right there in the moment. Tessa was handing me a trophy because I was the captain of the winning cricket versus skittle team. The information wasn't clearly written and didn't adequately describe the daft summer we'd had with the made up rules. I was completely lost as I looked at the picture and remembered.

'We were laughing. The so-called trophy was a snow globe of a village church that someone had stuck onto a piece of wood they'd painted black.'

I was speaking quietly, gazing at Tessa's face. She was holding a straw hat in the other hand, and was turned to camera, an expression of delight on her face. In the photograph I was in profile looking down at her. It was a small colour photograph, a half page of an A5 pamphlet, but it was a precious memento.

'You have my colour hair Su. But you're as pretty as your mother was. I don't have anything of her except for my memories.'

I stood there looking at the picture, seeing both our names in print. We really had known each other, we really had lived there, in that time, the words alone were proof. After that presentation we had walked off together, away from the pub and the noisy boozy silly celebrations and over the games field, over the stile and across the field to the copse. Just walking, holding hands and being together. We had talked about me leaving the village, it had almost been time for me to go back to Bristol. We'd discussed her ideas about working and I'd put an arm around her as we walked, promising that I'd look after her as soon as I was qualified. It was the first time I told her that I loved her. It was the first time we'd properly made love, there in the copse. It hadn't been planned.

When I looked up I realised that Su had moved away from my side and was sitting on a little sofa.

'You were very far away.'

'I was.' I sat down opposite her, still holding the magazine. 'I think that day was when you were conceived. Shortly before I left the village.' I hoped that wasn't too much information.

She didn't show any reaction to my statement. 'I have another photograph of mum taken at almost that same moment. Grandfather was a good amateur photographer and must have had his camera and tripod set up to record the event that day. Shall I get it?'

I nodded. 'Yes please.'

Su left the room as Rob came in carrying a tray with a coffee pot and a teapot on it and three mugs.

'Su doesn't drink coffee, she has peppermint tea after our evening meal. You're welcome to either Josh.'

I accepted coffee with a small splash of milk, enjoying being part of their little family rituals. Su returned holding a large framed photograph and handed it to me. I was glad I was sitting down. I exhaled slowly. There she was, her head turned and laughing at me as she so often had. It was a close head and shoulder's shot just of her. Her flower-sprigged green and white dress, her streaky toffee blonde hair, her pretty face. She looked so happy, caught in a moment of joy.

'Lemons.' I spoke aloud.

They looked at me and Su raised her eyebrows. Again there was that amused quizzical look that I used to see on Tessa's face.

'I just remembered your mum and the lemon juice.' I said.

'I'm none the wiser but go on.' Su was interested.

'That summer the landlord was trying out new drinks to encourage more ladies to come to the pub and support the teams, and he bought lemons to slice and put into the drinks. It made them more elegant or exotic and he could charge a fortune. Tessa used to take the unused slices home with her and squeeze the juice out. She used to comb it through her hair and sit outside in the sun to dry it. It acted as a natural bleach and gave her blonde highlights and streaks. She had lovely hair.'

'I must give it a try.' Su said.

'The lemon juice summer.' Rob said sympathetically.

I reached for my mug and saw that my hand was shaking a bit. The coffee had cooled but it was pleasantly strong and I drank it down.

'Phew, that's better.' It was all that I could say.

'We could get a copy of the photograph made for you if you'd like.' Su said.

I was thinking fast. 'I'm not sure how Marianne would feel about that,' I said. 'But if you don't mind I'll take a shot using my phone, and a couple of you two together would be good.'

We had a bit of fun doing all that and then Rob took some of me sitting with Su using my phone and their own camera. It had been a long day but a good one by the time I decided I should go back to the holiday cottage. They waved me off and Su said she'd come and see me later in the day. I promised to be in as I was going to be sorting out my stuff and packing.

I drove away smiling slightly. I slowed down on the bend by the copse but the lovely girl on the bicycle wasn't there in the lane any more.

THIRTY SIX

I was up early the next day and used the spare room to sort out all my stuff. No way was I packing used clothes and unpacking a stinky suitcase back home so I put the washing machine through its paces and got all my shirts on hangers on the rotary line outside and all the other stuff on the lines. It looked like a ship dressed overall for a harbour gala by the time Su turned up. This time she kissed my cheek which was rather nice.

'Rob enjoyed meeting you last night. He said you were genuine.'

'A genuine what? Pillock?' I smiled at her.

'It means you're an honest man.'

'I think that's true. It saves a lot of messing about and my mum always said you had to have a damn good memory if you wanted to tell lies. They will catch you out in the end.'

'She was right. I prefer the truth as well.' Su said.

I switched the kettle on. 'I found some herbal teas in the kitchen cupboard that someone had left behind. They any good for you Su?'

Su looked and wrinkled her nose. 'No thanks, they always taste like bath water to me. Builder's tea is fine by me.'

I looked at the packet. 'Doubt the original purchaser liked them either, they are way over their best before date.' I ditched the packet into the bin. Once again we sat down together in the kitchen.

'Better in here just now, I don't think sitting in the garden with a view of my smalls waving in the breeze is tasteful.' I said.

'Oh I don't mind. I appreciate a modern man who can take care of himself. Rob certainly can.' She sipped her tea delicately. 'This is when Rob likes his salty chocolate. He says it helps when there's a crisis.'

'Is there a crisis Su?' I asked her.

'No.' And she looked at me, right into my eyes and smiled. 'I was going to look for you, you know. I'd decided to write to the medical register people and trace you. After Rob and I got married it seemed the one thing left to do. And now you're here, for another day anyway. But at least I know who you are now. And I'm glad.' It was quite a speech.

'I'm happy to hear every word of that. And I shall tell my wife that you were going to look for me. It will help when I explain things to her.'

'You're happily married to Marianne?' Su said.

'Yes. Very happy. I've been lucky. It's a good marriage.'

'I've been on the phone to my in-laws this morning,' Su went on. 'I'm telling everyone that matters about you, everyone who knows about how Rob and I got together that is. Graham and Oliver are thrilled and have invited us all to drinks this evening. Do you mind?'

At first I thought it was all a bit much but then I thought what the hell. Su wasn't upset and there was nothing to be ashamed about.

'Sure why not, that's very decent of them. At least I shall have a clean shirt to wear.'

Su giggled, a delightful sound. I had a thought.

'Su we were looking at some of your photos last night. Do you want to see what your Australian family looks like? I've got photos on my phone.'

She nodded and I did that tedious bit that always bores people when you're looking through your phone for them. There were the ones of me and Nick at Altarnun and some of Anna's wedding. There were a few good ones of Marianne, she's very photogenic, and I explained about her music and the reason she wasn't here in England with me. Su examined the photos closely.

'You've got a good looking family. Nick looks a lot like your wife, I'm sorry I missed him when he was here. Who does Anna take after?' She said.

'She reminds me of my own mother, her people were Welsh although she grew up in the Welsh borders. Anna has a lot of work done on her hair, she's in fashion and design and changes her looks a couple of times a year. It gets quite startling sometimes. I think her designer ability comes from my mother too, she used to knit and make her own clothes.'

'Did you know mum was born in Orchard Cottage, and so was grandfather. It will be interesting to learn about your parents and their origins. I'm beginning to feel more complete in a funny sort of way.' Su said.

We talked some more and then made sure we had each other's contact details on our phones.

'Well Su, I never expected to be doing this. I came here to bury my sister and to see Nick and do a bit of family research for Marianne and now I've got new friends and family wanting to keep in touch.'

As I was looking at my phone it started ringing. The caller ID showed that it was Nick calling.

'D'you mind Su, I should take this, it's Nick.'

I answered the phone. 'Nick, how are you doing. Everything okay or have you run out of money already?'

Nick didn't laugh. 'Dad, what's going on down there?'

'What d'you mean what's going on? I've got my washing done and I'm about to start packing.'

For a moment there I was wondering if he'd found out about Su somehow.

'I've just read about you delivering Fiona's baby single-handedly in a violent thunderstorm. Did you know that Daniel Pencraddoc, the baby's father, is one of the guys who founded Whizztixx Media, the games company? He's gone on social media with the story, and he's got a lot of followers globally. It's going viral. My mates here are well impressed with you.'

'I had no idea. I don't know about any of that. Blimey.'

'It's quite a story. The PR arm of the RFDS have got hold of it. They've contacted mum and they are doing something about the Flying Doctor who can be relied upon to go anywhere anytime and is never off duty.'

'What?'

'So you did deliver her baby then?'

'Yes I did. But I thought that the only people who know are her family, and the landlord and his wife, and er a few other people here in the village,' I was looking at Su who Nick knew nothing about. 'Like people in the farm shop and so on.'

'I just thought you should know dad. I think you're going to be a celebrity for a couple of minutes back home.'

'Thanks for that Nick. Maybe for ten minutes but ladies have babies all the time.'

'Yeah but they don't have Daniel Pencraddoc for a dad. He's quite something according to my friends up here. I think he's a millionaire as well.'

'Oh surely not.'

I was thinking about the nice steady looking young bloke with his arm round Fiona, renting a small end of terrace cottage while she lived in her brother's side annexe. They didn't look like millionaires to me. Then I remembered his car and something he'd said about having a flat on the Thames I could use, and a house he was having rebuilt down here.

We ended the call and I checked my messages. Sure enough I had missed one from Marianne. I explained the story to Su and bless the girl she became very practical.

'It could be something or nothing. Message or call your wife and I'll get your washing sorted. Shall I iron you a shirt for tonight?'

She was already in action mode so I composed an email to Marianne telling her Nick had called me and that I was surprised. *"Like I told you before I was just doing my job."* I typed. *"I was in the right place at the right time, that's all."* I confirmed my flight details and finished off with a loving message.

Su was folding things and had pressed a couple of my shirts in case I wanted a choice, she explained, saying she liked the blue one that matched my eyes. It was very pleasant being fussed over, I liked the father-daughter thing that was unfurling even though at home I was used to doing my own ironing. I'd just switched the kettle on again when I heard knocking at the door. I answered and was looking at a very thin young woman wearing scarlet lipstick which didn't suit her.

'Dr Milton?' She had a very determined expression on her face.

'Yes, how can I help you?'

'I'm from BBC local radio and would like to do an interview with you for the local news slot this evening. About your wonderfully timely assistance with Daniel Pencraddoc's baby the other day. He's becoming quite the local golden boy.'

'Oh no really, I don't think so. The ambulance was there in no time and they did all the necessary. It wouldn't be right. I didn't have my kit with me and anyway I'm retired and on holiday.' I blustered a bit, trying to be honest.

'Wow, so you did it without any conventional medical assistance. That's really of great interest to our listeners. Didn't Mrs Pencraddoc have any pain relief then?' Her eyes were wide and glistening and she was hot on the trail of a story.

'Look miss,' I said. 'It wouldn't be right to discuss this, it's er inappropriate and probably disrespectful to the parents.' She obviously didn't know that Fiona and Daniel weren't married and for some reason her poor grasp of detail irritated me.

'But Daniel Pencraddoc has put the story out there on his blog. It's a wonderful story and our listeners would love to hear your side. It's heartwarmingly sympathetic.' She was overdoing the innocent bedtime story routine and I felt like asking for the sick-bag.

I shook my head. 'No miss, I'm sorry, but no. I really don't want to give an interview. Please don't waste your time here.'

As I closed the door I saw Daniel's muscle car going by on the road behind her, and not towards their place.

Su's phone started ringing so she answered it.

'Oh my goodness. Really? Yes, ok, yes I'm with Josh now and he just had a reporter at the door. He refused to give an interview. Okay, that might be a good idea, I'll tell him. Bye.'

She ended the call and looked at me. 'That was Fiona. I think Daniel's in the dog house for posting his blog. Fiona's moved over to the cottage with her parents for privacy and they've closed the gates and blocked access with her car. Daniel has just moved his car down to The Manor House because the boys can hide it in their garage. I think they're anticipating a siege. We can all escape to The Manor House later by the field footpaths at the back.'

'But why?' I said.

Su gave me a long look. 'You've been out of England a long time haven't you. This is the silly season for news. It's summer and Parliament is in recess. The news hounds need anything they can get their hands on to justify their jobs. And Daniel has already been interviewed a few times for radio and telly since he and Mike have put the West Country on the map with their Company. He's already a man of considerable interest.'

I trusted her local knowledge. And anyway I was enjoying the fact that I'd heard her say my name.

'Oh well, let's lock the door, raise the drawbridge and release the sharks into the moat. Shall we do some packing?' I said.

THIRTY SEVEN

From the upstairs window I could see that the young woman I'd closed the door on hadn't gone away. She was standing on the church path opposite and talking on her phone. I thought the poor girl looked a bit fed up. I started packing the stuff Su had folded up for me. I was a fairly light and efficient traveller after years of practice with the RFDS but there were a few presents to take home which I needed to squeeze in. It didn't take me that long. I had a clean shirt for tonight which I thought I'd wear tomorrow as well for the drive to London. I put the other clean ironed shirt into my cabin bag to change into during the flight. One thing about flying Business Class is that things are more spacious and you can stretch an arm out in the gents.

Su came into the front bedroom. 'I've just had a text from Fiona. She says the wolves are gathering on the lane up to the annexe. Apparently there's a television unit outside the pub now. It's weird isn't it. Oh and Daniel walked back to the annexe via the field footpath at the back and tore his trousers climbing over barbed wire on the paddock fence.'

I thought that Daniel could probably afford to replace them but I said nothing. I was used to Marianne giving the odd interview but that was almost always planned or booked ahead and undertaken in a civilised manner. This situation was different but I didn't think I had anything to worry about.

'Look, as soon as there's a whale washed up or the trains stop running they'll all rush away. We can deal with this. It's not that important and ladies have babies every day. Let's just ignore them.' I said.

There was another knock at the door and I moved to the side of the bedroom window so that I could see down to the path. Sarah from the pub was standing there. She looked up and saw me and started waving so I went downstairs and let her in, carefully turning the key in the lock after her. Sarah was rather surprised to see Su there and said so. I experienced a brief second of enjoyment as my daughter just waved the comment aside and asked Sarah what she wanted.

'I wanted to tell Dr Milton that the pub is full of telly people asking about him. They've already interviewed Tim. He said you'd been staying our holiday cottage with your son who's a dentist and that he'd seen you riding Fiona's horse. They asked him if you were a family friend of the Pencraddoc's but he didn't know so he couldn't answer that question.'

Her eyes kept flicking from me to Su and I could see that she was itching to ask why Su was in the cottage with me and I was thinking rapidly about how to answer that when she spoke again.

'So are you going to give an interview Dr Milton? You could come down to the pub and do it in the bar if you like. Probably easier and more space than in here. Or is there anything else Tim could say?'

'I think Tim has said quite enough already and no I'm not going to give an interview.' I said, keeping my voice calm and neutral.

'But it's the telly. There's cameras and everything.' She said it with a sort of desperation, as though all her dreams had come true.

I shook my head. 'I've already spoken to the lady from the local radio and said more than enough to her.'

'So why are you here then Su.' Sarah was having problems containing her frustration and irritation and was looking at Su with a mixture of defiance and curiosity.

'Oh I'm here on Fiona's behalf. Obviously Dr Milton can't and will not say anything without Fiona's permission. It's a very personal and private matter between them.'

Sarah was impressed and I was deeply proud. I assumed a sombre face.

'I'm just discussing the matter with Dr Milton now.' Su was standing there with one arm folded across her front, holding her phone in the other hand in an attitude that clearly said she needed to make an important and private call. She had a quiet authority and Sarah caved in.

361

'Oh well I'll be off then. I just thought you should know.' Sarah looked a bit peeved.

'Quite right Sarah. I'm grateful, you've done the right thing. Do thank Tim for me. But not a word more to anybody now. I'm relying on you.' And I packed her off.

Su and I exchanged a look. 'That woman is a trollop and a busybody.' Strong words from my daughter.

Su called Rob and briefly told him about the day's events and I could hear him laughing. She told him that she would go with me to The Manor House and meet him there later.

'We shall be skulking through the fields to where our marquee was. The boys have unlocked the wooden door so we can sneak in through the walled garden.'

Then she called the boys. 'Oliver can Josh and I come a bit earlier? Only we're hiding in the holiday cottage and will soon be climbing the walls.'

Again I could hear laughter. It was like being in a farce. I looked out of the front window, the reporter had gone and I couldn't see anyone out there.

'Come on then. Let's go.' Su said.

Before we left I grabbed my last bottle of wine, drew the front curtains and switched a lamp on. That should keep people guessing for a while. Su nodded approvingly and we let ourselves out of the back door and locked it. There was a wrought iron gate at the back of the little garden but as it was behind a small shed housing some garden implements and unused deckchairs I hadn't noticed it. We were out into the field and strolling along in the afternoon sun when I started chuckling.

'I haven't had this much fun for ages Su. I won't forget this. What a week!'

We had to walk down the field to a stile and then back up to get to The Manor House. We were soon there and went through the solid wooden door set into the high garden wall and straight onto the terrace in the handsome back garden. One of the dogs went ballistic until it recognised Su and one of their cats regarded us with misgivings before streaking off into the house. The doors to the garden room were open and Oliver appeared holding two glasses of white wine. I took one from him and gave him the bottle I'd brought with me.

'A light alcoholic beverage to calm and soothe your nerves. It's too early to call it a sundowner although I'm sure the sun has already gone down somewhere on the planet.' Oliver said.

We waited until he got his own glass and raised it. 'Cheers.'

I drank half my glass straight down. 'Hits the spot Oliver.' But I thought be careful lad, you're driving tomorrow.

Graham came bustling into the room with two bowls containing crisps and salted nuts. 'You could have waited for me. I've shut the bloody dogs up in the yard.'

He kissed Su on the cheek, took a glass from Oliver and turned to me.

'How does it feel to be famous?'

'I'm not. It's just a bit of hot air and nonsense that's all.' I said.

Graham was fizzing with excitement though. Of course, he knew our story too since Su had telephoned him.

'When you came round the other afternoon after the churchyard I was bursting to ask you about Su but you weren't giving anything away so I had to button it. Of course I'd remembered your name from when Su was doing her family research.'

'That must have been the hardest thing you've ever done Graham.' Oliver said, rolling his eyes theatrically.

Su was looking from Graham to me and back again. 'After the churchyard?' She echoed.

'Yes, I was walking one of the dogs and I found Josh by the grave so I invited him to eat with me. We were both on our own and desperately in need of cheering up.'

Su was looking at me now with her eyebrows raised.

'It was the afternoon you called round and I wasn't in. I went and put some flowers on Tessa's grave and Graham came along. He fed and watered me and got me through a difficult moment.'

'That was a lovely thing to do.' She said. She'd gone a bit pink.

'Oh it's all so exciting,' Graham interrupted us. 'My life is so dull. All I do is cook and clean and feed hens and pick up dog poo. Oh tell us everything.' Graham was bouncing on the balls of his feet and Oliver put a restraining hand on his arm.

'Let's all sit down. The others won't be along for a while.'

We sat eating crisps and nuts and told the boys an edited version of our story, even though Su had spoken to Oliver about it earlier that day.

'So Su knew your name but didn't know you were in the village and you didn't know about Su at all until Martha told you.' Graham breathed out in a long slow sigh. 'It's better than going to the pictures.'

They chatted about Su and Rob's wedding and I was shown the study where they'd had some special wedding photographs taken. I was quite touched since I'd heard some of the story. Then Oliver and Graham were both very interested in the role their house had played in Su's life and dwelt on the details for quite some time.

There was a knock at the front door and the door bell rang.

'Brace yourselves everyone. Hoards are arriving.' Oliver said, going off to answer.

I heard lots of voices and then there was a commotion as people I'd never met, apart from Martha, came into the conservatory. I was introduced to Rob's parents and to his sister Jay and her husband Phil. I recognised him as the one who'd given Su away at her wedding. There was lots of handshaking and more bottles were opened. I could hear Graham lamenting that he'd not thought about doing cocktails. They all wanted to talk about the events surrounding Fiona's baby and to their credit were pleasantly discreet about my newly discovered relationship to Su, but there was an awful lot of scrutiny going on. I wondered how Su was feeling about it but after her performance with Sarah this afternoon I had the feeling that my new daughter could, in fact, take care of herself.

Then the doorbell went again and there were more voices and shouts of laughter. Rob had taken his van onto the village road just along from the house that Daniel was renting from him and had picked him and Fiona up. They were both wearing hoodies and they'd left the baby with her parents.

I kissed Fiona hello and asked her how she was feeling.

'She's pretty fit Josh.' Daniel answered for her. 'This extraordinary woman only gave birth four and a bit days ago and she's already up and about and organising things.'

'Like they used to in the old days, pick the stones from the fields, have the baby under a hedge and then get the hay in.' Graham said provocatively.

That caused a fair bit of dissension from the women which was just what Graham enjoyed. He loved being at the centre of some excitement. As this was all going on Fiona turned to me and said Daniel owed me an apology.

'Whatever for?' I asked.

'His damn silly twitty book blog thing. He knows how uncomfortably I sit with all that and now the whole world wants to know about our relationship and my baby.'

She wasn't exaggerating. I considered her point and her feelings, trying not to smile at her expressive dismissal of social media. 'His parents aren't around to discuss fatherhood with him Fiona.' I said. 'And although Kate is wonderfully supportive I'm guessing he's overwhelmed on the one hand and very proud on the other hand. Maybe you should let him off the hook. He loves you.'

She treated me to her proud stare and then she softened and gave me a lovely smile.

'Yes, perhaps I should, getting Flora Rose is quite a surprise to us both.'

The gathering had moved into a large circle. Oliver came over and refreshed my glass and asked me when I was leaving.

'My flight is at a stupid time in the very early hours on Friday morning, hardly worth spending the night in a hotel. I've got to return the car though so I was thinking I'd go up tomorrow afternoon and do that, get a really good rest through Wednesday night into Thursday, and then hang around the airport for twelve hours. I can use the Business Class lounge to freshen up and relax and I shall sleep on the plane once we're processed through.'

People started agreeing about how awful travel was these days, especially getting up to London from Cornwall which added a day to the journey.

'I'm sure I could have made better plans if there'd been time, but with my sister passing away so unexpectedly I had to take what I could get.' I said.

There were more murmurs, this time a bit subdued. Su took hold of my hand and spoke out.

'You've done brilliantly. I'm proud of you. Everyone here is touched by what you've done for their own reasons. I'm so glad that you're my father.' And she burst into tears.

'Hey'. I said and I put my arms round her and gave her a hug, feeling a mixture of pride and tenderness. 'Hey that was nice.'

Rob was at my side and I released her into his arms while I fished in my pocket for a tissue to give her. I still had some from our previous emotional day together.

Of course that caused another commotion of which Graham was terribly proud. He was having a wonderful day. I could hear him talking to Rob's parents.

'Oh yes Oliver and I knew because it all came out of the family research thing last year. It's so exciting. Something that Liz Bradley from the library found in a parish magazine. Dear Su, we're so pleased for her. And he really is a lovely man, Martha will tell you.'

Oliver interrupted the proceedings. 'Everyone, the local news is on, come and look.'

We all followed him into the sitting room where a woman was talking to camera. She was clearly standing outside The Wheal in the village.

'Although Daniel Pencraddoc hasn't been available since he posted his blog last weekend we do know that mother and baby are doing fine since the extraordinary events during last Friday's storm. The landlord here at The Wheal knows both Daniel Pencraddoc and Dr Joshua Milton personally and here's what he had to say to me earlier today.'

I snorted. 'Tim doesn't know me at all.'

Daniel agreed. 'Nor me. I've eaten there a few times, that's all.'

'Shhhhh.' From several of the assembled company. Oh the power of television, I thought.

Tim was standing behind his bar looking as cool as a cucumber and already speaking.

'Yes, both Mr Pencraddoc and Dr Milton have been regulars here this summer.' I groaned aloud. I couldn't help it.

'Both are very nice gentlemen. My wife Sarah is friends with Mr Pencraddoc's sister and she told her all about what happened when they met in our local shop the following morning. That's the farm shop just up the road here.'

Tim was actually pointing in the appropriate direction. The camera moved sympathetically and caught Sarah bursting with excitement and smirking in the background.

I noticed Kate looked ready to explode. 'That woman is not my friend.' She hissed to Daniel.

Tim was still speaking. 'And after Dr Milton's timely help with the baby during the storm we gave him lunch on the house here. It was the least we could do to say thank you for helping someone in our community. Miss Frazer is an art teacher here and well liked as is Mr Pencraddoc. Although he's not an art teacher.'

There were some muffled giggles in the room. I glanced at Fiona. Her expression was complicated and her eyes widened slightly as she watched the screen.

'Free lunch?' Daniel spoke quietly, looking at me sideways.

'Sorry. He insisted. People in the pub were clapping at the time. I was put right on the spot.' I shrugged.

Daniel pulled a wry and knowing face at me and nodded his head. 'Right.' He said dryly.

The interviewer was now prompting Tim. 'And Dr Milton is Australian with the Royal Flying Doctor Service and he is on holiday here?'

'Is he?' Tim said. 'I thought he said he was English. He is on holiday though, with his son. I don't know anything about the Flying Doctors. Was that in Mr Pencraddoc's blog then?'

'Oh turn it off Oliver.' Daniel said.

'No, it's funny, let's see what they say next.' Graham said.

The camera was back outside with the live interviewer.

'As I said we've been unable to contact either Mr Pencraddoc or Dr Milton or, er, Miss Frazer personally, but we do have Miss Frazer's father here who has agreed to speak to us.

THIRTY EIGHT

'What?!' The exclamation in the room was unanimous. Fiona stood up, her eyes on the screen.

The camera pulled back to reveal Fiona's father standing there in the evening sunshine. He looked good, strong and imposing in chinos and a crisply ironed short sleeved shirt. The camera liked him, playing over the strong angles of his face, the sun catching the grey flecks in his mahogany coloured hair.

'Good evening Group Captain Frazer.' Someone had been doing their research well. 'Tell us in your own words how the events of last Friday have affected you.'

Fiona's father looked at the interviewer momentarily as though she was a dimwit.

'I just wish to say that I am delighted to have a new granddaughter. My wife and I are very, very proud of our daughter and of Daniel. They are a splendid couple. We are all extremely grateful to Dr Milton, and to the medical team who arrived so promptly.'

His Scots accent was beautifully modulated and his words were delivered precisely but politely. Fiona breathed out slowly.

The interviewer started to say something else but the Group Captain put his hand up quite casually and silenced her. She closed her mouth with an audible pop. This was not a man you could mess with, I thought, remembering that handshake.

'Let me also say that we all thank you for your interest, but the new parents would like to be left alone, and so would the rest of us. We have travelled a long way and it's a very special personal family time you understand.' There was an authoritative Scots inflection at the end of his sentence. 'I expect Daniel may do another blog in due course since media is his business, but now it's time to cease all the tittle tattle and leave them well alone. I think you will agree.'

The interviewer was dominated by his logic. To her credit she swung back to camera and concluded the non-interview rather nicely. Oliver switched the television off.

'That was fun. I especially enjoyed Tim's performance but your father was amazing Fiona.'

Fiona was still standing, a little bit of a flush in her cheeks. She turned and spoke to us all.

'I would like to be away now to my baby. And I want to hug my father. Will we go now?'

She was looking at Daniel and there were appreciative smiles as Daniel took her hand.

'I think I want to hug everyone,' he said.

I shook his hand and kissed Fiona goodbye and promised to keep in touch.

'I think I might be commissioning one of your family apple trees.' I told her.

Oliver and Graham saw them off through the wooden gate and the rest of us regrouped. Rob's parents wanted to talk to me, they seemed to like the fact that their daughter-in-law had suddenly become acquainted with her doctor father. I talked to them at some length and posed with my new family for yet more photographs, I didn't want to let Su down.

Eventually the gathering came to an end and amid the many thanks and expressions of good wishes people withdrew to their cars and left. Martha took hold of both of my hands.

'I'm delighted with you Joshua. And absolutely delighted that things are turning out so well between you and Su! And I do hope it all goes well at home.' She said.

I thanked the boys for their kindness over the recent days.

'Our pleasure Josh,' Oliver said. 'Next time you come please stay here with us. Graham does a fantastic breakfast.'

Graham hugged me and giggled archly. 'I've never actually hugged a doctor before.'

I got into the van with Su and Rob. It was only a hundred yards to the holiday cottage but Rob said it would keep me hidden from lurking journalists. The street was quiet.

'Everyone's down at the pub I think. It must be doing a good trade on the back of all this.' Su said.

They dropped me off and I held her hand through the van window.

'I shan't be leaving until lunchtime Su. Will I see you to say goodbye in the morning?'

'Yes. I shall be here to see you off.'

I said cheerio to Rob and he leaned forward in the driving seat and gave me a funny little salute with one finger.

'I've really enjoyed meeting you father-in-law. Hope the next visit won't be too far away.'

They drove off and I watched them go.

Inside the holiday cottage everything seemed indifferent after the emotions of the past few days. I checked the fridge contents and ditched a few things. After all the crisps and nuts I wasn't particularly hungry. There was enough bread for toast in the morning and I'd get something at a service station on the way to London.

I checked my phone and found a text from Nick and one from Anna. Nick just asked if everything was okay and I replied to him;

"*A bit of a leaving party and an item on the local evening news. Nothing out of the ordinary in my exciting life.*"

Anna had texted, "*Looking forward to seeing you home dad. Safe journey. Bring the sun back with you.*"

I replied saying I'd be glad to see her smiling face again. God, I thought, I miss home, and I messaged Marianne saying just that.

As I was putting my bags into the boot the following morning Daniel's muscle car growled into view and stopped outside the cottage. He jumped out, grinning broadly and called hello.

'Ahoy Daniel,' I said. 'What brings you here?'

'Fiona asked me to drop this off, I'm not stopping, I'm off up to Somerset to see my business buddy.' He handed me a small flat square parcel.

I took it and turned it over in my hands. 'Are her instructions that I should open it now or take it home with me?' I asked.

'She didn't say. All I know is that she was up in the night in the studio. When she has something on her mind she works any hour, it's something we have in common.'

I thought for a moment. 'I think I shall open it later, when I'm alone. But tell her thank you.' I stuck my hand out and Daniel shook it.

'Safe journey Josh. Don't forget the offer is there for you on the London flat. I really mean it. I hope we'll be seeing you again.'

He drove off and I enjoyed the sound of the engine. It was sex on wheels that beast. He'd definitely have to buy something else to ferry Fiona and baby equipment about but I couldn't see him parting with that car.

I was sorting out the Satnav in the hire car when Su drew up. She had a carrier bag with her.

'I've made you something proper to eat for the journey, just smoked fish and hard boiled egg sandwiches but the fish is from the local smokery and the eggs are from Martha's free range hens. There's a bottle of the farm's apple juice as well.'

I thanked her and told her she was a lovely thoughtful girl.

'It's just something to keep you going.'

'Come in Su, there's time for a cup of tea together and I have something for you.'

She followed me inside. The tea was already made and we sat down opposite each other at the kitchen table. There was silence between us.

'Oh I hate this,' she sounded passionate. 'I hate goodbyes.'

'Well I can't do anything about that love, but I can give you this. I think it should belong to you now.' I gave her a small gift wrapped in pink tissue. 'The tissue is the best the farm shop could offer at such short notice.'

Su took the little gift and held it for a moment, looking at me questioningly.

'Open it.' I said.

She gently tore the tissue and revealed a gold bracelet. Saying nothing she touched it with a finger tip and smiled.

'It belonged to your grandmother, my mother. My sister had it for a while but she had no one to pass it on to. It's a family piece and I think it suits your look. I think that my mum and Pam would approve.'

'It's very beautiful.' Su said picking it up and draping it over the back of her hand to look at it more closely.

I could see that she appreciated the bracelet with its sinuous shape, wide in the middle and narrowing to the clasp and fastening at each end.

'It looks old, unusual.' Su said. 'I've never seen a design like it.'

I took it from her and asked her to put her wrist out and fixed it into place.

'I think it's from the 1930s, it looks a bit art deco to me. I've never seen closed links like that. I remember my mum wearing it at Christmas, a very long time ago. You could check the hallmark and verify the date I guess.'

'I shall wear it and love it. And it will stay in our family.'

I was really pleased that I'd had the idea of giving it to her. We spent an hour talking about safe subjects, she was interested in my working life in Australia. I asked her if she'd any intention of going back to microbiology but she shook her head. Really it was just a way of filling in some time together. Finally she said she'd be off.

'Martha is expecting me for lunch. I'm not going to wave you goodbye, but I shall be thinking of you.'

I looked down at her serious face and kissed her on one cheek and then the other.

'You're very special Su. I'm so glad I know you now and that you're happy here with Rob. Now get off and give Martha my best. And thanks for the picnic.'

For a second I vividly remembered Tessa and our picnics so long ago, but Su was getting into her car and didn't see the flash of emotion tearing across my face. She blew me a kiss and drove away. I watched her go, weirdly conscious that her mother was lying in the churchyard a couple of hundred yards away.

'We did okay Tessa.' I murmured.

The last thing I had to do was drop the keys off at the pub. Tim was busy at the bar but came out from behind it to see me.

'Everything okay then doctor?' He didn't show any signs of embarrassment about last night.

I gave him the keys and confirmed that everything was indeed okay.

'I enjoyed your TV performance last night Tim. It was all rather exciting.'

Tim looked rather pleased. My feeble attempt at irony was totally lost on him.

'We've got loads of bookings enquiries, it's given the pub and the cottage quite a boost.' He'd pocketed the keys and was rubbing his hands together now, as though anticipating counting the money.

'Oh good. I'll have to see what I can do to put the place on the map again next time I come.' I kept my voice neutral. 'And thank Sarah for keeping it all so welcoming. She's a real gift for housekeeping and baking.' I was recalling Martha's acerbic words a few days ago. Only it seemed much longer ago than that.

'Oh thanks, I'll tell her that.'

I could see that Tim was keen to get back behind the bar and get some more money into the till. I copied Rob's neat little salute and said cheers mate, in a comedy Oz accent. It saved me from another handshake. Then I got into the car, set the Satnav and drove away.

It was as though the village and all that had happened just rolled itself up and was put away as I drove. All I could see was the road ahead. All I could think about was what I was going to tell Marianne. The truth, a voice in my head said. 'Nothing but the truth.'

The journey to Gatwick wasn't too bad because I took a leisurely route on A-roads and I quite enjoyed the greenery and the scenery. Daniel had suggested taking a break at Marlborough on the A4 and it was a very pretty place to stretch my legs. Finally I reached the drop off place and then checked into the hotel. I sent Su a text telling her I'd eaten all the delicious sandwiches and one to Marianne telling her stage one of the journey home was safely completed. Later on there was a reply from Marianne saying how much she was looking forward to seeing me.

I spent an age in the bathroom using all the complimentary products they provided and retired to lounge on the bed wearing the complimentary robe and smelling rather fragrant. I had the TV on low for company and took Fiona's parcel from my cabin bag and unwrapped it. She'd given me a superb little framed painting of Bel done in exquisite detail and with a pleasingly limited colour palette. She didn't paint to the edges of the paper and the effect was focussed but gentle, like a good memory. I recognised the setting and could see in my mind's eye where Bel was standing, with the fence and a bit of a tree and part of the roof of the annexe behind.

There was an accompanying card on thick deckle edged paper, a simple pen and ink sketch which she'd drawn herself of her sitting with Daniel and with Flora Rose in her arms. She'd written on it; "With our love to Josh, from Fiona and Daniel, I knew that our meeting had meaning." They had both signed it and it was dated the day of Flora's birth. I was charmed and wrapped it up carefully before repacking it in my case amongst layers of clothing. Nick had said that Daniel was getting quite famous and

I found myself thinking that one day Daniel Pencraddoc's signature might be worth something.

After a surprisingly good sleep I had a leisurely breakfast and then wandered into the airport and poked around the shops and the bookstalls for several hours, until I got fed up and took myself off to the Business Class lounge where I sat and rested, reading the newspapers and watching people. At last it was time to go to check-in.

The young man on the desk took my documents and made pleasant noises as he did his various checks. Then he paused, looking at me with a certain amount of interest.

'Oh. Dr Joshua Milton.'

'Yes. Is there a problem?' Please god don't let there be a problem I was thinking.

'No sir, no problem, not at all. I just have to ask you if you wouldn't mind stepping to this side.' He came out from behind his high desk and unhooked a purple barrier rope and handed me my passport and paperwork. 'Just over there sir, you've been vip'd for the flight home.' He indicated another check-in desk.

'I've been what?'

'You are a VIP sir. Have a very pleasant flight home.'

A pretty Asian girl was waiting for me and efficiently processed me through.

'I don't know how I've got lucky,' I said to her, a bit bewildered. 'Why me?'

'Oh we think there might be press waiting for you at Perth. It's easier for the airline to help you through in First, so that everyone else can proceed normally and not get held up. Your own steward will assist you with anything he can do to help. Have a lovely flight Dr Milton.'

Press. Oh great. I took my phone out and sent a text to Marianne, she was meeting my flight.

"I'm coming home First Class love and I've got such a lot to tell you."

Printed in Great Britain
by Amazon